Would I Lie to You?

a novel by

Mary Lou Dickinson

Inanna poetry & fiction series

INANNA PUBLICATIONS AND EDUCATION INC.
TORONTO, CANADA

Canada Council **Conseil des Arts**
for the Arts   du Canada

 ONTARIO ARTS COUNCIL
CONSEIL DES ARTS DE L'ONTARIO
an Ontario government agency
un organisme du gouvernement de l'Ontario

We gratefully acknowledge the support of the Canada Council for the Arts and the Ontario Arts Council for our publishing program. We also acknowledge the financial support of the Department of Canadian Heritage through the Canada Book Fund.

Would I Lie to You? is a work of fiction. All the characters and situations portrayed in this book are fictitious and any resemblance to persons living or dead is purely coincidental.

Cover design: Val Fullard

Library and Archives Canada Cataloguing in Publication

Dickinson, Mary Lou, 1937–, author
        Would I lie to you? : a novel / by Mary Lou Dickinson.

ISBN 978-1-77133-164-7 (pbk.)

        I. Title.

PS8607.I346W69 2014   C813'.6   C2014-905025-9

 MIX
Paper from
responsible sources
FSC® C004071

Printed and bound in Canada

Inanna Publications and Education Inc.
210 Founders College, York University
4700 Keele Street, Toronto, Ontario, Canada M3J 1P3
Telephone: (416) 736-5356 Fax: (416) 736-5765
Email: inanna.publications@inanna.ca Website: www.inanna.ca

For A. R. and a lifetime of friendship

Courage is what it takes and takes the more of
Because the deeper fear is so eternal.
— Robert Frost

1.

THE SOUND OF VOICES came through the wall beside her, but Sue could not make out what they were saying. She picked up a magazine from a small table, glanced through it and set it down again. The voices grew louder and she could hear people moving around. A woman came out into the waiting room and pulled a tan jacket off a hanger. Sue watched her push her arms into the sleeves as if she were punching holes in them and, sighing, head quickly to the stairs down to the main floor.

Had the woman made her appointment because she imagined it could change her life in some way? Sue wondered. Her own life was now determined by her husband's illness and that left her in ongoing fear that any breath might be his last. Who would not want to change that? She had seen the psychic's name in *Toronto Life's* recent list of bests that had gone on for pages. Best chefs, paint stores, physiotherapists, yoga teachers, hardware stores, and the best bakeries. Then had come the psychics. Just one was listed. Hans Jonker: "A make you feel good psychic."

The woman who had just left had not looked as if she felt good. Sue wondered if she should leave before she was called into the inner sanctum. Still, she was curious. It seemed unlikely that she would see a crystal ball or tarot cards. But beyond images of reading palms or tea leaves, she could not picture how a psychic might work.

A man with a tawny beard and long hair peered around the door frame of the office. His eyes perused her speculatively. About her age, mid-fifties, and tall, his rugged hands looked as if he worked in the fields or with tools or engines.

"Hello," he said. "You here to see me?"

Why am I doing this? Sue wondered. She used to go to art galleries to find solace. Or walk on wooded paths in ravines. Instead, she had told the woman who returned her call that she wanted an appointment as soon as possible. Nothing else could make her feel good. Just as nothing else could take away the fear of losing Jerry. She had left only her first name on the answering machine. Not Sue Reid. Or Mrs. Reid. She was just plain "Sue" for this appointment.

"He's very busy," the woman had said.

"I suppose he would be." Anyone who on the previous Saturday had been listed as the best of anything would have a rush of phone calls on Monday. But what did that mean? That he was popular, maybe. And if not, he soon would be.

"The first available appointment is in two months," the woman had said.

"That's far too long." Sue was irritated.

"I could call if there's a cancellation."

"All right."

Sue had not expected to hear at all. She had thought about his name. Hans Jonker. It might well have been Joker. At least she had known it was a Dutch name. She had visualized him, on skates, with his finger in a dike. She had pictures of people from their voices on answering machines and they inevitably turned out to be older or younger, to have a different colour skin, to be shorter or taller, almost nothing she imagined turned out to be so. Although once in awhile, there was some uncanny resemblance to her fantasies.

"I assume so," she said now. "But if you're the psychic, you'd know that, wouldn't you?"

She waited for his reply without any of her initial enthusiasm. Of course, she hoped he would tell her that Jerry would suddenly regain his health, proving all the doctors wrong. She wanted to have this man put his finger in that dike that was being overwhelmed the more ill Jerry became. The more he was in pain. But she knew no one could say anything that would change that. It would not be true. At the very least, she wanted to know what to expect.

"Well, that would be me," Hans Jonker smiled. "I ought to know." He gestured for her to follow him and began to move back into his office with an exuberant swagger.

Sue sat still and watched him, as if frozen to the chair. She should not be here. It was too bizarre.

"Come in," he said more gently.

As she stood up, Sue felt dizzy. Putting one foot in front of the other deliberately, she followed him slowly into his office. Gesturing to a chair, he sat down in an armchair on the other side of a small table. The room was not at all as she had pictured it, full of paraphernalia for his work. Instead, there was no hint of what happened here. It was more like a studio she might have created for herself. A place where she could paint and ponder.

Sue glanced out the large bay window where she could see the leaves of a tall maple, then at a Chagall painting that hung on the wall behind his desk. It was titled *Peasant Life*. The scene was of a man in a red cap with a yellow horse's head beside him and in the background was a red house with two tiny figures dancing in the vibrant sky around a horse-drawn carriage. She knew it from an exhibition of Chagall's works she had found when travelling one spring in Europe near the Riviera. Why does the idiot have to have yellow chickens on rooftops? she had wondered at the time. Even so, it had been then that she had begun to observe art more keenly and to think of putting brush and paint to a canvas of her own. Her glance moved to another wall where there was a large photograph of a yellow canoe in what looked like Algonquin

Park, a canoe similar to the one she and Jerry had taken on numerous trips.

"I don't know why I'm here," she said finally, sitting down in the easy chair across from him. "I know I don't want to hear bad news. There's enough of that already."

"First of all, let me introduce myself. I'm Hans Jonker. Call me Hans. And you must be Sue."

"Yes." She did not intend to give him her last name and he did not seem to want it. She was Sue Walters before she married Jerry. Odd to have changed her name so late in life, especially with her feeling that it was important to retain one's identity in a marriage. And yet, she supposed at that time, she had actually wanted to lose her earlier one and what went with it. All those things she was never supposed to talk about that she had managed to keep quiet. She watched Jonker press the button to start a tape recorder on the table between them.

"I'll give the tape to you at the end," he said. "No one remembers everything, so you can refer to it later if you want. I don't look for bad news. If there's something you can do to change things, I'll tell you. If the brakes on your car are going to fail when you leave, I'll let you know so you can get them fixed. But I'm not a forecaster of gloom and doom."

She relaxed her grip on the arms of her chair.

"There's something about your marriage," he said. "Your husband isn't well. You take care of him, but you have to take care of yourself, too."

Her hands shaking ever so slightly and her throat dry, Sue waited for what he would say next. How she missed Jerry's good humour these days. In spite of all the medication, he was more frequently in pain and often ignored even his beloved music. Only a few short weeks ago, he would have jumped up, calling out, "C'mon, gal. Let's show the world how to dance," and then twirled her around the living room. Soon, she would have been laughing with him as he danced in his slippers and an old dressing gown, or a pair of blue jeans and socks with holes in the heels. Irrepressible. That was Jerry. Or, it used to be.

"You'll get through it," Hans said. "You have whatever it will take."

"And then what? Will I manage that?"

"Yes, it will be a difficult time, but you'll find the light at the end of it. The painting you're about to start will help."

How could he know that colour permeated her life like a current in a stream? She watched him with a new appreciation, but she could tell his thoughts were already elsewhere. The lines around his eyes were sharper, as if he were deep in concentration. His lips were pursed so that for a moment they almost disappeared.

"There's something quite unusual," he said. "Quite unusual. I get something about a son you don't know about. Or someone who is like a son."

Sue shook her head. "No," she said, already dismissing his words.

"Yes," he said. "There is such a person. He's there and he'll appear soon."

"No."

"Just listen to me, Sue. Don't fight it. There's no point in fighting what I tell you. It's what I'm getting so clearly that there's no mistaking it. There are some things you won't believe, but time will prove them to be so."

"Will my husband die?" she asked.

"I think you know the answer."

"Well, that's what I came to find out."

"I don't think so," he said. "You came to find out something you didn't already know."

"And what is that?" she asked, showing more of the disdain she felt than she intended.

"I've just told you."

"Oh, *that*." She rolled her eyes.

"It's important." He looked at her so intently she wanted to turn away. "And you put your husband on a pedestal. He's a decent enough man, but he's also only human. It isn't going to help you to take care of things if you don't accept that he isn't perfect."

Oh yeah, well, he yells sometimes, Sue thought. Even picks his nose when no one is looking. But what the hell! So do I. She did not say anything out loud, but she imagined Hans Jonker could tell she was skeptical.

"You're going to take a trip later," he went on. "In the next year or two. Across a body of water."

Sue sighed. Where? She was not planning anything. Not with Jerry as ill as he was. The farthest she had gone for months was into the country for an afternoon, to sit by some lake or river. To eat a sandwich as she listened to the current. To draw a little sketch she might paint later. To mull things over. Would Jerry survive? And as it became apparent that he would not, how would she?

"There's something about music," he said. "It plays a big role in your life. Don't let it stop."

"It plays a big role in my husband's life," she said. "And sometimes he can't hear it anymore." She could scarcely bear the thought of that, more apparent with each passing day. It was as if Jerry were disappearing into some inner world where he heard only his own music.

"It's important to you, too. Don't give it up."

If this were supposed to make her feel good, Sue could not see how. She stood up.

"I think you still have some questions," he said. "It's fine to ask them."

"I don't remember any." Gripped by an overwhelming desire to get out of there as fast as possible, she handed him the envelope she had prepared for this moment. The woman on the telephone had not told her how to make payment, so she had put cash inside it. Seventy dollars had seemed preposterous. She had imagined a reading of tea leaves or a palm reading for ten or fifteen dollars. But then, she had found his name under the "Bests" list. And it had been the only name there. She'd had no idea of what would transpire here except it had never occurred to her that he would speak with such authority. As if he knew things about her life he could not possibly know. Or that could not possibly be true.

"Thanks," he said. "You're going to be all right. That's what I know about you. It's hard for you to see that now, but you will be." He opened the recorder. "Don't forget this. You might find it useful."

She took the tape and thrust it into the zippered pouch on the side of her bag. He had not actually told her anything that surprised her except the bit about a son, which was so far-fetched it had shaken any faith she might have had in him. The fact that Hans knew her husband was ill and that she was starting a new painting did not dawn on her as surprising in that moment And, if Jerry had a son, he would have told her long ago.

As she headed toward the door, her eye caught the Chagall painting again, the bright colours and curving lines of his depiction of Jewish village life. Her brush would also make sweeping strokes across a canvas one day. This visit had been meant to make her feel better, she thought, but aside from the sentiment evoked by this painting she was sure she had just wasted seventy dollars.

"Take care," the psychic said as she hurried out.

*

Sue was careful not to disturb Jerry, who lay dozing beside her, as she rolled to the side of the bed and touched her feet down onto the floor. The room was warmer than either of them would have liked before Jerry became ill. She reached for her light silk robe and tied it loosely around her waist. As she tiptoed down the stairs, she felt uncomfortable that she was hiding things from Jerry. They often had complimented themselves on how open they were, that they did not hide anything. She had known it was not true. There was an early part of her life she had never shared with anyone, but insofar as their lives together were concerned, there had been no desire to have secrets. No sense that what she left unsaid from a time so long ago could jeopardize their marriage. While she still found this acceptable, it struck her that she would not were it to apply to anyone else, a thought that she dismissed almost as soon as it occurred to her.

The newspaper was lying on the porch on the sisal mat in front of the door and she took it into the kitchen where she put on a pot of coffee. While the coffee percolated and the aroma began to drift through the room, she glanced at an article on an attack ad the Tories had released. It seemed they would do anything to win the election, but Sue thought this ad would surely backfire. It surprised her that they would stoop to such tactics.

She looked up when Jerry came into the kitchen in his flannel dressing gown. He had not shaved yet and his whiskers were like short stalks in a field, prickly.

"Coffee smells good," he said, leaning on the counter.

"Any minute," she said. Until recently, she would have mentioned the political events on the landscape, but Jerry had gradually become disinterested. He who could not talk enough about the last American presidency. She watched him straighten up and go to the window to look out at the yard. The leaves on the birch tree were beginning to fall and she knew he longed to be out raking them into piles. Last year, he had rolled in them. A tall man with greying hair and creases in his forehead, his sweater with holes at the elbows and his jeans and shoes covered in mud. Laughing. He was in his late fifties then, and still so much like a boy.

"It reminds me of growing up in Stratford," he had said. "Kicking the leaves on the way home from school and along the railroad track beside the Avondale Cemetery."

When Sue met Jerry at a party for a mutual friend who had decided to run for City Council, they were both in their mid-forties.

After long days of teaching for her and practising law for Jerry, they had worked evenings in Martin Drew's campaign office that fall. Later, a crowd would often go for a beer or coffee. A few months later, Jerry had asked her to marry him. To her own surprise, having long ago given up on the idea of marriage, she had hesitated only briefly before saying yes.

Some years earlier, she had lived for a while with a man who had insisted she wanted her own way all the time. It had baffled her, but no matter what she said or did, he found a way of twisting her words beyond her recognition. Then said *she* was the rigid one. Once, he told her she was always bumping into people and falling down, something so untrue that it had defied reason. She had been suddenly aware then why his wife had left him, leaving a house bare of furniture with only a note pinned to the mirror in the bathroom. Sue had been about to turf him when he left of his own accord. Even though she had been on edge all the time they had been together, she was still surprised at how relieved she had felt after he was gone. She could be herself again and knew she would never pretend or cater to a man's whims again. When her relationship with Jerry developed gradually over a course of months from friendship to romance, it had soon been clear he had not wanted her to be anyone but herself.

Now, Jerry could scarcely eat and he slept more all the time. It was a year since the surgeon had cut into him and found the cancer had spread beyond the scalpel's reach. He had been able to remove some of it and, for a while, Jerry had seemed better. After a round of radiation, Sue had even begun to believe that his health would continue to improve. But now she wondered. That was why she had made the appointment with the psychic. She had needed to know something no one else could tell her. Or *would* tell her. She sometimes wanted to yell at the doctors. They gave answers to her questions that were always vague. Now, her head and stomach ached. She reached for the Pepto Bismol and sipped a capful from the pink bottle.

"Is your stomach bothering you?" Jerry asked.

"As a matter of fact, it is," she said, unable to hide her irritation at the question.

Jerry turned away, sat down, and put his head in his hands.

She kicked at a pile of books under the table and watched them slide across the floor. Strung out like a taut wire, she felt ready to crack at any moment. It was not Jerry's fault. None of this was. But she did not like feeling she might be caught out, especially when she had only gone to see the psychic with the thought that it could help them.

"Oh yeah, sure," Jerry would likely reply. "How could something like that help me?" What he needed was a miracle. They both knew that. That was the tragedy of it all. Propelled toward a certain end, she had stopped paying attention to anything but her own fear. She started to pick up the books, trying to hide the fact that she was stifling sobs.

"Sue, just plain Sue, I hardly think so," Jerry used to say.

She used to think he would suddenly realize all her flaws and the criticism would begin. She was wary, knowing how charming a man could be at first and then turn into a bully. Instead, her husband had turned into a man who would not live much longer. She hated that he was going to die. But she could not stand to watch it happen either and sometimes she wished he would get it over with.

"Oh, Christ," Sue said. "I'm sorry." What guilt could do, she thought. Here she was snapping at him because he had asked her an innocuous question.

"I'm sorry, too."

"It's okay," she said finally. They seemed to irritate each other more often even when there was no tangible reason. And if she brought up some of the questions she would like to ask, that would likely incite another misunderstanding. She wished she had asked more about his first wife. He might die before she had a chance to find out. All she knew was that he had been married many years before. Although they had been wildly in love, he had said it was more like playing house than marriage. And then his wife was killed in a freak accident when a car had mounted a curb and pinned her against a building. If Sue asked him about that now, maybe Jerry would think she had not been listening when he had told her about it on one of the city walks they had taken exploring different neighbourhoods when they were first getting to know each other.

Maybe it was also because she did not think much about the earlier part of her life either; the part before Jerry. It felt as if it had taken a long time to move beyond the dreadful insecurities of her twenties. She had not probed deeply to find something she could do that gave her life a structure. Her favourite subject in high school had been history, but she was good at the sciences and there had been a need for teachers in that area. So, she had become a high-school physics teacher. She liked dealing with something she could write down as an equation. Liked to teach the material in such a way that the students understood *how* a particular point was reached. Isaac Newton himself had said he stood "on the shoulders of giants." Ideas had been in the air and the ideas of one scientist led to the next one's discovery, history in the making, people in any age always verging on discovery. She was able to incorporate her interest in history into her work by pointing out these connections to her students. Now, when people learned of her budding interest in art, it surprised them. But it had surprised her most of all.

"I feel sick," he said.

She watched him make his way across the kitchen and over into the living room. He was weaving, almost as if he had been drinking.

"Do you want help?" she asked, following him in case he lost his balance.

"I'll just lie down on the sofa," he said.

"Okay." For a moment, Sue continued to watch him. When these flashes of sudden weakness arose, she often seemed to be caught unprepared, and she had to be careful that he did not suddenly accuse her of being too solicitous. So, once he was settled, she went upstairs to their bedroom. She would fix her dark hair up in a swirl and surround her face with small curls, knowing how much that used to please him. Even though he might be too sick to notice.

When Sue returned to the living room, Jerry's eyes were closed. There were dark shadows across his sunken cheeks. She turned to leave the room.

"I'm awake, Sue," he said.

"Can I get anything for you?" she asked.

"I don't think so," Jerry said. "Surprise me." A wan grin crossed his face.

Shivers moved through her as she moved toward him and ran her hand through his curly hair. She kissed his forehead. "It's good to see you smile," she said.

"Pardon?"

*

Sun glinted on the front windows as Sue headed up the flag-stone path on her return from a short walk. She was sure Jerry would be sleeping again. He's going to die, she thought. It was not a nightmare she had awakened from, but what was going to happen. The psychic had not said so, but she could hear his voice nonetheless as if he were there so someone else could tell her. And, anyway, she had known it for a long time. So had Jerry.

"All the things I wanted to do with the rest of my life," he had said. "This isn't fair." He had punched the counter that day, sending a mug of coffee crashing to the floor.

"You've already made a difference, Jer." She had calmed herself by breathing deeply. "I love you," she said.

"So many more years I would have had with you." Then he mouthed his response to her last words. "I love you, too, Bird."

He never called her "Hon" or "Sweetheart." Those names she associated, for no good reason, with suburbia. She was his "Small Bird," his "Chickadee," names unique to their relationship. She wanted to bury herself in a book or a piece of music to make her forget that one day soon her husband would leave her, that she would be all alone. How could she have imagined that going to a psychic would make any difference? What foolishness. Still, colour had begun to fill her life in a most satisfying way. She might dream of the impossible in wanting her husband to recover, but her need for colour was already finding expression as it filled the void that stretched wide open ahead of her. She needed colour. Golden sunshine. The white bark of the birch with flecks of purple and green. Sky. A jet contrail, a pale white strip against an expanse of blue, high above.

"There you are," Jerry said when she came through the door. "I've missed you, Bird." Music filled the room. Jazz. He had not listened to jazz for a while. It was Joshua Redman. It was almost as if the music flowed magically through the saxophone, each note and phrase touching her with its perfection. She never had the ear for music Jerry had, but she knew when something moved her.

"There were a couple of phone calls," Jerry's voice greeted her now. "I wrote messages."

Sue smiled at the sound of his voice so clearly saying he had been able to deal with the calls. This was one of his better days. Sometimes he let the answering machine take messages. Some days that was all he could do.

"Did you have a good swim?" he asked.

Sue went regularly to a nearby pool and Jerry must have thought that was where she had been. "I was shopping," she said.

"Isn't it Halloween today?" he asked.

"Yes," Sue said, although dates and events were a blur these days. She had almost forgotten to vote in the federal election, and was surprised the next day when the Liberals had won so handily. The electors had overthrown the first female prime minister and left her without a seat in the House of Commons. It seemed they were really punishing the former prime minister who had relinquished control of the party already.

"I almost forgot about Halloween this year, but when I remembered I bought chips and chocolate bars. And I brought home a pumpkin, too." The store at the intersection of their street with Bloor had the orange squash in a pile on a table outside the door. There were larger ones on the sidewalk. "I left it on the front porch. I'll bring it inside to cut eyes and a mouth in it."

"Oh, good," Jerry said. "Can I carry it in for you?"

"It's not too heavy. I brought it home without rolling it along the street." Sue visualized an orange ball pushed slowly with an outstretched foot and passersby stopping to stare. Surely the stuff of slapstick comedy.

He laughed and she was glad that he was amused by that scenario.

"What are you going to do with the pumpkin?" he asked, after she had brought it inside.

"Just watch me," she said, pleased as his face lit up again. She drew a cat's face on the surface, then carved out the pieces. Afterwards, she put a candle inside and the cat smiled mischievously, as if he had a secret.

"I'll help put it on the porch," he said.

The gremlins appeared at the door as dark began to fall. By then, jack-o'-lanterns were lit at most houses and children of various ages traipsed along the street in their costumes. The little ones climbed the stairs awkwardly, gripping trick-or-treat bags. A princess. A puppy. Shy children tentatively said, "Thank you." The parents stood on the walk near the street, watchful. From where Jerry lay on the sofa, dozing, he could see the callers and occasionally raised his head enough to comment.

"Are you a pirate?" he asked one small boy.

"Yes."

Sue could tell both Jerry and the child were delighted.

"That was one of my favourite costumes when I was a kid," he said to the boy.

The older children descended in hordes toward half-past seven. They rushed from one house to another in a clamour of noise and laughter.

After Sue gave out all the treats, she turned off the lights.

"What would you like to eat tonight?" she asked.

"Roast beef," he joked, "with Yorkshire pudding."

Sue chuckled, knowing he was rarely hungry anymore. Beef consommé perhaps as a substitute. He still managed finely cut meat and vegetables some days. Going out to the kitchen, she spied the cassette tape Hans Jonker had given her where she had left it inadvertently out on the counter the other day. She tossed it into a drawer filled with recipes, fuses, string, and some old pill containers. She did not imagine she would ever play it. The psychic had been an interesting man, but likely a charlatan like others she had heard about.

Jerry. Jerry. Jerry.

They had had so many plans until the diagnosis of cancer. Even then, they had taken a trip out west where in the mornings on the coast, their bodies touching in bed, they had listened to the thunder of the Pacific pounding on the beach just beyond their window. Later, wearing green nylon ponchos, they had walked on the beach in the rain, watching sandpipers run along the shore, leaving little three-pronged foot markings on the wet sand.

Sue had wanted to go to the far coast of Vancouver Island and Jerry had promised to take her. She had known by then they would never make it to Tuscany or Provence together. Or even back to Quebec City where they had wandered the narrow streets of the old town, exploring the historic buildings. They had moved among the throngs milling on the boardwalk in front of the Chateau Frontenac. The Plains of Abraham, where they had followed trails above the river, had been a mass of golden leaves the year before. They had spoken French to the owner of the small hotel where they had stayed. He had told them the names of restaurants, some of which were well-kept secrets of the locals.

There were still so many things left unexplored.

Sue put the consommé down on the table beside Jerry, glad to see a contented look on his face. The thought that they would soon have to talk about his funeral flitted through her mind.

"Do you mind if I go out for a few minutes to see what's going on at the other houses?" she asked. The thought of talking about what would occur after his death, or about his death, made her shudder.

"No," he said. "I don't mind."

"I won't be long."

Just that weekend, they had had to turn the clock back one hour, and dark had begun to descend much earlier. Leaves shone in the lamplight. Skeletons hung from trees at one house, like small bobbing buoys. At another, lit pumpkins lined the walk. Some of the adults also wore costumes. Sue did not want to go back inside the house. When there had still been more time, they had had long discussions about their lives together and how that soon would end, but since it had never felt quite real to her then, she had been able to manage those conversations. Now, it felt as if the next time she came out onto the street it would be winter and a season would have passed almost overnight.

"How was it?" Jerry asked, his face heavy with fatigue.

"People are having a good time."

As he smiled, the trace of freckles across his cheeks crinkled. "I love Halloween," he murmured.

"I know."

"I fell asleep when you were out," he said thoughtfully, his eyes following her. "When I woke up, I thought I'd like to talk about our plans. You know, for after. I want to be cremated," he continued. "I think I'd like some kind of memorial later. A celebration."

Relieved that she did not have to raise it, Sue hoped she could have this talk with him now without breaking down.

"Where?" she asked, brushing her hand through her hair. She could see in the pane of the nearby window that the bangs fell on either side to form a part and that there was a white streak through the front wave that she had been told looked striking. Jerry had often said so.

"If we don't get around to deciding, I'd be glad with anything you come up with."

"But I don't want to decide something that important for you." She bit her bottom lip and waited for him to answer.

Instead, he looked bewildered, even hurt. "Why not?" he asked.

"It's something I'd rather you knew about." Still, concerned that she might upset him further, Sue tried to think of some place that would feel comfortable to him. "Maybe on the island?" All her memories about the archipelago across the bay from downtown Toronto were ones of relaxed exploration and discovery. Before she knew Jerry, she had often cycled there and found a spot to read on rocks just below the boardwalk. It was a place where she had watched sailboats dance in the waves on fine summer days and kayaks with lone paddlers streak down the shoreline.

"Yes," he said. "Near the water. Where we were married. Martin could make reservations for the clubhouse."

He flashed a conspiratorial smile, one she had not seen in a long time. One that indicated they had resolved something significant. And then, he fell asleep again. Just like that. His face was lined and craggy, but he still looked peaceful in sleep. She had a momentary image of finding her husband gone. A body. Gradually getting cold.

"I'm not ready," Sue murmured.

"I know, love." Jerry was not asleep after all. He had only closed his eyes.

"No funeral?" she asked.

"Yes, I guess. It would be a formality," he said. "Look, Sue, there's something I'd like to tell you." He looked suddenly worried.

"What is it, Jer?" What did he want to tell her that she did not already know? Anything was possible, she supposed. She had protected aspects of her own life she had found impossible to explain. After a while, it had become too large a hurdle, something she feared might change everything. Would Jerry have been less loving had he learned about that early pregnancy?

Sue thought about Jerry's childhood in small town Ontario where he had first known Martin. Surely, a man who had practised family law and accepted legal aid so he could see clients from across the spectrum would have been able to hear her story. What had restrained her had been threats her mother had made that could still make her tremble. Even at the prospect of telling her husband. She had revelled in his love of wine, of fine food, of music, of walking on the Bruce Trail. Of the tiny cabin they had near the water on a lake up north. Of how sensuous and affectionate he was. And she had chuckled when she had seen his hand go to his head as he spoke to scratch at some sudden itch, then toy with a tuft of hair. Or to his forearm. Maybe his leg, just behind the knee. His crotch. She knew he could also become impatient at times, but that was not why she had not told him.

"You know that I've made you the beneficiary of my will."

"Yes, but if you want to change anything, just tell me," she said. He had always been generous with his good fortune and could well have made arrangements he had forgotten to tell her about.

"I don't," he said. "But after I die there could be some disputes when Martin, as executor, goes looking for anyone else who might have a claim."

Suddenly, she thought of the psychic's words, but she still thought he had been so wide of the truth that she discounted them. It occurred to her the man might have confused her own hidden past with Jerry's. That must be it, she thought, but she was still baffled by Jerry's words.

"Is there anyone who might have a claim?" Something about the way he had said it put her antennae suddenly on alert.

"I don't know," he said.

"How could you not know?" she asked. At least he must have some idea.

"I just don't," he said, his voice rising. "That's all. I don't like it when you sound as if you're accusing me of something."

"Calm down, Jerry," she said, lowering her voice. "It's not good for you to get so agitated."

"I am calm."

"Listen," she said. "I just asked a question. That's all. Let's drop it." Whatever it was, she would rather not know if it upset him so much.

*

Sue climbed the stairs to where Jerry now sat on the edge of the queen bed where she had left him earlier to rest again. The sheets were rumpled and the duvet had fallen almost to the floor. His eyelids drooped as he pulled himself under the sheets and drew the duvet up. Sue finished placing it around his shoulders as she crawled in beside him. None of this would be happening if she had not become involved in Martin Drew's campaign that fateful fall. She would not have met Jerry. He might be dying, but she would not know about it.

"I'm sorry, Bird," he whispered. Then fell asleep.

Sue lay awake beside him for a long time. She could hear the wind moaning and shafts of light from a nearby street lamp came through the blinds. Somewhere, boards creaked in the old house.

Although she had not known it at the time, her life had changed the day she had walked into Martin Drew's storefront office near Honest Ed's on Bloor Street. A tall man in a black turtleneck and jacket stood near the table of pamphlets and sign-up sheets. A handsome man, she had thought at the time, admiring his red hair and aquiline nose. The man she had not known would become her husband.

Martin came from behind to greet her, giving her a hug.

A neighbour who had been involved in the local ratepayer association, Martin had helped her deal with racoons raiding garbage next door and strewing potato peelings, bones, and eggshells across her garden. He had put her in touch with the local councillor. Not too many months later, Martin had decided to run for the position.

"Jerry," he said as she stood in the office that day. "Meet my neighbour, Sue Walters."

Both of them were quiet. Sue felt she had been caught staring. The man finally put out his hand. "I'm Jerry Reid," he said. "Hello, Sue."

"Hello," she said, taking his hand briefly.

The telephone on the table rang and Martin reached for it. "Yes," he said. "The meeting will start in half an hour." He hung up and then beckoned to her. "Have a coffee, Sue."

There were lawn signs piled against the wall and maps overhead showing all the streets in the ward in minute detail. A large photo of Martin also hung on the wall. Sue had been involved in other kinds of campaigns and was nervous about whether she would have enough time for this one. As well as all the preparation she already had to do for her students, there were the extracurricular meetings she was by then involved in. Not to mention the *Take Back the Night* march once again. She had been there in the ranks through years of struggling for women's rights, for adequate daycare for children, for the rights of diverse peoples. It was discussions about those issues that had shown Martin was supportive of initiatives that mattered to her.

"Let me get it for you," Jerry said. He went to a table where a large urn was plugged into a wall outlet. She watched the dark stream of hot liquid fill the mug, noting that he wore no rings.

He pointed to the chairs on the far side of the room and her eyes followed his gaze to a spot where people had started to gather. "Martin's going to speak," he said.

This was a year or so after the departure of the man she had lived with for longer than made any sense to her later. He had packed up most of his belongings in a large brown suitcase with a strap around it. As well as whatever remained in cardboard boxes he had brought back from the supermarket at the corner. She had filled her time with work since then, thinking she would never be interested in a man again. The principal at her school had asked her to be on a committee and she was treasurer of the provincial association for teachers. In the evenings, other meetings, concerts, or skating on the rink in front of City Hall took up her time. She frequented the local pool, swam laps, and occasionally met with a friend for coffee afterwards.

She had wanted to support Martin even if it meant taking on a bit more than she could handle. She knew part of it was that even with all her activity, she was feeling lonely.

"How do you know Martin?" Jerry asked.

"He lives near me. I met Emily first. His wife. And you?" She did not say she found Martin friendlier than Emily. That was often the way, that one person in a couple was more outgoing or warmer. She also felt Emily was wary of her, but had never understood why.

"We grew up together," Jerry said.

"Where was that?"

"Stratford."

"I didn't know Martin came from Stratford."

"He does."

"And how did you get involved in the campaign?" she asked.

"I suppose because I encouraged Martin to run," Jerry said. "So he asked me to be his campaign manager. That gives me the privilege of asking if there are things you might like to do."

"I haven't decided yet. I just know I want to do something." She looked at the map again. "Lots of territory to cover," she said. "Probably canvass. I like meeting people."

"Great," he said.

Canvassing also meant she would be away from the office and not find herself feeling uncomfortable around this man.

Not having suddenly to explain to herself that she was staring at him again. All she needed was another ill-fated love affair. Anyway, he did not seem more interested than he would be in anyone prepared to volunteer and when the door opened again, he turned to greet the man and woman who came through it.

"Great to see you," he said. "Martin will be speaking soon. You can hang up your coats over there. And there's coffee. I'm Jerry Reid, Martin's campaign manager."

This was how Sue knew Jerry for weeks, as Martin's campaign manager. He seemed well-organized and invariably polite. But once when she came into the office, she heard him cursing into the telephone. When he hung up, he yelled at one of the volunteers who was sitting quietly, waiting for instructions.

"Can I help you?" Sue asked, aware that his tone and language would create a profound impression on the young woman. It would not contribute to the smooth campaign Sue had known by instinct was desirable. What's the matter with him? she wondered. He was showing a side of himself she had not witnessed before. Surely, he knew better. By now, she also had learned he was a lawyer and while that might be typical behaviour for some of them, it was not reflective of the image he had thus far portrayed.

"I'm sorry," Jerry said, shaking his head. "Thanks, Sue. Maybe you can get things organized for Cathy. She's going to take a kit for her poll so she can canvass the blocks nearest to where she lives."

"Karen," the young woman said.

"Hi, Karen." Sue smiled at the woman who appeared to be no older than nineteen or twenty and very nervous. She had covered for Jerry, Sue thought, even though she hated the "important man" image he projected as he turned to deal with a reporter from the newspaper, a man she recognized from photographs in the media. A distinctive flourish of white hair. Somewhat oversized ears. Insouciant smile. He started talking to Jerry. She assumed he would ask the direct questions he was known for, digging for pertinent information. This interview would be important to the campaign. But even so, there was no reason for Jerry to have been bad-tempered with the new volunteer. "What is Martin going to do about the homeless situation?" she heard the reporter ask, instead of asking about the plans around a proposed high-rise, a question the local residents had raised repeatedly.

As soon as the reporter left, Jerry grabbed his jacket and rushed out of the office.

It went on like that. Sue would come in after canvassing on at least one evening every week. Almost always, she would encounter Jerry. She did not see him lose his temper again and might have forgotten the incident, except every so often she would hear an underlying tone that sounded on the verge of impatience. A rising voice. A heavy sigh. Perhaps not anything she would have particularly noticed if not for the earlier incident. If she came in near closing time, she also noticed two or three people who left together. One night, Martin asked if she would like to join them.

"Please do," Jerry said.

"Thanks," she said.

At the nearby Brunswick House, they all sat in two adjoining booths. They ordered beer and talked in animated voices about the progress of the campaign. Martin wanted to know what reaction the canvassers were getting at the door.

"What about you, Sue?"

"Oh, it's mixed," she said. "I'm disappointed in how little many people seem to know or care. But if they'll give me a moment, they ask questions and seem interested in your platform. A number have asked for lawn signs or have said they'd be willing to take one. I pass those requests on right away."

"Of course," Jerry said. "Sue's amazing."

Oh, she thought. I didn't know he noticed. She recalled the night he had stormed out of the office after he managed to

deal with that reporter. He had thanked her for giving information to the volunteer, who, by then, had probably thought
of leaving without her canvas kit. Sue supposed she was
granting that situation too much prominence in that nothing
like it had happened again and he had apologized not only to
the volunteer, but also to her. Surely, everyone was entitled to
some impatience.

After one beer, Sue took out her wallet. "Have to get up
early in the morning," she said.

"I'll pay," Jerry said, slapping a bill on the table. "Could I
walk you home?"

"I'll pay for my own," she said quietly even as she wondered
why she found it so difficult to accept this gesture from him.
To say, "Thanks" and smile politely. Ordinarily she would, but
in assuming this he had misjudged her. No more men like that
last one who attempted to take over, an almost unstated motto
by then.

"Okay," he said. "May I walk you home?"

"All right." She only hesitated for a moment.

So, he accompanied her along Bloor to the foot of her street,
a short one that ran north.

"I live only a couple of blocks away," he said. "Maybe I could
call you some time."

"Maybe after the campaign," she said, thinking he would
forget by then. This show of interest felt uncomfortable to her,
and besides, she knew she would continue to see him at the
campaign office until the election.

He looked disappointed. "All right," he said. "We'll celebrate
the results."

She nodded. Her assessment of him could be wrong, but she
was prepared to wait to find out.

*

When Jerry's pain increased, a nurse began to come in daily to
check his drugs and monitor dosages. He had more difficulty

going upstairs by then and one of the nurses recommended a hospital-type bed for the living room. There were rails on the sides he could use to pull himself up and the mattress could be raised and lowered. Sue felt as if he were getting thinner by the hour. Indeed, his legs and arms were like sticks. He had to be moved regularly to avoid painful bedsores. One day, when his eyes opened, he pressed his lips together and groaned.

"I can't stand this. The pain is unbearable. For God's sake, put a pillow over my head," he begged. "End this misery."

"Oh, Jerry." Sue understood no one needed to live in this kind of pain and that carefully titrated dosages should be able to contain his agony. The doctor had agreed, telling them there could still be pain that broke through and that he had approved special doses in between the regular ones when that happened. But sometimes, even before they could be administered, Jerry was desperate.

"This is no way to live," he groaned.

Sue flinched. No, she thought, it isn't, but everything was suddenly moving so much more quickly than she had anticipated. She did not know what to do.

"Would you like some visitors?" she asked, her voice sounding as if it scraped across marble floors and glossy countertops in another realm entirely.

"You must be joking."

"I was thinking of your friends in the meditation group." They might provide some distraction for him.

Jerry nodded then. Yes, he knew these people were ones he wanted to see. He had belonged for a while to a small group that met early on Friday mornings. He had told Sue that those quiet times had changed his perceptions of what was significant. And so, the members began to appear one at a time at his bedside for an hour or two, their presence accentuating in a different way Sue's awareness of time growing shorter.

"How are you, Sue?" one of the women asked as she came through the door.

"I'm tired," Sue admitted, her face crumbling slightly before she breathed in deeply. She knew Jerry was fond of Jane and was embarrassed to think that even though she had trusted her husband, she had been jealous of this woman without even knowing her. She had also been aware that some of her past experience had left her more wary than she ought to be and she had worked hard at dispelling those feelings of jealousy.

"Will you go for a swim while I'm here?" Jane asked, the dark brown eyes of the younger woman radiating concern.

"I think so," Sue said. "If you're comfortable with that. Jerry's looking forward to seeing you." She had mentioned when Jane arranged her visit that swimming was her means of relaxation. Even so, she sometimes felt guilty when she did things to please herself. Even though otherwise, she was sure she would be so stressed that she might say or do things she would regret later. She was grateful that she had been able to get this time off, that the principal had arranged for someone to take her classes and told her to take as long as she needed. It seemed sometimes that her interior monologue was so painful that this time that she had been given was useless. Then, when she swam a few lengths, the buoyancy of the water and her limbs creating a steady rhythm, soothed her. Jerry would be the first to recognize that kind of connection and even acknowledged he had taken up running with Martin and working out for the same reasons.

Jane turned toward the living room. At the sight of Jerry, she winced, frown lines forming between her eyes.

"He's so wan," she whispered.

Sue nodded. "It's all right to go in." She felt Jane's ambivalence. "It is."

Jane moved tentatively toward Jerry and settled in a chair beside his bed. Picking up a zippered bag with her bathing suit and cap in it, Sue kissed him on his forehead. "I'll see you shortly," she said.

At the pool, Sue slipped into the cool water, quickly ducking under the surface. It reminded her of skinny-dipping off the sailboat with Jerry. He had reached for her underwater and stroked her breasts. It was so long since they had been able to hold each other and make love that her body felt deprived. That body that she had carefully guarded for so long before she met him. She swam with an even crawl up the pool and back again. After the first lap, she settled into the breaststroke. Her movements and her breathing became her whole world then and it was forty-five minutes before she emerged and went into the change room to dry her hair and put on her clothes.

Back at the house, the nurse was leaning over Jerry, changing his diaper. A slight paunch sagged now into folds at his waist above his greying pubic hair. His penis hung limply, tiny and almost grey in colour. The skin was wrinkled. She looked at his face, trying not to look shocked or upset, knowing how difficult this indignity was for him, he who had always been so proud of his virility, who had had no idea how his body would fail him. Now his eyes were almost closed and Jane was on the couch behind the bed where she could not see him. Sue realized she had likely moved there to give him privacy until the nurse was finished, saw when he reached his hand over his head and dangled it in the air that Jane, this younger woman who had probably never been more than someone also seeking tranquillity, stood up with eyes averted and took Jerry's hand into hers. Looking toward Sue, who turned away to put her bag down on a chair, she also gently touched his forehead. When the nurse stepped away from the bed and moved to pick up her jacket, Jane then went around to the other side where she reached for a bowl and put a spoonful of applesauce to Jerry's lips. He slurped on it and coughed.

It was only after Jerry dozed off again that Jane joined Sue who now sat at the table at the other end of the room.

"Have something to eat," Sue said, gesturing at the food on the table that people had brought. "I'll make coffee."

"Thanks." Jane took a bagel.

Sue stared out the window at the street where the children passed by on their way home for lunch. She heard the lilting sounds of their conversation and an occasional laugh. Crimson fell from a small Japanese maple as if the tree were undressing, leaf by leaf. It occurred to her that ordinary life went on as usual while her world seemed to have become very small, Jerry's breath, voice and needs almost her entire focus.

On Sunday, Martin came to see Jerry. Sue listened to them talk as she put out towels for her sister, Maggie, who would arrive later that day from Vancouver.

"Remember swimming at the quarry?" Martin asked.

"How could I forget?" Jerry said.

"We jumped from that high rock into the water," Martin said. "Our parents told us not to, of course. How deep the water was, how cold. We felt immortal."

Both of them had grown into strong swimmers and sailboat aficionados. What would happen to Jerry's boat? It was a thirty-foot beauty with a blue line around it and blue canvas covers for the sails. In honour of their marriage, Jerry had named it *Prime Time*.

"Sue won't want it," Jerry said.

"Well, ask her about it," Martin said.

"No, I won't want it," Sue said, going into the room to join the conversation. Not about to become a solo sailor, she would be glad to see the boat go to Martin.

"I really can't think about it now," Martin said.

"All the trips we've taken together. All the races we've entered."

"And lost," Martin added.

"We won the important ones," Jerry said.

Martin was silent.

Sue's thoughts drifted to the trips she and Jerry had taken on the sailboat. He kept it at a marina up north not far from their cabin, a cabin she had always loved but no longer wanted to visit as long as she could not do so with Jerry. Some summers, they had sailed out into the gleaming ripples of Georgian Bay and down the rocky shoreline or through the islands. It was possible to get to many parts of southern Ontario by water. Jerry had maps of all the waterways. But he was right that she would rather Martin have *Prime Time*.

Before she met Jerry, she had been on a sailboat only a couple of times. Once to see the Toronto skyline with a man she had later discovered was dating three or four other women and using his boat as a means to court them. Sue had always known quickly when a man was the wrong one, but not how she would know the right one. Sometimes, she had wondered how that might feel. That was until Jerry came along and she understood finally why no one could really explain it to you until it happened. It was something that transcended words. It had not struck her like a flash of lightning. It had happened over time. Either way, there was a moment when it had become so clear that she had almost wanted to jump up and shout, "Eureka."

Jerry drifted off, his breathing sounding like a rattle in his throat. Martin put on the coffee pot and Sue followed him and stood at the door. He looked up at her with a sad smile, his moustache following the lines of his lips. Tears glistened in his eyes.

"I can't sail in that boat without Jerry," he said.

"He wants you to have it."

"I know that. I understand it. I still find it impossible to think about."

They both knew it was not the boat they were talking about.

"It won't be long," Sue said.

He nodded.

"My sister is coming today." Maggie had offered and Sue had accepted without hesitation.

"Yes, Jerry told me. Is someone meeting her at the airport?"

"No. She'll take a cab." Sue had not thought to ask him. Now she wished she had.

"I could go," he offered.

"Thank you."

"Or I could stay with Jerry while you do."

"That's kind of you. I'd really like to meet Maggie." Sue realized this suddenly now that he had offered. He knew she would not leave for quite that long if anyone else were here. Although Jerry did not have long, it felt as if he had at least another day or two.

Martin found her coat in the closet and held it up while she put her arms into the sleeves.

"Drive safely," he said.

She went into the living room and kissed her husband. "I'll be back soon, love," she whispered.

*

Outside on the street, Sue inserted the car key and attached her seat belt. She looked blindly at the dashboard, thinking of the day she and Jerry were married. Everyone had crossed to the island on the ferry early that morning. The water was cool as she walked along the beach, dipping her bare feet. She had worn a long pale blue skirt and loose blouse that tied in the front. Skirt held high, she had tiptoed through the ripples rolling up onto the sand.

Jerry wore light trousers and a pale shirt that matched hers. Cavorting in the water beside her, he took her hand and pulled her along. Laughing, her hair streamed out behind her in the breeze.

"This is our wedding day," she sang.

"Finally!" He had thought she would never say yes, he had told her. "You were so standoffish for a long time, I didn't even dare ask for a date."

She smiled slightly as she reached to put the key into the ignition. She thought of Martin and Emily who had fallen behind to walk with the young minister. The lines of the ceremony Sue and Jerry had worked out with him were ones they had struggled over as they had looked for ways to make what they would promise to one another reflect their own beliefs.

"I'm not going to obey anyone," Sue had said.

Jerry laughed. "For sure." She was like a bird, he had often said. "And you have to let a bird fly free." The minister had struck out the offending word.

Walking along behind were Maggie and her husband, Angus Milroy. The minister talked with them, their words lost in the wind. Only Maggie and Angus had been invited from either of the families so altogether there were seven of them there that day. Sue bent over and cupped her hand in the water, lifting it to throw droplets at Jerry.

"Bless you," she chuckled.

"Why are you doing that?" he grimaced.

"Because I'm happy."

"What an odd way to show it."

Shards of shadow fell across Sue's face and for a moment she pressed her lips together and was quiet. Only the day before, Jerry had turned and walked out of the restaurant when she had joked about the remarks Martin might make at the wedding. He came back almost right away, but his face was drawn and for a while it was difficult to engage him in conversation.

Is this a mistake after all? she had wondered. It had not been too late. She could have said, "I've changed my mind."

But Jerry had leaned toward her with a contrite smile. "I love you, Suzy Q," he said. "I'm happy, too." Her thought was that he had likely been nervous. She was relieved when she saw everyone with them had relaxed again also, the moment forgotten. Now, as she pulled out of their driveway, she was relieved that those early portents had not turned into future problems.

They had all moved to the patch of grass under a tree picked for the ceremony. The minister looked around, seemingly trying to decide where to stand. The others surrounded them as the vows were spoken. Martin handed the ring to Jerry who put it on Sue's finger. The couple embraced, and Sue felt Jerry's lips on hers, familiar yet different. She had done what she thought she would never do. Marry. What would her mother have said? By now, her parents had both died, and she wondered why fear of their disapproval still kept her from telling Jerry what her mother had told her she must never tell anyone. Surely, he would understand, she figured. Still, she had not told him. Instead, she had thought of Maggie's children who had sent their best wishes and small gifts; these children who had become almost as close to her, even at a distance, as she thought one of her own would have been. But she could not know that and tried not to think about it as she moved into new territory by marrying Jerry. Nonetheless, her mother's admonitions still rang in her mind. She must never speak about her secret. Like a safety deposit box for which she had lost the key, it had to remain forever closed.

And she was Jerry's bird, his chickadee. A bird they both assumed would fly free. This was what Jerry seemed to promise. There was such an aura of hope in those first days that had never entirely left her.

After signing the documents, Martin opened a large wicker basket and handed out wine glasses. He peered into the basket again and with a triumphant smile pulled out a champagne bottle.

"A toast," he said.

Pop.

Soon, they were raising their glasses.

The minister left after that. "I have to get back to the city," he had said. This had been understood, that he would not stay beyond the ceremony. The rest of them had brought food for a picnic and searched for a table that would give them some privacy. Emily laid out the checkered tablecloth and someone placed cutlery on it. Sue and Jerry had wanted their day to be simple.

Sue recalled that she had thought maybe it would not have been so easy to call off the marriage after all. She was glad it had not come to that.

*

Signs above the highway indicated the locations of various traffic jams, and, at every juncture, they seemed to be where Sue was heading. She had not considered all the lights that would stream toward her as people drove back into the metropolis, and she had not left herself any leeway. She hoped she would arrive at Pearson before her sister's plane did.

Maggie was older, with three children, and had been married for thirty years to the same man. Sue thought about how different their lives had been. Even so, they had shared a childhood spent in a house covered with white asbestos shingles in the northern Quebec bush. Their father, one of the earliest to live at the mine site in what became Ile d'Or, had designed the hoist for a new mine. The company had provided the houses. Their mother, a lively woman from Toronto, almost seemed a northerner by birth as she became a skilled poker player and handled guns so well during hunting season she often took other women along with her to show them the best places to shoot partridge. She had also taught Sue how to use a gun. This was something Maggie had commented on more than once. Why not her?

Sometimes, Sue wondered if her childhood had been easier than Maggie's. When her sister was eleven and twelve, no one knew whether their father would come home safely from one of his trips into the bush. But, more often than not, he would arrive singing loudly as he navigated his way from the back door to the kitchen. Maggie said she had been so relieved, she had jumped into his arms to hug him. Their mother had sometimes said that he would have to stop flying in those little planes that landed on the lake or she would go back to the city. Sue had thought it was all a joke, but Maggie had seemed to take it seriously. Sue only knew that by the time she reached her teenage years, he was a quiet, rather droll man, often buried in mysteries by Agatha Christie and books about the Second World War by Winston Churchill. He had also liked helping her with her homework. Never the student Maggie was, Sue had needed all the help she could get.

Time was running out to make it before Maggie's flight landed. Sue thought of snow-capped mountains overlooking English Bay. Maggie's husband, Angus, often drove through Stanley Park to the Lions Gate Bridge to the West End so he could see the mountains more clearly. He loved to take photographs of his and Maggie's trips as well as spots discovered not far from his own doorstep. Like Jerry, Angus Milroy was a lawyer. He worked for one of the mining companies, Amarpec, with an interest in large copper deposits in Chile. Maggie, who had not wanted to move west, now loved it there; yet, as her children moved away, she had become less certain. The Rocky Mountains created a psychological barrier between Vancouver and the rest of the country, she had said. And, as the children gradually reversed their parents' migration, her focus had begun to shift east again. Never intimating that she would move back, she had said enough to make Sue wonder if it might not happen one day.

At the luggage turntable, the bags were already circling. It was five or ten minutes before she saw a familiar lime pompom bouncing back and forth on the handle of a black suitcase. When she looked up, she saw her sister coming toward her. Maggie was still trim and youthful although with an abundance of grey hair to which she had stopped adding highlights.

"You look so tired," Maggie said as she drew nearer.

Rarely did Sue think of their age difference anymore. However, with both their parents gone, there was something reassuring in having an older sister. She'll greet people at the door when I can't face one more person, Sue thought. She'll make coffee in the morning and reorganize all the food in the refrigerator.

Maggie was here to see Jerry one last time, expecting an imminent funeral. Tears streamed down Sue's cheeks.

"Oh, Sue," Maggie said softly, moving to hold her sister.

"How's Angus?" Sue asked when she stopped crying, her voice shaky.

"He sends his love," Maggie said. "He'll fly in the moment we call him."

That moment would come soon, with the bed in the living room and the portable toilet looming up beside it, as much omens as dark ravens or skeletons.

"It won't be long," Sue said. "Not more than a day or two."

"That soon."

"I think so." Only to Martin had she voiced this prescience that the days of *Prime Time* were over. "He wants to give his boat to Martin," she added.

"Oh my."

"Umm."

"Will he know me?"

"He'll know you."

Maggie pulled her suitcase as they began to walk to the elevator that would take them to the parking area. Sue took a small backpack her sister had been carrying and placed it over her shoulder.

"The book I was reading on the plane is in that pack," Maggie said. "And a small something for Jerry."

Sue did not ask what that might be. She wondered if Maggie knew that all Jerry needed now was love, touch, warmth, and the sound of their voices.

When they arrived at the house, Maggie put a CD of country music on that was soft and lyrical. Jerry was asleep, but Sue could see a small smile creep across his face.

"He hears it," Maggie said. "He hears it."

Martin and Maggie went out into the kitchen, leaving Sue alone with Jerry. Their voices, low and gentle, rose and fell quietly in the background. Sue was aware only of the rhythm of their conversation. Jerry's eyes opened and seemed to hold hers. His mouth formed the shape of some words. The first was "love." After awhile, he also mouthed the name, "Maggie."

"She's talking to Martin," Sue said.

He nodded so imperceptibly that if she had not been watching, Sue would have missed it. Shortly after, Maggie walked out of the kitchen and across the room to the hospital bed. From where Sue stood on the other side, she could see the fireplace with a painting over the mantel of northern scenery — rock, birch, and a lake gleaming in sunlight. To the left was a photograph of Jerry and her taken ten years earlier. A handsome couple, he used to say. And happy. For ten years, most of the time they had been. Occasionally, when there were angry words, they had learned to dispel them with good humour and patience. Usually. The prospect of death had made that harder. She felt guilty about the surges of anger that would come over her unexpectedly.

"Jerry," Maggie said gently. "It's Maggie."

He knows, Sue thought. He knows you.

"Angus sends his love," Maggie whispered.

Martin gestured good night from the door. He told Sue he would be back the next evening. When he left, Maggie backed away from the bed and turned to watch her sister. She seemed to ponder something.

"Do you think I might have a chance to do a little shopping tomorrow?" she asked finally.

Sue was momentarily speechless. Shopping? "Oh sure," she said. "Take all the time you want." If that's what you came to do, go shopping. She did not add that final thought to accompany her sarcastic tone.

"I just thought I might be able to find a birthday present for Angus," Maggie said quietly. "I wouldn't be gone all that long."

"Whatever."

They moved around in the kitchen, skirting each other silently.

"I could feel Jerry squeeze slightly when I took his hand. And he had such a smile for me." Although he was too weak to follow through with words, could summon nothing more than a murmur.

"Yes," Sue said. "He gets tired so quickly." This was often how he was now, weak and listless with occasional moments when he showed that something was significant. It could be as simple as a wan smile when she brought him a glass of apple juice or a cup of tea, or perhaps on seeing Maggie, who had come all the way across the country. Sue was grateful and in that recognition also knew that Maggie had had to leave things undone at her home in order to make this trip, such as, finding a gift for her husband.

"Do you have some ideas what you want to buy for Angus?" she asked.

Maggie took in a deep breath. "A book maybe," she said.

When Maggie came back from her walk along Bloor Street the next day, Sue heard her open the front door from where she and Martin sat at the table. Jerry was sleeping.

They both greeted Maggie quietly.

"Did you find something?" Sue asked.

Maggie held up a small package. "Incense," she said. "A book." It was one on politics. "I'll take everything upstairs."

"May I stay overnight?" Martin asked after Maggie disappeared.

"Of course," Sue said.

He could sleep on the couch in the den at the back of the house while Maggie was using the upstairs guestroom. There was a nurse at the house at nights now also. Most often, Sue slept on the sofa to be there when Jerry woke up, to touch him, to sing softly.

That night, when the nurse left the room for a while, Sue knew she would not be gone long and was close enough to be called easily. Sometimes, she read in the kitchen, sitting at the counter while Sue lay beside Jerry on the narrow bed, holding him. Creeping into the bed with him now, she fell asleep with the warmth of her husband beside her, but was soon awakened by his soft moan.

The nurse appeared at the sound and Sue thought she must have extraordinary hearing.

"I'll give him a bit more," the nurse said. A bit more of the painkiller, she meant.

Martin came out into the room and surveyed the scene. He watched Jerry's slow, laboured breathing.

"G'morning, buddy," he murmured. "I'll put on the coffee," he said, turning to Sue.

When that was ready, Maggie brought mugs on a tray. Sue took one, but did not drink it. Jerry's eyes opened and fluttered. As soon as he saw her, he sighed.

"Jerry," Sue whispered.

He stopped breathing. She stared at him. One moment he was there, and now he was not. "He's gone," she said quietly with the sense that she was part of a surreal occurrence.

She could feel Maggie's arm around her as she spoke. Martin was on her other side. All of them were beside the bed now. Sue leaned over Jerry and whispered in his ear, her tears falling onto the pillow beside him.

"You were a good friend, Jerry," Martin said. "The best a man could ask for."

As she heard Martin's voice, Sue thought of him and Jerry as boys at the quarry. Fearless. Voices echoing over water. Martin, saying, "Come on, buddy, your turn now."

And then the whack of a body hitting the surface. They were not divers who entered it as if from a high diving board. Rather, they were boys on an adventure, unaware of peril.

"What would you like me to do?" Martin asked.

Sue appeared to be in a trance.

"Anything at all." He would do what needed to be done without being asked if that was what she wanted.

Sue's eyes rested on Jerry as she spoke quietly to Martin. "Go ahead," she said, unable to say more. Go ahead with whatever needs to be done. A doctor would have to come, but she did not feel ready. If everyone would leave, she could just sit with her husband.

Martin went to the telephone, and she could hear his steady voice in the background. He would take care of things. No one came into the room. Gradually, her breath became even as she held Jerry's cold hand and looked at his face. She wanted to sit there at his side as if she were guarding over him. She was not sure how long she remained like that, aware of nothing but the silence.

"Goodbye, Jer," she whispered, breaking into sobs again. Nothing had prepared her for this. Not even these last days. Everything seemed suddenly so different from only a few minutes before, as if she had been in a storm on a ship and only just managed to fall into a small raft on open, rough water.

Finally, Sue put her husband's hand carefully by his side and pulled a sheet up to a spot just below his chin.

Martin appeared beside her. "I've called the doctor," he said.

"Thanks."

"Jerry said there would be a list of people to call."

He had finally given her instructions and a simple funeral had already been arranged.

"There is," she said. "There's a telephone tree somewhere near the phone." Martin would only have to make four or five calls.

"I'll do them in Jerry's study," he said.

"When you're finished, I'll call Angus," Maggie said.

Martin nodded.

"Anyone else you want me to tell?" Maggie asked. She repeated her question when Sue appeared perplexed.

"Florence, I guess."

"Who's she?"

"A cousin of Jerry's. I don't know if she'll be up to coming to Toronto for the funeral. I just know she'll want to know. We'll plan the memorial far enough ahead so she can make it." Sue was not sure what else she wished to convey to Florence. It felt as if she were missing something important, something beyond the stark reality of Jerry's death, of his lingering presence that she was afraid would dissipate too quickly. She wanted some sense that he was still watching. A spirit.

"Where is she?" Maggie asked.

"She lives in Blenheim. In southwestern Ontario. I've met her. Lovely older woman. Jerry's kept in touch with her. Mostly by phone. She doesn't like coming into the city so after his diagnosis, he went to see her. She's going to be terribly upset."

"Maybe you'd like to make that call," Maggie said.

"I think you're right," Sue said. "I would."

*

From the door at the front of the chapel, Sue could see blurred shapes filling the pews. Men and women in business suits. More people than she had anticipated. No one Jerry was related to would be at the service. As it turned out, Florence was too ill to make the journey. She had said she was grateful for Jerry's last visit when he could still travel.

"I would have come if I could, my dear," she had said. "Please keep in touch with me."

Besides Martin, Florence was the only link she had with Jerry's past and Sue scarcely knew her. It all felt so tenuous. She walked into the front pew with her eyes on the coffin, feeling herself move from numbness to tears then back again. Only the presence of Maggie and Angus, who had flown in the night before, and Martin and Emily on the other side, kept her anchored. She could have been floating on the ceiling, watching from there. When she began to quiver, Martin put his arm around her. She curled her fingers around a tissue. The thought of Jerry in the coffin scratching at his elbow and trying to raise the lid was almost her undoing. She wanted to go and snatch away the flowers she had bought for him and raise the lid before he suffocated.

The minister entered and moved to the front of the chapel and her attention turned to him. A small goatee and thick glasses with narrow wire frames gave him a distant air, but she knew that was an illusion. He was the same minister who had married them and had come to the house to talk with Jerry when he was ill. Each time, his warmth and friendliness had soothed Jerry. On his most recent visit, the two of them had discussed the music for this service. Jerry had considered Mozart, but the gospel piece the pianist now started to play was one Sue had chosen. *There will be peace in the valley for me.*

"What about Beethoven?" the minister had asked.

Mostly, what they had settled on was music anyone who knew Jerry would expect. After the cremation, Martin would arrange for the ashes to be put in an urn and brought to the house. Sue would keep the small brass container on the mantel until she took it up north to scatter the ashes over water near their cabin. That was what Jerry had requested. Also she would plant a small spruce tree there in his memory. The celebration of his life was left in Martin's hands. They would gather on the island in the spring or summer when the weather was warmer.

Once they were seated, Sue's eyes were drawn to the white cloth over the coffin again, then to its centre, where one spray of lilies rested, a white bow tied around the long green stems. Otherwise, Jerry had requested donations be made to Amnesty International.

"No flowers," he had said. "Except yours, Sue."

Sue could feel Maggie's hand holding hers throughout the service and her sister's eyes on her every so often. She also sensed Angus's repeated glances. Martin and Emily, their eyes red, held each other. A textured wall hanging with bright yellow interwoven strands reminiscent of a Van Gogh palette reminded Sue of their father's funeral held here years earlier, then, more recently, their mother's. Her parents' move to Toronto had not been anticipated, but in their more frail years they had chosen to live in a city. Maggie would think of their funerals, too. Around the corner were their plaques, their ashes in urns behind the carved letters of their names, birth and death dates inscribed in gold letters. The hesitation she had had about scattering Jerry's ashes rather than have a cemetery plot or niche was prompted by the knowledge that there would be no outward mark of his existence anyone could visit. Even she might not continue to go to the cabin up north and see the tree she might plant eventually grow. No one would come into the mausoleum, as she did occasionally, to put some small token on the ledge just below her parents' names. A small stone or an acorn. Once, a TTC transfer. She thought her parents would have appreciated those gifts, knowing that from her they were significant. Without children, there might be no way to trace a family that ended with Jerry's passing.

Her father had loved genealogy, showing her and Maggie and, eventually Wally, the charts he had inherited, which had been written at least a century earlier. These charts had traced back through layers of ancestors. He was happy when he could read the hallmarks on family silver and let them know these connections were what made them firmly rooted. The idea of roots had made little sense to Sue in a northern town carved out of the bush, a town that existed with rocks beside and underneath everything. What was solid was the rock. Sue had tolerated her father's enthusiasm, but she had never shared it. Perhaps because he seemed, in that fervour, to look only to the past. The people on the gravel streets and wooden sidewalks of the mining town were the ones who had interested her. Although French was the language mainly spoken there, it was all the different languages the immigrants from Europe had spoken, that had intrigued her.

As a child, there were so many things she had not understood about migration. Only as an adult, when she and Maggie had made homes so far apart and their parents were deceased, had it dawned on her that the way most people lived was in motion. Some, due to upheaval in their countries had been forced to flee; others had imagined a better life somewhere else; and others had simply ended up where they were by happenstance. Like her. She had never intended to live in Toronto. Only when she had met Jerry had she felt at home. Now, she would come in through the foyer of their house to an empty living room, looking for him. Then, she would head for the stairs against the far wall and go up to his study or to their bedroom with the skylight where the sun shone in on bright days, only to feel his absence.

Tears fell onto her blouse and something heavy rose in her chest. Her face turned red. She could scarcely breathe.

"Sue," Maggie whispered. "Sue."

She let out a long breath as her head fell onto her sister's shoulder. Maggie's arm tightened around her. The strains of Oscar Peterson's "Hymn to Freedom" surrounded them. As the service ended, Sue could hear noses blowing and muffled whispers. People started to get up.

"They'll wait for you to go out before they do," Maggie whispered.

Slowly, Sue rose and walked with Maggie and Angus to the steps at the front of the mausoleum. People followed, stopping at the door to offer their condolences. Sue did not hear much of what anyone said, although she pretended to.

"I'm sorry for your loss."

Similar words echoed over and over.

"Thank you for coming."

"Thank you for caring."

"Yes, he was a wonderful man."

"Yes."

There were quite a few people Sue had not previously met. She hoped everyone had signed the visitation book. Later, she would ponder over some of their names, wondering about their connection to Jerry. She recognized two women he had met in law school and introduced to her one evening on the crowded sidewalk on Bloor Street. A young man standing off to the side also had a slightly familiar look. Sue turned to ask Martin who he was, but Martin had moved away to the other side of the church entrance where he was speaking with people who were also strangers to her. She tucked away the question for later.

"Jerry was such an extraordinary man. So competent, yet so gentle," a woman said. She was dressed in a charcoal grey suit with a deep purple silk scarf.

"I don't know if you realize, Sue, but he was one of the bright lights of the profession," said the man who spoke to her next. "We need more like him."

Sue nodded. And he had the nerve to die, she thought. Damn him. She caught herself. She must not be angry today. But with the only other option a flood of tears, she could only draw in a breath and bite her lip. As she looked around, people seeming part of a far-off tableau, she saw the young man again. Her gaze lingered on his reddish hair. Again, he seemed familiar. He stood somewhat apart from everyone else, and looked as if he were waiting for someone.

"It isn't fair," another voice said. "He still had so much to live for."

Sue turned to look at the couple in front of her.

"Yes," she sighed.

*

Only by chance had he seen the obituary in *The Globe and Mail* at his dentist's office in Stratford, Thomas thought. He didn't even know the man in the coffin at the front of the chapel. Who would go to a funeral where he knew no one? The newspaper had been on the table in the dentist's waiting room only two days earlier. He'd fished out the sports section and started leafing through it from the back. On the first page he came to, there were death notices.

As he started to turn the pages, a name caught his eye. A familiar name. *Gerald Foster Reid.* It had startled him so much he had almost left without seeing the dentist. Could it be that this man was his father? The birth date had made it possible. He had read the full obituary then. *Born in Stratford, Ontario.* It had to be the same Jerry Reid he had been told about. It had not taken him too long after having his teeth cleaned and examined to decide to go to the funeral and be a spectator at the last rites of the father he had never met.

From the dentist's office, he had quickly driven home to the bungalow he had shared with his mother until she had died earlier that year. He had not gone through her papers and scrapbooks yet. Every time he started, he could not continue. It always upset him too much. But now he was looking for something. A photograph, maybe, of his father. There had to be at least one photograph. But he found nothing, that is until he had scoured her old high-school yearbooks.

He observed the mourners carefully from his seat at the back of the chapel. The woman he had seen sit in the front pew with a couple on either side of her must be the widow. He had read her name, Susan, in the paper. If he had found his father earlier, would this woman have been an obstacle for him? He did not see Florence and wondered if she knew about the funeral. She must know. He was not sure what her relationship to Jerry Reid was. Maybe she was an older friend of his mother's who had also known his father. It was clear she had somehow known both of them. Florence had come into his life again since his mother's death. She had been at that funeral. He had wondered why she had never talked about his father. Even when he asked her, she was quiet, as if she had been asked not to say anything. It was so unlike the Florence he had known otherwise. A woman with an enormous hug and warm banter that belied her age. She seemed more like his mother's age. He missed his mother's hug more than he wanted to think about.

After the service, people streamed out of the chapel. Thomas stood under a tall tree with spreading branches, the sun shining through to brighten the dull day. He watched a man speak with the widow and then turn to walk to a parked car. As he looked at her, Thomas saw her glance in his direction. He was not sure if she had noticed him. A lot of people were likely strangers to her. Business associates of his father's? Friends from college? He did not see anyone from Stratford. At least, not anyone he knew.

As people got into cars and gradually left, the young man lingered under the trees. He wanted to speak to the woman, but was afraid he would upset her. This did not seem to be the time or place for that. What would his mother have told him to do? He stood there for a long time, until almost the last car pulled away and two men closed the doors to the mausoleum. A breeze brushed gently through his hair and dark clouds began to form overhead. When he heard thunder, he returned to his car and sat behind the wheel. How strange it was to have been at his father's funeral without ever having met the man about whom he had had so many fantasies. He had often wondered what his father looked like, especially when other children asked about him. When he had asked his mother, she had been evasive. He learned there was no sense in trying to find out very much from her. Most of the time, this had not preoccupied him. He did all the things other children did. Read books. Played hockey. Swam at the quarry. His mother always had treats for his friends, so they had been glad to come and exchange hockey cards or play some game. Over time, there were many other children also living with only one of their parents or with a new stepmother or stepfather who had moved in with them.

He turned the key in the ignition and drove away slowly. It was only when he had looked in those high-school yearbooks that he had found anything concrete. In a class photograph, Thomas had found a Jerry Reid, one of the taller boys in the back row. He was also in photographs of the football and hockey teams. What had surprised Thomas most, and at first given him shivers, was how much he resembled this man.

He passed by the mausoleum again before heading to the exit onto Yonge Street. He was hungry, but anxious to get back to Stratford where he now lived alone in the house left to him by his mother. He might sell it, but he was not sure if he was ready yet for the changes that would ensue from that. If his father were still alive, he might have had an entirely other life. As it was, his father would remain a stranger.

*

Rain streaked down the windowpanes where Sue sat looking out through bare branches at a bleak landscape. All she could see were sagging staircases on the backs of houses beyond the fence. She had cried so much in the days and weeks since Jerry died, it seemed impossible there could be any tears left. The ringing of the telephone interrupted the steady patter of freezing rain. For a few seconds, she considered not answering.

"May I speak to Mrs. Jerry Reid?" a male voice asked.

"Who is this?"

"My name is Thomas," the unfamiliar voice said. "Thomas Crossar."

"Yes?" she said.

"I think your husband was my father."

"I don't think so," she said. "You must have the wrong number." She resisted the impulse to hang up.

"Just before she died, my mother finally told me where to find him. And I have a birth certificate."

"Do you?" Sue was skeptical, still thinking it was likely a wrong number. On the other hand, she had heard there were people who read obituaries and contacted vulnerable widows. Such a scam was not going to succeed with her. "I really have no reason to believe you."

"I was at his funeral," the voice said. "I wanted to give you a little time." So it's him, Sue thought. The young man with the reddish hair she had seen at the mausoleum in Mount

Pleasant Cemetery. It was as if this vision had merely been waiting for an opportunity to reappear. Yes, he was the one who had seemed familiar. The one, she now realized, with a striking resemblance to Jerry whom she had not wanted to notice that day.

She suddenly recalled what the psychic she had visited shortly before Jerry died had said about someone who was like a son. That, too, she had not wanted to register.

"What are you looking for?" Sue asked, not at all sure she wanted to hear any more. If she had gone to visit on the West Coast as Maggie had suggested, she would not have been here to receive this call.

"Were you married to Jerry Reid?" Thomas asked.

"Yes," she said. "I was." But her husband was, of course, a different Jerry Reid. He was not anybody's father. And she told him so.

"Could I meet with you?" Thomas asked, as if he had not heard her.

"I don't know," Sue stammered. "I simply don't know. Not today."

"Could I call you back? I'll be in town for a few days."

"Where do you live?" she asked.

"Stratford."

That left Sue speechless. The town Jerry had come from, where they had gone to the theatre and had shared picnics at the edge of the Avon River. Jerry had showed her the hotel his grandfather once owned down near the railway station where travelling salesmen had stopped to show their wares. They had gone inside to see the long curving bar with a wooden top below a tin ceiling with filigree design around the edges.

"Why don't you give me your number?" Sue did not know what else to say or do. Surely, if Jerry had a son growing up there, he would have visited him. Or if he had not wanted to, he would have been apprehensive about running into him or the boy's mother. "Then I can call you in a couple of days?"

"All right." Thomas sounded nervous as he gave her the number. He did not ask any questions. Not if or when she would phone. Nothing.

"All right," Sue said. "I'll think about it." As she hung up, she tacked the number to the bulletin board near the telephone. If she'd had her way, she would have preferred to remain oblivious. Maybe Martin would know something more. She also wanted to tell him what Jerry had said about someone who might have a claim with regard to his will. Suppose the only reason for this call was to claim an inheritance? Her hands were trembling.

"Martin," she said when he answered her call. "Would you have time to drop by? I have something serious to discuss with you."

"Are you all right?"

"I ... I guess so. But I do need to talk with you."

"I'll be right over," Martin said.

When she hung up, tears ran down her cheeks again. For so many months, she'd had to feign strength. Now, she was alone in a house full of memories. Jerry's clothes in closets; his muddy shoes on the sisal mat in the front hall. Photographs in frames throughout the rooms. His plaid umbrella at the back door that she could see from her seat at the kitchen counter. Still, she thought she would have regretted not being here when this Thomas person called. This surprised her. Her curiosity had, however slightly, diminished the seemingly ever-present grief, the despair that on one occasion had her pushing numbers on her cell phone as if it were a remote control that would open the refrigerator or turn on the television. Everything designed to make life easier, had, lately, seemed to conspire to confuse her.

Martin had called at various times since Jerry died and had come by to sit with her.

"Whoever would have thought it would be Jerry who would go first," he had mused on one occasion. At their age, in their fifties, whoever died would still have been a surprise.

She heard a knock at the front door and went to open it. It was Martin, who had arrived so fast she had not yet expected him. She smiled then, relieved. After he hugged her, he sat down in the pinstriped armchair in the same place Sue had last seen Jerry before he spent all his time in the hospital bed in the living room. That bed had disappeared the day after the men came from the funeral parlour and took away Jerry's emaciated body. It was all a blur in her mind.

"Coffee?" she asked.

Martin's face appeared haggard. He tapped the fingers of his left hand on the small redwood table beside him.

"Is it made already?"

"Yes," she said. "It is."

He followed her out to the kitchen where he took cream and sugar from a small glazed set Jerry had bought for her. "I've been meaning to come round," Martin said. "I know how difficult it is for you."

"One minute I think I might move to Vancouver to be near Maggie," Sue said. "A condominium maybe, looking out over English Bay and up at the mountains. And in the next minute…" her voice trailed off. She did not think she would get around to moving or even visiting for quite a while. First, there had been the cremation. Later, there would be the scattering of ashes and the memorial. One day, she would have to return to teaching. And, as people kept dropping by, at times she would expect Jerry to appear also. She knew it was irrational, but she would forget momentarily and want to call up the stairs to him that their friends were there. All had stories to tell, stories that continued to connect her to the circle she and Jerry had shared.

"You don't have to do anything quickly," Martin said. "It's probably better if you don't."

Back in the living room, they sat as they had before, he in Jerry's favourite armchair and Sue on the sofa.

"Did Jerry have a son?" she asked, studying his face for a reaction.

"What?" Martin said, sitting up straight. He stared at her with an expression of disbelief that she could ask such a question.

"Did Jerry have a son?"

"What makes you ask?" Deep furrows continued to line his forehead.

She told him about the phone call and about what Jerry had said about his will.

"That's most unusual," he said. "I'm sure he would have told me. Not to mention something like that to either of us! I hardly think so." That sounded final and his expression became calm again.

"This young man says he has a birth certificate."

"What young man?" His tone was gruff now.

"The one who called me earlier today." She visualized again the stranger she had seen at the funeral.

"What's his name?" Martin asked.

"Thomas." Would Jerry have named him that? "Thomas who?"

"Something like Crossar."

"Well, at least that's what he's telling you." His impatience was palpable now.

"Martin, he comes from Stratford."

Martin was silent then.

"Suppose he's after Jerry's money," Sue said. "I don't mind if he wants what's his. But how am I to know he's really Jerry's son?"

Martin sighed. "I don't know," he said. "I need to think about it."

"Should I see him?" Sue asked.

"Crossar," he mumbled. "Crossar. I had a girlfriend with that name."

"Should I see him?" Sue repeated.

"That's really up to you," he said. He seemed to have settled something for himself, perhaps some acceptance of mystery existing in a friend he had known so well. "But if you say no, you'll always wonder."

And she would, Sue nodded.

"What would you like me to do?" Martin asked. "I can stick around a while. Or you can call me if you need to. Of course, you know that."

"Thank you," Sue said. "I guess I'll arrange to see him."

And soon after Martin left, she dialled the number Thomas had given to her. There was no point in waiting.

"Hello?" she said. "Thomas?" Part of her wanted to believe this might still be a hoax. If it were not, she hoped that it was not only money that had prompted his phone call to her.

"Yes."

"What about the Second Cup on Bloor Street? Near Bathurst?" she asked.

An hour later, the same man Sue had seen at Jerry's funeral came into the coffee shop. In that first moment, all she could see was Jerry as a young man. Six feet tall, angular features, bushy eyebrows to match the reddish hair, a certain jauntiness about his gait. A slight bump in her husband's nose, which she had always thought was an injury, was duplicated here. This was no impostor.

"Hello," she said. "You must be Thomas."

He nodded and put out his hand.

"Will you sit down?" she asked as she shook the proffered hand.

"I'll get something. I see you have coffee." He put his gloves on the table.

"Yes."

When he returned, Sue watched the dark liquid form tiny bubbles as he stirred sugar into it. It was awhile before he met her eyes again.

"Thanks for meeting with me," he said.

Sue nodded.

"I'm trying to understand why I never saw my father." When his mother died recently, he told Sue, he knew he had to look for him.

"I knew Jerry had been married, but he said she was killed in a car accident."

"Maybe there was someone else," Thomas said. "I wanted to look for him sooner so badly. Mom begged me not to."

To Sue, he appeared genuine, but she remained detached. She felt awkward that she distrusted him when she would have preferred to like him. If she let herself, she feared it would leave her too vulnerable.

"You know," he said. "It's not money I'm after."

"What then?"

"I want to know more about my father." Thomas reached into his pocket and pulled out a card.

It was a birth certificate and, glancing at it, Sue thought about her own deception and could still scarcely believe that she and Jerry had both managed to conceal such significant matters from each other. In ten years of marriage, she had never offered even a clue, and with him, there had been no hint, no subtle reference or mystified tone in a phone call that might have alerted her. Nothing. Their secrets had still been buried in silence even as Jerry drew his last breaths.

"He couldn't have known," she said. "He would've been involved in your life somehow if he had."

But would he have been? And would Jerry have married her if he had known about those months as a young teenager when her body grew and changed? Those months when her mother told her never to talk about it, never to tell anyone. Even after both her parents had died, she had kept her secret. Now, she knew that both she and Jerry had been far from honest with each other.

"I don't know," Thomas said. "Mom only told me he lived in Toronto. She said he didn't come back much after his parents died. There was no other family there after that. There's a friend of hers called Florence who's related."

"Did you ever meet Florence?" Sue asked, feeling doubts now about Florence also. What might Jerry's older cousin also have concealed for all these years?

"Yes, but she didn't live in Stratford so I only saw her a couple times when I was a young kid," he said. "Until after my Mom died. Then I saw her again."

Florence likely won't know very much she can tell me either, Sue thought. Or might not want to tell what she does know. But what could be more compelling than this young man across from her? He could have visited her and Jerry. He and Jerry could have sailed together.

"Mom never married," Thomas said. "Maybe men don't want to marry someone who already has a kid."

His wistful tone, the way his brows came together when he cocked his head, and the way his eyes lit up and the small specks of green in the hazel background glistened, started to reach her. He was so like Jerry, it was uncanny. She could also tell he had begun to feel comfortable with her. He would have been ten or eleven when she had met Jerry, possibly a little older. As these thoughts came to her, there was, as well, something hovering at the edge of her perception of her marriage, untangling the stitches there. As if the fabric of what was over with Jerry's death could even so unravel with the onslaught of new discoveries.

Jerry must have known about Thomas. She wished he had told her. It might have been catalyst enough for her own disclosure.

"Mom always said I looked like my father."

"You certainly resemble Jerry." No doubt about that, she thought.

Thomas picked up the plastic card and handed it to her so she could read the name printed on it, "Thomas Gerald Crossar." He also had a roughly drawn family chart that showed his parents as Joanna Crossar and Gerald Foster Reid. Sue's eyes blurred. Could it possibly have been a pregnancy Jerry had not known about? He might have gone diving in the quarry, happily ignorant of the new life he had set in motion. She could not figure out how in a town like Stratford, he would not have known sooner or later. But no one in her family had suspected her predicament when she was a teenager either in an even smaller town. In those days, unwanted pregnancies were never acknowledged. So, perhaps Jerry was home from university for the summer and Joanna Crossar was a fling for him, a youthful exploration.

"My Mom said she knew Jerry when they were kids," Thomas said. "They were in their thirties when they met again. He was in court for an old friend and met her there. Mom was a clerk in the court. She said he stayed a week for the case. They had dinner and talked about old times. After he left, they didn't see each other anymore."

"So when she discovered she was pregnant, didn't she let him know?"

"I don't know," he said. "Money came from somewhere. More than a court clerk would have made." He paused, and then added, "We had a small house and I'm in university now. She left me everything."

"I find it hard to believe the Jerry I knew would never have seen his child."

"Maybe it made it easier for him."

If Thomas had found Jerry still alive and well, she was sure she would not have objected. She would probably have been baffled. Still, it would have been better, for both her and Thomas, to have heard all of this from Jerry. What they were left with was conjecture. A few facts. A birth certificate. His resemblance to Jerry.

"Grandma and Grandpa Crossar are both dead," he said. "I remember Grandpa. I was fifteen when he died. Grandma had cancer when I was really little, maybe three. I do remember her a bit, sometimes. Mostly from pictures. I think she read, *The*

Wind in the Willows to me." He smiled. "Of course, I didn't know my father's parents."

So here they were, she and Thomas, joined by Jerry.

She studied him for awhile as one would in such a situation. Would he turn into a grasping stranger? She did not think so, convinced now that he was genuine.

"What do we do now?" Sue asked.

"I don't know," he said.

"Would you like to come back to the house?" she asked finally.

"Oh, yeah," he breathed out the words quietly.

"Let's go then," she said.

Out on Bloor Street, past small shops and restaurants, Thomas kept pace with her. When they arrived in front of the house, she rummaged in her purse for keys. They went into the front hall and from there into the living room where she invited him to sit down.

"I'll look for some photographs," she said.

While she searched for albums, he sat on the sofa with his coat draped awkwardly across his lap.

"Look at this," Sue said.

A photo of Jerry on his sailboat with one hand on the tiller, the blue-and-white sail unfurling in the wind. Another on the island on the boardwalk by a bench where he sat looking out at the lake. His framed law degree, his university graduation photograph. Some genealogy charts.

"Maybe you'd like to have this," Sue said, holding out a watch with a wide brown leather band. She was surprised at not feeling a need to hang onto everything of Jerry's.

Thomas held the watch carefully, running his fingers over the face. "Thank you," he said. Then he put it on, still looking at it.

"I'm thinking of studying law," he said after awhile.

Maybe one day she would give him the law degree also and the photograph. At this moment, she could not do more than imagine that.

She brought out some soup and crackers to the small table

in the sunroom where she and Jerry had taken most of their meals. He followed her, holding an album and placing it open beside him on a shelf. Sometimes they talked. At other times, he stared at photographs or out the window. Long silences were punctuated by short bursts of conversation.

When they parted, Sue stood at the front window and watched Thomas walk down the street. Would she let that psychic know about this unexpected appearance?

"Of course," he would say. "Someone like a son. That's what I told you."

But it was not Hans Jonker she wanted to tell. Something so strong welled up that it was like being engulfed by waves in a storm even as one runs for higher ground. With one hand to her throat, she stood holding onto a scream. All that emerged was a loud, raspy whisper.

"Jerry!"

How could he have ignored this young man's existence? If she could grasp her husband's scrawny neck right now, she might throttle him.

*

A week, a month, two months later, Sue had heard nothing from Thomas. As suddenly as he had come into her life, he seemed to have disappeared. She had imagined giving some of Jerry's clothes to him. Her late husband's closet was still full of jackets, shirts, sweaters, ties. She still could not bear to look at all of it, but if Thomas could have used some of the clothes and accessories, that might have made it slightly easier. She could hear him calling it "stuff" and then being delighted to find some item fit. Perhaps Jerry's dark winter coat or a tweed jacket.

As long as she kept Jerry's clothes, Sue could imagine Jerry might return. Oh, what foolishness. She knew by now that was never going to happen. Had Jerry considered this sort of scenario happening after he was gone? That she would meet his son? No, he must not have known. But then, why had he tried to warn her about someone else who might have a claim?

Sue knew it would be simple enough to trace the lad. There would be a listing in Stratford. But if he did not want to hear from her, she felt she had no right to disturb him. As his late father's wife, she would likely be perceived as a nuisance. It surprised her that it mattered to her. But meeting him had taken the edge off her sadness for a while and she had begun to paint a little again. If her mother were alive, she would say that Sue had begun "to pick up the pieces." She could hear her mother's voice, rife with the clichés of her generation, the clichés that had ensured Sue's silence. Her mother's voice telling her never to talk about why she had been sent away to the city for a few months awakened her at night now with endless questions about what might have been. And what she might still do about it.

Maybe she should have gone back to teaching after that first bleak Christmas without Jerry so that she would now have that to preoccupy her. Martin and Emily had tried to make the season a little cheerier and she had spent the day with them and their grown children. There had been stories and memories and Emily had been very kind. "Would you like to spend the night?" she had asked. Sue had been surprised at Emily's thoughtfulness, having become so accustomed to the raised eyebrow or dismissive tone that had so often revealed itself when Sue was around.

"Thanks, Emily," she had said. "But if you two would walk me back to my place, that would make me feel comfortable with going home for the night."

They had done that and the next day had called to see how she was doing. January would have been a convenient time to pick up with the students, but it was only two months after Jerry's death. She had not been able to do it. Also, she had wanted to keep on painting. And if Thomas contacted her to have time for him for what she thought a selfish reason, the sense that in the presence of someone so similar to her husband part of Jerry was still there. Now, she felt herself in a vacuum, except for all the paperwork that had to be attended to in dealing with Jerry's estate. Fortunately, Martin was executor.

Eventually, Sue called the psychic's office. It was the end of January by then, although she found it hard to keep track of time. She had told the principal she would like to return to teach in the fall. She had thanked him for the leave of absence, knowing that the last thing she had needed as Jerry hovered near death had been to deal with teenagers and the pressures of preparing lessons and marking papers. Now, she felt it would all come crashing in on her if she went back too early.

She spoke to the woman who made appointments, not surprised this time to find the psychic booked well in advance. But when the woman said she would call if there were a cancellation, Sue thought that possible and in less than two weeks, it happened.

"Tomorrow afternoon," the woman said. "At two o'clock."

The address was a mere few blocks away from where Sue lived, but she had not walked by Jonker's office since the day she had first gone there. She thought there was a tall maple in the patch of yard between the front door and the sidewalk and that she would see the high branches of that tree through his bay window. Even bare, awaiting the appearance of tiny buds, it likely had a stark beauty. But what she recalled and wanted to see again were the bright colours of the paintings and photographs on his walls.

"Yes," she said. "Thank you."

The next day, she would climb the steps to the door of the brick building again, and then continue to the second floor. It had not changed her life the first time, nor even made her feel good, but his comments had stayed with her.

2.

SNOW SWIRLED IN THE WIND like genies escaping from bottles. Hans pulled his collar up as he stumbled along the path he had shovelled from the house to the barn. He had not liked living in a city where houses often seemed to press in and obscure the sky. Even with his whiskers encased in tiny bits of ice, he had no regrets about moving to the country. Heather was the one to suggest buying a farm when they had talked about finding a house with a bit more land. Since she had expressed no interest before, he had been surprised. But then, Heather was always full of surprises. Her English accent normally so refined then turned into a caricature as she leapt across the bed imitating some American western she had seen. Yelling that she would lasso him and, "Watch out buddy, you're going to get laid." Although, come to think of it, she had not done that for a long time.

"I want chickens," she had said. "Chickens and roosters and peacocks and piglets and…"

"Do you have any idea how much work it is to farm?" He had grown up on the family farm in the Netherlands.

"We needn't be farmers. We could find a place where someone already uses the land."

"Well, I'd like to do a bit of farming," he had said. The thought of it had created visions of new calves, fresh eggs, walks across sun-stroked fields, tomatoes ripening. "Just not all of it."

So fifteen years ago, they had found this house, built of stone and buried in the hills behind a screen of trees. From the road you could not see it or the long driveway that circled to the front door. In the summer, flowers grew up through the steps, tall purple and pink hollyhocks that looked as if there might be a fairy tale waiting. Behind that was a large barn where the horses Heather had wanted had their stalls.

"I'm going to be a jockey," she had said.

He had almost laughed, had wanted to tell her she was too tall, but then decided to keep quiet. He admired her spunk. Especially when she started to do jumps and enter competitions. Heather had never lived on a farm, but she had learned to ride where she grew up in the south of England, something she had convinced her parents was so important that she would spend her own money on lessons.

Before long, she and Hans had also started to board and groom other horses to cover some of their expenses.

"You could teach people to ride," Heather said.

"No. I'm going to go on doing readings. And I'll be a gentleman farmer."

Not quite as it turned out, the gentleman part. There was never enough money to hire help. So, every morning, he was up to his ankles in dung. But as he entered the barn, he savoured the earthy odour of animals, the sweet scent of hay. He also had a small henhouse where he collected eggs for omelettes. French toast. Pancakes. At first, he put on weight, but soon the work was enough to keep him trim. They planted a vegetable garden in summer with all that they needed for the season, green vines twirling upward to meet the sun. Or crawling along the earth in tendrils to birth cucumbers and zucchini. When they made relish with the tomatoes, all the neighbours received a jar.

When Hans returned to the house, Heather was at the counter in the kitchen. She glanced over at him with a slight frown as he brushed snow from his beard.

"I'm going to fly to London," she said, flinging her long fair hair over her shoulders. "And take a train to Devon."

He draped his coat on a hook over a heat vent. "In February?" he asked.

Her parents lived in a village outside Exeter where her father was the postmaster. They were getting older and she went to visit each year in early spring.

She sat down with a cup of coffee at the large wooden table in the centre of the room, tapping her fingers in time to unheard music that seemed to float around her.

"Why now?" he asked when she did not respond to his first question.

"My mother needs me," she said.

"Why haven't you mentioned it?" He liked visiting her family. But she was sometimes inscrutable. Before he figured it out, she would often be out on one of the horses, riding off into the woods or down the road as it got dark. He wished she would say more. It was an ongoing tug of war between them, that he wanted her to be more forthcoming. And she figured, like some of his clients, that he ought to know.

"I didn't know either," she said. "Until Dad called this morning."

"So fill me in." He sat down at the table across from her.

A tinge of red crept across her cheeks and the bridge of her nose. "I'm worried," she said. "Dad said Mum isn't taking her prescription. And she won't use her hearing aid."

Hans sighed. "I'd like to go with you. I really would. But I don't think we can afford it right now."

"It's all right," Heather said.

"It doesn't feel that way to me."

She stood up and moved around the kitchen in the hurried way she always did before she left to head into her job in the city. He watched her as she picked up her purse and put on her coat, waiting for her to say something else. She did not.

"What is it?" he asked.

"I told you," she said.

"I get the feeling there's more to it."

"You always do." She shook her head and raised her hand to her mouth to blow a kiss to him as she opened the door

"I always do what?" he asked, but she was already out of earshot.

When Hans left three hours later, rush hour traffic was over. Snow still blew across the highway and just before he reached the 401, he hit a patch of black ice and began to skid. He tried to stay in his own lane and as the car edged over onto the other side, he was relieved no other vehicles were close enough for him to hit. As he coasted forward, the tires gradually regained a grip on the road.

After that, he drove more carefully than usual and was already tired when he arrived at the office in Toronto. Grateful to rest for half an hour before his first appointment, he put his feet up on the small table in front of his chair. His clients were booked for Monday, Wednesday, and Thursday afternoons. His mornings started early on the farm when he milked two cows and fed the horses, chickens, and goats before he left for the city. He closed his eyes and waited for his mind to become blank. Instead, he thought of Heather. There was a chill in his marriage and he could not figure out what was happening. He wondered if it might have been there for a while without him noticing it. When he tried to think about that, nothing particular emerged. He must clear his mind or the images that emerged from whoever sat across from him would be blocked. It was only with that blank slate that the rhythm of his day in the office would begin to unfold well.

He heard shuffling that seemed to come from the waiting area on the other side of the wall. His first client? He breathed deeply and moved toward the door. When he opened it, he saw a young woman who had come a few times before, the last visit about a year ago. She would want to know what most people did. About her boyfriend. Would she find a new job? About her health. Mainly, his clients seemed to seek reassurance. If they knew how uncertain his own life was most days, they would not want it from him. After she was seated across from him, he saw her furniture in another city and told her she would move there.

"I don't think so," she said without hesitation. "I don't want to leave Toronto."

"Well, you're going to," he said.

"No," she said. "I'm not going to."

Then why had she come? He had things to tell her and she did not want to hear them. This was often how people reacted, but it never ceased to surprise him. "You're going to," he repeated. "There'll be work there in your field and you'll be given a car to drive."

"I don't think so," she said again.

"Well, let me know when it happens," Hans said, almost as if he were throwing up his hands. But he saw something more. "A silver car."

"Yeah, sure." Ironic tone.

"Yeah, sure." Certainty.

Nonetheless, she continued to be resistant to most of what he told her. At the end of the reading, he handed her the tape. If she listened later, she would be surprised at how much would transpire and for all he knew would call to tell him. Some did.

As he said goodbye, he listened to the sound of her footsteps going down the stairs, then to the front door below that closed with a bang. Going over to the bay window, he reached his arms above his head and let out a sigh. His work was exhausting when there was so much resistance. Sometimes, he would say he could not do a reading for that person and forego payment. "You'll have to be more receptive," he might say. "Come back if you are." But he figured this woman might find the information useful when the offer came in. She would at the very least be prepared for it.

As he continued to stare out the window, his eyes were drawn to a woman approaching from the west. Her walk looked familiar and this made him curious. When he heard footsteps enter the waiting room and the rustle of a magazine, he was alert. What is it about her? When he invited her into his office and she sat down across from him, he knew she had been there before. She twisted her hands in her lap and he could see her wedding ring, something about a husband who was ill. And he knew what had happened since then had altogether changed her life.

"I often stand and look out at the trees and the sky," he said. "And the people. When I saw you on the street just now, I knew you were coming to see me."

"Maybe you recognized me," she said.

He rarely recalled much about anyone until they had come more than once or twice. "Yes," he said. "But just something superficial, like the way you walked. And you might have been going somewhere else." Years before, a man had sat in that same chair, eyeing Hans piercingly, and speaking in a rapid staccato that Hans had found uncomfortable. He had wanted the man to leave. At the end of the session, he had handed over the tape and quickly ushered the man to the door. A few months later, there had been some confusion surrounding his bank account and when he got to the bottom of it, this man had been forging his signature. The police arrested the man, but Hans never figured out what had been taken from his office to make him vulnerable. He had theories. A letter he could not find that he had signed and left out ready to put in an envelope? He had often wondered how the man had known anything about his banking account.

But Hans did not feel there was anything sinister about Sue even though he felt uneasy. It was strange that seeing her approach on the street had inexplicably filled up some emptiness in him, a void that had begun to open around the time his sister, Anna, had died in Amsterdam. She had been the sibling closest in age to him. The one he had loved the most of all in his family, so often was she his ally when they were children. Heather, busy with her new job at the hospital when Anna died, had not been able to go to the funeral or seemed fully aware of the extent of his sorrow. Sometimes of late, Heather seemed so remote, like a hawk, circling. Maybe it had been a mistake to marry someone fifteen years younger. He had had children in his first marriage and had not wanted them in his second. Men might marry because the woman wanted a child, but, in some ways, he had married Heather because she had not. Already with a daughter who was a young teenager when they had met, she was fine with having one child and glad that Hans had wanted to raise Vivian with her. Hans had loved Heather for her spontaneity, her plucky sense of adventure, her love of hollyhocks and horses, and for Vivian, if truth be told. He had not minded starting over with a teenager.

He saw Sue look around at the hangings on his walls and recalled how carefully she had inspected them the first time. Now, her eyes were on the shells he had gathered on beaches in the Caribbean and Florida. Some day, she would use bits of what she was observing in a painting.

"So," he said, turning on the recorder. "Everything's changing. Everything. Your work, where you live, and the people you know. But you'll be all right." He told her that although she would return to work, she would continue to find a way to create images on canvas. And listen to music.

"How do you know?"

"I don't know where it comes from," he said.

"Then how do you know?"

"I get something about whoever sits down in front of me."

"You get something," she said. "What in the world does that mean?"

"Only once I didn't and then discovered that the man had AIDS and didn't have much time ahead of him."

"So you drew a blank."

"You could say so."

"I did."

"But you have plenty of time. And what you're doing and will do is to question everything. The whole pot will get stirred."

"What does that mean?'

"I just tell you what I get. I don't know what it means." He was irritated with her and did not mean for her to know that, worried it was apparent in his tone. People always seemed to think he ought to know, either some fact about them or the meaning of what he did actually know. For him that was irrelevant and if he looked for more it might block the channels for the images and sounds that arrived naturally. If she did not understand anything thus far, she certainly would not understand that either. "But I do know you're now a widow," he said. "And that's a big change already. It's huge."

"I didn't believe what you said when I came the first time," she said.

"No, I could tell. But you do now, I guess, or you wouldn't be here."

"You said there would be someone like a son. And after my husband died, I had a phone call from a young man who said Jerry was his father. I didn't know what to do, but when Thomas said he wanted to see me, I said yes. Not at first, but later."

"Of course," Hans said.

"But it wasn't as if I knew he existed."

"Well," he said. "You knew."

Hans could feel that resistance, the distrust again. What did she think she was paying for?

"Why didn't Jerry tell me? It's not as if he didn't have an opportunity. Now I think I lived all those years with a stranger."

"Everyone has some secrets. It doesn't necessarily make them strangers."

She hesitated. "When Thomas came to see me, he looked just like Jerry did when he was younger," she said. "He'd never seen his father. As we talked, there was an instant rapport between us. But then, he disappeared again. I don't know why."

"He'll come back." So this was what she was seeking to know this time, he thought. He looked down at the tape machine to make sure it was recording.

"How do you know? You must have some idea."

"I don't," he said, trying not to sound impatient. But she asked even more questions than his most annoying clients. Even so, he liked her, though he was not sure why, except he thought her a striking woman and likely a kind and gentle one. He was reminded of his delight in the early years of his three children. Their expectation that he knew everything and their endless questions. The innocence. The wonder.

It also reminded him of Vivian when she had found out he was psychic and asked him what she was going to do when she went to college. He had laughed and said, "Can't do it, Vivian. I leave that stuff at the office." His former wife had done everything she could to turn his children against him, but gradually they had come around as they had wanted their father in their lives. So now, his adult children brought their families to the farm. Just recently, his son had helped him cut down a dead tree just before more snow had fallen

"I wonder if you might have lunch with me some time. Or coffee." Her voice trembled slightly.

"Pardon?" he said, perplexed. This kind of situation was unfamiliar. A client came for a reading and left. Perhaps over a few appointments, there might be some kind of rapport established. But he did not make arrangements to meet anyone elsewhere. As soon as his last client left, he would be on his way out of the city, letting thoughts of the farm take over. He glanced at her again, saw her even features and her piercing glance.

"Well, I suppose I could," he said, aware this was something he was considering not only because the woman created a spark of longing in him, but because Heather would be away. And there were, as well, the puzzled feelings around this woman he could not yet decipher. What harm is there in it? he wondered, as he felt himself nodding. He gripped the arms of his chair.

Sue started to talk about her husband again, almost as if the conversation had not taken a turn for a moment. Almost as if nothing had passed between them, that there had not been a tacit decision.

"He was married before. A long time ago," she said. "She was killed in an accident soon after the wedding. He told me about that, but he never told me about Thomas. It sounds as if he had a brief fling with a childhood friend when they were in their thirties. I was married to him for ten years and I thought we knew each other well, but I didn't know something that important."

"And did you tell him everything?"

Her body turned rigid, like an animal caught at night in the beam of a headlight.

"All the same, you did know each other well," Hans continued as if he had not noticed her revealing body language. "And you know that you loved each other. What about his son?"

"I gave him a watch of his father's and we talked and talked. He seemed to like and trust me, but I guess I was wrong."

"I don't think so," Hans said. He turned off the tape.

"Why did you do that?"

"Oh, it's almost finished," he said. Whatever was hidden below the surface would have to wait. Whatever secret she had lived with for such a long time would be hard for her to face yet. "Anyway, there's nothing else for me to tell you. Not at the moment anyway. Should we decide when to have lunch?"

His work brought him into contact with many people, but often he felt isolated. Even his friends and neighbours regarded him with a certain amount of awe or suspicion. He was looking forward now to the prospect of getting to know her better, and away from his office routine.

"All right," Sue said, sounding doubtful now, perhaps wishing she had said nothing. Almost echoing Heather who had also sounded that way all those years ago when he had first called her. But in every other way, these two women were different. Heather was taller and with more angular features than Sue's. She was younger. This woman, Sue, was his age and less likely to notice his lines and wrinkles. Or so he thought. And she had lived through the war, too, although in a different country than him and undoubtedly with other experiences.

"Maybe next week?" he said.

The war still haunted and intrigued him. He often read books about it and tried to put together pieces that as a child had not cohered. He was curious now, suspecting he and Sue would have a common language around their early lives. As the child of a British soldier, Heather understood what he had told her, but Sue would have memories of the same time frame.

"Or the week after."

"That's fine," he said. "You pick a date. I don't come into the city on Tuesdays or Fridays."

She took a calendar out of her purse and looked at it. "Thursday then," she said.

He wrote it down. "There's a little Thai restaurant over on Bloor Street near Spadina," he said. "I forget the name. It's on the north side."

"So I'll meet you there at what time? Noon?"

"That's it then," he said. "Noon."

*

Two weeks later, Hans walked from his office through drifting snow to meet Sue at the restaurant, not in the least surprised to find her waiting at a table. Not because he had known she would be there, but because he knew she was a punctual person. She would be apologetic if she arrived somewhere even five minutes late. She had not told him these things, but he knew. He might also have guessed as much.

He smiled broadly as she waved at him, shaking the snow from his boots.

"I hope you haven't been waiting long," he said. She had picked a good table. It was off to one side, on its own, where no one would be straining to hear their conversation.

"Not long at all," she said. "I just got here."

As they waited to give their order, Sue looked at him with a quizzical smile. Are you really here? her eyes seemed to ask. He was convinced this rendezvous was out of character for her. Ordinarily, she would never have gone to a psychic in the first place either. She must have acted on a whim when she had suggested having lunch with him, something he knew should elicit caution. Nonetheless, here she was across from him, making conversation.

"I noticed the photographs in your office. A lake. A barn. Are they places you've been?" Sue asked.

"Oh, yes," he said. "I took them myself. I love taking photos."

He smoothed his white paper napkin on the table and began to sketch. Since he had stopped smoking, it was difficult sometimes to keep his hands occupied. In only a few seconds, he created the winding curve of a river flowing through a forest.

"You're an artist," she said, surprised at how quickly the strokes began to form a picture.

"I doodle," he said. "I drew everything when I was a child. It wasn't until I was in my teens that I saw some of the great masters in the galleries in Amsterdam. We were too busy on the farm. It had to wait until I went there with some of my friends."

"What's the name of the main art gallery in Amsterdam?" she asked. "I remember going there. I've been trying to remember. You know the gallery where I would have seen *The Night Watch,* Rembrandt's famous painting."

"The Rijksmuseum." He wrote it on the napkin underneath the sketch and gave it to her.

She opened her purse and tucked the napkin inside her calendar.

Suddenly, he felt a need to touch her with something personal even though he seldom talked about his past. "I was a child during the war," he said.

"Me, too," she sighed.

"At five, I spent three months in a concentration camp."

"How could that be?" she asked. "I thought you were Dutch. Where was the rest of your family?" She spoke as if she mistrusted this information.

"In other camps. I was alone. But I escaped," he said. "I spent the night in a ditch before finding someone who would hide me."

"That's an amazing story. How did you get out?" She still looked as if she were not sure whether to believe him or not.

"I just did what children do and went through a gate that was open and kept on walking. No one was looking for a child to leave. I can't remember too well really. Maybe someone helped me."

"Why were you in a camp in Holland anyway?" Sue asked.

"My family had a bedroom in an attic where they hid Jewish people. Someone must have told the Nazis." Anyone could have betrayed them, seeking some advantage.

"Did you know what was going on?"

"Only that I was never supposed to tell anyone about the people in the room. And I didn't. But they found out. It was horrendous. I saw things that day I'd never want to repeat. I don't know if I even had words for what I saw then." He still sometimes had nightmares of men attacking their house, men wearing dark clothes and carrying torches and guns. He almost forgot Sue was sitting across from him.

"I remember the war, too," she said. "Or at least the end of it. This man I didn't know moved in. He turned out to be my father. My mother talked about him when he was away and read bits of his letters to us. He called me 'Baby.' I didn't like that. Before he came, I heard my mother talking to people about 'overseas' and I thought it was a place, maybe like Toronto where we went once to see him when he was on leave. I know that because there are pictures and later I was told what they were. That was before he sailed. By the time he came back, I had heard enough about guns and tanks and people murmuring maybe he would die that I thought he was someone in a story. Not a real person at all. My older sister, Maggie, prayed every night though that he would come home safely."

Yes. It would have been frightening for her also, but in such a different way. A time of waiting, not knowing, yet in a safe haven.

"A lot of Dutch people came to Canada during the war and there were a lot of Canadian soldiers in Holland," he said. "So this seemed a natural place to emigrate after I was married. I learned English working in restaurants. That was at the end of the fifties."

Waiting on tables had bored him before long, but without any other Canadian experience he had not been sure what else to do. With the four languages he knew — Dutch, English, German, and French — he had thought he might be able to freelance as a translator. Not able to make enough at that alone, he had found seasonal work in city parks as a gardener, and, later, part-time work with at-risk-youth in a community centre. That was where he had met Heather. Married at the time, he had been careful not to show his attraction to her. When his first wife left him, he thought of Heather often and finally went back to see if she was still there. His former boss told him that she had gone to work at a downtown hospital and agreed to call to ask if she would give permission for Hans to have her telephone number.

"I guess my story is growing up in a frontier town," Sue said. "In the northern bush, far south of the actual frontier now. I guess the frontiers are in space these days."

"Or somewhere else entirely." Like a parallel world, he wanted to say, where spirits guided those who were open to them, but he refrained. He sensed that such a statement might make her leery of him. It might even frighten her. As if he were a creature from another dimension himself. Little did people know though how much like them he really was, relying on intuition and a gift he had been given. Nothing more spectacular than that. And it had seemed natural to follow the path this gift had opened for him.

"You told me in my last reading that I'm a nomad," Sue said. "Why?"

"I think what I said was that everything would change for you."

"I guess that was it, but I seem to recall you used the word nomad."

"Whether I did or not, you are like one. There'll be no arriving for you. You'll find a new path, a new direction, and when you reach the horizon, you'll seek another."

"It sounds as if you've likely done that yourself."

"Yeah." And he had always found surprises as he approached those horizons.

The waiter stood beside the table. "Are you ready to order?" he asked.

Hans looked startled and reached for the menu. As Sue asked for lemon grass soup and stir-fried rice, he supposed she had probably already read it.

"No, nothing to drink," she said. "Water."

"A mango salad," Hans said. "And a Blue."

"I've changed my mind," she said. "I'd like a beer, too."

Hans told Sue more about the war then and what he remembered of the soldiers who came to question his parents, of the fear he had felt when the soldiers had taken him away. It was an era they had shared even though they had lived in different circumstances. They had all been fighting the same war, the Nazis the common enemy.

"It was a strange time," Sue said. "Not understanding what Maggie was praying for. And then one day we had a flag on the lawn. The Union Jack. Or so I was told as we looked at

pictures later. All the neighbourhood children gathered underneath the flag for those photos. It wasn't long after that my
father turned up.

"'How's Baby?" he asked. I ignored him, climbed down
from my chair and went to find my teddy bear. "Maggie was
really happy."

"Um," Hans said. It was not at all similar to what had happened to him, but she had experienced a profound absence
that war brings and seemed to have an almost visceral reaction
when anything to do with the battlefield or the life of soldiers
was mentioned. He was aware he had not told her that his wife
had grown up in England after the war and was considerably
younger than he was. Nor did he tell her that Heather had
flown to London only a few days earlier.

*

Sue walked along the sidewalk in the bright sunlight, feeling
strangely euphoric. Her body, which had seemed dead for
months before Jerry died, felt something stirring. As if from the
ashes, a sprig of grass was poking through. She was worried
someone might have seen Hans hug her when they parted.
As if her judges — her long dead parents, or Martin — were
watching over her shoulder. Although it would more likely
be Emily who would say her judgment was lacking, that her
behaviour showed a lack of propriety. She would not even be
able to tell Maggie.

Walking down Spadina, she saw an art supply store. Thinking about how Hans had sketched so effortlessly, she recalled
a photograph she had taken of a planter full of bright yellow
and orange nasturtiums. Watercolours would not capture the
vivid effect she needed. Some paintings in that medium were
bright enough, but she knew she wanted vibrant colour.

"You might try acrylics," the clerk said. "They're easy to
use. They're water-based and dry quickly." She pointed out
tubes with labels in different colours.

Ah, Sue thought. Alizarin crimson, ultramarine blue, cadmium yellow, burnt umber. She would need white and black, of course. Titanium white. Carbon black.

She also bought a charcoal pencil. Her ironing board was set up in the kitchen with a thin piece of board on top where she had left a sketchbook open. The night before, she had drawn two elephants with intertwined trunks. When she arrived home, she painted them red, blue, and purple. On a larger sheet, using the photograph she had taken as her guide, she drew a planter full of nasturtiums. The largest painting she had attempted, she saw it now gradually beginning to take form and shape. Ultramarine and then the crimson mixed with it created a vibrant purple. When she was finished for that day, she thought she would move everything upstairs to the desk in Jerry's office where the rest of her art materials now were.

A sound came from the back porch and, looking out through the window, Sue saw a squirrel run across the wooden slats, pushing a piece of bread. Some neighbour must put out food for the animals. The crumbs ended up often in an empty crevice under the roof where birds built nests in summer. The previous year, there had been a robin with her family living there, little heads reaching up, beaks open for worms. When Sue had gone out onto the porch, the mother robin had dive-bombed her, then sat on the rail of the porch next door and shrieked. Sue was relieved the raccoon that had pooped on the back porch seemed to be gone. For ten years, one had made his mound of litter right outside their back door, always on the same spot. Could it have been the same racoon for all that time?

Suddenly overwhelmed with loneliness, the painting on the ironing board had no meaning for her. What would her husband want her to do? She did not know. Surely, in having embraced Thomas, she was being loyal. But a little voice, some judge sitting on her shoulder, murmured that what she and Jerry had needed was to tell the truth to each other. And now she was compounding everything with persistent thoughts about another man and not even Jerry would understand about Hans. She was not even sure she understood herself except that she could not stand the empty house. She could no longer stand talking to Jerry and knowing he was not there. At least Hans was alive and tangible and whenever she thought about him, something stirred in her.

She turned on the radio to a station playing classical music. Jerry would have been able to tell her who the composer was. If she could become absorbed in painting again as he had in music, she would feel better. And so she worked on the shades of plants and trees in the background of the nasturtiums. She wondered what Hans would say about her work. At some point, colour and form usually soothed her, but instead she kept thinking of Hans. Recalling also that once when she had been deep in meditation, all the famous paintings she had ever seen had streamed across what seemed like a screen as she watched in wonder. Vincent van Gogh's, *Fishing Boats on the Beach at Saintes-Maries*, da Vinci's *Mona Lisa,* and Picasso's *Guernica*. It was not like that now. Nothing worked and she could not concentrate as thoughts of this unknown man flitted in and out of her mind. And why had Thomas not called at least to say goodbye? She was relieved when the phone rang to hear another voice entirely.

"How are you doing?" Martin asked. "Emily and I want to have you over for dinner."

"Thank you."

They picked a date.

"I thought we could ask one of the lawyers from —"

"Too soon, Martin," she said. "I'd like to just spend an evening with you two."

"All right," he said. "I also wondered when I might come round to start planning the memorial for Jerry. Would today be possible?"

"That would be fine," she said, even though her heart was saying no. I can't. It's too soon. But when would it not be?

"I know it's difficult."

"It feels good to be able to do it together," Sue said because she knew she relied on him for this. "It would please Jerry."

"Have you heard from Thomas?"

"No."

"I feel badly about that. For you, of course. But I also hoped to meet him."

What could she say? He seemed so reasonable and his disappointment, which mirrored her own, suddenly annoyed her. "He'll come back," she said.

"Oh my goodness," he said. "Don't set yourself up."

She could not tell Martin a psychic had told her she would see Thomas again or that she felt attracted to another man already. Although Martin had a sense of the absurd, she did not imagine that he would be any more receptive to the intuitive knowing of a psychic than Jerry would have been.

"It's all right," she said. "I'm not going to be disappointed."

"Okay." He sounded doubtful, but her feelings about Hans and her belief he would be right again reassured her. She hoped Hans would get in touch with her to suggest another meeting. And when Thomas turned up, there would be some straightforward explanation about where he had been and why he had not contacted her. It could be months before she would hear from him, but one day when she was engrossed in something else, it would happen.

"I'll be over around seven," Martin said.

When he came, he stood in the kitchen in the spot near the counter where he had engaged in lively conversation with Jerry so often, pouring more beer or coffee. What were Jerry's thoughts on a particular initiative being taken by the city? he would ask. Or, Martin would be interested in some case of Jerry's. More often than not, the talk was about sailing. And they often jogged down the back streets south and north of Bloor, returning hot and sweaty, their faces glistening.

Martin leaned over to look at the painting on the ironing

board she had not yet taken upstairs. "I like it." He paused. "Where do you get your inspiration?"

"This one's from a photograph I took." She showed it to him. There was something about the shape of the flowers and leaves pouring out of the container that had a tropical feel. The flamboyance of orange flowers and greenery she associated with Costa Rica or Jamaica. Her tiny philodendron that grew so well in the house was a miniature next to the huge lush plants in the painting.

"What about having the memorial in June?" he asked. "By then, the weather should be warmer and the leaves will be out. Flowers will be in bloom, too."

She leaned over the counter, trying to hide her tears even though Martin would be the first to put out a hand to reassure her. What she did not want for him to know was that part of hiding her eyes from him was a feeling that they might betray something else.

"I could see about getting space on the island for a Saturday or Sunday. I remember when you and Jerry were married over there." He stopped when he heard her sniff. "I'm sorry." He took out a clean handkerchief and handed it to her.

She took the hanky, beginning to blubber.

"Oh, Sue," Martin said.

She tried to wipe the tears away, but they went on flowing. When they stopped enough for her to speak, she asked, "What do you want me to do?" surprising even herself with the sudden resentment in her voice. He could not help her deal with the internal furor that had begun to rise in her. Nothing she could tell him would make for comfortable conversation.

"Could we make a list of people now?" He looked as if he were trying to stay calm, as if he disapproved of her outburst.

"I can't." What was the matter with him? "I don't even want to," she said, her voice rising again. "How could he do this to us? Leave you with a boat and me with his son. Sometimes, I wish I could kill him."

Martin stepped back as if she had hit him. "Maybe not today then," he said.

Although Sue realized she was now verging on the irrational, she wanted to hit him. Why could he not show some emotion? "Was Jerry always Mister Nice Guy?" she asked. "You knew him longer than anybody."

"Whoever called him that?"

"I just did."

"He was human," Martin said, his voice remaining level. "You saw him lose his cool more than once. And before you met him, long before that, he was a bit of a drinker. Not enough to interfere with his work, but more than I wished for a while. And he was a risk-taker."

"Ah," she said, but she did not feel as if this made anything better. How could it? Mixed as it was with something else that she was only beginning to grasp herself.

"You can call and tell me when you're ready to talk about the memorial." He edged toward the door.

"Surely sometimes you feel angry with Jerry."

He lowered his head. "I guess," he said. "But you sounded so sarcastic, so vindictive just a moment ago."

"I'm sorry," she sighed. "Maybe you and Emily could make a list."

"All right. We'll take a stab at it." He put his hand on the knob of the front door. "I'll get in touch with you."

When she saw him disappear down the street, Sue fell onto the couch and covered her head with a pillow, sobbing. She felt so alone, as if no one had ever shared her deepest feelings, but as she gradually calmed down she had a glimpse of the possibility of that openness with someone like Hans.

*

Books lined the shelves in what used to be Jerry's office, reflecting his interest in history, political biography, and crime fiction. Peter Newman beside Josephine Tey. *The Thirty-Nine Steps*. A history of the Boer War. Nothing was organized, the titles having found homes where space existed. Sue's art materials were now on the desk and on the floor.

Standing back to consider the easel she had finally set up, she picked up a brush. She dipped it into the burnt umber on her palette and started to paint a tiger. Next, she would add vivid stripes and bring to life Rousseau's jungle. The brightness from the overhead skylight made the colours stand out and a smile crept across her face as she contemplated her work again. Startled by the telephone, she almost knocked over a ceramic mug full of paintbrushes as she jumped back from the canvas.

"Hello, Sue. It's Thomas."

A deep intake of breath. "I missed you," she said.

"I'm sorry I didn't say goodbye before I left the city."

"I must admit I wondered."

She had worried that he would not turn up again until Hans had said he would. How ludicrous to plan her life around what she was told by a psychic. But so far, he had been accurate. What had the ad said about him? A "make you feel good psychic." She might not go that far.

"I had an interview," Thomas said.

Again, Sue waited for him to continue.

"And then I got a job. Starting something new. I bet you know what that's like."

"Um," Sue said. "It takes all your time for a while, doesn't it?

"Almost, even though it's only part-time." He was keeping on with his studies. He seemed to hesitate. "And then, there's Kate."

"And who's Kate?" She stood further back from the painting. It was only partially finished, just the tiger's head and shoulders so far fully formed.

"I'll tell you," he said.

"Go ahead."

"When I see you."

"Do you have time for a visit?"

81

"What about today?" he asked.

"Sure," Sue said, trying not to sound eager, not wanting to be disappointed again. "Today would be fine. Where are you?"

"Union Station," he said. "The train just got here. I'll walk over."

Well, that will take some time, she thought. Time to get the paint off her hands and for a quick shower. She hung her splattered smock on a hook. In the bathroom, the water came out hot after running briefly and, sighing, Sue stepped into it.

Just under an hour later, the bell rang and Thomas's frame was visible through the glass, as startling as the first time she had seen him — this vision of a younger Jerry.

"Come in," she said. Under his open jacket he was wearing a shirt with fine navy-and-white stripes and dark trousers. Then, suddenly, no words came. Turning toward the hall, she managed to hide that she was at a loss for what to say at the sight of seeing Thomas in clothes that might have been Jerry's so closely did their tastes overlap.

"I won't lose touch again," he said.

"Um," she said. "I hope not." Although why she cared enough already to be hurt that he might not baffled her.

"I won't," he said, leaning on the kitchen counter. A few dishes lay helter-skelter in the sink under the window. "Is that one of yours?" he asked, pointing at a small painting on the wall beside the door to the pantry. It was an island scene with a curving walk and lamppost with branches twirled around it. There was a sailboat in the distance.

Sue nodded.

"I like it," he said.

"I imagine something will appear at any moment from around that corner." What might she be waiting for? Who?

"I like the colours of the leaves."

When they went into the living room, Thomas sat on the sofa at the opposite end from Sue.

"Do you need any clothes?" she asked. Then she stopped

abruptly and put her hand to her mouth. She could not bear to look at that closet.

"Do you want me to go through stuff with you?" he asked, almost as if he were repeating the lines she had imagined for him. *Stuff*, she thought. She had known he would call it that and it took the sting out of it slightly.

"Would you?" She was relieved, surprised at how quickly he had understood her. When she got up and started up the stairs, Thomas followed her to find the clothes that still hung in the closet just as Jerry had left them.

"Here." She took out the tweed jacket.

"Thanks," Thomas said, holding it for a moment. Then he tried it on.

As she held out a pair of tan cords, she noticed that the jacket looked as if it were made for him. He tried on another, with a hood, that was almost new. After he nodded at the sight of himself, he took it off in exchange for a dark winter coat that Sue had imagined he would like.

She took out a scarf and a flannel shirt, which she hugged tightly. "I'll keep these," she murmured. "He wore this shirt when he sat in front of the fireplace on winter evenings."

Even if he were pondering that it had belonged to his father, she thought he couldn't possibly feel the emotions this clothing aroused in her.

"Thanks for all of this," Thomas said. They spent another half an hour taking out garment after garment, waiting for Thomas to decide what he wanted. When Sue thought they might have gone through most of what was there, she sighed. "I'm tired now," she said. "Thanks for your help." He started to tell her about Kate then. "She was behind me in high school," he said. "Her brother's a buddy. I ran into her a couple months ago and ... I must have been blind. Or she'd grown up since the last time I saw her."

As Sue watched his face, a smile creeping across it, she was reminded of seeing Jerry's face like that on the day they had married. There was an album full of photographs. She visualized Thomas looking through it as they went downstairs again to the kitchen.

"How old was my father then?" he might ask. "What was he like?"

He had not asked those kinds of questions yet. In some ways, she had looked forward to this, in others she had dreaded it, fearing that she would not be able to paint a picture of someone who would have been a good father. When Thomas was born, she understood that Jerry might still have been drinking too much or too often. Martin had alluded to that, and, to the stories of his exploits in back country after his first wife was killed, stories of almost being caught in an avalanche or of breaking a leg skiing down a treacherous slope. Stories of adventure, but of unnecessary risk also.

Thomas pulled up a chair and grinned as he pulled out a wallet from his back pocket. Inside a plastic sleeve was a photo of a young woman holding a tennis racquet. She had long fair hair, and wore a white sleeveless top, short skirt, tiny hoop earrings, and a striped terry-cloth band around her wrist.

"Ah," Sue said. "A ten?"

"You bet," Thomas said. "The love of my life."

"That's good news."

"She's going to study law, too," he chuckled.

"It's too bad you won't have a chance to talk about law with Jerry," she said.

He nodded.

"I'm glad you're telling me," she added.

He smiled slightly and raised the mug she had just given to him. Steam still rose from dark liquid and the smell of cinnamon was in the air.

"There's going to be a memorial for Jerry," she said. "I'm planning it with a friend of his. Martin would like to meet you."

"Martin?" Thomas said, pursing his lips. "Well..." he fidgeted with his keys, pulling them out of his pocket and then putting them back again.

She waited for some comment, but he was quiet, his eyes cast down toward the floor. Sue had considered he might not be comfortable about the memorial, but for him to become suddenly evasive surprised her. What was it about? She looked beyond him to a black-and-white photograph Jerry had picked up in Paris. It was of a stall on the Seine.

"I can't," he said.

"Why not?" she asked.

"I can't say." He turned away again.

"I don't understand."

"I'm sorry. It's just too much," he said. "Maybe some day."

"Some day what?"

He shrugged and put his mug on the counter. "I'll give you my phone number." He took out a pen and wrote the number down on the edge of a newspaper lying there. "You can call any time."

"You just got here," she said. "And I think you need to get in touch with me when you figure out what you want to do."

Thomas had suddenly changed when she had mentioned Martin. Would he know what this was all about? Maybe Jerry's childhood friend had his secrets also, but she had always felt that you knew where you stood with Martin. If he knew anything, he would have told her, especially if she had asked him. That was the way he was. Even in her recent anger at Jerry, it had been clear that Martin was upset with her. Thomas leaned over to pick up his jacket where it had fallen into a crumpled pile on the floor.

"What if I call him?" he asked cautiously. "I could do that."

Now it was her turn to write numbers down on a piece of newspaper. He put the fragment she handed him in his pocket. "I may," he said. "I don't know."

"All right," she sighed. "Of course, it's up to you." As she turned around, a photograph on the refrigerator of Jerry at the tiller of *Prime Time* caught her passing glance. The day she had taken that photo, they had swum from a beach on an island and were just preparing to sail back to the marina where Jerry kept the boat. How odd to think that on that day, they had both had secrets. She could not comprehend the happiness she had experienced then knowing what she now did about this secret of Jerry's, so tangibly revealed, standing before her. Why, Jerry? And why had she kept the secret of her baby from him? Why had they kept such huge secrets from each other?

Sue followed Thomas to the front hall, clutching her palms. There was so much she could say, but she was afraid if she showed how much she wanted contact with him he might never come back. And she began to wonder if she were using this same kind of thinking to avoid looking for her own child.

"There are lots of things of Jerry's you haven't seen yet," she said.

He reached for the doorknob. "Not now," he said.

"Would you mind if I took your photograph?" She had a desire to record things more often recently, as if that would keep her from losing them. Although all the photographs she had taken of Jerry over the years had not kept him from dying.

He shrugged, "Yeah, sure. Go ahead."

Sue went to the shelf under the front window where her camera was lying in an open case. Thomas stood, jacket already on, looking at his watch.

"Ready?" she asked.

"Yeah."

She took a profile shot of him standing in the hall, and another of him opening the door, and yet another of him standing on the porch before he turned to go down the stairs. If he never returned, she would have these images.

"Bye," he said.

His stride was fast and determined and he did not look back to smile or wave before he disappeared around the corner. When she went out to the kitchen and picked up the half full mug he had left on the counter, it was still warm in her hands. She sat down, holding the cup. She thought of how she had felt at sixteen when the baby had kicked inside her. Sometimes, when her belly had moved, she had been sure she could actually see the shape of a foot. Sitting and holding her hand on her large abdomen, she had wondered what the baby would look like. Would it be a boy or a girl? Conceived in a moment of awkward, even painful, adolescent passion and confusion, she had wanted to keep it. But even as she had not wanted to give it up, she had not known what else to do.

When she fell asleep, she dreamed of a foetus floating in clear liquid in a bottle. Sue knew it was the baby she had carried in her uterus. She herself was floating on the surface of the water in a pond, frogs chirped nearby and plants grew underneath and became caught in her legs. Grabbing great mounds of slimy green strands, she threw them out onto the rocks at the side of the pond. There were always more entwining her. When she swam on the surface, the frogs stayed on the rocks, but tiny tadpoles darted at her shoulders. Finally, she pulled herself up onto the rocks, exhausted.

As she started to look again for the bottle, she could not find it. It must have sunk. Where was it? Sue woke up in a panic. What about the baby? What am I to do with the baby? It was as if she were still sixteen. But the nurse had not let her see her daughter.

"We've taken care of her." The white uniform had towered over her, the voice disembodied. No warmth, no touch.

"But she's my baby," Sue had cried. "I want to see her once. I want to see her."

"It's better that you don't, my dear."

*

Martin put a glass of orange juice on the small table on Emily's side of the bed. He always liked greeting the city as it started to awaken. He had already been up for an hour and left coffee brewing. Emily could only be roused at the very last minute and now she murmured and rolled over.

"Bye," she said in a muffled voice.

He saw the soft sag of her shoulders as she drifted off again.

"Bye," he said.

Long before anyone else would have come in, Martin would be at his office. He would study the case he was taking to court later. When he did get there and settled in, it took over an hour to go through everything he had left on his desk. Then he walked to the outer office to get the blood in his legs circulating again. At the water cooler, he was surprised to see someone sitting on a chair next to it.

"Here to see someone?" he asked.

As the young man looked up, Martin was startled. Jerry! he thought. This man could be Jerry.

"Martin Drew?" the young man asked.

"Yes," Martin said. "Did you call to make an appointment?"

"I guess I should have."

Martin sighed. Then it struck him. "You must be Thomas," he said.

The young man looked relieved. "Yes," he said. "Thomas Crossar."

Martin thought quickly of his calendar for the morning. He had to go to court, but that was not until the afternoon. And while he had some preparation still to do, he did not have any clients for another hour.

"Come on into my office," he said.

Thomas followed him down the hall and into the large space where a tree just outside the window cast long shadows into the room. Heavy legal binders and books lined the shelves. Leaves dangled down one side from a hanging earthenware pot.

Thomas looked at a photograph of Emily on a swing.

"My wife," Martin said

"My mom said you went steady in high school."

"That's so." Martin gestured to a comfortable brown leather

armchair across from his desk and pulled one out for himself on the same side.

"What happened?" Thomas asked.

"Well, we were young," Martin said. "She broke it off after a year or so."

Thomas frowned. "But she told me you came back."

"I did from time to time. My parents lived in Stratford until they died. But I never saw her on any of those visits."

Thomas pulled out an envelope. "This was with her papers in a safety deposit box."

Martin could see his name on the outside and that the back was sealed with tape. It seemed odd that Joanna would have left anything for him. He had left Stratford for university and only returned occasionally with Emily. Often, he had run into someone he knew on the main street and he might have been told that Joanna had a son, but he had not remembered that. He put the envelope on his desk, not planning to open it until after the young man left.

"She said you did."

"Well, I don't remember. Why would she say that?"

"She only told me a year ago that Jerry Reid was my father."

"You didn't know until then? Good grief. What did she tell you?'

Thomas's face turned bright red. Martin got up and went to the window. The quiet stretched unbroken. "She told me *you* were my father," Thomas finally said in a low voice.

Martin whirled around. "What?" He could not believe it. What he recalled about Joanna was her unwavering honesty. Even when she had told him they should not go steady anymore, it had been as clear a statement as he had ever heard.

"I don't get it," he said.

"Don't ask me," Thomas said.

"Well, she told you the truth at some point. And there's no doubt about that. You look so much like Jerry that were I to see you on the street, I would likely stop you to find out if you were related." He paused. "But if you thought I was your father, why didn't you look for me?"

"I wanted to, but Mom told me you wouldn't want to see me."

Martin sat down again, this time in his chair behind the desk. What was he supposed to say? "I tell you what," he said. "I have clients this morning and I have to go to court this afternoon." He held up the envelope. "I'll try to read what's in here some time today and perhaps we could meet later."

"All right," Thomas said.

They decided on a pub Martin knew.

"Six o'clock?"

Thomas nodded.

Martin's court appearance was on a divorce case with the wife as his client. The husband was still fighting custody. It was not settled that afternoon and the woman was disappointed. He did not blame her; not only was she left in limbo still, the legal bills kept climbing.

Afterwards, he stopped in a small restaurant nearby where he could sit in a corner undisturbed. Even though he had had enough coffee for one day, he ordered another cup, dubious about opening the envelope Thomas had handed him that morning. Sweat began to form on his upper lip. His heart pounded. Whatever was inside likely was not going to make his life any easier. He slit the envelope open with a jackknife he carried, one he had used since he was a teenager. The single page was plain with only a brief typed message on it and Joanna's signature at the bottom.

Dear Martin, he read.

By now you'll have met my son. I apologize for having told Thomas for many years that you were his father. I don't know what I was thinking of. You would have known immediately that wasn't so. He's the image of Jerry. And Jerry knew about him, but I didn't want him to see him. I'm really sorry now Jerry didn't know him earlier.

So, Martin thought, he was not going to find out any more than he already knew. What was her point in writing to him?

Often, I wished I'd listened when you begged me to stay with you. I was too young, I guess. I hope you'll consider my request to be involved in my son's life. I hear that you and Jerry have remained friends so likely you would be anyway. But I want you to know that's also my wish.
Joanna Crossar

Martin stared at the letter. It was like a knife in his heart. After all, when they were all in high school, Joanna had been Martin's girlfriend. Even though it would have been years after that, it was odd to think of Jerry sleeping with her. Why had Jerry never told him? Instead, he was left to pick up the pieces and he did not know how. Glancing at his watch, he saw he would be late for the pub if he did not leave now. All there really was for him to do was to get there and tell Thomas about the memorial.

A cold wind blew across the streetcar tracks as Martin loped to the stop. Emily would be at home by now. Before he reached the pub, he would call her. The revelations of the day were ones he thought he ought to share with Sue, though he was unsure how to deal with her. Her recent conduct had made him more uncomfortable with her than he had realized.

After calling Emily and alerting her he might be quite late, Martin joined Thomas at the pub. They each drank a couple of beers and talked about Stratford. Thomas asked some legal questions and it was not long before a stranger would have guessed they had known each other for a long time.

The waiter stopped by their table and took the empty bottles. "Another?" he asked.

"Thanks, no," Martin said. "A hamburger and fries."

Thomas ordered also.

Later, on the street outside the pub, where by then darkness had wrapped itself around the city, Thomas became suddenly awkward.

"Keep in touch, will you?" Martin said. "You can call any time."

"Thanks," Thomas said, his face relaxing. He shook Martin's hand and turned to go.

As he moved out of earshot, Martin took out his cell and dialled Sue's number. He would say he wanted to drop by, hoping he would be able to deal with however she reacted. At the same time, he continued to bask a bit at the thought of the young man who had sat across the table from him in the pub. While it had been almost too warm near the fireplace, it had been a comfortable spot to chat in private.

Stopping momentarily, he called Emily again.

"Just out of the pub," he said. "And off to Jerry's house now. I mean, Sue's."

Must be almost a full moon, Martin thought as he stood on Sue's porch. It was late, but also still very bright.

When Sue answered his knock, he followed her into the living room.

"Those are new, aren't they?" he asked, pointing at photographs of Thomas on the mantel.

She nodded.

"I met Thomas," he said.

"Really?" She sat down on the sofa.

"Yes, he came by the office. You gave him my number, didn't you?" He turned around to look at her, frowning slightly.

"Yes, of course," she said. "But I'm surprised he went ahead and called you."

Martin walked across the room to the window. He leaned against the sill, staring out.

"I don't get it," he said, without turning around. "Why wouldn't he? And why would you be surprised?"

"Well, his initial reaction was disinterest."

Martin twisted around to look at her. "He seemed glad to

chat," he said. "I think his mother might have told him about me."

Sue reached toward a bowl on the glass table in front of her and took a handful of almonds.

"Want some?" she asked.

Martin shook his head. "Did I tell you I dated her in high school?" he asked, continuing without waiting for an answer. "I was heartbroken when she broke it off, but that was years before she and Jerry saw each other again. It might explain why Jerry never told me about his interlude in Stratford or about Thomas."

Sue tried to imagine the anger Martin might have felt if he had known about Jerry's fling and about the pregnancy. She could not, but suspected he would have been concerned about the child and insisted Jerry be involved. Maybe that was why Jerry had never told him.

"I was stunned by the resemblance," Martin said. "Even though you'd told me."

"You have to see him, don't you?"

She recalled her first glimpse outside the church at Jerry's funeral, the sense that Thomas was someone she knew.

"Mannerisms as well. The way his head moves to one side when he's listening," Martin said, moving his own head in a way Jerry had. "Yet they never saw each other. It's like being thrown back to my childhood."

Sue wondered if Thomas had also gone swimming at the quarry. Probably all the local teenagers had.

"What did his mother tell him?" she asked.

Martin drew in his breath and turned toward the window again. His head was lit up by a streetlight that shone through into the room. There were shadows of the plants on the sill and on the rug. Before he spoke again, he moved to lean against the wall where he could look directly at her. "It's amazing and I can't even imagine why. But for a long time, she told him I was his father."

Sue gasped. "What?" She gathered her wits. "Why on earth would she do that? It must have been obvious to her if he ever found you that you would recognize the resemblance to Jerry immediately."

"Oh, yes. And I keep mulling it over, wishing she was still here so we could talk. But she's not, so we'll never know," Martin said. "For one thing, I don't suppose she thought he'd ever meet me. Or Jerry either, for that matter." He looked at the photo of Thomas on the mantel again and one of Jerry on the other side of it.

He hesitated before he spoke again. "Probably when she knew she was dying, she thought it wise to tell him the truth."

"Would that Jerry had done the same." Her voice was low, as if she wanted to speak aloud but at the same time hoped Martin would not hear her.

He sat down on the sofa. "He didn't, Sue," he sighed. "You can be upset. You can be sad. And it won't matter. He didn't."

"Well, you ought to be upset, even angry. Imagine telling Thomas you were his father."

"He's a neat kid," Martin said. "I almost wish I was."

"Oh God!" She turned and walked to a pair of glass doors that looked out over the small concrete area at the back that was just big enough for a few pots and her bicycle. A squirrel darted through a beam of light across a wire that stretched from the porch to a pole at the end of the yard. Martin followed and stood beside the long oak table in the dining room, bright red place mats on either end.

"You know what," he said. "I can't change anything. If I could, I might try."

Sue turned to look at him with tears streaming down her face. "I'm sorry," she said.

He moved to put an arm around her shoulders until her sobbing lessened. She stood back. "Maybe we can start to plan the memorial now," she said.

He nodded.

"You were going to make a list?"

He reached into his trousers and pulled out a crumpled sheet of paper. "I did get started," he said. "Have a look at it."

3.

HANS LEFT THE OFFICE EARLY, anxious to get on the road before the heavy traffic. It always took longer in winter to drive back and forth between the farm and the city. Although by March, there was usually less snow and ice. When he had picked Heather up after her flight from London just two days earlier, she was nursing a slight cold picked up on the plane. She had stayed home that day and while he supposed some of it might still be jet lag, he hoped she felt better.

"I'm glad I went," she had said. "I think we sorted some things out when I was there." She had chattered on about her mother's prescriptions and her father's painful knee, but he had sensed there was something she did not want to talk about. It was not any prescient knowledge, just intuition derived from his awareness that she had started sleeping closer to the edge of their bed since her return.

Pulling over to the right lane to exit onto the road north that would take him to the farm, he wondered why he thought it would make a difference to how she felt if he arrived home earlier than usual. Whether it did or not, he felt compelled to have whatever conversation was lurking in the background sooner rather than later.

As he parked his car over by the fence across from the side door, his dog, Rusty, ran to greet him. The moment he stepped out, the dog jumped up against his trousers.

"Hey, pal," Hans chuckled. "Good to see ya."

Opening the door, he saw Heather on the telephone. Turning toward him, her frown startled him. He had not thought it had reached a point where she was not only surprised to see him, but not particularly pleased. He saw that being interrupted had put her on the spot somehow.

"I'll speak with you another time, Dad." She hung up then as if she did not want Hans to overhear her speaking with her father.

It did not make sense to him. Poppa, as he called the older man, always wanted a word with him, too. He could not recall any occasion when she had not handed over the receiver before ending her conversation.

"How is Poppa?" he asked.

"Fine." Without looking at him, she went to the stove and started to stir something in a large pot.

He had visualized finding her in bed, damp and hot from the bug. Instead, she looked as if she had stayed home for what she would call a "mental health day." She sometimes did that, using the time to cook or go riding across the fields and down a trail in the backwoods. Now, he smelled the scent of garlic and onions wafting through the air.

"Then why didn't you let me say hello?" he asked.

"Well, we'd already been talking for a while."

"Is that a reason?"

She sighed, turned to put a lid on the pot and walked out of the kitchen up the stairs to their bedroom. If that was the way it was, he would leave her alone. He put his boots on again and went out to the barn. As soon as he opened the door, he was met with the scent of hay and horses. Breathing deeply, he moved to the stalls and patted the mare.

"Don't know what's goin' on, gal," he whispered. Heather's curious behaviour baffled him, but, after all, she was not feeling well. It was likely no more complicated than that.

A few days later, life having fallen back into the more or less regular pattern of work on the farm and in the city, he had almost forgotten his initial suspicions. It was then that he found a letter on the table in the den.

Dearest Heather.

How could he not read it? Open right there as if left for him to do so. He frowned as he read that the writer was sorry not to be able to travel to Canada for a few months. But hoped she would still be there for him.

Still *there* for him? Lights exploded in Hans's head like fireworks. So that was it. There was a man in England. But she had rushed off in the middle of winter as if there were a crisis with her parents. He was mystified.

The letter ended, *All my love, David.*

"David," he muttered. Who the hell was David? Where had she met this man? Why had he not heard about him? He was so angry by then that he was almost glad he would have time to calm down before Heather arrived. It was much later, after he had showered and had a coffee, when he saw her car turn into the driveway and heard the engine as she drove toward the house.

She burst in the door, arms full of plastic bags from the supermarket.

"Tell me what's going on," he said.

"What are you talking about?"

"David," he blurted out. "Who is David?"

He ought to have known. He, a psychic, should already have figured it out. But he knew that psychics were poor readers of their own lives, and, as usual, the traumas in his unfolded just as trauma unfolded for anyone. Unexpectedly. Like his sister's death. Anna. He had loved Anna more than any of his brothers; she, the one he had turned to all his life to help him out of scrapes with his parents, with teachers, with anyone. She had had cancer in her pancreas and died quickly. Not even sixty yet. He wished he could talk to her now.

"Have you been reading my mail?" Heather asked. "What right have you to read my mail?"

"Well, if you don't want me to know you're carrying on an affair under my nose, don't leave your damn letters scattered out where I can't help but see them."

She kicked her boots across the room and stomped into the kitchen. He heard the bags thump onto the floor. Following her, he stood watching as she shoved vegetables into a plastic bin in the refrigerator.

"Leave me alone," she said.

"I have a right to know."

"Know what?"

"Who is David?"

"You're waiting for me to say he's my lover, aren't you? Well, you're mistaken."

He felt the vein in his forehead throbbing, even worried he might hit her. He picked up a plate, but quickly turned in the opposite direction and threw it against that wall. As it smashed into shards, he shuddered.

"Such melodrama," she said. "I told you he wasn't my lover."

"So I smashed a plate," he said. "Big deal. What about my feelings? I'm supposed to like it that I might be getting diddled? Fuck it all, I love you," he said as if at this moment it surprised him. How could he still love her? The thought of this David infuriated him.

"I'm sorry, Hans," she said. "But he understands some things you don't and so we talked a lot when I was there."

"Well, did you even try to talk with me about it?"

"I just know you wouldn't understand," she said. "But I do love you."

"This is crazy," he said. "Whatever it is sounds as if we need to talk about it."

She reached toward him, almost touching his cheek. "Right now wouldn't be a good idea."

"So what are you going to do about David?" he asked more gently.

"I don't know." She pulled away. "Probably nothing."

He wondered if he would break something else or if he would run outside and start screaming. But he waited.

"There isn't anything to do," she said. She picked up a tin from the counter and put it in a cupboard.

"So, are you having an affair with him?"

"Of course not. I told you I wasn't. You're just so willing to believe the worst. Dad asked me if I could come to England to help him deal with Mum. You know all that."

Hans did not know what to believe. He hated how he looked in the bathroom mirror of late, lines creeping in around his eyes. And his belly was getting larger. It was easy to believe that Heather might find someone else more attractive.

"So why didn't you just tell me that? And how he happens to be helping your family?"

"I haven't had time."

"There's been plenty of time. You've been back long enough to make phone calls, to get this letter."

Her eyes blazed. "I think I'd rather talk later," she said.

"When?"

"Just a little later. I need to get some air."

"Wouldn't it be better if you just told me something to set my mind at rest?"

She reached for the wall and propped herself against it. "I'm not trying to keep anything from you. I don't know where to start. Dad was upset."

"You said something about your mother's prescriptions before you went."

"That, too." She sat down against the soft cushions of a chair in the nook beside the kitchen where one of them often sat reading the newspaper. "We got them straightened out, as I already told you. I went to the doctor with Mum."

Hans watched the lines between her eyes recede. She looked younger. She was younger, but perhaps age had nothing to do with any of it. He did not know. Just that he was increasingly conscious of it and how could she not be?

"I'm glad you were able to go and help," Hans said. "You know that."

"Yes," she said. "I do."

But there was still something that niggled at him and he willed her to erase his suspicion. It bothered him because they had always trusted each other. He looked toward the window. Snow fell beyond it on the rolling hills of the farm, onto the leafless maples beside the house. A horse neighed in the barn, the sound echoing in the distance.

"David is a neighbour who found Mum wandering outside and brought her home. That turned out to be because of the medication. I didn't meet him when I went to visit before because he lives in London. His parents live next door. He's coming to Canada to do some research. I said we could help him out with contacts."

"All my love, David?"

"He's a kid, Hans. All of twenty-three. And expressive and affectionate. That's all."

So for her, was that all? He was not sure. The phone calls. The way she often turned away from him when he pressed against her. Something he had to admit now had begun long before her trip.

Hans went out into the snow, large flakes dropping onto his cheeks and melting. He kicked at some chunks of ice that went skidding down the driveway. Maybe she was telling the truth, but there was something more to it. He picked up a shovel and began to lift the snow that lay along the path to the barn. He threw it into mounds beside the fence. In the summer, the two goats would be peering at him, but all the animals were inside their sheds or the barn today.

An hour later, he went back into the house. Heather handed him a mug of hot chocolate.

"Thanks," he said, although he wished she would also hand him his pipe that she had been asked to hide while he stopped smoking.

"I'm going out to see the horses," she said. "They missed me when I was away." She had her boots on already. The door closed behind her.

Hans sat at his desk, sorting through papers he needed to take into the office. Among them he saw Sue's number. He picked up the phone and dialled it. A recording came on. *Please leave a message. Veuillez laissez un message, s'il vous plaît.*

"I haven't forgotten you," he said. "This is Hans. So when are we going to have lunch again?"

He left a number for her to call, a private number.

*

Sue listened to Hans's message. She could hear his playful good nature and something ingenuous about him. Of course, the quintessential question, too. How did he know the future? He had told her that people went to see psychics because they were unhappy or curious. Sometimes both. She had asked him if he had thought her unhappy.

"Not an unhappy person," he had said. "But how could you have been happy when your husband was dying?

Now, she questioned whether to return his call. People came to him for something to hope for, he had told her. That was what she needed, something to hope for. Likely, she would call and after doing so set out, feeling almost light-hearted, to meet him at a coffee shop not far from his office. And although he was full of the unexpected, when she did reach him the next day that was exactly what he suggested.

"You know that little coffee shop not far from the corner, near my office?"

Well, yes she did.

"In half an hour?" he asked.

When she arrived, Hans rose with a grin that stretched across his face.

"I brought some photographs," she said. These were shots taken in various locations around the city. Horses sculpted out of black iron on a green bridge over Yonge Street just north of Mount Pleasant Cemetery. Later, the horses would disappear, but she would know they had been there.

"They're very good," he said, looking at the images.

"Most of the shots are experiments. I take them when something suddenly appears that demands to be painted. I love horses."

"We keep horses," Hans said.

"Do you ride?" She was aware of the "we" that stood suddenly between them. He might not have noticed saying it, or he might have done so intentionally.

"Oh yes," he said. "I feed them in the early morning and then again in the late evening. When I go into the barn, they shuffle around, swish their tails, and peer over the edges of their stalls, waiting for food. I clean up after them, too. I don't mind." Shovelling the shit was good for him, he said. It made him feel strong. "They belong to my wife though. She's the one who rides most often. I like cows. We don't have many. That's what we had on the farm where I grew up."

She showed him the rest of the photographs. One was of a streetcar near St. James Cathedral, another of the boardwalk on the island.

"I like the curve of that walk," she said. "I've often tried to paint it."

"I spent months working as a gardener in my first years in Toronto, digging up those flower plots on Centre Island with the breeze blowing in from Lake Ontario," Hans said. "Sometimes it was so cold, my whiskers were full of ice. I worked in Edwards Gardens, too."

She could visualize the manicured, carefully laid out flowers where many wedding photographs were taken.

"I like working with plants as much as with people. In those first years, I missed the animals on the farm."

"I thought you worked as a translator."

"I did," he said. "But there wasn't enough money in that.

When I started to look for something else, I looked for work outdoors that would give me a break in the winter so I could start to do readings."

"Where did you do readings?" she asked.

"At first in a shop down on a side street off Bloor. People heard about me through friends who came to see me. I never had signs out on the sidewalk or in windows," he said, tossing his head. "I made appointments over the telephone."

Sue could tell that he was proud of this and considered himself in a different league than those who advertised that way.

"How did your wife feel about it?" she asked.

"She wasn't too keen," he said. "She didn't really believe I could make a living that would support a family of five. We had three children. And she was tired of working as a cook for women who saw her only as a servant. I didn't notice what was happening to Maxine and our marriage didn't last. Not surprising. I'd be more forgiving if she hadn't started to call the readings the devil's work. And worse than that, turned the children against me. I'm relieved that as they've grown up, all of my children have come looking for me. 'We need a father,' they said. 'We need a grandfather for our children.'"

Not having known anyone like him before, Sue was intrigued not only by the scenarios he drew, but also by how demonstrative he could be.

Thank you, thank you, and thank you, an expression that had surprised her the first time he used these words in multiples, although it had also made her smile. He'd said it after they had laughed and talked together, he seemingly grateful for their good humour.

"The ring," she said, looking at the wide gold band on his finger.

"I married again." He did not seem about to go into it.

"What's her name?" Sue asked tentatively.

"Heather."

Sue sipped her coffee, not at all happy about something so

stark as a name that was now known by her. Consequently, she knew this woman existed. But what right did she have to feel jealous? This was not something she had experienced with Jerry, except possibly momentarily when he had joined the meditation group and spent time with Jane. Otherwise, he could be involved with his work or listening quietly to music or out with friends or on a political rampage over some injustice, but she had not really ever felt her place in his affections seriously threatened. That she should now be jealous of the unknown wife of a man who was almost a stranger was ludicrous. She, a woman who would never knowingly become involved with a married man, or so she had always believed. But her marriage had been a dance full of secrets and deceit. Now, it seemed she might not be who she had always thought she was either. An honest woman. A woman not easily fooled. One who would not deceive her husband. It seemed she had been wrong about everything, and possibly, most of all, about herself.

"Is her last name Jonker?" she asked, not sure why it mattered.

"No."

"What is it?"

"I wouldn't tell you that. That's her business."

Sue felt he could sense her jealousy. "Is it all right to ask if you met her in Canada?" she asked.

"Yes," Hans said. "She comes from England and has an accent that immediately places her. Although when I first learned English, it was such a confusing language I thought all the different accents were part of it."

"Does she have children, too?" Though aware that she could stop at any moment, she kept right on probing.

"One daughter." He eyed her quizzically, then continued as if her curiosity were not unusual, as if he might even want to tell her. "Heather and I raised Vivian together. A young teenager when we met, she spent every second weekend with her father. I love children, but neither of us wanted any more." He said they had been able to follow their dream to own land in the country. Rolling hills where the wind from the lake came rushing through and you could feel the weather changing and when a storm was coming. And they had fields of oats for their horses and for the ones they boarded. They had a pond where he fished and swam, where Heather's daughter still swam when she came to visit.

"Chickens. Roosters. Pigs. And my dogs, of course."

He described it as an oasis from his work in the city. She could almost visualize it and it intrigued her almost as much as he did.

"I don't think about psychic premonitions there," he continued. "I spend my time planting and weeding or mowing hay. We grow fresh vegetables and freeze them for the winter. And catch fish. Sometimes we have a big fish fry with the neighbours."

"Does Heather do the farm work, too?"

"Not much. A little. She works hard in the city. Often, I scarcely see her."

He did not say it as if this bothered him though Sue imagined it did.

"Tell me more about your work," she said. Would he be here with her if there were no cracks in his marriage? She did not think there had been any women in Jerry's life she did not know about, but now she could doubt even that if she let herself. No, she must not do that. Nothing that she knew or had discovered suggested he had been unfaithful.

Hans paused and seemed to ponder what he would say. "Usually, unless I know through the media or they've left that information, I don't know a last name," he said. "Yet I know a lot more about people in the first moment than they could possibly imagine. I get a sense right away, as with you when I saw you in the waiting room. A son, but not one you knew about. I'm never good about time frames. Usually, I just know something is going to happen. I want it recorded because often it helps a person later. If they're unsure, they can check. They can also see I didn't make idle predictions." So, he had known that first time that she already knew her husband was going to die.

"It's draining to take in so much of another's pain," he said.

"Soon there'll be a memorial for my husband," she said. "On the island."

"Yes."

"You know," she mused, "One day I will probably be a grandmother without ever having had children."

"If I'd told you that when I first read for you, you wouldn't have believed that either."

But Hans did not seem to know about anyone except Thomas. She wondered if she ought to feel reassured about that, proof that he was ordinary, that his knowledge about Thomas had been a lucky guess after all.

"I wouldn't have wanted to think about it," she said. "So it's just as well you didn't. Did you know then?"

"I can't remember."

An answer she was glad to hear.

When they left the coffee shop, Sue walked with Hans along Bloor Street toward his office. They dodged a fast moving group of children and stepped around a man leaning on a bicycle. He invited her upstairs for a moment, indicating a chair she now recognized that let them sit across from each other. In the waiting room outside Hans's office that was used by everyone on the floor, the radio played Mozart and the soft music drowned out the voices for anyone who might arrive for an appointment. The kettle there was also boiling, likely plugged in by someone down the hall who was making tea. Sue watched him start to fiddle with the papers on his desk and thought whatever else he was or was not, his face and physique appealed to her. Her type, although he was quite different from Jerry.

"I need to clear my head," Hans said. "I have a string of appointments, then a long drive back to the country."

"I'll get going." She stood to leave and he came across the room to put his arms around her in a friendly hug. Her body stiffened momentarily and then she leaned briefly against him.

"See you," he said.

*

Sue walked through the house to the sliding doors that led into the dining room. The morning newspaper was strewn across the long wooden table where so often friends had gathered, she sitting at one end and Jerry at the other. Off the dining room was a bright pantry with a skylight her husband had installed. It sprinkled light into one end of the living room and onto a huge abstract painting with red shades predominating, as well as onto the old piano Jerry had often played to relax. He had often sat there, picking out chords before launching into ragtime or jazz. Sue searched the empty spaces as if he would be there, imagining him turning to smile at her. Light flashing across his face from above, crinkles where the laugh lines were.

"Hey, gal, where've you been? Sing along, I'm playing something wondrous," he would have said.

Huge, gulping sobs suddenly engulfed her and she fell to her knees by the fireplace where, gasping for breath, she grabbed onto an arm of the sofa. Then, she found herself entwined around a huge pillow.

"Jerry," she wailed. "JERRY."

My love. My love. That had not changed. She had loved him and still did.

When she finally calmed down, she went into the kitchen where a pile of dirty dishes on the counter glared at her. She put them in the dishwasher, then began to peel and chop carrots for soup. As she sliced onions, her eyes started to water. After that, she took a shower and scrubbed and scrubbed until she felt bits of skin coming away with the soap. Perhaps she had been foolish to see Hans again rather than friends who knew her already. Friends from the school where she taught or from the gym. But since the early days after the funeral, most of them had not called. Nor did she take the initiative. Jerry would not want her to grieve too long, but she thought he might be hurt by her lack of discretion in seeing a married stranger, especially one with whom she thought she might already be slightly in love. She picked up a book when she left the bathroom, but after reading a few lines of a chapter on Picasso, let it drop.

Was Hans also thinking about her as he fed the animals? As he walked across the fields? Would he thrash in his bed at night, his wife beside him, until a cat jumped down onto the floor? She was not sure if he had mentioned a cat. It would be Heather's cat. The dogs probably slept in the barn. She thought of his stories. A man who had said it was impossible that he would get a new car even though that was what Hans had predicted. Then called later to say he had landed a new job with a car as part of the package. The woman he had told would study law. And that she would go to Africa where she should listen to what she heard. She wanted to, but thought she was too old. After that reading she had gone anyway, and, while there, had visited a small village where the people had taken her to a witch doctor. He told her she was going to help others sort out messes between people, which for her was a good enough description of a lawyer to be the deciding factor.

Sue fell asleep and dreamed about Jerry, his voice and touch so real he could have been there.

"You're doing fine, Bird," he said.

In the dream, she wanted to argue with Jerry that because of Hans she was not doing well at all, but he insisted she had nothing to worry about. And when she woke up, she felt peaceful.

Calls from Hans came when Sue was not there to pick up the phone. Then she would find his messages, disappointed to have missed him again.

"I've been thinking about you," he said one day in a new message.

Sue replayed it a couple of times, listening intently to his voice. She wished she had not ever encouraged him as his interest now made her nervous. Yet she knew his attention took the edge off her loneliness. And something else, too, she was drawn to him.

Two days later, unable to get through to him by telephone and not wanting to talk to his machine, Sue wrote a note. A butterfly in bright colours on the outside of the card suggested happy news was enclosed, a cheerful note that conveyed only good wishes.

As she went out onto Bloor Street, Sue thought Hans might go to some of the small restaurants or shops in the neighbourhood like the Thai place with the golden lion in the window where they had had lunch or the sushi place or the Hungarian deli that had been there for decades. She might even run into him, in which case, she could give him the note with her invitation.

What was more likely was that she would not see him and with no other choice she would go to his office and slip the card under his door. Quickly, even stealthily. But when she arrived there, she was greeted by an open door through which she could see the Chagall painting on the opposite wall. Likely he was in the washroom or down the hall. Having looked for him in the faces on the street, hoping to see him, now all she wanted was to be able to leave her note and disappear. Dropping the envelope onto the floor just inside his open door, she went hurriedly down the stairs.

What about dropping by for a chat and tea or coffee on your way into the office one day, she had written. *Sue.*

She imagined him looking at his face in the mirror on the back of his door, at his longish, curly hair. At his moustache. He would grimace and a small grin might then creep up into his eyes. Whether or not he intended to accept her invitation, she somehow knew those eyes would sparkle. She was not surprised to get a telephone call later that afternoon.

"What about if I come by on Thursday after my day is finished?" he asked.

It was not what she had intended. Her thought had been if he came on his way into work he would not stay very long. She was worried about the longing she felt, about how she might allow what she would regret later. But weighing it over quickly, she decided he was unlikely to do anything unless she let him.

"Okay," she said.

When he called on Thursday to tell her he was finished his appointments, Sue gave him directions.

"Not that far from your office," she said. "Just north of the supermarket and the church on Bloor Street, up the first block."

In less than fifteen minutes, he walked up onto the cedar porch, holding lightly onto the wrought iron rail. A small gas lamp lit up the number. At the sound of the bell, she opened the door. Could he tell she had been waiting expectantly?

"The No Flyers sign worried me," he said, pointing at the mailbox. "I thought maybe you wouldn't let me in."

"I'll make an exception."

He sat on the sofa and she on the armchair covered in striped material. Both of them were tentative, even awkward.

"Coffee? Something to eat?" she asked.

"Just coffee." He followed her to the kitchen. "Your house has a good buzz."

She supposed he knew there were almost too many memories and was grateful he did not say so now. She could see him watching her as she moved. It was so long since a man had done that. It was disconcerting, and yet, what she wanted was for him to notice her.

"It's nicer in the day time with the sun streaming in," she said. "But I'd like to move. I don't know where or why or anything." Saying so surprised her, because she had not thought of it before except for the vague notions about living on English Bay.

"If the spirit demands it, you will."

He followed her to her studio. No longer was she using the ironing board in the kitchen now that she had turned Jerry's office into an art room. Her paints were out on the desk.

"May I?" he asked, moving closer to the canvas on the easel. Studying the animals in bright colours, his body leaning forward slightly, he moved his head at different angles. It was as if he wanted to see it from as many perspectives as he could.

"Wonderful," he said. "Keep it up."

Sue smiled and nodded.

"Do you have a pencil and some paper?" he asked.

Sue reached for a pad of paper in the top drawer of the desk. Taking the pencil she handed him, Hans put the pad on the desk beside the canvas and began to sketch her scene in black and white, shading details as he drew animals resting on the jungle floor, a tangle of vines and trees behind them. She watched how his perspective happened so naturally, was surprised to see a new angle she could emphasize in her work.

"That's amazing," she said.

"I'm just doodling," he said. "If you were a racehorse, I'd put my bets on you. You're the artist."

"Well, that may be a stretch," she said. "But thanks." She smiled as they proceeded down the hall past the guestroom and bathroom. As they passed her room, he peered in at the large bed where she and Jerry had slept. A new green-and-white duvet was flung over it. Paintings hung from floor to ceiling and a hanging plant was suspended in one corner. She had moved many things into another room and changed the colour scheme of the walls to a pale grey with underlying highlights. She had bought new linens. She was not about to mention anything about these changes, but she did point at her CD player.

"Because of what you said last year, I bought that."

"What kind of music do you like?" he asked.

"Classical best. But I have pretty eclectic tastes. Jazz."

"Me, too. Why don't you put something on?"

"Like what?" Sue asked, aware of not wanting to go into that room.

"Oh, something you like."

"Well, I could, I guess," she said. "There are speakers downstairs connected to it so we can listen there." She moved quickly across the room and picked out a disc. The *Trout Quintet*. After starting the player, she walked to the door again. He did not move from the spot just outside the room.

"I heard from my husband's son again," she said.

"Oh," he said.

"You said I would."

"I did," he replied. "But that's not what I'm thinking about."

She looked down at the floor, inspecting the lines of the hardwood.

"Right now I'd like to kiss you."

Her eyes widened and she could feel her heart beating hard and her throat constricting. At the same time, her body ached from the absence of touch. She took in a long breath, slowly letting it out again. The silence hung there as a kaleidoscope of images rushed through her mind. Jerry. In his blue dressing gown. In a familiar sports shirt. Corduroy trousers. Blue jeans. It was ridiculous to be standing in the door of their bedroom with another man and a man who had just said he wanted to kiss her. Yet Sue knew she could smile and step quickly out into the hall. It would be as if his words had not been spoken. She knew that was what she should do. But she did not move.

Hans put his arms around her lightly and their lips touched. She sank against him, his arms encircling her and tightening a bit. Mouths slightly open, bodies warm against each other. The kiss went on and on before she drew back to find him staring gently at her.

"It would be easy to make love to you," he said, almost in a whisper.

She sighed, afraid of what she might answer.

"Because I already have. In my mind."

"Well, it's different as long as it stays in your head," she said. "It doesn't turn your life upside down. It doesn't change you from the person you are to someone you might not want to be."

"It wouldn't change who I am," he whispered. "It would just add something wonderful to my experience."

Sue scarcely breathed as he leaned forward and kissed her again, and then ran his fingers down her nose. Over her lips. Around her chin. It seemed natural to move with him to the bed where they sat on the edge. His fingers traced her breasts tentatively and she ran hers down his shoulder. Lifting her sweater upwards, he reached to undo her bra. She undid the buttons of his shirt. Gradually, after removing one layer after another of clothing, they lay beside each other. Leaning forward again, he kissed her breasts and traced a line down to the hair over her pubic area.

"You're so beautiful," he said.

"Do you know that music?" she asked.

"Umm. It's Schubert," he said. "*Trout Quintet.*"

She did not show she was surprised.

Their bodies started to move together. He reached out to his trousers for something, then tore open a small package. She was relieved when he put on a condom as she had not thought about protection. As he entered her and moaned, she heard herself moan also.

"It was wonderful," he said afterwards as they lay still in the dark in the cold room, barely touching. "Even better than I imagined." He ran a finger over the lines around her eyes and down beside her nose to her chin. It was as if he were sculpting her features and it surprised her to sense that his mind had moved elsewhere.

What have I done? she wondered. So soon after Jerry's death. To have made love so wantonly to a married man. He would never be able to see her except in short intervals. Everything they did would forever have to be clandestine.

"The dogs," he said. "They'll be hungry and barking to go out."

*

As he buttoned his shirt, Hans looked at a photograph in a pewter frame on the bedside table.

"Your husband," he said, although he knew he was stating the obvious.

"Yes."

Hans leaned toward her and ran his fingers gently through her hair, breathing in a mild scent that could have been her shampoo.

"I thought I'd become used to his dying," she said. "You think you're prepared and I guess you are in some ways after a long, lingering illness. But even so. Even though we met late and were married ten years, not twenty or thirty or something, for a while it was as if my whole life was taken away from me."

"What's your sign?" he asked.

"Gemini."

"I see."

"What's yours?"

"Scorpio," he said. "I'm going to be sixty, but I feel about twenty-three right now. Still, sometimes I wonder if the knowing is gone. It isn't that I have a problem doing readings, but some days it is harder than it used to be. I wonder then what it would feel like not to have the gift anymore. I've seen it happen to others and I've started preparing myself." He watched her slip on a mauve T-shirt and a pair of navy sweatpants. "I always thought I'd be sad or frightened at the prospect," he said. "But instead I'm excited. It's bizarre."

She reached out and ran her fingers down the arm of his shirt, then turned to the door. He followed her downstairs to the kitchen where she plugged in a kettle and took out some herbal tea.

"I'll call you," he said.

"Sure. Okay," she said as she followed him to the front of the house. He stopped to pull on his shoes. "Do you know where we're going?" she asked.

"I leave that at the office," he said. "Except if I have premonitions, I don't ignore them. The first was when I was a young child. I saw my uncle's skull with a date on it. Can you imagine? I told my mother. 'I think Hans has something,' she said later to my father. She sounded worried. I don't think she knew I was listening."

He had not known what they were talking about. Later, his uncle died on the date he had seen. "But I don't want to be seen as extraordinary. When I leave the office, I go fishing. And catch bass. Or catfish. Trout. Maybe a pike. I plant vegetables and flowers, clean out the barn and walk the dogs. Just ordinary things." He was often frustrated by people's expectations that his entire experience might be removed from the rhythms of regular life.

"It's all right," she said. "I knew from the beginning that you were just another person. You might have a gift not everyone has, but is that so different from your talent as an artist?"

He sighed and before he opened the front door to leave, he kissed the tip of her nose and touched her breasts fleetingly. Turning to wave when he reached the sidewalk, he saw her watching through the window, and felt her eyes still following him as he opened the door of his car. He crawled in behind the wheel. Something visceral was rising in her, he sensed. Something like a scream. Still missing her husband so much she could barely stand it. To her, he was a stranger and he could almost hear her strangled cry. He had lied to her about leaving *everything* at the office. Mostly he did, but sometimes he had these insights and they told him something he could not ignore. So, although he had just told Sue he would call her, he was not sure he would. The last thing he wanted was either to hurt or complicate her life.

There was a red light at the corner of Bloor Street and as he waited for it to turn, he thought of Heather arriving at the farm and finding he was not yet there. Then he recalled that she had a meeting after work that would keep her downtown so late that she was staying over with a friend. That was why he had felt free to drop by on Sue, not constrained by a designated dinner hour. He would pick up a pizza for himself on his way to the farm.

When he arrived, Rusty barked and ran to the door on Hans's side of the car. Jumping against it, dark nose pointing upwards, it was as if the dog were saying, "C'mon, get out of there. I want to play," just as he did every day.

Hans turned off the engine and stepped out onto the gravel road. "Hi, Rusty," he said. "C'mon." The black, rust, and tan mongrel always ran beside him when he fed the animals, barking at the horses. It was a game for him. When Hans drove the truck, Rusty sat right beside him and peered out the front window as if he were driving. Sometimes, someone in another car would look startled at the sight of the dog, leaning forward like a person without a seat belt. He reached under Rusty's chin and tickled his neck, then bounded along beside the dog to the house. There was one light on in the hall and the door was slightly ajar. The dog pushed in ahead of him.

He had forgotten again to pick up the mail from the box at the edge of the highway. As soon as he fed Rusty, he would walk down to get it. He seemed to think he had seen the small flag pointing upward that indicated the postman had left something. A letter from his family in the Netherlands? His sister used to write more often than any of the others, but there was an occasional note from one of his brothers.

As he headed out the door, Rusty was on his heels, and then dashed on ahead of him. Every so often, the dog came back to look up at Hans as if to check he were still following him. Rusty stopped at the road and waited while Hans looked into the metal box with flowers and a horse painted on it. Just a bill and a flyer. The mailbox an excuse to walk outside in the fresh air and bask in the sounds of the country. Crickets. When he headed back the way he had come, he heard the horses in the barn. Time to feed them, too.

Sue would love the farm, but he would never be able to show it to her. Likely, he would never see her again.

*

Thomas stood in front of the house in downtown Toronto where his father had lived, pondering his conversation with Martin. Why had his mom lied to him? Snowflakes landed on his forehead, reminding him of the rink in Stratford where he had learned to skate. He had missed having a father when other dads were out on the rink with their kids. It had not been quite the same to have his mom show him how to stand up on skates or to cheer him on when he started to play hockey. Sometimes, she had worried too much, hovering over him in a way none of the dads did.

Joanna Crossar had given him her surname. He had not known why, if he were Martin Drew's son, he was not Thomas Drew. His mom must have had a tough time not wanting him to know who his father really was. But surely she had known he would have found out eventually even if she had not told him.

The light from the sun glinted on the front window of the brick house and he imagined Jerry coming out the wooden door and looking up at the sky before proceeding down the walk.

"Dad," Thomas would have called when he saw him on the porch. "I'm over here."

He thought of jogging with his father down the streets in Stratford. They could have talked about hockey. And books. Jerry would have read to him when he was a young child. Dr. Seuss. *Green Eggs and Ham.* Maybe Dennis Lee. Now, they would talk about law school. It struck him as ironic that he had decided to follow in his father's footsteps. But maybe not, after all, his mother had worked in the courts for his entire life. He could do anything, she had often said, which was why law seemed possible. She had told him about the law from his earliest childhood, showing him where she sat under the judge's seat, taking notes. Sometimes, she said her eyes were crossed from it all. Or that some lawyer spouted hot air.

"I shouldn't have said that," she might say, quick to add, "You didn't hear that."

She had also told him that Martin was a lawyer. And later, that Jerry was also. Still, it was only when he had done his undergraduate work in history and philosophy that he had realized he wanted to make law his profession also.

His glance caught Sue looking out the front window and he waved at her. His mom had not been very old when she was rushed to hospital, maybe Sue's age. It was her heart. He could see his mom pulling her hair back into a ponytail, swishing a terry-cloth robe around her. Now he knew where his height came from and the reddish hair that was like Jerry Reid's. But, he had his mother's smile.

His head was a jumble of impressions. His mother at the stove, stirring something, porridge maybe, which he had hated because it glued itself to the top of his mouth. C'mon, son, you need to have a good breakfast. If he was going to be strong. If he was going to grow tall. "Like my father?" he had asked and she had said, "Well, you know boys want to be tall and strong. You never know. There might be tigers or elephants." It had taken him a while to figure out she had been teasing him, that it had been her way of encouraging him to eat something he had not been that fond of, although he had liked most things: the rare whiff of steak on a Sunday, applesauce from a bottle in the refrigerator. Sausages. Green beans. Baked potatoes.

Sue opened the front door and called out to him. "C'mon in."

Her words startled him.

"Hi, Sue," he said, moving toward her. She waited while he went up the steps. Inside, he studied the paintings and photographs again, feeling his father's presence.

"Martin probably told you I called on him."

"I gather." She had the door of the refrigerator open and pointed at beer on a rack on the door.

He shrugged. "Just some Coke," he said.

"Sure," Sue said, reaching further back to get a can.

"Martin said you and my father were married on the island."

Sue nodded. "It was lovely," she said. "New leaves coming

out on trees. Birds singing. A red cardinal swishing through branches. A jay. Cheerful sounds. Water rippling against the shore. Now life is more often a nightmare. I dream Jerry is alive, then I wake up and call him and he doesn't answer."

She brushed her hair back and ran her fingers through the white slash in the front. Like the white strip down the back of a skunk, he thought. He did not know what to expect. She might turn against him. Why wouldn't she? He was the reason her memories would have gone sour, making his father into some kind of fraud.

"But he wasn't," he said.

"What?" Sue asked.

"My dad," he said. "He wasn't a fraud."

"I didn't say he was."

"Well..."

"Sometimes I get angry that he never told me about you. But, you're right, he wasn't a fraud."

"I'd like to come to the memorial," Thomas said, upset by the way his feelings kept changing. He had been angry with her and now he felt protective.

4.

MARTIN AND EMILY STOOD on either side of Sue on the deck of the ferry, arms around her shoulders. Sue knew Maggie and Angus were at the back rail, watching the large buildings of downtown loom up to create a postcard view. This was the skyline Sue now called home. Once upon a time, she would never have dreamed she would come to love Toronto. But after she and Jerry had cycled and walked its ravines and parks, it had happened. They would start near the downtown campus of the university and then wend their way through traffic, eventually finding a trail that led to a stream that felt as if they were in the country. The Don River. The Humber River. Wind blowing and rustling through leaves, the sound of water over pebbles and rocks. Both rivers flowed into Lake Ontario through lush greenery in summer, the brilliant oranges and red leaves of fall, the drifting snows of winter.

They had also walked downtown streets, exploring the architecture of buildings they passed by quickly most days. Old City Hall with its gargoyles at intervals, and New City Hall with the dome in the centre and the two tall towers looking down on it. They had visited St. Lawrence Market occasionally on a Saturday, where the earliest business of the city had been carried out in the building that now housed shops and stalls that overflowed with fruits and vegetables as well as fresh fish, meat, cheese, and probably everything she needed if she had lived close enough to walk there. Her route more often took her to Kensington Market with its old-world atmosphere of narrow streets and small shops brimming with goods and people from many cultures.

Angus knew how she felt about Toronto now. At her prompting, he had photographed its historic buildings in neighbourhoods he had visited, like the dome inside St. Anne's Church with murals by young artists who later became members of the Group of Seven. Old brick houses in the Annex. The CN Tower. Union Station. The natural beauty of the parks and trails outside the concrete core. He had sent her these photos and gradually began to speak about Toronto as one of the cities where he enjoyed spending time. So many visitors became snarled in the traffic and cursed the city, she thought, and because they were frustrated or in a hurry, they did not look further. They often would malign the city to her, something she would never have considered doing about wherever they lived. At least in the early years, when she had not much liked Toronto, she had known enough to keep it to herself. She had not talked about how much better it was to live in a town up north where everyone was friendly. Or how much livelier it was in Montreal. Gradually, she too had come to appreciate the variety of a city that kept on changing as new waves of immigrants settled in, as old buildings were preserved after much outcry from people who cared about history, and as new ones were built within guidelines for development that more often seemed to work in the people's favour.

Sue closed her eyes, thinking that home was largely a myth you created as you carved out a place for yourself. No one else saw it as you did. Jerry had given her a sense of being rooted in this place. As she watched the CN Tower and the Royal York Hotel, the island airport off to the west, the waves the ferry left in its wake, she knew that the sense of place evoked for them was why they'd married on the island. That archipelago was so integral to the whole of the city and was why, several months after Jerry's death, they were about to celebrate his life there.

"Such a gorgeous day," Emily said.

Even if at times Sue was not sure of Emily, her presence today was soothing.

"Thomas said he'd bring Florence," Sue said.

"I never thought to take care of that," Martin said. "I knew Florence as a child."

"I thought you must have."

It still felt foreign to her that she had known nothing about such a large part of Jerry's past when he was alive. Although she remembered that Florence had come and stayed with them once. A tiny woman with large breasts, twisted fingers, huge brown eyes and arthritic knees, she had struggled up the front steps.

"It's all right, dears," she had said. "In about a month I'll get to the door." An irrepressible grin had spread across her face. "I'm just so happy to be here." Sue recalled how her eyes lit up as they drove her through downtown Toronto. "I'm just a country bumpkin," she had said. "But, you know, I love it here." She had pointed out the big towers and the flowers in the middle of University Avenue.

"I remember coming into Union Station as a child," she had said. "When we walked into the large main hall with the high ceiling, I would stop and stare up at it. My poor mother could scarcely get me to go any further until she reminded me about going over to Centre Island."

"I'm so glad it's a clear day." Sue could see a small airplane taking off from the runway at the far end of the island. Jerry had had a pilot's license and had liked to fly. Once, he had taken her over Niagara Falls in a small, twin-engine plane. As the wings tipped, she was almost sick, but she looked down on the land below with a new sense of the Welland Canal running from Lake Erie to Lake Ontario, and of the landscape as they approached the island airport over the lake with the view of Hamilton to the west. It was then she thought of what the earth must look like from outer space. All the astronauts had commented on it. They went all the way to the moon and the most memorable moments seemed to be the view of earth they had then.

When the ferry landed at the dock at Ward's Island, Sue walked with Martin. Emily, Maggie, and Angus were just behind them as they crossed the grass and went over a wide wooden bridge to Algonquin Island. At the clubhouse, tables were laid out with baskets of bright yellow daisies, irises, and lilies, alongside plates of pita, hummus, baba ghanouj, and tabouleh.

Jerry would have loved this feast, Sue thought. He would have loved the speeches, basking in the limelight when the occasion provided it. A roguish grin would have appeared on his face and Sue would know he was about to say something that would cause everyone to burst out laughing.

Jerry. Jerry. What happened with Hans does not change things. She wondered if she had not learned about Thomas if she would have let it happen. Had she felt a sense of betrayal that had needed something to ease it? She was not sure that Jerry would have understood, but she knew that certainly Martin would not. So it was clear to her that she could never tell him.

"Martin, thanks for arranging all of this. It's breathtaking," she said.

Martin leaned over and hugged her. "You know how much I loved Jerry," he said. "And I hope you know that Emily and I love you."

"Yes, I know."

Although sometimes she sensed that Emily would be the first to suspect her of inappropriate behaviour, the kind she would never condone. She also felt sometimes that Emily already had an inkling of the secret that lay under Sue's entire life. But how could she? Suddenly, Sue saw Thomas coming toward them with Florence beside him. Now these people who had been strangers to her until recently were here on one of the most difficult days of her life. They moved slowly as Florence hung onto Thomas's arm. She seemed smaller and one foot dragged even as she walked on a flat path.

"The arthritis," she said when she saw Sue watching her. "But I'm here. I can drive around in the country, but that's all now. Except perhaps to London because I know it so well. And, of course, it's so much smaller than Toronto. Thomas came from Stratford to pick me up and drive me to the city. Isn't that wonderful? It takes over three hours from Blenheim. The bed and breakfast is lovely. Thanks for making the arrangements."

"I can walk to it from where I live," Sue said. She felt slightly guilty as she observed them, but also consoled by the thought that aside from her sister and brother-in-law who comforted her when they saw she needed that, no one had more right to be here than Florence and Thomas. She smiled at them then. "And Thomas has said he'll drive you over to the house," she said. "My sister and her husband are here from Vancouver or I would have asked you to stay with me."

"Well, my dear, this is very nice," Florence said. "And it's very kind of you to have taken care of it for us."

"Jerry would have wanted that," Sue said, knowing no matter how much he had concealed from her, he would have been relieved that she now knew. "And so do I."

At that moment, she heard someone playing a flute and turned to hear where the music was coming from. It was one of Jerry's favourite pieces of music, but she could not remember the name. All she knew was that she had heard it with him at some concert. Martin had found this group of musicians especially for the occasion, as he had known there had to be music, as well as particular selections. Mozart. Beethoven. Handel. Martin had known exactly what would be appropriate. More than anyone, even more than she herself had, he had known Jerry's musical likes and dislikes, that his taste had been eclectic. He had liked Joe Henderson and Dizzy Gillespie. Of the jazz musicians, most of all Duke Ellington. She remembered how he had asked her to put on some of the Duke's music in the days when he could no longer reach the discs and change them himself.

Thunder rumbled in the distance and she noticed Martin go to the door and watch the sky. They had planned that most of the day would occur outdoors, but if it rained, the food, drinks, and speeches would be under cover. Martin looked at Sue and nodded. She thought he meant it looked as if it would pass over quickly, but he could have meant anything.

For a while, she watched Thomas taking care of Florence. Reddish hair and beard, engaging smile, leaning over to hear what the older woman was saying, attending to her. She felt as if she were in a time warp with Jerry dead and yet this mirror image instead.

As if she were back in Martin's campaign office where she had met Jerry, seeing him again for the first time. After Martin had been elected, Jerry had suggested they go for a walk on the island, from Hanlan's Point at one end to Ward's Island at the other. She had wondered after the third or fourth walk through city parks whether he was looking only for a friend to share nature. It had all evolved slowly, and yet she had been relieved as well. There had been no pressure to jump into bed and wake up the next morning with the taste of some horrible mistake lingering. One day, Jerry had simply asked if they could go out in the evening.

"You know," he had said. "A *date* date."

Even then, it had been casual. But when he had looked at her over wine at a table in a small downtown restaurant where the grill was close enough to watch the steaks and vegetables cooking, she had known they were slowly moving into new territory. When he had reached out his hand to touch hers, there had been no mixed message or missed cue. She had felt her body tingling even though it would be hours before they would return to her place in the Annex. And they had sipped wine there, too, before tacitly agreeing that he would spend the night.

"Sue," Martin said. "I think we need you over here for a moment."

"I was remembering," she said.

"I could tell."

Thoughts of Hans had been obliterated, but now they surged forth once more. Was it possible to love again? She supposed it must be because she had already started to, even though the circumstances were fraught with complications. Forget about all of that, she told herself. This day is for Jerry.

Sue surveyed the photographs she and Martin had put together. Jerry as an undergrad; Jerry in his gown as a lawyer in court. Martin had found one of the two of them at the quarry. There was another of their wedding as well as one of a canoe trip she and Jerry had taken. A couple hundred photographs that told the story of a man's life, yet not a single one of Thomas. Someone could come to the memorial and not know this important facet of Jerry's life. But Thomas was there and anyone who saw him would know.

Sue's mind often wandered as she continued to greet and hug people. Yet, she was also fully present with their relatives and friends. Perhaps everyone lives a double life, she thought as she caught herself thinking of Hans once again. Anyway, Hans did not know what would happen in his own reality and she had discovered he did not trust any other psychic to tell him.

Suddenly aware that Martin was about to speak, she focused her attention on him. Old stories were retold and different twists were put on some of them. Perhaps some were embellished for the occasion.

"He knew how to laugh at himself," Martin said. "And how to enjoy life. He cared about people and you all know he took on the toughest legal aid cases. And that he was my campaign manager when I ran for City Council. When he was younger, he took risks that were sometimes foolhardy, but Sue settled him in ways we'd all hoped for. Not because she asked him to change. I think he wanted to spend more time with her and less doing things like back-country skiing. He'd still take on a mountain slope since she enjoys that kind of adventure, too. They were a great pair. No one will miss him more than Sue does. Although for me it's like losing a brother and I don't have another friend like Jerry. No one else goes back as far as my childhood." Sue could see Martin's eyes were misty. She wondered whether he would continue. He took out a handkerchief, but did not seem to know what to do with it.

"Thanks to everyone for coming," he said. "You're here to have a good time. Jerry would be happy to see us celebrating. It's a party he asked Sue to arrange. And I'm glad to have been able to help."

Then he surprised Sue. "There are a few people you should meet," he said, inviting Florence, Jerry's cousin, and Maggie and Angus, to raise their hands. "And Thomas Crossar," he said. "Jerry's son. Unfortunately, they never met, but we know him now. And what an amazing young man he is."

Sue trembled. Would this cause people to turn to look at her? Would there be gossip? And she wondered how this could help Thomas. But it made sense. She trusted Martin. He was a man a child could have counted on. Thomas had his head down, but then looked up and smiled across at her. As a quartet started to play, Martin moved to the tables with food on them. Sue went over to join him.

"Thanks," she whispered.

"You don't mind about Thomas?"

"Someone had to say so sooner or later," Sue said. "I could see people looking at him when they thought no one else noticed. Now it will appear there isn't anything to hide."

They listened for a moment to the music.

"Did I tell you that Joanna left a note for me?" he asked.

The day he had read that note, he had gone to tell Sue. He recalled now that he had not, feeling it was not the right time for it. "She wanted me to be involved in Thomas's life."

Sue tried to stifle a sudden rush of jealousy. "Yes, you did tell me something like that," she said, sighing. "It was a good idea. He needs a family. And for starters, he has you and Emily. And me, too, if he wants that."

Thomas approached and stood a bit apart until Sue saw him and beckoned to him to come closer. They hugged.

"Thanks," he said.

Martin stood quietly beside them and only spoke when Thomas turned to him. "Thank you, too."

Florence was next, reaching out to take Sue's hand. Sue wanted to thank her for coming, but her body began to heave with dry sobs before she could say anything.

"It's all right, dear," the older woman said. "You're meant to cry when you lose someone you love."

It was then that the sky darkened more. Thunder began again and the wind rose in the trees. Lightning was followed by an immediate crack of thunder. The next crack was even louder. Then the clouds seemed to move on, driven by wind and lashing rain. In less than fifteen minutes, it was over.

"Thank heavens," Maggie said.

Her sister might remember the time in the northern bush, looking at land their parents had found for a cabin, when Maggie had been near a tree hit by lightning. The trunk had fallen right behind her. Maggie had claimed that they had all ignored her. But they had only learned what had happened when she caught up to them. Piling hurriedly into the little green Austin, they had huddled in the back seat as their father put it in gear and were still huddling as he drove out in blinding rain to the main road.

The musicians continued to play, but Martin had discs for when they left. There was a line of people now at the food table, filling the colourful plates. At another table, a bartender, hired for the day, served wine.

After another number by the quartet, Martin announced that he would play music for dancing as soon as everyone had their food. Or they could dance now and eat later.

"Imagine how Jerry would enjoy being here," he said. "We'll play all his favourites."

Sue smiled. Jerry had been a wonderful dancer. She was not nearly as good as he, at least not at the beginning. But he had made it easy to follow and had made her feel that she was adept at it. But now, she had an overwhelming sense that all of that had been superficial, like the icing on a cake that was there simply for decoration, that hid the cake so that you only knew the flavour when you bit into it. She and Jerry had lived their lives on the surface. And although what he had hidden was now revealed, he would never know about the child she had given birth to who would now be in her forties. Someone out there who could be any woman Sue ran into of that age or who could live anywhere in the world.

"May I ask you to do the foxtrot?" Martin asked.

Startled, Sue thrust her thoughts aside. "Of course," she said.

After that, there was some big band music and she and Angus swung to it. East coast, West coast. Before long, the room was alive with rhythm. Nearly everyone danced with Sue. And she smiled with them, looking at the photos of Jerry, sharing memories. And then Thomas excused himself from Florence and asked if she would dance with him.

"It's the only one I know how to do," he said.

"Of course." A waltz.

"Was my father a good dancer?" he asked.

"Oh yes," she said. "The best."

"Kate has asked me to learn to dance. She likes the waltz."

When the music stopped, they went on talking.

"You're so much like him," she said. In the same breath, she thought of how dishonest it would be to Thomas to act as if he were her son when she had never acknowledged her own daughter.

"I see that in the photos. Florence says she has lots of when he was even younger than I am."

"I don't mean to disturb you children," Florence said. "But

I don't think I can hold on much longer."

She sat on a chair not far from where they stood, her glass on a table beside her. Her eyes were heavy and her body seemed to have shrunk even further.

"I'm sorry," Sue said. "I should have asked you sooner how you were managing."

"No," Florence said. "You shouldn't have to think about me today. I've been fine until now. Thomas has taken good care of me."

"I'll take you home now," Thomas said. "We can see Sue in the morning."

As they helped Florence to her feet, Martin rushed over. He and Thomas walked on either side of her down to the ferry. Sue went too, telling them when she would pick them up. "And Thomas, take a taxi up to the bed and breakfast."

"Yes." Martin pulled out his wallet and handed Thomas twenty dollars.

"I have enough money," Thomas said.

"It's all right," Martin said. "Jerry would have given it to you. He'd want me to."

Sue and Martin stood watching the ferry move steadily in their direction from across the inner harbour. They could see the tall buildings on the other side clearly etched against blue sky although the sun was getting lower and it was clear that evening was descending. Soon there would be stars and a sliver of moon. Before that, those who remained would gather in a circle and hold hands. It would all last for at least half an hour, perhaps an hour. She was not sure. Then they, too, would take the ferry back to the city. They would go on with their lives.

Sue supposed that that was what she would do, too. She just did not know what that meant yet. Maybe it was time for something different. Could she face the reality of the woman who had grown up without her, who might not even want to know her? She thought if Jerry were still alive now, she would tell him her whole story and ask him to accompany her on this journey to find her child. But he was not ever going to come back. And gradually, the full impact of her life being forever altered began once more to penetrate.

Jerry. Jerry.

She would dream about him, look at photographs, talk about him to friends and family, and see his image in Thomas. But never again would she touch him or hear the sound of his voice. Never again.

She wanted to stay on the island. Her husband seemed to be there. In the shadows under a tree. Down by the water. If she went to the other side of the island, out on the boardwalk where they had gone on their bicycles, and looked into the vast expanse of Lake Ontario, would he answer her call? Would he tell her what to do now? Could anyone do that?

"Sue," Martin said gently. "We're pretty well cleaned up now. Let's walk for a while and then catch the ferry."

She looked around to see that only Martin, Emily, Maggie, and Angus remained.

"Where did they all go?" she asked. "When?"

"Gradually, "Martin said. "In the last hour."

"Did I speak to them?"

"Uh-huh," Martin said. "It's all right."

*

Emily observed Martin as he stood beside Sue at the rail of the ferry, watching the storm clouds gradually dissipate. They had a camaraderie she could not seem to share. They stood shoulder to shoulder, leaning forward as the water formed a wake and she would only have to walk over and say something, but she did not feel like intruding. And besides, whatever apprehension she felt, this was not the time for that. It was Jerry's day. All the same, there was something strange about Sue today. She seemed distracted. Every so often, she would flush and sigh. That did not seem like sounds of grief to Emily, but she had no idea what they were. Martin would ask why she was suspicious of Sue. But she could not help it.

"Sort of a lightweight, don't you think?" she had asked Martin when they first met her.

"Oh, c'mon, Em," he had said. "A physics teacher. She seems pretty solid."

That had not convinced Emily. She did not measure people by their occupations. It was their capacity to be human, to be compassionate. Sue had always struck her as rather cold, as if she were a physics teacher by default rather than by conviction. That it acted as protection. Even so, Emily had loved Jerry almost as much as Martin had and had wanted him to be happy.

Daughter of a mother from the Ukraine, Emily had come from the prairies outside of Winnipeg, where endless fields stretched into the western landscape. Emily and Martin had one of those weddings where money was collected and they were given a large chunk that they had used to buy their first home near the railroad tracks in Transcona. That was before Martin had established a law practise in Toronto. She had thought she wanted to be a minister, but to be ordained in those days had been unthinkable and once they had children, she dropped it. Now that their two daughters were grown up and worked elsewhere, she was studying theology as a mature student even if she never used the piece of paper except to frame it. It was important to her to finish what she had started so many years ago. She was interested in preaching and in bereavement and what she could do to help people going through loss. So, she also volunteered with a hospice and visited a man who was dying of cancer. Mostly, he had family on his team, but there were a couple of volunteers he saw and she was one of them. Sometimes, when she went to visit, he was grumpy but he'd had a good day this week. He'd wanted to talk about his funeral, and make phone calls to his relatives. Sue had been diffident with her after Jerry died, a coolness that had surprised Emily. She and Martin had shared many meals with her, had walked together in High Park, and gone sometimes as a threesome to the theatre. But Sue remained distant. Emily did not think Martin noticed, so in need to chat about Jerry to anyone who would listen. Who better than his widow?

"She was a good wife to Jerry," he had told Emily. "I feel sorry for her."

He had been shattered to find out Thomas existed, something so important from which he had been excluded, like Sue. It gave them a bond. But a rather flimsy one, she thought. She felt like the solid one of the group, but then she was once removed from Jerry. She with the stolid mien and square face, brown eyes peering out above forward slanting cheekbones. Honey hair that hung straight to her shoulders. Prairie stock. The daughter of farmers. All that she and Sue seemed to have in common was their appreciation of Canadian winter. Hers of winds racing across flat fields and temperatures so low that it froze breath in the air, white bits of ice attached to the scarf tied across her face. Sue, from another northern landscape, knew the snow and wind also and talked of icicles forming inside her window as a child. At times they had laughed about being thrust out to play in temperatures so low that only their eyes were visible behind the layers of clothing.

Martin turned and gestured to her to join them. "Stars are out again," he said.

Emily stood on the other side of her husband, the water bubbling up below. No ducks at night, no gulls flying over the wake. Orange life jackets were arranged in rows in the ceiling just behind them. A couple stood with bicycles at the bottom of the stairs where they would all leave the ferry. Into the traffic. The city. The subway.

"Would you like to come back for a drink?" Emily asked, touching Sue's arm.

"That's kind of you," Sue said.

But Emily felt her recoil from her touch.

"It's a good idea," Martin said. "We could walk you home later."

So, sitting across from each other, they took the bus up Bay Street past tall towers and both old and new City Halls. Then, they walked to the Annex along one of the back streets above Bloor. The leaves on the trees were heavy with the summer night's damp heat. Only a week or so earlier, they had been little more than a light lattice above the street.

"We haven't talked much about Thomas," Martin said.

"I'm glad he came today," Sue said.

"Emily and I want to keep in touch with him. He's a great kid. Well, scarcely a kid. It's the least we can do for him. And for Jerry."

They arrived at Emily and Martin's walk where a light on the porch cast its beam almost to where they stood.

"You'll be good for him," Sue said.

"We'll all be good for him," Martin said.

Sue stood to the side as both of them started up the walk. "Yes," she said. "I think so."

"Please come in," Emily said.

"I think I'll go on home," Sue said. "But thanks. Thanks for everything."

Emily moved forward to give Sue a hug with the feeling that the other woman would merely tolerate her embrace. Would Martin's be more welcome? she wondered, as he stepped forward. She watched as Sue walked further up the street and turned onto an adjoining one that would take her to the house where Martin had spent so much time for all the years Jerry had lived there.

"Do you think she minds sharing Thomas?" he asked.

Emily pondered before she answered. She had no idea, but there was still something she could not fathom about Sue.

"If she does, it's too bad," she said. "He needs all of us."

Thomas might be the catalyst that would draw them all

more closely together, but it was as likely that it might do the opposite.

*

Sometimes, Sue did not know what day it was or even what month. Time passed in a haze. When Hans called, they met for coffee. Sitting across from him in the restaurant, Sue felt her hands tremble. She wanted him to say he loved her, but she was afraid of feeling anything. Instead, she became apologetic, as if what they had done was almost criminal. Of course, adultery was not laudable. But surely loving someone was at least something that could be forgiven. Instead, she wanted to distance him.

"I'm not sorry about what happened," she said "But it bothers me. I can't help it." If she did not stop talking, she would soon start going around in circles. It seemed theatrical to tell him someone else had made love to him. Her lips pressed into a thin line, holding her hands tightly together on her lap, she watched his eyes flicker away momentarily before he replied. Make this better, the child inside her begged. Leave your wife. Sweep me off my feet.

"I understand," he said quietly. "Of course I do. It was wonderful, but I do understand."

They did not linger over the coffee as they might once have done. There seemed little else to say. As Hans took the bill to the counter, Sue went outside and waited for him on the pavement.

"Well," he said, emerging from the restaurant and standing in front of her. "I guess this is farewell then."

Unable to say anything, she nodded.

"All right then," he said, walking away. Once he turned back and waved before disappearing around a corner on a road that led to his office.

Sue walked along Bloor Street, looking into the windows of the shops. She had wanted to say, "See you around," but thought better of it. It was too dismissive, too superficial. Something else was over. She would not see Hans again. She wished it was a moral sense that had fuelled her decision, but knew it was rather the fear that with him she would ultimately have to dive below the surface. She slowed slightly in front of a shop with trendy jewellery where she had once bought earrings for her sister, but her eyes clouded over. It was time to go home and sort through the papers that had accumulated. Old tax and hydro bills, piles of half read *Maclean's* magazines. But she did not feel any better now that she had ended whatever it was that she knew she had also started. What else could she have done? she wondered. What else? Sooner or later, whatever had started would have ended in disaster. An irate wife who found out about Sue and came to throw things at her, to swear at her, to call her a home-wrecker. Or the demands she herself would make on Hans would be ones he could not fulfil and that would make her increasingly bitter.

When she reached the house, she went immediately to her easel and stared at it. A blank canvas. Her life felt that way now, too. With no idea how to deal with either, she picked up a brush and began to work with the acrylics on another version of the curve on the island boardwalk that she had photographed. Vibrant reds and purples in the trunks of trees or slashed across the sky. She wanted to know what was around the corner and would probably go on painting until that happened, and go on living until she knew what direction to follow. Suddenly overwhelmed by tears, her body ached to be held. What had she done? All she wanted was to call Hans. She could not keep changing her mind, but it was as if she were driven, unable to keep from lifting the receiver, unable not to dial his number. She reached for the telephone. Would he be angry?

When she did hear his voice, Sue was speechless.

"Hello," he said.

And then again, "Hello."

"I was wrong," she said.

"Is that you, Sue?"

"Yes," she said. "I'd like to see you."

"You mean you miss your husband."

"Yes, I do. Of course I do," she said. "But I think I miss you, too."

He hesitated. "I'll come over," he said. "If that's what you want."

When Sue greeted him at the door, what she saw first was the smile that widened his face and took in his eyes. Almost dancing into the room, he raised his hands toward the ceiling.

"Hallelujah," he said.

"Hey," she said. "Hello."

He reminded her of a large puppy. He saw things, he knew things, and yet he seemed such a boy. Such a delightful man. He was full of optimism and enthusiasm, looking skyward with a sense of wonder that suggested the world was treating him well. She wished she could be like that.

"It's nice to see you," he said.

"I'm glad." She would not tell him how afraid she had just been that he would be angry.

She moved into the kitchen. "Beer?" she asked. "Juice? Coffee?"

He shook his head. "No thanks," he said. "I don't want anything to drink. I came to see you."

She let him put his arm around her. "Hey," he said, slipping his hand under her blouse. She moved back a little. "There are a couple questions I'd like to ask," she said, feeling that she was about to become almost ridiculously formal. "I don't have any right to and obviously you don't have to answer. Like how you deal with your marriage."

She could see his eyes veer off to the left. But it was important to her even though she knew she had acted without really considering it, as if they lived in a bubble that would protect them. Now she had asked him to return, said she missed him, knew she wanted him. She thought she needed to know even though when he did answer, it did not clarify anything.

"They're quite separate." It was clear this was all he was about to offer about his overlapping relationships with two women. "Have there been others?" she continued. Was she special in some way? Or was he a philanderer? But if he were, surely he would not tell her.

He looked at her sadly, as if he were disappointed she had to ask. "I don't screw around," he said softly. "But there was one once. At a conference. She went back to Hawaii afterwards. Those two weeks at a retreat in California were like a dream." He remembered the ocean, he said. Rocks with shells embedded in them. The sun drenching their bodies. "I knew I would never see her again." Although she had written later to tell him how her life had unfolded after their encounter, that she had finally made the choices she needed to make.

"What was it for you?" Sue asked, not at all clear as to why she imagined there might be a simple answer.

"It was about flying," he said.

She thought she probably looked as baffled as she felt. Flying? What on earth did that mean?

"Finding out I could still fly."

"Oh," she said. "Is that what this is about?"

"No, this is a gift. And I wouldn't want to clip your wings. You need to grow them again. You need to be free."

Sue did not comment. Like a bird, she thought. Jerry's bird. This conversation felt as if it had proceeded as far as it was ever going to. If she fell deeply in love with him and he went on keeping his life in boxes, how would that feel? All she could do for now was to drop it all.

"Do you want to listen to music?" she asked.

"I wasn't thinking of music, but we can just talk if that's what you want."

What would they talk about? She wondered if he shared her love of travel, he who had come to a strange country and built a whole new life here. What else did they share? She had no idea.

"I remember a story you told me about riding your bicycle

around Europe," she said. "About living with gypsies for a while."

"Where would you like to go?" he asked as if he knew this was a question that masked what she really wanted to ask.

"Maybe New Zealand."

"It's beautiful." He had hiked some major trails there and driven around rocky cliffs above the sea.

He mentioned Russia.

"I'd like to go to South Africa," she said. "But I wouldn't have wanted to go in the days of apartheid."

He could understand that, he told her, although he remembered visiting the former Yugoslavia when Tito was still in power. "It was one of my best trips. The people were so friendly."

They were close to each other again and he bent down and kissed her breast through her blouse. She watched his long fingers with fine hair on them stroking her as if she were watching a tableau as well as being part of it.

"Is that all right?" he asked.

She nodded. That part of her that was open to loving again could not do otherwise.

After they made love again, he looked at his watch. "That was wonderful," he sighed "But I still have to drive back to the country. It takes over an hour." He stood up and started to pull on his trousers.

Sue fingered his green silk shirt on the chair beside her. "Would you give me an old shirt some time?" she asked, knowing he would soon be gone and if she did not see him for days or weeks her memory of these moments would fade and she did not want that to happen. She wanted to hold onto them.

"A shirt?" he asked, his tone bewildered.

"Just something of yours to wear," she said. "Something that makes me feel close to you when I do."

He did not say anything. When he was dressed, he started down the stairs, stopping halfway down to look at a group of paintings on the wall.

"My shirt," he said.

It took her a few seconds to figure out what he likely meant was the paintings created images with the same impact on him as his shirt would create for her. Then she smiled.

At the front door, he grinned. "See you in New Zealand." He turned to wave from the sidewalk before crossing the street to his car.

It was then Sue realized he had not said he would call, although she thought he had intended to. And as the days went by, she was baffled. She began to worry that maybe she had annoyed him. She could imagine him looking at his calendar to see when appointments were slotted in. At the first opportunity, he would call. What would he say? "I'm sorry. Can we meet and talk?" But that did not happen either and as more days went by, then weeks, Sue did not know what to do. She felt the dilemma of being a new widow overwhelmed by the implacable strength of her desire. Hans had said something about not hurting people. Yet she suspected he did not think he would hurt either his wife or her as long as they were both in their distinct compartments. She had known enough men to know they could create these separations more easily than most women could. If he wanted to find time, he could. She knew that. Maybe he realized it was not actually possible to carry on without someone getting hurt.

He had filled some of the emptiness after Jerry's death, but she also realized that by now there was more to it than that. She carried on conversations with Jerry still, but also ones with Hans. And it was Hans she yearned for. She told no one, her life replete with compartments also, like the mailboxes standing by the roadside in a rural community.

*

Hans looked in his agenda to find out who his next client would be. The name written there was "Elizabeth." He remembered adding it himself when the answering service had called to give him his most recently booked appointments. When he opened his door, he was surprised to see Sue look up at him. For some reason, he thought of a woman he had seen some years earlier who had her paper open to a section that looked like international events. Before she dropped it on the table next to her, he had seen a headline about the Americans starting to deploy troops to Kuwait. Not a good omen, yet he had already known from the flashes of the future he had received from the universe that day that it would all soon end in a withdrawal of Iraqi troops. At least for the time being. He wondered why this crossed his mind now, perhaps a foreboding sense about Sue's presence.

There was no one else in the waiting area and he realized the last time he had seen Sue in his office was in early summer after the memorial for her husband. He was embarrassed now, knowing she would have expected him to call her. He cleared his throat. "Do you have an appointment with someone in the building?"

"I have an appointment with you."

"My next client is..."

"Elizabeth," she said. "That's the name I gave. You didn't call. You didn't seem to want to see me and this was the only way I could find out why."

He stepped aside as she went into his office to sit in the arm-chair on the other side of the tape recorder. She put a package down beside her. In his mind's eye, he could see and touch the curves and lines of her body. Shaking his head, he turned to the task before him, to read for her when he knew so much about her on an intimate level. Maybe he should start with something he had not told her in her first reading.

"Did you bring a tape?" he asked quietly. "Because, as you know, I wasn't expecting you." He could tell she was nervous, but then he was also.

"No. Maybe you have an extra one."

"There must be one around somewhere." He reached into

his desk drawer. "No," he said. "I don't think so." But he continued to reach further back and finally brought out an unopened tape. He ripped off the plastic wrap, then put it in the machine on the table.

"Actually, I'm going to do the talking," she said, suddenly displaying a confidence he had not previously witnessed.

He squirmed in his chair, but at the same time it pleased him to see her like this.

"I see your life changing," she said. "Everything. You're going to question everything. Someone from your past, your not so distant past, is going to turn up and it would be wise for you to reflect carefully on how you handle it."

When she finally stopped, he was quiet. "Why not turn off the tape?" she asked. "You can tell me what happened."

"This is difficult," he said. "I didn't intend that things would be so murky and to leave you wondering. But you were right. You knew about turning a life upside down. I didn't believe you. Or didn't want to. Everything is still pretty unsettled and maybe I'm a coward."

She picked up the package from the floor and handed it to him.

When he opened the mauve paper fastened at the top, he smiled at the sight of the single iris with a long stem.

"Van Gogh."

As she stood up, he wondered if he would let her go down the stairs without saying anything or calling out to her. He was not even sure he was capable of simply listening to her footsteps disappear, of watching through the window as she walked along the sidewalk and vanished in the distance. He might never see her again.

The leaves on the maple were starting to change. Were he about to take the trip to Russia, by the time he returned, the leaves would be a mass of brilliant crimson. But he no longer wanted to go there without Sue. He could see the two of them standing at a check-in counter at an airport, smiling as the man behind the desk put destination tickets on their luggage.

He had to discern whether this was an imaginary story or something his psychic sense intuited. What about Heather? This story was not unlike the ones he had created for himself as a child. No one had to know. He had sat in the concentration camp and visualized what it was like outside the prison, the fields he would have to cross to escape this horrid place. It had stunk, he had heard people moaning, and there had not been enough food. He had been hungry. But that story he had created for himself of what was outside the prison had led to his escape. Most of his stories had preceded some action.

"Are you leaving?" he asked quietly. Would she really leave after all the trouble she had taken to come here?

"I've said what I came to say," Sue said.

"You didn't say everything."

"Like what?"

She can't say that she's begun to love me, he thought. It did not take a psychic to know that. Or that she felt she was betraying her husband. Jerry's his name, he recalled. She still loves Jerry. She'll always love Jerry. That much was clear.

"Sometimes you're angry with Jerry for dying."

"I'm not."

"Oh yes, you are. And about what he never told you."

She sighed.

"A double-edged sword, isn't it? Because from that secrecy has come something of value."

"You know too much."

"That's my job."

She smiled slightly as she turned to leave. "And anyway if he'd told me sooner, we would have been able to share it," she said over her shoulder.

"There's something I didn't tell you in your last reading," he said, willing her to stop and listen. "Do you remember when I saw a trip across water? I thought you had enough to handle when I saw you then."

"It doesn't look as if I'm going to take any trip."

"You will. And when you do, something will happen. But that's not what I didn't tell you. Let me reassure you about the trip. Afterwards, you'll have trouble walking for awhile, but it will be all right."

"Oh gee, thanks."

"It's better to know," he said. "Then you'll know that you'll be all right."

"But I'm not taking any trips."

Ah well, he was used to her now, always rejecting anything he told her that she did not already know. "As I said, you will," he said.

"And what about you?" It was clear she wanted to know his intention.

"I think I need longer," Hans said. "Will it be too late to call you then?"

"I don't know," she said with a tinge of sarcasm. "I'm not psychic."

"Listen," he said. "Coming here and saying what you said took a lot of courage and I don't want to take away from that, but I'm getting something right now." He peered off into the distance. He knew this was important and was part of what he had not told her before.

She brushed her hair back impatiently, but she waited.

"Don't let all your disappointment become focused on me," he said, returning his gaze to her. "There's something else you haven't looked at underlying everything you've said to me. When it surfaces, you'll have to deal with it. Don't try to push it away."

"I don't know what you mean."

"Nor do I. But I think you do know." That was as much as he felt he could say if he did not want to frighten her.

She squeezed her eyebrows together. He could tell she was back in time now, thinking about what it was that troubled her. Her secret. He knew she had one, but not what it was.

"It's funny," he said. "I see this picture." He did not think this had anything to do with what he had just said because it seemed innocuous enough to be irrelevant. But it did have to do with her and it might distract her enough to help her look sooner at the deeper secret. "There are two swans," he continued. "Very graceful. I can see their reflections in the water. I'm getting them very clearly. It reminds me of telling a woman her life was going to have a great deal to do with horses.

"'I hate horses,' she said. 'They make me ill. My life couldn't possibly have anything to do with horses.' I didn't hear from her for a long time and then she came back and said, 'You know, Hans, you were right after all. I met a man not long after I came to see you and we married. He's a jockey. Horses run my life now.' So you see, I may not know the significance of what comes to me, but I know when it's important."

"Sure," Sue said, visibly trembling now at the same time as she struggled not to show it. "I'll let you know."

He smiled, his eyes and nose crinkling up even though she was no longer looking at him and was moving swiftly to the door. When she reached it, she turned again. "Do you miss me?" she asked.

"That's beside the point," he said. "Of course I do, but I can't give you what you want or what you deserve. And there's nothing wrong with wanting it. I was wrong to think I might be able to in spite of all the odds against it. I was naïve, too. I'm sorry."

He was not prepared to leave Heather and even though he had vaguely considered that possibility, he had decided against it. So he had not called Sue. And as he watched her leave, he felt relieved he had said what he had. Also, he felt very sad. Their paths had overlapped for what he thought must have been a reason, but it did not feel as if there would be another intersection. Her pride, her dignity, or something of that ilk would prevent her from contacting him for even as profound a reason as what she discovered about herself when she eventually faced what lay buried. He wondered if she even knew what it might be. No, she knew. He was convinced she did.

*

The message on Sue's machine came a few weeks after her visit to Hans's office. She had not anticipated a call this time, feeling from what she now knew that he was not someone to toy with her feelings. His voice, raspy as if choked with a cold, was nonetheless easily recognizable.

"Hello, Sue, this is Hans. It may not sound like me, but it is...."

It had not dawned on her the first time she had gone for a reading that she would ever see him again. Preoccupied with survival, she had been like someone hanging onto a life raft or trying to hold at bay a horse rushing toward her in headlong flight. Nonetheless, she had to acknowledge, if only to herself, that she had noticed his rugged good looks then and had been slightly disappointed to find that he wore a gold wedding band. What struck her now was how she had assumed, at the time, that any world he inhabited would be very different from hers.

As she listened to his voice, she was surprised how much her body relaxed at the sound of it. The year just past when they had seen each other at intervals no longer seemed a chimera. She had known better than to imagine a married man would leave his wife. Nor, most of the time, would she have wanted him to. She probably could not have handled it. Yet a large hole had existed since last she saw him that was no longer just about Jerry's absence.

"Keep painting," Hans's message continued. "I have images of the work you are doing."

Well, yes, that she would continue was now a given. She wondered about his life in the country, the farm with animals, and the place where he grew vegetables. If he lived in a house in downtown Toronto, she wondered if their affair would have happened. She supposed it would have, given the electricity of his piercing awareness.

"I've been lying here, trying to recover. And all I seem to be able to think about is you," he said. "I'll get in touch when I'm feeling better."

As soon as that happened, he would probably be busy. Ever since he was interviewed about his psychic ability on a recent television show, she presumed that he would have become swamped with new clients. Just as he had been when the issue of *Toronto Life* gave him the plug that had led her to his office. Still, he had called. That surprised her. Looking at the telephone, she considered what she might say to him.

"I've missed you," Sue said to his answering machine. "Get well quickly."

So there it was. She thought his laughter and spontaneity were what she missed most. For a while, she had actually imagined he would arrive one day to tell her his wife had left him. The fantasy had continued with an invitation out to see his place in the country where she would meet his horses. *Sue, meet Velvet. Meet London Fog.*

Sue listened to his message again, aware there was every reason to back away, to dismiss him. Instead, she had already responded. She supposed both curiosity and loneliness motivated her. But it was more than longing. There was some magnetism between them. Why me? Why now? Such questions were now constant companions. She had thought men had affairs with younger women, not with someone the same age. All along, every time she thought about him, or saw him, there had been this intrigue. He had told her stories without revealing any personal information. Maybe he liked that she listened.

Once, he had said, "I like it that you always knew I'm just another person."

She guessed he had forgotten that at first she had not. It was almost as if she fed a deep hunger in him, a hunger for contact with someone who was as mysterious and yet opaque as he was. She was of his own generation, too, even if from the comfort of small town Canada. She knew the music he knew, a song like, "Lili Marlene," evoking something for her also.

At intervals after that message, she found his voice again on her answering machine and was reassured, but about what she was not sure. That he existed? That he was still out there? That one day he would come for her? Then came the moment he actually did reach her and she found herself fumbling for words. On the waves of memory came tumbling out all the long-ago times before she met Jerry when she had realized a relationship with a married man would reach some stagnant and rotten core that became insurmountable and backed away from it

"I've been waiting until I felt more settled to call," he said. "There's stuff. And I'm not sure I can deal with it."

"Stuff," she said, that word again. "What kind of stuff? Did your wife find out?"

"No, not that."

"Well, what then?"

"I'll call soon," he said. "We'll plan something."

"All right."

He did not say goodbye, nor did he hang up. Sue waited, imagining him sitting at his desk, looking up over the top of the reading glasses he sometimes wore on the end of his nose. She thought about his long, curly hair, of the intense blue of his eyes. She did not like the thought that theirs might be a tawdry affair, nor that his wife might be hurt by it.

"Listen," he said. "I feel so dislocated somehow. I'll call you soon. Okay?"

"Yes," she said. "Okay. But please don't take too long."

When she went out the door onto the street, a slight breeze blew leaves around her feet. The oppressive heat of yet another summer had lifted. All around were signs of fall, a season that presaged the grey gloom of November and the first anniversary of Jerry's death. She remembered him that last autumn when the leaves flamed crimson, when the grass needed to be raked, when the first gentle flakes of another winter began to fall. She had a jigsaw puzzle in which all the pieces were askew. In the worst way, she still missed Jerry. And yet, she had done what she had promised herself not to do. She shook her head in disbelief. A vision of Jerry's gaunt face, eyes filled with pain, momentarily obscured her vision. And she recognized that she had fallen in love with a man she still scarcely knew and he had already been her lover. Such passion as she felt for Hans she had never expected to feel again. And, even if she could, she would not erase the memory of him. His exuberant gesture after the first time they had made love was still clear in her mind. A dozen pale peach roses he had sent, wrapped in transparent paper, tied with a bow. The sense of discovery that they had both acknowledged that had made them feel like teenagers. As she crossed Spadina and wound her way between the people on Bloor Street, she thought how little she knew of what was going on in Hans's life. At the same time, she longed to see him.

Overhead, a plane flew across the city toward Pearson International Airport. Watching it begin its descent, Sue imagined herself on one leaving for the West Coast where at the furthest edge of land the Pacific pounded ceaselessly against the shore. Or she imagined crossing the Atlantic to a city in Europe. Anywhere where she could escape. But she knew there was no place where she would not think of her unexpected lover.

Climbing the steps of the porch, Sue felt a heaviness descend and an awareness that she was entering a house with memories that might cave in on her the moment she opened the door. Maybe I'll move, she thought. She needed a place to be another woman, not a widow who watched her husband die of cancer, not a woman whose thoughts were consumed by a man who was married. This would be some other woman entirely. She did not know yet who that would be.

There was a pile of mail under the slot in the door. Sprawling across the sofa, she started to slit open envelopes and idly scan their contents. There was a flyer from the University of Toronto, only a few blocks away. She read it carefully and decided she would do something to distract her. A week later, after registering for a course on scientific illustrations she had come upon quite arbitrarily, she began to attend lectures. Looking around on the first evening, it seemed likely she was the oldest in the small group and she was glad when one of the younger men, a gay man she surmised, took the seat at the table next to her.

The next week, he sat beside her again.

"Hi," he said. 'Mind if I park here again?'"

Of course she did not.

Soon, she was immersed in the nerve impulses of a cockroach and discovered little spines emanating from its legs. Next, they were told to chop off the legs and stick electrodes into a spine to stimulate it. The young man flinched as she stuck the instrument into one insect and she felt her curiosity expose her cruelty. Her curiosity won as she watched the legs that were connected to an oscilloscope measure any reaction that was amplified by another machine so that the class could also hear it. She did not yet know what the point was unless they were about to be asked to do sketches of different stages in the torture of a cockroach.

"Your turn," she said, turning to her colleague.

"Carry on," he said. "I'll watch."

He was not at the next class, or the one after, but by then Sue was so engrossed she scarcely noticed. At home, she had begun to paint the insects. It was not long before she realized small, precise illustrations did not interest her and suddenly a cockroach took over almost an entire canvas when she returned to her study in the house on Walken Avenue. It was at least three feet across and reminded her of a Magritte rock almost filling a large room. She was aware of following a dual path, the one of careful presentations on paper for the classes and another where she was creating huge bugs and animals in vivid colours. One was a spider in hues of purple, yellow, and red caught in a huge web on one canvas. There was also a cockroach in a leopard skin. One night, she had nightmares about hurting the cockroach.

The next weekend, she wondered if acrylics were really her medium. Her subject was an ant with rectangles making up its body. Maybe water colours? When she finished, it would become one of her *Bug Series*.

Hans, why don't you call? she wondered. I need to know why. As time passed and she did not hear from him, it was not at all okay even though she thought she ought to give him the time he needed.

*

You have to see it, Maggie wrote about their new piece of land. *High on a hill, overlooking the landing for the ferry from Vancouver Island, the view alone is magnificent. We haven't decided what to build there yet so we're going to rent a place nearby for Christmas. What about coming with us?*

The enclosed photographs of yellow broom in bloom were beautiful. A piece of a dream. A dream Maggie had talked about of a road with trees on either side, winding upward on the edge of a steep incline over a harbour.

This invitation came at an opportune time, Sue thought. Otherwise, she would spend the whole season longing for Hans, the plight she supposed of any woman who became involved with a married man. And even more difficult when she did not know when or if she would hear from him. She had returned to teaching and would have a long enough break at Christmas to make the trip. The thought of moving there had vanished, but she still loved the beauty of her sister's surroundings above the water in West Vancouver. And Saltspring Island intrigued her. Even though her sister's world had always held endless fascination for her, they had not been close as children. When Maggie had gone away to university, Sue had actually been excited when she returned home and listened hungrily as Maggie and their mother talked, sitting together at the kitchen table. She remembered thinking that maybe now Maggie would see her as more than a little kid. But Maggie had acted as if nothing had changed and turned to ask her to get her slippers. It had made Sue feel like a dog asked to go and fetch. If she did go, she would not hear what Maggie and her mother said next, but if she did not Maggie might not ever tell her anything. Or she might have started to ask their little brother, Wally, who was five years younger than Sue. Then where would Sue have been?

Everything had changed when they were older. Sometimes, Maggie had been there for Sue, as she had been during Jerry's illness and after. Or, she would call during a grey, wet spell in Vancouver. It had also been awhile since Sue had seen her nephew and two nieces. Or Vancouver. She recalled standing in Stanley Park, looking out over English Bay and up at the mountains on the north shore. Counting the ships in the harbour. She'd had time to wander or sit on a log or rock near the water, looking off into the distance. She had watched the sun set over mountains and had gone around the sea wall on a bicycle.

The prospect of spending the holiday season with Maggie and Angus and their family would be a way of celebrating some of what was going well in the world. Also she would know they would all honour Jerry's absence. She thought also of telling her sister about what had turned into her good news about Thomas. She was not ready yet to tell Maggie about Hans.

So it was that Sue flew across the continent in record time on the Friday just before Christmas, glad to be away from Toronto and the endless waiting to hear from Hans. The hope that she would, but never knowing what to expect. As she descended on the escalator to the carousel in Vancouver where her baggage would soon appear, she could see Maggie standing off to the edge of the crowd. She waved and they moved toward each other, meeting in a warm hug.

After Sue had collected her suitcase off the conveyor belt, the two women walked out to the parking lot where it had started to snow lightly, not at all what Sue had anticipated in Vancouver.

"Surely this won't last," she said. "Doesn't it melt between one day and the next?"

"Usually."

Instead, it went on falling and on the morning they were to leave for Saltspring, the car was covered and the branches of surrounding trees were laden. After listening to endless weather forecasts and missing the early ferry to Nanaimo, they decided to make the trip in spite of the weather and set off with a frozen turkey in the trunk along with an array of tins, boxes, and wrapped presents. On Vancouver Island, they drove south to Crofton and took another ferry for the short ride to Saltspring. From there, Angus said, it was only a short drive to the cabin he had rented at a lodge a few miles from their piece of property.

"Across a body of water," Hans had said. "There will be some unexpected occurrence and afterwards you'll have a difficult time walking."

Surely, this was not a significant body of water. Sue thought he had meant something like an ocean. Although the bodies of water that make up the British Columbia coast in and around all the various islands could be considered "significant," she supposed. And if something was about to happen, at least Hans had also predicted that everything would be all right soon after. The thoughts of those words of his were fleeting. Even when she saw cars off to the side in the snow, two of them so twisted and damaged that it was hard to imagine anyone had survived, it did not occur to her that any harm would come to her here. After all, Angus had grown up in the north and was an experienced winter driver. Something she thought as she saw ambulances and police cars surrounding the accident scene.

At the dock in Crofton, after a short ferry ride across a thin strip of water, only a few miles on the road would separate them from the lodge. By this time, the snow had become so dense that they could scarcely see a foot or so ahead of them, but the ferry nonetheless pulled away from the shore. On the other side, Angus, followed by their son in their old red car, drove off the ferry. He turned gingerly out onto the road that wound its way upward out of the village. From her seat in the back, Sue's shoulders relaxed as she watched the snowflakes. She hoped they would find a fireplace ready to light, with logs laid carefully across each other so they would burn easily.

"Oh no," Angus said suddenly. "Oh, no."

Swivelling her head to look, Sue saw a dark blue pickup truck sliding toward them and she cringed. Immediately after that came the impact and a loud crunch. As she was jolted forward, Sue could feel her whole body vibrate and their car slide toward the steep incline next to the road. Everything seemed to happen in slow motion and she was convinced the car would flip over. It was a surprise when it stopped moving, all of them still upright, the back end of the car almost hanging over the precipice. Sue waited for the drop to come, the final crash. When nothing happened, she dared to look around.

"The door won't open," Maggie said.

Sue looked down at the steep slope beside her, not keen to get out. Her door would not budge either, but after hearing a click when Angus released all the door locks, she tried again. Sliding out onto the snow, she realized she had landed precariously on a slight slope but that she was safe there if she was able to keep from slipping onto a steeper one that was so close she could not bear to look at it. Pulling herself to her knees, she reached for Maggie's door. Sue's purse and Maggie's glasses lay on top of some luggage where if she leaned forward she could just grasp them.

"My face," Maggie said. "My face."

"It's red," Sue said.

"The air bag hit me in the face and knocked my glasses off," Maggie said, her cheeks burning. "I can't hear out of my right ear." Gingerly, she too slid from her seat, landing next to Sue on the snowy slope.

Angus stood beside the other side of the car, watching anxiously to see that they were able to get out of the car safely. Then he moved toward a house close by where the driver of the pickup that had bumped into them was now trying to park.

"It doesn't look as if anything is broken," Sue said as she and Maggie carefully stood up.

Colin, Maggie's son, inched carefully down beside them. Tall and lanky, he towered over them, his face ashen. "Are you all right?" he asked.

He took Maggie's hand to help her up the bank while Sue scrambled along behind them. Colin said he and his two sisters, in Little Red, had watched helplessly, unable to do anything to stop the collision. The girls were standing at the top of the bank.

"Are you all right, Mum?"

Maggie nodded.

There was a dull ache down the middle of Sue's chest. She could not figure out why because she had not hit anything. Colin reached his hand to her, but she was afraid if she took it the pain would increase.

Finally, she reached the top of the incline where they all stood, dazed, at the edge of the road. Near the house that Angus was now approaching, a young ponytailed woman in blue jeans and a heavy sweater struggled to get out of the pickup truck. She gestured wildly with her arms and spoke frantically to the man who came out the front door. They could hear her say it was the first snow she had ever driven through and she had put on her brakes the same way she would any other day.

"I was just about here," she said. "I was just about home. And instead of the truck coming into the driveway, it slid the other way. It went out of control." A little tow-headed boy hung onto her. "We weren't hurt," she kept saying.

"Thank heavens for that," the man said, picking up the boy. "I'll have to give you some lessons for driving in winter."

Angus walked up to them. "I need to call the police," he said. "And the insurance company."

It was then that both the man and woman noticed the occupants of the other vehicle.

"Come into the house," the man said to Angus, brushing the boy's hair with one hand, the other placed on the small of his wife's back, gently urging her inside. "Are you folks all okay?" he asked, turning to Sue and Maggie, who had joined them with Colin and the girls close behind.

They followed the man into a room littered with children's toys, dirty laundry, and boots stacked on top of each other. Sue leaned against the wall. If the young woman had known how to drive on icy roads, this would not have happened. Almost unable to breathe from the pain across her chest, she waited for the woman to say she was sorry. Instead, she kept on moving, rushing back and forth and round and round like a headless chicken. Finally, Sue sat down on the floor and watched Angus, who did not seem to be hurt, dial a number. Colin and the girls lingered near the doorway. The child who had been in the vehicle with his mother also seemed to be in constant motion. When the woman passed by close to Sue, the two of them ignored each other. Finally, an hour later, a man from the lodge came to pick up their luggage. Thankfully, Angus had also called him. Sue, Maggie and the girls accompanied him in a four-wheel drive, sitting quietly in the back. Colin waited with Angus for the police to arrive.

Drive slowly, Sue thought. Please drive slowly. Her arms and legs trembled.

*

The next morning dawned bright and cold. A plough went by in the distance on the other side of the water, but no cars arrived at the lodge. The only vehicle to turn up was a tow truck that came to haul the Camry into town with Angus and Colin following behind in Little Red.

Pristine snow lay everywhere around the slope behind the lodge and there was scarcely a sound except that of a truck or plough on the highway miles away. Sue picked her way through the snow, breathing in the fresh air. With every breath, she could feel pain in her chest that had increased in the hours since the accident. But Hans had said she would be all right, if not right away, in the not too distant future. He had been attempting to reassure her, she thought, so probably the pain would not last.

When she went back up to the lodge, Sue found Maggie in the kitchen busily putting everything back into boxes. It seemed that while she was not able to hear out of her right ear that otherwise her sister was all right.

"What're you doing?" Sue asked, trying not to breathe too hard and baffled by her sister's actions.

"We're going back as soon as we have this stuff ready. Angus and the kids rented a car."

"Why?"

"A good question," Maggie said. "It seems Angus feels that after the accident we wouldn't enjoy Christmas here. You're in pain and my face hurts. I can't hear properly. And maybe more to the point, it sounds as if the storm could get even worse. We don't want to get trapped here."

When Angus and the children returned, Sue and Maggie were sitting in the living room. "Are you all right?" Angus asked when he came into the room.

Sue's face was pale and she was slightly crouched over now. Most of all, she was terrified of ever getting back into a car.

"I want to go back to the ferry docks in the four-wheel drive," she said.

They all looked at her.

"I was just in a car accident," she said.

"Me, too," Maggie said finally, breaking the awkward silence.

So once that was arranged, the owner of the lodge drove the two women while Angus, Colin and the girls drove the rental car and Little Red. They picked Maggie and Sue up at the dock.

On the way up the highway to Nanaimo, they were all quiet. There was almost a collective sigh when the ferry pulled into Horseshoe Bay with its ring of stark rock and trees above them. After that, they all sighed again when they finally parked in the driveway of the house. Angus turned brusquely away from everyone as he walked hurriedly toward the stairs that led to the basement

"I need to watch television or do something mindless," he said. He was more affected by the accident than he had let on over the past couple of days.

"I'm going out," Colin said and stomped out the door, slamming it behind him.

Sue could see him walk quickly down to the street and disappear around a bend at the corner. She wanted to shout or scream herself, to let off all the emotion of the last few hours, but she did not. Later, she heard her nephew's poorly concealed footsteps as she was about to drift off to sleep.

On Christmas Day, Maggie stood at the counter in the kitchen, peeling and chopping. Everyone talked cheerfully and it felt as if nothing had happened. Sue sensed her sister did not want to hear anything more about their aborted trip, and especially not about the pain in Sue's chest. So Sue stayed as still as she could in an attempt not to exacerbate it.

"Angus," Sue finally said quietly. "Would you drive me to the emergency at the hospital?"

Maggie looked dubious. "My face is still sore," she said. "And I can't hear out of my right ear."

"I'm sorry," Sue said. "I'm really sorry."

Angus was almost through the door and he did not stop when he heard his wife's words.

"I have to make the dinner," Maggie said. "So, I can't come."

Sue bristled slightly, feeling no one cared if she were in pain. No one cared whether she had broken anything. If Maggie needed a doctor, she ought to ask Angus, or even one of the girls, to take over. Colin could have driven both of them. But no one suggested anything like that and Sue went out the door to the car.

"You can leave me here," she said when Angus stopped at the hospital entrance. "I'll call when they've seen me." She waved him away, figuring he could still help out back at the house.

In the waiting room, she picked up a magazine. It was two hours before her name was called and she was directed to a cubicle where she sat on a bed with a white curtain draped around it. Finally, a young female doctor came in.

"What happened?" she asked.

Sue described the accident.

"Ah," the doctor said. "A seat belt injury. We see a lot of them." She said she would not X-ray because the treatment plan would not be any different whether there were broken bones or not.

Sue nodded.

"We can give you some painkillers," the doctor added. "It may be invisible except for some bruising, but that doesn't make it any less painful."

Angus arrived soon after Sue called and by the time they returned to the house the turkey was already out on a platter and someone had made white paper stockings and put them on the drumsticks. The smell of onions and sage stuffing wafted through the entire lower floor.

"Merry Christmas," Maggie said.

Sue thought of the car almost hanging over the side of a mountain, the woman running around her house ignoring them, the four-wheel drive that seemed safe in a world suddenly more vulnerable.

"Merry Christmas," she replied.

"The turkey travelled well," Maggie said.

Yes, Sue thought. As a summary of their adventure, that would do. And while she would like to tell Maggie about Hans and what he had said, that was another story. Had the whole trip been pointless? Perhaps to the island, but certainly not to visit her family. It had been a way of spending the holiday season with them rather than alone. Even the snowstorm was now a shared experience they would likely recall in years to come. They would probably laugh then, even though now they avoided talking about it since clearly it had unnerved all of them.

Sue wondered how Jerry would have reacted to the whole experience. Her face reddened. How could he have kept the existence of a son from her? And even from his closest friend, Martin? Still, not even once had she contemplated telling him about her baby. Nor had she sought to find her. She felt so convoluted that she willed the thoughts away. She would have to face them again soon enough when she arrived back in Toronto.

"I never saw the property," she said, nevertheless relieved, as they all were, to be back in what was a warm, comfortable house rather than in pain and disarray on the island.

5.

THOMAS RIPPED OPEN a slender envelope that had just fallen onto the floor from the mail slot. The return address was now familiar.

What about coming for a visit? Sue had written. Although she had invited Kate also, he had told Sue when he called that he would be coming on his own.

Walking up the front steps, his limbs shook slightly. He thought this silly, as he was not nervous about seeing Sue. He picked up the knocker and let it fall against the plate under it. Sue answered right away, almost as if she had been waiting just inside the door.

"Hello," he said, feeling more shy than he had when he first met her. "I've missed you," he added quietly. There was a vein in his forehead that throbbed from time to time. His eyes were bloodshot.

"You look thinner," she said. "Are you all right?"

"Yes," he said. "Just tired." There was more work to these university courses than he had expected, he told her. "How about you?" He was surprised at how much time had passed since he had last seen her at the memorial for his father. But he had been preoccupied with Kate and with his courses. Also, he knew Sue had returned to teaching.

"Mostly all right."

She told him about the accident and that it had taken two months for the pain to disappear entirely. That sometimes, when walking down Bloor Street on a windy day, she still felt tightness in her chest when she breathed.

"I miss Jerry," she added. "But I'm often angry with him, too."

"I was angry with my mother after she died," Thomas said. "You know, how could she do that to me? Leave me alone? Behind? But after a while, I stopped being so mad. She should have told me about my father sooner though. And I've been thinking a lot about that."

"I've been angry with Jerry for not being that father." She brushed a strand of hair off her forehead and backed into the hallway, gesturing for him to follow. In the kitchen, she pulled out stools. They both sat down at the counter.

"Maybe he did what he could." What else could explain it? He already had the impression of Jerry Reid as someone who would have found it difficult to conceal his own son's existence for all these years.

"If he'd ever let himself meet you, there would have been worlds more he could have done. He likely knew that."

She did like to go on and on, Thomas thought. This might be part of why he had taken so long to make contact again. It was tiring. He was grateful for her unexpected friendship, but he could not deal with the feelings that often seemed to pour out in his presence. He had enough of his own to deal with. Still, he and Kate wanted her in their lives. He also intended to visit Martin.

"Kate and I are getting married in June," Thomas said.

The worried lines on her face evaporated as a smile softened her features. "I'm happy for you," she said.

"We'd like you to be there." And he told her that he was sorry he had not been in touch sooner. "Time passes so quickly. My mother used to say that and I'm beginning to understand why with so much going on all the time."

"I know," she said. "It's been like that since I returned to teaching."

"You'll be my only family member at the wedding other

than Florence." He did not add she was related to him only through Jerry. He did not need to.

"I'm going to invite Martin and Emily, too," he said.

"Of course."

She did not look particularly pleased, but he decided to ignore that. "Next time I come to the city, I'll bring Kate."

"Will she like me, do you think?" The smile gave way to a doubtful look.

"What's not to like?"

"Well, we'll hope that whatever there is not to like, she won't notice." Sue's face relaxed again.

"She said something like that, too." That was Kate, wanting to make a good impression on his relatives, as if Sue had been in his life for a long time.

"Where is the wedding?" Sue asked.

"Stratford," Thomas said. "Kate's family all live there. I think I told you I've known her since high school. Now we're both at Western."

"Where will I sit?"

"On my side," he said. "Where else? Close to the front." He would leave his mother's place empty. "You would have liked her," he said.

Thomas thought she looked unsure about that. Or was it his father she was having doubts about again?

"Jerry took me to see plays in Stratford," she said, disbelief ringing in her intonation. "He didn't even try to see you then. Do you suppose he never told me because he was afraid that I'd try to convince him to?"

"I don't know. How would I know?"

"I'm sorry," she said. "I scarcely realized I was talking out loud. Will Florence be at the wedding?"

"Yes."

"Let's have coffee," she said.

Thomas stood up.

"Oh, don't rush off," she said.

"Just looking for something." He emptied one of his pockets. She moved to plug in the kettle. "Do you mind instant today?" Thomas shrugged and smiled. It made no difference to him. He handed her a small folder of photographs of him with his mother. He liked that she seemed to want to know him. She was a bit like an aunt. Maybe his relationship with Jerry would have been similar, like finding a long-lost uncle.

"Thanks," Sue said as she began to go through the folder.

"Do you mind if I give Kate a call?" he asked.

"Of course not," she said. "Go ahead."

*

There was a photograph of a white calla lily on a card on the shelf that caught Sue's eye. Any distraction from marking papers was welcome. Florence had sent the card after the memorial to thank Sue for making arrangements for her stay at the bed and breakfast and for brunch the day after with Thomas, Emily, and Martin. Sue wondered why she had not thought of going to visit Florence until seeing this card again. It would be better if she could go before the wedding, she thought, and decided to call her.

"I wondered if I might visit," she said to Florence after they chatted for a while.

"Oh yes, my dear. I'd be delighted," Florence said.

"Are there any bed and breakfasts nearby?"

"I wouldn't hear of it," the older woman replied firmly.

So, with spring on the verge of arriving, Sue drove to Blenheim, a small town near Lake Erie on a weekend. Not long before Florence's husband died, they had moved from their farm into a modest brick-and-vinyl bungalow across the street from the local swimming pool. The room where Sue was to sleep had a bright, patchwork quilt on the bed and a pine rocking chair in the corner. The window overlooked a backyard with a wooden swing. On the walls were black-and-white photographs of people in clothing Sue thought was from the twenties.

"That's Jerry's mother and my mother," Florence said, pointing at two women with their arms around each other. "Sisters. Jerry and I were first cousins."

Her mother had been the oldest in a family of eight, and his mother had been the youngest; hence, the age difference between Florence and Jerry.

"Did Jerry ever tell you about Thomas?" Sue could not wait any longer. There was utter silence behind her and she turned to find Florence standing awkwardly beside the door. She acted as if Sue had not spoken. Maybe she was slightly deaf, Sue thought, so she cleared her throat.

Florence looked at her and Sue could tell by her eyes that the older woman had heard. Her throat tightened. She had taken advantage of this kind woman only to put her in an unpleasant situation.

"You know, dear," Florence said. "I *am* a little weary. Perhaps we could have a cup of tea and I could rest for an hour. You must be tired, too, after all that driving. We can talk about things later. Whatever things you came to talk about."

"Thank you," Sue said quietly.

While Florence rested, Sue closed her eyes for a while. Then, she studied the photographs in a copy of the *National Geographic* she had brought with her. When Florence came for her, they went for a slow walk out onto the road. The older woman held onto her arm for balance. Florence knew everyone they encountered on the main street that ran through the town. Since there were only four or five thousand inhabitants, Sue thought that was not surprising. It was similar to her own childhood experience in a small community, except that no one spoke French here and the land was so flat it seemed like the prairies. Not reminiscent of the rocks, bush, and water where in the fall, when the leaves were a brilliant gold and crimson, she and her mother had driven out on tiny dirt roads to shoot partridge.

Early in the morning, Mum would tap on her bedroom door.

"Sue," she'd whisper. "Time to get up."

Sue remembered the old Nash, two tones with dark blue around the body and light blue on top. She had learned to drive in that car. Around and around the block. Sixty times. Seventy-eight times. She had also practised on the road to the lake, where if you had encountered another car, it was always a surprise. One had yielded then and backed up until the other could squeeze by, the road had been that narrow.

"Jerry used to come and visit here," Florence said. "He slept in the room you're in. Not often, but especially after he learned about the pregnancy. That was long before he met you. Later, he sent money through me and I always saw it got to Thomas's mother." She also had visited with Thomas when he was a boy, and, more recently before his mother died.

"Did you ever tell Jerry about him?"

"Oh yes, of course, my dear. He called every month or two to ask questions."

"Why did I never hear about this? Why didn't I know?"

"Maybe Jerry was afraid you wouldn't accept what he had done."

"Did he say that to you?"

"No. We didn't talk about you or his marriage, except that I knew he was happy with you."

"Of course I would have accepted his son." Sue felt irritated at the supposition that she might not have. She watched the older woman walk slowly a step or two before stopping and turning, her lips tight as she faced Sue.

"Are you sure?"

Sue flinched and looked away. She did not really know. One of the miracles of meeting Jerry had been that neither of them had children and there was had been a certain relief at that. Lies, she thought. Tragic lies. Now that she had met Thomas, she could no longer understand any of it.

"I don't know anymore," Sue said.

At breakfast the next morning, Sue sat at the table near a

kitchen window that looked out on birds clustered at a feeder. A cat skulked around the foot of the feeder, its eyes fixed on the birds.

"Kate's a special young woman," Florence said.

"I'm looking forward to meeting her," Sue said. "I thought Thomas was going to bring her into the city, but it hasn't happened yet. Martin and Emily went to Stratford to meet her."

"Didn't they offer to take you with them?"

"I didn't expect them to." Sue frowned and looked out at the birds again. There was a cardinal there now, but before she could point it out Florence spoke.

"I see," she said, her puzzled expression making it clear that she did not. "We'll sit together in the church," she added. "You and I."

"Thanks," Sue said. There would be one person she knew at the reception other than the bride and groom. Well, of course, she would also know Martin and Emily.

Sue was sorry she had not made more of an effort to be in touch with Florence. Maybe if Jerry had made her feel part of a family, it would have happened. Instead, they had been a couple, seemingly without any attachments. Now, she doubted that that had been enough.

They had had Maggie and Angus and their family, of course, out on the West Coast, but they had been too far away for much on-going contact. And Wally, in California where he flew a Pacific route for a large American airline, had seldom been in the picture. Aside from the occasional birthday or Christmas card, Sue would scarcely know her brother existed unless she happened to call him. Then, he was invariably friendly and said he would call the next time. To her surprise, he had done so since Jerry died.

"How will you get there?" Sue asked. It was a long drive for Florence.

"I haven't decided. I could take the train. But it's a bit of a roundabout route."

Sue said she could go down a day ahead to Blenheim and they could drive to Stratford together. It was a genuine offer to help the other woman, but she also knew it would make arriving at the wedding easier for her.

"Thank you," Florence said. "But let's see. That's a lot to ask of you."

"Not really," Sue said. "I'd like the company."

"Thank you," Florence said again. "At the moment, I'm wondering why you wouldn't drive to Stratford with Martin and Emily."

Sue looked out at the birds again. There were mostly small brown birds now, swallows perhaps. She fidgeted with her hands and finally put them around her cup, feeling the warmth of the coffee through it.

"It's awkward," she said. "They've been very kind since Jerry died. It must be difficult for Emily because she's never liked me."

Florence was silent, then walked over from the counter to sit down across from Sue at the table. "I find that hard to believe," she said.

Sue was uncomfortable after finally articulating the suspicion she had held for such a long time. It would have been better not to have said anything. For a long time, she had sensed Emily's feelings about her and now that Thomas was in the picture, she had noticed that she was subtly excluded from some conversations. She knew there would always be people whom she disliked, as well as ones who disliked her. But Emily! It meant a continuing uneasiness because Martin wanted to keep in touch with her, or felt an obligation to do so, and sometimes she could tell how awkward it was for him. Especially now that he assumed an extended family with Thomas and Kate that also included Sue. There was no way around seeing Emily. Sue would have to go on facing the unpleasant scrutiny that seemed more intense since the memorial. And yet she had liked Emily when they had first met years ago, had even known her *before* Martin. Was it possible that she was wrong and it had something to do with Hans? Was it possible that Emily knew about him?

"Oh well," she said. "Maybe I imagine it." But she knew whatever Emily felt about her was not that simple.

"I hope so," Florence said. "Because it's not worth spending time worrying about it. Better to look for ways to make *her* comfortable."

Sue was startled at those words. What could she do to make Emily comfortable? This trip was not turning out at all. She realized she had hoped that Florence would do something to fix whatever worried her. How ludicrous! This was a kind and concerned woman, but nothing more. Sue would have to figure out this new constellation of people in her life a step at a time. If she had not already bungled it.

*

When he listened carefully, Hans could hear birds singing. He watched Heather reach into the refrigerator for something in the fruit container. Warmth radiated from a heater by the wall and he stood near it while she cut through the yellow skin of a grapefruit.

"Want half?" she asked.

"Save it for later."

"I haven't been fair to you," she said. "You need to know what I've been thinking about."

Only moments earlier, they had been chuckling about the way one of her cats had snuggled down between them during the night. Maybe that had given her an opening to share something that he knew she had been worrying about.

"It's about Mum and Dad," she said. Ever so calmly, as if she were calm.

"Yes," he said. This was a conversation he had hoped for, but at this moment it was a surprise and he did not know what to say.

"Let's be clear," Hans felt compelled to say. "I've always loved you and I still do." He had never intended his affair would end his marriage. But why was he making a statement as if he were apologizing for something she did not even know about. He hoped she would ignore it, especially since it had nothing to do with what she was trying to tell him.

"I know that," she said. "And I love you. But there's something that's creating a lot of stress for me." She stopped and moved slightly closer to him. "I have to go to England again. I can't leave them alone. I want to take a leave of absence from work."

"Oh," he said, his spirits plummeting. It was odd how the one thing she came up with would be something he had not even anticipated. And although he knew her parents were increasingly vulnerable and even more so since her visit that helped sort out medications and her latest visit a few months later, he did not think he could stand the thought of her being so far away for as long as a leave of absence implied. Nor had they ever talked again about David or what he meant to her. But it hardly seemed like the right time to raise that again, especially after months had passed.

"I need to think," he said. "I need to go outside." At least at this time of year, it was light out earlier. He went to the back door and put on a pair of boots. There were chores to do that would keep his mind from circling around his own fears.

For a while, he wandered the farm aimlessly, unable to concentrate. What had happened to change everything so much that she would consider being apart for so long? There was a time when she did not want any separation to last for more than a night. He was confused and whatever had to be done on the farm did not feel like the usual antidote. There would be an early haying to take care of and he wondered when he would get to that. So unlike any previous summer when he had relished the hard work, it felt as if his will had vanished.

On the path leading to the pond, one of the horses came up

beside him and nuzzled his shoulder. The dog, Rusty, barked at the horse's nose. He could hear Heather's voice.

"Hans, I'm going to have to go into the city. Please, let's have this chat now." Her words floated across the pond to him.

He could not bear it. He already missed her. This was one of those times when he wished he had the power to intuit what would happen, something that would help him decide what to do. He felt lost and guilty. He would never be able to see Sue. That would undermine his marriage completely. He could hear the sound of footsteps and turned to see Heather approaching him.

"I don't want to leave without having this talk," she repeated. "And it's almost time to go to work."

Just when he thought she was the one who evaded communication, here she was pressing him to talk.

"All right."

He did not have any idea what might be coming. There was no image that suddenly appeared for him as his uncle's skull had. That skull with the date that still sometimes haunted him. At first, he had thought maybe he had made his uncle die.

"Hans."

He nodded.

"I'm thinking of asking for six months," she said.

"That's a long time." He understood her concern for her parents, but it felt as if it had now become an excuse for something deeper.

"Yes," she said. "It is. Maybe you could try to come over for a while?"

"What about David?"

"There's nothing there, except we did talk about this a couple of times because I had to ask someone whether they thought it made sense for me to be there."

"Do you really think he was neutral?"

Heather sighed. "I don't know. I assume he was. He didn't say much one way or another. He just listened."

"Just what I'm not doing," Hans said. "Not that I've had much of an opportunity."

"C'mon," Heather said, tugging at his arm. "Let's go inside and just sit for awhile and…"

"All right," he interrupted her. "Let's." It is time to be clear, he thought. That was what he had wanted for quite some time now.

Inside, they settled on opposite sides of the counter that separated the kitchen from a large dining area that looked out toward the road. He stood leaning on his elbow, waiting.

"I'd like to go as soon as the end of the month."

"You know I want you to do all you can for your parents, but I also want our marriage to hold together. This kind of separation isn't going to help that."

Heather looked down at her hands. When she raised her head again, he could see the confusion and pain in her eyes. "I don't know what else to do," she said.

"Okay," he sighed. "I guess we'll just have to figure it out."

After Heather left for the city, Hans took his lunch and papers out to his car. He had no idea how they would weather the upcoming months, but he had to start to focus on his trip into the office and the appointments scheduled for that afternoon. There would be five that day. Rusty barked beside the car door and he let the dog in beside him. Sometimes, Rusty came with him into the office where he lay on the floor beside Hans's chair while clients came for readings. As Hans drove to the road that ran past the farm, he saw a crow struggling in the gravel and slammed on the brakes. The bird looked up at him as he stepped out beside it and leaned over, grasping it carefully so as not to cause further injury. He would have to find a box for it. He would also need a small bottle to feed it water. There were seeds in the house. So he went back and put together a small kit for the bird with some loose newspaper and a towel in a cardboard box as well. He settled the crow in the carton and placed it carefully on the back seat.

"You sit here with me, Rusty," he said. "Leave the bird alone." He made the sound of a crow. He loved birds and the wonderful calls they made. Such an obvious one, that of the loon, but it was a sound that evoked deep feelings of loneliness as well as of beauty. It made him think of the Big Dipper, of water in a quiet lake, of photographs he might take or had taken.

The conversation with Heather rose to the top of his mind. If he had had the chance to go to Anna's side and support her through her illness, he would have gone. It had never dawned on him that more than a visit to his sister was possible. It would have been inconceivable to do that and pay the bills. He was not sure Heather had thought of that either. To keep up the payments on the farm, he would have to work a lot harder.

If no one cancelled an appointment, his trip into the city would be worth it. That was one thing about this kind of practise. If someone did not turn up, he did not get paid. Sometimes, he would drive all the way and there would be two cancellations, a "no show," and a list of excuses. If it were a regular client, he could count on that appointment, or at the very least, a message in enough time that he would not have to make an unnecessary trip. It was not so bad when there were other clients who had appointments. But today, feeling the pressure of earning more than usual, he was not about to cancel anything.

He drove down Mississauga Road to the highway. When he pulled onto the 401, he turned the radio on low, to classical music. It would soothe the crow. The poor bird was thrashing around in the box. It seemed to have a broken wing and maybe a leg, too. He wondered if an animal had attacked it.

In a few moments, he was surrounded by trucks loaded with cargo, beating up the roads he considered belonged as much to him as to these huge transports. It seemed as if there were more of them all the time. All those goods that were now transported by truck slated for same-day delivery, he supposed.

Rusty sniffed at his ear.

"C'mon, dog," he said. "Too much traffic for nuzzling."

Rusty recognized the tone. This was not the time for play. He folded himself down onto the passenger seat, resting his nose on his paws.

In his office, Hans put the crow in the corner and gave Rusty a rubber bone and a toy doll to play with. Closing the door behind him, he went down the hall to the washroom. When he came back, he set up the tape recorder and looked at his Day-timer. Would this be a good time to call Sue, he wondered, even though he knew it would be better not to do that. It was tempting, even though he had been the one to say he could not offer her what she wanted.

Fool! he thought. Why had he gone to her house? He could have suggested meeting elsewhere or declined her invitation. And how would he explain that to Heather if it ever came to light? It had only happened because he thought she would never know. Now, he had to make certain that she never did.

The crow made a low noise and Hans went across the room to peer into the box. What would he do with the bird now that he had rescued it? He leaned over and gently dripped a bit of water from the small bottle into its open beak. Carefully, he slid some seeds closer to it, hoping it would be able to feed itself without trouble. Later, when it was better, he would find a safe place on the farm to release it. That might take a day or two.

*

Sue drove to Stratford on the 401 highway. The wedding invitation, a white card engraved with two swans, was lying in an envelope on the seat beside her. These swans did not feel to her as if they were the ones Hans had seen. Or if they were, then this image was not complete in itself. Although she had talked quite a lot with Thomas, she did not know many of the wedding details. Perhaps the swans would turn up as part of the décor at the wedding and the reception.

Florence had found someone who lived closer who was able to drive her to the wedding, so Sue was on her own, speeding along under blue skies. She wondered why she was taking on a role in Thomas's life and ignoring that somewhere out there she had a daughter. Why was she not looking for her? Surely it was time. She swerved slightly as a car started to move over into her lane and then pulled back again, as if the driver had suddenly seen her car for the first time.

Martin had suggested she accompany them, but she found Martin had become more distant of late and she scarcely saw Emily. It had made her nervous to come under the other woman's scrutiny, afraid that her affair with Hans was written all over her. She wondered if Emily would feel she was betraying Jerry if she mentioned Hans. Surely, after almost two years, she should not feel this guilty. She could hear the contemptuous voice of whatever judge had been assigned to monitor her thoughts: *C'mon Sue, that's not the point.*

Emily would not say it like that, but it might as well have been her voicing her disdain.

Are you stupid or what? Sue asked herself. How could she tell anyone about Hans? He was married. It was like her long-ago daughter; there were too many reasons for her to keep her secret.

With a deep sigh, she tried to shift her thoughts. How would Florence get back to Blenheim? Would the nephew who drove her over to Stratford come back for her after the festivities? Sue felt awkward and nervous about the family dinner to which she, Martin, and Emily had all been invited. It seemed that Jerry had not kept any connections in Stratford once he left. All his relatives had lived elsewhere and the one friend he had retained over the long haul was Martin who had told her that he and Emily would arrive in time for the rehearsal dinner.

It was a relief to leave the 401 and drive west along a two-lane highway through farms and fields. She parked in Stratford on the road beside the water and took a picnic cooler from the trunk. It reminded her of the times Jerry had carried it down to the river and over a small wooden bridge to a tiny island.

They had often had picnics at one of the tables and sat and watched the swans on the river. Hans had said the two swans he had seen were intertwined. It would be very peaceful, so serene that you could see their reflections. He had not known what it signified. Eating her lunch, the swans became part of the ambience of the day, floating on the river followed by tiny, brown babies. One black one stood out from the others, the first she had ever seen, lending more reality to *Swan Lake* for her. But no tableau appeared that fit Hans's description.

A breeze wafted through the leaves. Jerry seemed close by, throwing a Frisbee up into the air as he had the last time they had been to Stratford, almost as if it were happening now. A moment carved in time. She could remember that day and the sense there was something eternal about what had lasted less than a minute. Perhaps love was all that was eternal. Soon, she would be at a ceremony in a church where the solemn vows of matrimony would be taken. This was a day Jerry should have been alive to share. Instead, she would go alone and she dreaded it. But had Jerry been there, she felt there would have been a coolness between them, an argument brewing. One they would never have and one she felt ought to have happened.

There were nametags in small holders at each setting on the long table. As Sue had suspected, her place was with Martin and Emily. He would sit in the middle with the two women on either side. She put her purse on her chair and looked around to see if they had arrived yet. Instead, she saw Thomas beckon and went over to talk with him.

"This is Sue," he said to the young woman beside him who was clearly Kate.

"Hello, Kate," Sue said, taking the young woman's hand. "I'm delighted to meet you."

"Thomas has talked so much about you," Kate said.

Just as Sue was about to say something more, a young couple came in and threw their arms around Kate. She tried to introduce them as her brother and sister-in-law, but the words were lost in the general rush of other people arriving. Sue backed away and returned to her table to find Emily standing there, ready to pull out her chair.

"Hello," she said. "I'm glad to see you."

Sue smiled. "Me, too."

"Martin is hanging up our jackets. He'll be right here."

They both seemed at a loss for words then. Emily moved to put a glass of white wine on the table and to sit down. "How was the drive?" she asked.

Sue said that it had been uneventful, that she had had a picnic in the park. Then, she had settled in at her lodgings. "Up above the river in a quiet, residential neighbourhood."

"We made good time," Emily said. "Martin went into the office before we left. He had some files to go over. But we did get here in time to have a quick nap at the hotel. We had a late night last night, but I don't suppose we have to stay too late tonight, do you?"

"No," Sue said. "I wouldn't think so." She was surprised by Emily's candour. At that moment, Martin came up and gave her a kiss on each cheek.

"We're so glad you're here," he said. "We must try to see each other more often without having to have an excuse. How have you been?"

"Most of the time, quite well," Sue said. "I'm glad to be teaching again. There are times I think I might like to spend more time painting though." She shrugged slightly.

Other people began to take their seats. Martin pulled out his chair and sat down between Sue and Emily. They introduced themselves to a young couple almost across from them who turned out to be part of Kate's family. Just as they began to chat, Thomas brought Florence over to their table. There was a slight commotion as he looked for her nametag and then found it right across from Martin.

"Oh my dears," she said. "How glad I am to see you."

She had been to her hotel to have a nap and a splash, as she put it. And to freshen her lipstick.

"And now it's time to begin the celebration."

"Isn't Kate wonderful?" Emily said.

Heads nodded.

"A toast," a male voice called out.

Clinking glasses. "Kiss," someone else called. "Kiss, kiss…" Voices joined in the chorus. Kate and Thomas took their places next to each other at the head of the table. They kissed shyly. More wine was poured.

*

Sue was surprised at how emotional she felt during the wedding service the next day. She was transported back to her and Jerry's wedding as they stood in the late afternoon sunshine on the island. Jerry, too, had shown that sudden flash of emotion. Sue had known how seriously he had taken their marriage, but perhaps not till then had she realized how deep his emotions ran. He had told her afterwards it was his happiness mixed with memory of his first marriage, when, within months, he had seen the young woman he had loved tossed into the air and thrown to the pavement. Dead on arrival at the hospital. With those memories rising to the surface, he had cried on his and Sue's wedding night with tears that sent his body into spasms.

"This isn't something to do with you," he had said. "I love you." She had held onto him until, exhausted, he had fallen asleep. That first night of their life together as husband and wife had been disconcerting. He had slept for hours, and finally, she had lain against him and slept also.

When Thomas had tears at a crucial moment in the ceremony, grasping for the words he needed, Sue pressed her lips together. She watched with relief as he turned to Kate and found her smiling. Then, his voice rose from a whisper and he said his vow in a strong tone.

"I, Thomas, take you, Kate…."

Kate's long hair was held in place by a pearly hairpiece set on top of her veil. Sue could see her red cheeks and a small mole on the side of her neck.

She now watched Jerry's son repeat his vows. Florence beamed. And when the ceremony was finished and before the reception an hour later, Florence agreed readily to a drive around town. She showed Sue the brick house on Britannia Street where Jerry had grown up and the one around the corner on Mornington where she had.

"I don't think I'll ever understand why Jerry didn't see his son," Sue said.

"Joanna Crossar didn't want to marry him," Florence said. "She didn't love him. She didn't want to make his life difficult. She asked him never to contact her directly. It was her decision about the child, that he shouldn't see his father."

"Why did Jerry accept such conditions?"

"He was confused," Florence said. "He was hurt. He could have made it into a legal struggle, but he decided that wouldn't be in anyone's best interests."

"I still don't understand why he didn't tell *me*."

"I expect he knew you'd never accept those conditions. You would have wanted him to know his child. You would have insisted that it was good for Thomas. Even though you never had or wanted children, you knew what would be good for them."

"Is that what he told you?" Sue asked.

"Not in so many words."

"I guess it makes as much sense as any other reasons I've come up with," Sue said. Yet, at times, the thought she had been married to a stranger still haunted her. Maybe this was what Hans meant when he talked about not fastening her disappointment on him. Fortunately, she had not.

"It makes me wonder if he had other secrets," she said.

"I don't think there would have been any big ones. Anything else I suspect was oversight."

"It just totally confuses me to find that something so immense could have been there all the time. Surely I would have noticed something that big even though it was only a shadow."

"Maybe you didn't want to."

"Maybe." Once again, her own secret thrust itself into her awareness, as she thought she might have been glad Jerry had not been interested in his child because that would have allowed her to keep her secret from him. As she had been sworn to do — to keep her secret from all prying eyes. And she had been silent for so long that sometimes she actually forgot it. Oversight, she thought. Is that what her own deception had been? She hardly thought so but she carried on about Jerry as if he ought to have done what she had not been able to. "I don't know."

"Well, let's enjoy this day," Florence said, eyeing Sue with a piercing look, as if she might even suspect something. "I think it's time for the reception."

They proceeded to the patio of Kate's parents' home where Thomas made sure Sue had a chance to chat with his new family and they treated her warmly as they had at the rehearsal dinner. Kate also made sure that Sue met everyone. Then, took her aside for a short walk down to a pond where goldfish, bright orange flashes in the sunlight, flitted between rocks. There was a gnome at the edge with a red hat, green jacket, and a fishing pole.

"Make a wish," Kate said.

"I wish you a long and happy marriage."

"Make one for yourself, too," Kate said. "You can keep this one a secret."

Sue could not think of what else to wish for, except that Jerry might be there, but what point was there in a wish like that? She wished at least to feel that he was aware of this moment. Hans had talked in terms of guardian angels.

"You have a good one," he had told her. "Someone who has passed on."

Well, they both knew who that was.

"Sure we know," Hans had said. "But he didn't have to take on that role for you. He could have moved to some other realm."

Oh sure, Sue thought. Oh sure. But at this wedding, in this garden, she felt Jerry's presence. And then another presence. Her own daughter. She must be out there somewhere, living through all of life's experiences. Weddings. Births. Did she resent that she had been abandoned?

"This certainly is a beautiful spot," she said now to Kate.

It was then that Sue saw, on the other side of the pond, a canopy over a cake with two tiny swans under a small white arbour. She made her way over to the cake for a closer look. The swans were set on a mirror on top of the cake and seemed to be both upright and floating beneath the mirror's surface in a circle of tiny coloured flowers.

"Oh my." So this was the motif that Hans had said would reflect peace. It was these swans he must have seen. When Kate rejoined Thomas, Sue watched the young man move with his bride to place the first cut in the cake. He felt like her son now. Or, at the very least, someone like a son. But instead of feeling happy, she felt guilty.

When she looked around, Sue saw Martin watching her. With a small gesture, he indicated that he knew she had caught him. It was not one of those looks that sought an answer, but rather a speculative one. One that suggested he could not figure her out or where any of this might be going.

He came over to her and smiled warmly. "Lovely wedding," he said.

"Yes," she smiled back. "Where's Emily?"

"I think she must have gone to the washroom. But I've wanted to speak with you on my own. It's been a while since we've talked."

"Yes."

"I think we'll enjoy this new family, don't you?"

"They're very welcoming."

"That they are. I'd like to suggest…" but, he stopped abruptly as Emily appeared beside him.

"How long are you staying?" she asked Sue.

"Overnight. What about you?"

"We're going to head back fairly soon. I wish you'd come and visit us in the next few days. We've missed you."

Sue was startled. This was not something she had expected, especially after the opportunity for saying so had already been there at the rehearsal dinner.

"I've been busy. Teaching, you know. All that involves. I'm sorry if it has felt as if I'm neglecting you. It's probably a good time to invite both of you to dinner."

Now it was Emily who showed surprise. "Well," she said after a moment's hesitation. "That would be lovely."

Martin took out a handkerchief and blew his nose. "Allergies," he said. "Emily, I started to suggest to Sue that we invite the children in for dinner when they get settled."

"The children?" Emily said. "Oh yes. The children."

"I'll call you," Sue said.

Emily nodded, her face warm and expectant. "You know, if you've met someone it would be lovely to meet him. You don't have to hide anything from us because of Jerry. You deserve to be happy. You took good care of Jerry and you loved him."

Sue was speechless and blushed. Had Emily or Martin seen Hans? Or was this the natural expectation about her circumstances?

"Thanks, Emily. I'll bear it in mind."

"Well, you never responded to any of our suggestions that we include some eligible man in gatherings."

"I wasn't ready then." She was not about to give any information. This was the plight of the other woman, she knew, and she did not like it. There was no one she felt she could tell about Hans. This secretive life no longer suited her. But, she had not cheated on Jerry. Now he was dead and she was free to make her own choices, even ones that surprised her.

"I have been seeing someone from time to time," Sue said with relief. "Trouble is, he's married. I wouldn't say so to anyone but you two."

Martin took in a deep breath and almost choked on it, coughing loudly. To Sue's surprise, Emily smiled. It could have been a relieved smile or it could have been a triumphant one.

*

As Kate put her hand on the knife to cut the cake, Thomas looked around at the wedding guests.

"Thomas," she whispered his name. He turned and reached out to put his hand on top of hers.

Would she comment later that he had seemed distracted? Thomas wondered. Sometimes, she became irritated with him and he was not sure what it was about, but it was usually fleeting. The train of her dress flowed from her waist, her hair hanging to her shoulders. She seemed almost always to be smiling. Her mother said she had been like that from early childhood, the optimist in the family. Most of the time that pleased him. Oh, Mom, Thomas thought, you'd love her.

He put a bit of pressure on Kate's hand and the knife slipped down through the icing and cake to the plate beneath. He could feel something sticking to his thumb.

"What's the matter?" she asked.

He licked his thumb as surreptitiously as he could. She wriggled her nose and smiled at the sight. As he leaned in to kiss her, he heard clapping. Kate sighed and Thomas could feel her shoulders relax. Music drifted out through the French doors onto the patio. He looked around to find Sue watching them. He felt unexpectedly resentful that she was the only one alive to be there. His children would never know their grandparents. This stranger would be all he could offer.

"Let's enjoy ourselves," Kate said as if she sensed his tension. "It's our day."

He hugged her more tightly. "Of course," he murmured.

He felt a light touch on his shoulder and looked up to find Sue standing there. His body became rigid. "Please," he whispered.

"I wanted to wish you happiness," Sue said. "And to say how wonderful you both look."

"My mother should be here," Thomas said.

Sue flinched and stepped back.

"Thomas," Kate said, touching his arm.

"I'm sorry," Thomas said. "I don't know what I was thinking. I had an image of Mom's face."

"I wish she could be here, too," Sue said.

"I wish I'd met Thomas's Mom. She sounds like such a courageous person," Kate said. "And I'm glad you're here, Sue."

Thomas tried to think of something welcoming to say, but he wished Sue would stop intruding. It felt as if she did not quite belong and he would be more comfortable if she faded into the background. Her eyes flickered nervously and he thought she was probably as uncomfortable about her presence as he was. His mother might even have liked her. "Yes," he said.

Sue nodded and moved away to a canopy over a long table covered with a white cloth. He watched her merge with others, taking a glass with wine in it from someone.

"Thomas," Kate said. "I love you."

He smiled. "Me, too."

They were surrounded once more with friends taking photographs and collecting their pieces of cake.

"And soon we get to dance," Kate said.

Thomas had a sudden flash of horror of missing some steps in the waltz sequence they had learned for the wedding, but did not say so. Instead, he sniffed in the gentle scent of his bride's hair. He would fumble through those steps and she would never know how difficult that was for him. Leading her out onto the patio where the music would soon invite everyone to join them, he thought she would never know how much he dreaded dancing.

*

The mattress in the old brick house in Stratford sagged slightly in the middle. A ceiling fan circulated slowly above the bed. Sue lay between the grey-and-white striped sheets, thinking about Thomas's eyes following her at the wedding. At times it had felt as if he were blaming her for the absence of his parents, finding her presence unwelcome. Surely he knew that she did not want to be his mother. She wondered if the time would ever come when he would simply accept her.

Turning on the radio on the night table, she found it set to a station where news came on right away. There were reports on crime and arson was suspected in a house fire. Reaching for the knob, she turned off the string of stories that connected her to a world she did not want to know so much about at that moment. After a while, she drifted off to sleep and images of Jerry's childhood in this town flowed past her eyes like the reel of an old movie. Then came dreams that made no sense to her. She opened the trunk of a new white van to discover there was no spare tire. She asked the salesman about it. He shrugged — if she needed a spare, he would see she got one. He spoke as if it did not matter, as if only a fool would not be able to manage a flat tire on a crowded highway or on some deserted road in the country without anything to fall back on. When she woke up, it was so hot and muggy that even the gentle whirring of the fan provided no relief.

As she sat on the veranda after a full breakfast of bacon and eggs, Sue was relieved to feel a breeze. The host of the bed and breakfast brought coffee. Tiny, about Sue's age, with curly tawny hair and a nose with one nostril that was slightly larger than the other, the woman spoke with an Irish accent.

"We bought the house so my husband would have some-thing to do," she said. "He has to have a project on the go all the time. Now, it's new flowerbeds all around the sides of the veranda. I'm the one who looks after breakfasts, laundry, changing the beds, and cleaning. He does the bookkeeping."

"Have you lived in Stratford long?" Sue asked.

"About ten years."

Sue was disappointed, knowing this woman would not be able to answer any questions about what it was like here when Jerry was a child. She would not know the people he had known. Sue realized she had no more questions to ask. She wanted only to finish her coffee before leaving to walk by the river, go through the park, and then wander on the main street. After that, she would drive back to Toronto. It seemed odd that only after Jerry's death was she destined to come to know this place.

"Like it?" Sue asked.

"Oh yes," the woman said. "It's such a relief after Toronto. It was getting too big for us. And too many immigrants. You know what I mean."

Sue was aware the woman was likely making a statement about colour, about people from the islands or the Philippines or refugees from Sri Lanka. She had heard this sort of remark as the face of Toronto kept changing and over time had learned it changed nothing if she were overly confrontational in expressing her own opinion. Carefully considering her words, she said, "One of the things I like most about Toronto is the variety." Then she added, "I love riding on the subway. I don't think there's any other place where you can get a microcosm of the whole world so easily. Although when I first moved to Toronto, it wasn't like that." She stopped then, not surprised when the other woman turned and seemed to scurry back into the kitchen.

"More coffee?" she asked cheerfully ten minutes later.

"Thanks. I'll be on my way now."

When she left, Sue parked in a lot down by the river. Her plan was evolving in her mind as she locked the car and started walking. She would go over a bridge and around a corner to a main street until she found Britannia. The address she was looking for was one Florence had shown her, a red brick two-storey house on a wide, deep lot with an enclosed porch at the front. It was the house where Jerry had spent his childhood. The trim was painted white.

A woman stood on the porch of Jerry's childhood home, watching the street. When she came out onto the steps, Sue saw she was over eighty. Her back was tall and straight and there was a slight tinge of bronze in her white hair. It was as if she had touched it up and the colour was now fading. She wore bright lipstick. Her pale blue dress was clean and fresh even on such a hot day.

"Are you looking for someone, my dear?"

"I was looking at your house," Sue said. "I hope you don't mind. I was told that my husband grew up in it. "

"Would you like to come in?"

"Oh, I couldn't do that. I'm sorry to have bothered you."

"I live alone, my dear. I'd be glad to have you come in for a while. Who was your husband?"

"Jerry Reid."

"Reid," she said. "Reid. Well, I don't remember that family. I've lived in the house for about thirteen years. My husband and I used to live out in the country. When he couldn't handle the farm anymore, we bought this place in town. Soon after we moved here, he died. Now I'm saddled with it."

"I'd rather not see the inside," Sue said. "But might I see the garden?"

"Yes, of course," the woman said grudgingly.

Sue suspected the woman was disappointed that she would not have someone to chat with over tea. A guest was less likely to linger in the garden.

"Oh my," Sue said as they went around the side of the house and the huge backyard opened up in front of them. "It's really beautiful." In the middle of the lawn was a white trellis with red roses climbing up and over it. Sue could see Jerry rolling in golden leaves when the large birch tree at the end of the yard shed its autumnal glory.

"Reid," the woman said again. "Is that your name then?"

"Oh, I am sorry," Sue said. "Yes, I'm Sue Reid."

"Charlotte Todhunter," the woman said. "I don't remember anyone called Reid owning the house. I have looked at papers. But, you know, I do remember the story of some lawyer who died in jail after a drinking binge. Joe Reid. Jim Reid. I don't remember. Maybe it wasn't Reid at all."

Sue thought a husband would have told her something like that also. But if he did not mention a son, why would he mention a father, grandfather, or uncle who was picked up for drunkenness and subsequently died in a jail cell? Even without this history, it did not surprise her that when Jerry left Stratford, he cut his ties with the place. In the mining town where she had grown up, stories such as these were only too familiar. After a while, they became legendary. Her father had been somewhat of a drinker for a time. The story that had circulated was that although he sometimes drank too much, he was a gentleman. A family held onto a myth like that as if it were their link to survival, Sue thought. Likely it was. Likely that had been the case with her father. Sue had not known at the time that that was what she was doing. When she looked back now, she saw it clearly.

Nonetheless, when her father died, she had been bereft, missing him so terribly it was often almost visceral. She had been relieved that he had stopped drinking and images of him floundering had not remained as vivid for her as they likely had for Maggie. The strongest image of her own childhood was instead of the white house covered with asbestos shingles next to the bush. It was near the path to the mine. Sue would walk out the back door and head over a small footbridge, onto a path that led to the highway. As she came out from the gravel path alongside the road that led toward Montreal, she could see the mine shaft rising above the scrawny trees that were left on the property. Out behind were the slimes, the waste from the rock that was brought up from underground and processed in the mill. Hard rock miners went underground looking for gold. She used to think when she was a child and heard about veins of gold that they would find large rivers of it underground.

Charlotte Todhunter walked laboriously toward a flower-bed full of lilies and stooped to pull out some weeds. When she stood up, she sat on a green bench with ivy growing up a lattice behind it.

"I could make a cup of tea," she said.

"It's all right," Sue said. "I have a long drive back to Toronto."

"As you wish," the woman said. "Did you come for the theatre?"

"A wedding."

"Would I know anyone?"

"The groom's name is Crossar."

"Thomas Crossar? Oh my goodness," she said. "How do you know him?"

"My late husband was his father."

"You don't mean to say that your husband was his father."

Sue nodded.

"Oh my goodness," the woman repeated. "I knew Thomas's mother well. Such a brave young woman, raising that child on her own. I never knew the story, but I assumed some man deserted her."

"Well, that's not exactly the story I've been told. Unfortunately, I knew nothing when Jerry was alive so I never had a chance to ask him."

"Are you saying he never told you?" The voice was imperious.

Sue nodded, although it was none of this old woman's business.

"Oh, you poor dear." Now she sounded more pitying.

Sue stepped away, annoyed. "Do you think you knew everything about your husband?"

"Well, of course I did," Charlotte Todhunter said, sniffing.

Sue wanted to get away as quickly as she could. She would have to tell Thomas she came to look at this house before someone else did. This kind of information would travel like a new fire in dry grass. She hoped it would not make him even more resentful.

"My dear, you can't imagine who came to my house this morning," the old woman would probably say.

"Well, Mrs. Todhunter," Sue said. "Time to get back on the road." She could imagine Jerry cutting the grass, throwing a football or a baseball in the large yard. Charlotte Todhunter looked at Sue with piercing green eyes.

"You know," the older woman said. "Harold, that was my husband's name, found old newspapers in the attic that might tell you something about the house. I think he put them in a file somewhere. Maybe in a scrapbook. He was a great collector. I've thrown out some things, but I don't think I threw out those papers. I might be able to unearth them. If you want to come in and wait."

"All right," Sue said finally. She saw a look of triumph pass fleetingly across Charlotte Todhunter's face. She followed the older woman into the house where a staircase went up to the second floor along the left side of the front hall. The kitchen was connected to a large room behind it that looked out over the garden. It was finished in wood veneer. From the window, Sue could see the spot in the yard where they had been just a few minutes earlier.

"Let me show you around the house," the older woman said.

"No, no," Sue protested. "It isn't necessary."

The woman was making no attempt to find the file she had mentioned. When could she say something without seeming rude, Sue wondered. She felt like Hansel and Gretel, trapped by a witch and she feared there would be repercussions if she said something to anger this woman.

Mrs. Todhunter stood up and headed toward the dining room. Everything, the colour scheme, the rather old-fashioned damask upholstery on the chesterfield in the living room, the photographs of children, reflected this woman's taste. Sue was determined not to ask about anything.

"Now my dear, the upstairs."

"Did your husband keep his papers there?"

"Some of them."

"Mrs. Todhunter," Sue said, reining in a tone of impatience. "I'm very sorry, but I don't have time. I can leave an address and if you find anything, you can write to me. I'd be prepared to come back if there's something of interest." Sue was not about to tell her that she would let Thomas know so he could follow up on it for himself. Nor that once she left, she did not expect to hear anything.

"I'm sorry, my dear," Charlotte said as she emptied a drawer in a desk. "I could have sworn my husband found something."

"Yes, of course." Sue backed away, turning toward the door. "I have to go now," she said.

"What a shame. Do come to visit when you come back to Stratford."

Sue was so relieved to reach the street that she sighed loudly. Sometimes, trying to retrace the past was a mistake. But she was glad at least to know where Jerry had grown up. When she walked to where she had parked the car and drove down to the river, a breeze was blowing from the west. Small waves rippled on the surface of the water and leaves stirred on the trees. A beautiful spot, she thought. But she did not stop.

Trucks passed on both sides when she finally reached the highway. As she drove in the middle lane, they hurtled up behind and even though she was going above the speed limit, overtook her. As she got closer to Toronto, the number of lanes increased until it felt like she was surrounded by a mass of hurtling metal. From a distance, the large buildings began to rise ahead until they sprawled across the entire landscape.

Disappointed not to find a message from Hans when she returned from Stratford, though no longer expecting one, Sue slept fitfully. After her morning coffee and some muesli, she walked over once again to the old brick house where he met with clients. There was a note on the door to Hans's office — *Please do not disturb the session in progress.* An arrow pointed to the waiting room. Sue sat down. What would she say to him? She anticipated his displeasure, even his anger. Only once when she had asked him to stay over had she seen anything like that in a trapped look as he shook his head and walked across the room to the chair where his clothes hung lopsided on the back.

"Don't you see that I can't do that?" He had reached for his trousers and socks and dressed quickly, then headed down the stairs to the front door.

"What is it?" she had called, following him with only a blouse she had grabbed flung around her.

"I can't stand it. You're not doing anything wrong in asking for what you want. But I can't give it."

"It's all right. I understand."

"No, it's not all right. It's not all right at all that I can't give it to you."

"Then I won't ask." Please stop and talk. Please. She had heard these words in her head, but had not said them.

"That's not the point."

Probably it had not been the point. Probably it still was not the point, but she wanted to see him anyway, to hear what he would say, especially after he had called a few weeks earlier to tell her Heather had gone to England to be with her parents for a while. She had suspected he might be frightened to find he had no excuse not to see her.

The door of Hans's office opened and a man came out. He reached for a coat on the back of a chair. Another woman had come in by then and Hans nodded at her. Then he saw Sue.

A smile crossed his face and then his brows furrowed. "Hello," he said in his deep voice. "Come on in for a second." Closing the door behind her, he indicated a chair. "I have a few minutes before seeing the next client."

"I didn't want to make any assumptions when I didn't hear

from you," she said, knowing that her sense of time had become distorted, that a week or two of no call felt like months.

"What do you mean?" he asked. "I've called. I must have left at least half a dozen messages in the last week and you never returned them. Then, finally, I got through to someone and asked for Sue. When you came on the line, you said you'd never heard of me. What was that about? I thought you didn't want me to call you anymore. I thought you were angry."

"I don't get it," she frowned. "I didn't get any phone calls. And I didn't talk to you. That wasn't me."

"What do you mean? It wasn't you? I certainly thought it was."

"I don't understand."

"Well, neither do I." He took out his desk diary and read out a number.

"That's not my number," she said. "Whose number is it?"

"I thought it was yours."

"Well, it isn't. That's why I haven't returned your calls. What kind of psychic are you anyway?" she asked. "You've called me before. You had the right number then."

"I lost your number and when I looked it up, I must have used the one for another Sue. At least I got the right name." He was suddenly playful, as if trying to distract her. "Mostly I don't add surnames to my client list because I don't know them."

"You know mine."

He shrugged.

"You told me once not to make assumptions. So I didn't. But now I don't know what to think." Still, she was relieved to know he had not been avoiding her. She looked at his left hand. The gold wedding band was still there.

"What was that number again?"

"Here it is. It's all yours. It's no help to me, obviously," he said. "Call it. You'll see."

"Maybe I will."

"Go ahead."

So she picked up the telephone, expecting to get an answering machine. *Hello, this is Sue* — another woman's message — *I like getting messages, so please leave one.* What she did not anticipate was that someone would answer.

"This is going to sound preposterous," she began. "I have a friend who's been trying to reach me and he seems to have used your number instead. Are you Sue?"

"Yes, I'm Sue."

"It's my name, too."

"Well, I guess that explains it. I've had these weird calls and the guy thinks he knows me. I've told him I've never heard of him."

"He has the right number now." She wanted to say he was a psychic and that he'd had everything wrong in spite of that, but that had nothing to do with this stranger.

When she hung up, Sue looked at Hans and rolled her eyes. "I don't think I'd trust a psychic's telephone book."

"Looks as if I shouldn't have either."

She smiled nervously.

"I need to talk to you," he said. "But there isn't long enough now. Can we arrange a time?"

"Coffee somewhere on Bloor Street?"

Hans's voice was warm, but almost detached at the same time. She supposed it was because he would be seeing a client as soon as she left.

When she walked away down the street, she imagined birds taking seeds from the feeder outside a window at his farm and bright flowers in beds around the house. She had seen them in a photograph on his desk. Then there would be the pond where he swam early, where he sat with his coffee and watched the sun rise.

Hot, tired, and pensive, she soaked in the tub until she became sleepy. After that, she cut her toenails and finally dropped into bed with a book to read. She was not prepared for the telephone when it rang after eleven o'clock that evening. What flashed through her mind was an emergency of some kind, a call from a hospital. Her heart started racing.

"It's me," Hans said.

"It's kind of late, isn't it?" she said. "Are you all right?"

"I was thinking about you."

She noticed his words were slightly slurred.

"You know what I've been doing," he laughed.

"I don't think I want to know." She was taken aback, but not entirely speechless.

"Well, I'll tell you anyway," he said. "I had a couple of good stiff drinks and I've been...."

He was undressing her. She did not want to hear it. "Please, Hans," she said. "Don't say any more." She did not say so, but she would have minded less if he were sober.

"I won't bother you," he said abruptly and hung up.

Was this the man she had fallen in love with? The entire day had been bizzare, including Hans's story of the wrong phone number. And now this drunken phone call? It seemed crazy. What was going on? She lay awake, trying to make sense of what was happening until finally she rolled over and fell asleep.

*

When he woke the next morning, Hans was embarrassed. He would have to wait to call Sue when she returned from school late in the afternoon. It was just after five o'clock when he reached her.

"It isn't even flattering," she said coolly. "To have someone telephone when they've been drinking to make sexual allusions."

"I'm really sorry," he said. Rusty nuzzled at his knee. He heard Sue sigh.

"I'll see you at the restaurant tomorrow," she said.

"All right." He wondered how he could tell her he could not stand the tension, that he could not go on seeing her. He tucked his fingers under Rusty's ear.

"What do you think I think when you don't call? What do

you think that's like?" she asked. "And then you get drunk and insult me."

"I said I'm sorry." He wondered if he were more worried about his marriage or that he could not live up to her husband, that there would always be a ghost between them. "I feel guilty about having become involved with you," he said. "I'm just a basket case. Why would you even want to hear from me?" He was convinced of what he said, but when he heard it out loud, he hated that he was almost whining.

"Well, that's a good question. But I do want to."

Oh Lord, he thought. He could remember every line in her body and their hunger when they had been together. He could not resist. "So could I see you tonight?"

"Tonight?"

"Uh-huh."

"All right."

"I'll grab a chariot." He would change and have a quick bite and be right over.

"Where are you coming from?" Sue asked.

"The country. The drive takes just under an hour."

She did not ask who would feed the horses.

By seven, he was at her door. He let the knocker fall lightly. *Tap, tap, tap.* She did not answer. It felt as if this might be retribution, driving down the highway to find an empty house. He went back onto the sidewalk and looked up at her window. There was not even a light anywhere, but as he stood and wondered what to do, the front door opened. She beckoned to him and he cleared his throat, suddenly nervous again.

"Hello," he said, walking across the grass.

Once inside the door, he put his arms around her. Then he backed away. He was suddenly so uncomfortable that he wanted to turn and run. He wished he were back at the farm. It had been exciting before, but the allure of the mysterious had disappeared and there was more at stake now.

"I think I'd better drive back tonight," he said. "I didn't

make any arrangements for the animals."

"Do you have to leave right away? You've scarcely arrived."

"No," he said. "But fairly soon."

"C'mon up to the studio," she said. "Let me show you what I'm working on."

He followed her, determined that he would not initiate or get drawn into anything. He was surprised to see a huge cockroach in bright colours on the canvas on her easel.

"This is something new," he said, looking more closely.

She told him how she had been drawn to these insects. "They seem to have a life of their own. They've turned into canvasses that would only interest some dealer or collector with eccentric taste."

"There'll be someone."

"Is that psychic knowing?"

He looked down and noticed he had a hole in his sleeve. His stomach would bulge slightly over his belt if he raised his hands over his head and his sweater would rise also. She turned to look at him. "Do you have others?" he asked.

She pulled out a few sketches and another painting.

"What about the perspective?" she asked.

He picked up a charcoal pencil and began to draw a ladybug on a sheet of sketch paper. "See the shading on the body. And on the ground behind it." He began to relax as the lines flowed.

"I don't get that very well, do I?'

"I wouldn't say that. You've only missed a stroke or two."

"Let me try." She drew another bug and highlighted it.

He stood behind her, smiling. "Way to go."

As they walked downstairs, she asked if he would like a cup of coffee.

"No, but let's sit for a few minutes in the kitchen," he said. "It was a bit of a rush to get here." Something reverberated through him that seemed to portend some insight. He ignored it.

"On Saturday I marched in a protest," she said. It had been a beautiful, sunny day when over two hundred people had converged on Queen's Park. "Jerry would have added his own flair and passion," she said. "Many people say they miss him at these events. For them, I guess he's still an inspiration."

"Good for you," he said. "You know, you're such a caring woman." He supposed she was unaware how much it bothered him when she spoke so glowingly of her husband. It was not something he would mention as he knew it was petty of him and that she had every right to do so.

Sue merely smiled.

"I have a new puppy," Hans said. "Takes time to train. And I've been worried about one of the horses. There's been a lot on my mind." He paused. "And I think I told you Heather has gone back to England. She's coming back, but it's a long time to be apart. I miss her."

Sue flinched. "Oh," she said. "Is missing her the stuff you mentioned?"

"Yeah." He sighed.

"I'm having trouble figuring out where to go from here," she said. "Sometimes with you I've felt as if I'm on cloud nine and then I fall through a hole. Like now."

He found he could not respond because a message started to emerge. "There's something happening," he said. "I don't know what. Hold yourself open for whatever it is."

"What do you mean?"

"I don't know. All I can tell you is that it doesn't have anything to do with me. You'll figure it out."

She put a slice of lemon in a glass of water. Light from overhead glinted on the golden peel. "I don't see how whatever it is can have nothing to do with you."

"I saw a woman this week who wasn't ready to believe anything I said," Hans said. "I wondered why she came. At some point, I asked her what her mother was worrying about, why she was hanging around. 'My mother's dead,' she said. I told her I knew that, but she was still worrying about something. She looked at me as if I were crazy. 'What happened to her teeth?' I asked. 'Teeth?' she repeated, her face white. 'Yes.' Then, she sat up straight as if a current of electricity had run through her. 'How did you know? My mother would never go anywhere without her teeth. Even to bed. But somehow she was buried without them. We found them afterwards. And it's bothered us ever since.'"

"God, that's eerie," Sue said. Although not more eerie than sitting there together.

His face brightened and he took her hands in both of his. "You've been such a gift to me," he said. "I'm grateful. Thank you for offering me your heart."

"It's a bruised and battered heart, you know."

"It's gone through a lot, I won't deny that. And I've been the cause of some of it. Is it out of the repair shop now?"

"I hope so."

"Me, too. And I'm sorry to have to disappoint you tonight. I want your friendship and respect, but I can't go on with the other. Even though it was amazing." He felt badly when he saw the sadness that flashed across her face, then relaxed when she smiled slightly.

"I suppose it was destined to crash," she said. "Not because we don't care about each other."

"Maybe because we do," he said.

They sat quietly for a few minutes.

"Sue," Hans said finally. "Go back as far as you can and look at what comes up. There's something there you need to grapple with."

"I'm too tired."

"Do you know what I'm talking about?"

She sighed.

"It won't destroy your life as you've always imagined. It will give you what you need to go on."

"Guilt. Pain. Remorse. Sorrow. Isn't there enough of that already?'

So she does know, he thought. "Yes, there is enough," he

said. "But this isn't new. It's already there and it's worse because it's never been attended to. It's like a cyst or a wound that goes on festering."

"I've been happy."

"You know as well as I do that it's possible to find happiness even when there are huge pieces of our lives that are painful."

"Okay," she sighed. "Okay."

6.

SUE RETURNED FROM A BRIEF WALK to red flashes on her answering machine. Calls were more rare since Hans had stopped contacting her and she was surprised from a cursory glance at the machine to find at least three of them. The first was a colleague reminding her of a meeting. Then Thomas asking her to call. Another call from Thomas.

"It's about Florence."

His voice sounded frantic. Sue had talked to Florence only two or three days earlier. Trying to prepare herself for anything, she drew in a long breath and released it slowly. She had no way of knowing if this call was as urgent as Thomas's increasingly worried voice made it sound. She did know it was important to get back to him quickly.

"Oh, Sue, I'm so relieved to hear from you," he said.

"What is it?"

"Florence was in a car accident late yesterday. She's in hospital in London. Her chances aren't great."

"Oh my goodness. What happened?"

"I'm not sure. She was in London. She goes there for appointments for her heart and things like that. She has angina sometimes."

"Yes, I know."

"I think someone hit her broadside, turning left. I think she had the right of way."

"Poor Florence."

"She keeps asking for you."

"I'll go right down," Sue said, surprised that Florence wanted that. "As soon as I can throw a few things in a bag and get in touch with the principal at my school."

"I'll meet you at the hospital," Thomas said. "I was in London last night and I'm going back now."

"Could you find me a bed and breakfast there?"

"I'll check the Internet."

On the way to London, it was all that Sue could do not to think of what it would mean to have Florence die. Florence was the keeper of all the memories connected to Jerry before Sue knew him. Well, Martin was also. But Florence was the significant link between Jerry and the son he never knew.

When Sue arrived at the hospital, she parked and rushed across the street. At the information desk, she learned that Florence was no longer in intensive care. She spoke to a nurse on the floor who told her it now seemed likely that Florence would recover.

"Don't stay too long," the nurse said. "She tires easily. Or, if you do stay, sit quietly with her."

The moment Sue walked into the room, the older woman's eyes lit up. She was covered with bruises and bandages and her left arm was in a cast. "I'm so glad you're here, my dear," Florence murmured. "This is such stupidity. The drivers nowadays are an outrage."

"Yes," Sue said, grateful Florence could still say so.

"I don't remember if I told you that I've made you executor of my will. The main beneficiary is Thomas. Not that I have so much to leave, but Jerry set up bank accounts in Thomas's and my name that I promised to see went to Thomas. I have everything written down and in a safety deposit box in Chatham. Thomas has its number. I can't remember it right now. The key is in my jewellery box." She dropped off to sleep as soon as she finished her sentence and slept for an hour before she woke up again. Sue moved back to the side of the bed from the window where she had stood for a while staring out at the sky.

"There's something I want to know," Florence said. "I want you to tell me why you never had children."

Sue was so surprised she took a step backwards, almost as if the words had a physical impact. "You're too ill," she said. "You need to rest. Why are you asking me this now?"

"Because I've meant to. Because I know there's something there you haven't talked about and I think it's time, my dear."

Sue looked down at the floor. The question was so unexpected. "I did have a child once," she said. Her eyes were suddenly full of tears she could not control. She had never said this aloud before. She had willed herself not to. "I was sixteen," she said. "My mother made me give it up for adoption. I never could face having another."

"Why?"

"I don't know."

"And you never told Jerry?"

"No."

Florence was silent. She might have fallen asleep again, but when Sue looked at her, she was fully awake, her eyes unfathomable.

"I didn't feel as if I was concealing her. I never even saw the child. I wasn't allowed to. I know it was a girl and that she was taken from me and given to someone in an adjoining room. My mother told me I was to forget all about her. We never talked about her again. I had to go away from home for the last five months before the birth, to a place where no one knew me, so no one in the town would find out. It was a shameful thing in those days and you carry the shame of it, you know. You carry it forever."

"I know, my dear."

Sue wondered if Florence had had a similar experience, but the older woman was drifting off again. As she did, Florence reached out and held Sue's hand. When Thomas arrived,

Sue told him the older woman was doing better. And that Florence had told her about the will in the safety deposit box in Chatham.

He bent over and whispered to Florence. When he stood up, his face was puckered from holding back tears. They went out into the hall just outside the room.

"I hope she makes it," he said. "I pray she does."

"I think I told you the nurse said she would likely recover. She will be fine, Thomas."

He calmed down then. "Do you know, she wanted to talk to me about having a baby? Can you believe it?" he said. "She wanted to tell me things I would want to tell my children as they grew up. About my father. Often, she seemed to talk gibberish. It was as if she wanted to get it all said in case she died."

Sue reached out to hug him.

They went back into the room and sat quietly beside the bed until the nurse came to tell them visiting hours were over. As they walked slowly out of the hospital, Thomas commented that he had found a place for her to stay. "I'll take my car and you can follow in yours." Then he would leave and go back to Stratford.

"I can be here in an hour if you need me," he said.

"Yes, of course."

She rang the bell of a large brick bungalow on the bank of the river. When a woman came to the door, Thomas waved and drove away. The woman showed Sue to a room downstairs at ground level that looked out over the water. There was a breeze blowing the waves into white crests. She wondered if there would be a storm, but the sky was blue with only an occasional cloud.

"How long will you be staying?" the woman asked.

"One night. Perhaps two."

"I'll give you the rate for a hospital visitor rather than a tourist."

"I appreciate that. Thanks."

When the woman left, Sue closed the door and sat in a chair overlooking the water. She thought about what Florence had said. Hans and Florence had both known there was something buried even without her telling them. Neither would judge her, she knew that, knowing the even greater problem now would be if she continued to ignore the most significant event of her life. This was a truth she had known and yet been able to ignore. Suddenly, it was incomprehensible. Most of all, she wished she had told Jerry. She could not imagine now what their marriage would have been like had she done so or had Jerry told her about Thomas.

And what about her baby now? What could she do about her? All she knew was that she had carried a life inside her that was taken away when she was still a child herself. That there had never been permission until this moment to acknowledge that child or to acknowledge that something in her had died with that birth. Sue felt she had been robbed.

There was a tap on her door and she stood up and went toward it. The woman was just outside with a cup of tea on a tray. Her copper hair gleamed in the light, much as Sue's had when she was younger. Although her eyes were never the clear blue this woman's were. She looked like an angel, Sue thought.

"If you'd like a swim in the morning, you're welcome to use the pool," the woman said.

"Thank you." Sue thought she would want to get to the hospital the moment she finished her morning coffee, but she appreciated the offer.

"Did you bring a bathing suit?"

"No. I didn't think of it." As far as she was concerned, it was likely too cool.

"I'll leave one for you. You're about my size. I'll get it for you," the woman said, already halfway across the room.

Sue watched the retreating figure of the woman, thinking she was around the age of the daughter Sue had never seen.

*

That night she dreamed about the foetus in the pond again. A white uniform towered over her, denying her the sight of her own baby.

"It's better that you don't, my dear," the disembodied voice of the nurse said.

Waking to a dark, unfamiliar room, Sue wondered, better for whom? It was better that the boy not know, she had been told. Indeed, he never had known he made a child, that out there somewhere was a baby they had made together. Sue had stopped dating him as soon as she missed her first period. His family moved away the next year to another mining town, a new job for his father, a familiar tale in the world of mining. Before he left, he never asked her why she was gone for more than five months. He never talked to her at all. She used to hear about him from people who worked in that other town. That was how she learned that he had gone away to university the same year she did, but in a different city. It was not fair that she had had to go through all of it alone, whereas he never even knew it happened. Or so she had thought at the time. Told there was nothing he could have done about it anyway, she had known that had she told him, her mother would have punished her somehow. Nor would she ever have been forgiven.

This secrecy had haunted her entire life, compelling her not to tell even Jerry. It had lived with them, crowding the rooms of their time together. She fell asleep again. And when she awakened once more, even as she imagined holding a baby in her arms, she could remember the joy of being with Jerry.

The scent of coffee brewing and muffins baking permeated the room. She was aware there had been no phone call during the night and she sighed with relief as she stepped out of the bed. Before she drank her coffee, she would call the hospital.

"She's still sleeping," the nurse said.

"Has she been awake at all?"

"Well, not really. But she's very peaceful."

Sue wondered why Hans had not forewarned her about Florence's accident. Perhaps she expected too much of people. Even a psychic did not know everything. When he imparted some knowledge, it had more to do with growth and healing than it did with predicting an entire future. And yet he had told her he enjoyed the visions of something he could not figure out that pertained to the life of the person in front of him. More than once, he had seen such things in her future, like the swans.

Before she dressed, Sue decided to put on the bathing suit the woman had given her. Lying on her back in the pool, she looked up at a bright red, orange, purple, and yellow hot air balloon floating above the green trees on the other side of the river. She stayed suspended for a few minutes before swimming two lengths and climbing out of the pool. When she arrived on the deck after changing into her street clothes, she ate some pancakes overlooking the same river before driving slowly to the hospital. She was surprised to find Florence trying to move. And wailing.

"It hurts," she said.

"Did you ring for a nurse?"

"No one pays any attention."

"I'll go and make sure someone does." Sue was annoyed that a person in so much pain could simply be ignored. At the nursing station, two doctors were going through files and consulting with each other as well as with one of the nurses. Sue stood impatiently, waiting for them to notice her. She cleared her throat. Finally, the nurse nodded in her direction and as soon as one of the doctors started down the hall, came over.

"Look," Sue said. "My cousin has been ringing for a while. She's in considerable pain and…"

"Which room?"

"316."

"Florence Davis?"

"Yes."

"We gave her some painkillers an hour or so ago."

"Well, she still needs to see someone."

"Just let me check her chart," the nurse said. She headed down the hall to Florence's room with Sue behind her. One of the two doctors who had been at the nursing station stood beside the bed. There was a woman in the other bed as well, lying flat on her back with her eyes closed, grey hair streaming across her pillow. She looked to Sue as if she had had a stroke or heart attack. But she knew there was no way of knowing just by glancing at her.

"So Mrs. Davis," the doctor said. "Can you tell me what the matter is?"

"Everything hurts."

He checked her dressings and tried to soothe her. Sue was surprised at how gentle he was as he lightly massaged her forehead.

"You've had a rough time, ma'am," he said. "We'll see what we can give you. I think you're going to pull through, but you may be here for quite awhile."

When Thomas came, he said that perhaps they ought to start planning. If Florence were bedridden, she would not be able to go back to her house.

"Could she go with you?" he asked.

"With me? To Toronto? With all those stairs?"

"Well," he said. "Maybe it's too soon to figure it out."

They stood in the corridor, avoiding each other's eyes.

"What about you, Thomas?"

"Oh come on," he said. "She'd be so bored. Besides it was you she was asking for."

"I don't understand what's going on," Sue said. "I haven't known Florence nearly as well as you have and I'm not here to interfere in any way."

He turned and walked away. She did not follow him, nor did she go into Florence's room. Instead, she found the room for visitors where there was a television set and chairs with orange vinyl covers on the seats and backs. A man with haggard lines of fatigue across his face sat staring at the screen. He had been there the last time she had sat in the room.

It struck her that when Florence went home, she or Thomas might go down for the first week. It was fifteen minutes before Thomas returned with cups of coffee for both of them.

"Sorry," he said. "It's just I don't know what to do."

"'I'm sure we can figure something out."

"I suppose so. But it still feels odd that you knew my father and I didn't."

"Do you think I would have prevented him from seeing you?" Sue asked, puzzled. "You know very well I never knew you existed."

"It doesn't change what I feel sometimes," he said. "Sometimes, I imagine that if you hadn't married him, he would have come back to Stratford and found me and my mom."

"I don't think so. I don't think you do either. Although it is the sort of fantasy that children have, I imagine."

He grinned slightly, an abashed look crossing his face.

"Florence could come to Stratford with Kate and me for awhile," he said. "You're right. Those stairs at your place would be too hard for her. Our place is all one floor with the door at ground level."

"I suppose we're being a little premature. But I think it's a good idea to be talking about it. When Florence begins to worry, we'll be able to reassure her. She may want to go home and have us spell each other for a while, but whether she wants to go to Stratford or not, I'm sure she'll appreciate your offer."

"How is the B&B?"

"Very comfortable, thank you."

She wanted to tell him about the baby, but it did not seem like either the right place or time. Although Sue supposed eventually she would. It was all so confusing. Her daughter would be much older than he was. Yet, for Sue, she was the baby she had never seen. And the one to whom she felt attached in a way she could not to Thomas, content as she was that he had found Jerry's world even if only after his father had died. As for her own child, she now knew she might go looking for her. She might put her name on a list with some government ministry indicating that Sue would like to see her if she so wanted. What were the odds of that? And what would she say to a daughter after all these years? This was the kind of question one could ask of a psychic. Sue smiled a little at that thought.

"Something funny?" Thomas asked.

"Not really," she said. "Let's go back and sit with Florence."

All of life seemed contained within the walls of this room, with its florescent light and white sheets, where Florence lay. It struck Sue how many worlds there were that we never entered, or only entered for brief periods. Yet, while in them, they seem the entirety of existence. It had felt like that during Jerry's illness, both in the hospital and beside his bed in the living room.

Florence was calmer as the day wore on and it seemed that their company soothed her. Also, it was almost as if the doctor had wielded some magic by acknowledging her and paying attention. A nurse came into the room and greeted them pleasantly, but later, another was curt and dismissive. She talked down her nose at Florence, as if Florence were a child.

"She can hear you, you know," Sue said.

She could see this surly nurse talking loudly to older people routinely and likely as well to those for whom English was not their first language. It appeared she viewed them as trespassing on her territory. Sue could remember similar experiences with Jerry when he was so ill. Finally, she leaned over the bed to kiss Florence's forehead.

"I'll drop in tomorrow in the morning before I head back to Toronto."

Thomas kissed Florence also, and then he and Sue ate dinner in the cafeteria. He left shortly after to drive to Stratford, and she went back to the bed overlooking the river and lay awake in the dark. She was almost afraid to drop off to sleep, aware of what darkness might unleash in her dreams again. She was relieved to rest easily and not to remember any dreams the next morning.

She packed her suitcase early and went up to the dining room to drink coffee and eat home-baked muffins. There was fruit in a large pale blue bowl in the middle of the table.

"Help yourself," the woman said.

"Thanks." Sue took out her purse and paid her bill. "You've made what is a very difficult time easier."

"If you need to come back, give us a call."

At the hospital, Florence was smiling. "It's very kind of you to be here again. I hope I wasn't too hard on you."

"No, not really. Knowing how much you care made it possible to start thinking about what I never dared talk about before." She began to tell Florence what it had felt like to be pregnant, how it felt not to know what had become of her child.

"Tell me more if you want to."

"She's over forty now. My daughter. I don't suppose I'll ever see her."

"Would you like to?"

"I don't know. One moment I think I do, and then soon after I change my mind."

"You could go to the government and see if your child is looking for you. You could do it for her and if nothing comes of it, then you would have done all that's required."

"Do you think it's required?"

"Well, I'm not equipped to say really, am I? It's your life. But yes, I think it would be a good thing to do. For you. And if she's willing, surely for her."

Sue nodded and pulled the sheet and thin blanket up to just below Florence's chin. She was asleep again before Sue could formulate an answer. I'm not sure I want to, Florence. She wished she did not keep changing her mind. But how could she say that to Florence as she lay bedridden in hospital? And even as she stood there resolved to do nothing, she began to wonder about her baby, her daughter, again. It was time to find out what it would be like to meet a woman of over forty to whom she had given birth.

*

Sue procrastinated for days, almost afraid to uncover the long history that was now her daughter's life, her birth a distant shadow. But was it possible to ignore this reality any longer? What would she find if she actually pursued this search? The child she had borne could be a teacher or a doctor or a midwife, she supposed. A diplomat assigned to a posting in some foreign capital. Islamabad? Canberra? Or the Canadian embassy in Washington? She might be a hairdresser or a cook. Anything at all.

All these prospects seemed more like the story of a woman in some romantic novel, and not the story of a real person. But she realized she had no choice about starting this search now that the door had been opened. It was something she had badly wanted to do even though it was frightening. There would be a family somewhere. Did her daughter have children? It was likely she would have siblings.

When she could no longer take all the possibilities her imagination conjured up, Sue finally began to plan. She called the Ministry in Toronto, surprised at the lengthy process required. Forms would be mailed to her. She would fill them out and there would be a waiting period. If someone came forward, she would be notified by mail.

"All right," she said, her voice shaking slightly. "I'd like you to send me the forms."

Afterwards, she watched for an official envelope among all those others the postman dropped off each day through the mail slot in the front door. Then one day, there it was, a large manila envelope with her name on it. Her fingers fumbled with the edges, but she could not bring herself to open it. The contents would change her life in ways she could not even imagine and she put it on a small table in the hall. When she could not ignore it any longer, she finally took a letter opener and slit it open. She looked at the spaces she would fill in. *Surname ... Walters. First names ... Susan Catherine.* There were other particulars, but without that name no one would be able to tell her anything.

After Sue returned the form, it seemed like forever before a letter came telling her there was a match. *What information would you like revealed?* the government representative in the Ministry had inquired.

Sue was ecstatic now that she knew her daughter was actually looking for her. But when she felt the impact of this, she wondered if this young woman would be angry or merely curious. And whether, knowing how long it had taken her to do anything, if she, Sue, could even face her.

Having gone through those inevitable feelings, Sue wrote back that she would like to meet her daughter and to answer any questions she might have. Even then, she would have to wait to see if her daughter still wished to proceed. She was not sure how she would feel either way. She only knew that if the answer were positive, it was not a clear path even then as mandatory counselling by the adoption disclosure personnel would be required before they could go further. But all of that seemed worth it. As Florence had likely known it would be. That it was important.

When Sue went into the Ministry to meet with the counsellor, her hands were trembling. She sat behind a desk perusing the forms she had filled out.

"Well, Ms. Walters," the counsellor, a woman who wore thick glasses and appeared to be in her thirties, said. "My name is Shirley Meacham. I'm pleased to meet you and to know that it's good news. As you know, someone has been looking for you. Actually, for quite a few years now. It will be a surprise to her that you've come forward. Once we contact her, we'll let you know what her wishes are."

"I see," Sue said, wondering why she felt so numb. This woman who was her daughter might well tell her what a failure she had been as a mother. I don't want to meet her, she thought. What am I doing here? "I think I've changed my mind." Then she wanted to retract the words she had hardly realized she had just spoken aloud.

Shirley Meacham looked up. "Most mothers get nervous at this point," she said kindly. "Tell me what you're feeling."

Sue was frightened, but how did she tell a stranger that?

"Usually, there's some kind of resolution for people to find out who their birth parents are," the counsellor said. "And then, there are the health issues, the ones related to biological parents."

"I don't know anything about the father's side. He never knew about it, so he didn't even know she was born."

"That happened often in those days."

Sue wondered how long it would take for Shirley Meacham to form an opinion of her. Would she guess Sue was ambivalent and deem her irresponsible? Even with her kind face and gentle voice, it was this woman's job to draw conclusions about people.

"You'll figure out what to tell your daughter if you meet. It will depend also on what questions she asks. Do you want to proceed?"

"Yes, I will." She could not keep this secret any longer. And if there were, all these years later, anything she could do for her daughter, she owed her at least that much in amends for her silence, for her original betrayal. What mother gives away a child? Even as she knew she could not have done otherwise under the circumstances.

"We'll be in touch again as soon as we have more information for you," Shirley Meacham said.

"All right. My name is Sue Reid. I changed it when I married."

"Fine, Mrs. Reid."

As Sue walked out onto the pavement, the reflections in the glass of the windows she passed revealed the walk of a confident woman. She had expected delays and disinterest on the part of bureaucracy. And that such delays, all the red tape, might give her the time she needed to get used to the possibility of meeting her daughter. That did not happen.

"Jerry," she whispered. "We both had secrets. Secrets so huge we were sitting on minefields."

And she wanted both Hans and Florence to know, suspecting it would make both of them happy. She wondered what Maggie knew. She must have known something. Their mother must have given some explanation for Sue's long absence to her older daughter.

When she arrived back at the house, Sue hung her jacket in the hall closet before going to the telephone and dialling the familiar Vancouver number.

Sue did not know if her sister would be at home that afternoon or what she would say to her. She was a bit apprehensive when Maggie picked up at the other end.

"Hi Maggie," she said.

"What a nice surprise to hear from you," her sister said.

"Florence was in a car accident," Sue said, not able to say why she had really called yet.

"I'm sorry. Is she all right?"

"Well, it looks as if she'll make some kind of recovery, but no one knows for sure to what extent yet. She's still in hospital in London."

"I didn't really get a chance to know her except at the memorial." Sue could hear a clinking sound and thought her sister must be tapping her spoon on her habitual cup of coffee. At least Maggie would not have to run off to make coffee as they approached what promised to be a difficult conversation.

"What an incredible woman she is," Sue said. "She pushed me to look at some things about my past I've never acknowledged before."

"How would she know about them?"

"That's what I mean by incredible. Intuition, I suppose."

There was silence at the other end and Sue continued. "What do you know about what happened, Maggie?"

"What do you mean?"

"You know."

"You're going to have to be more specific."

"About when I was sent out of town as a teenager."

There was a pause and then her sister's measured voice. "There were kids who said you ran away with the circus and for a while I chose to believe that, I think."

"Why have we never talked about it?"

"You never brought it up."

"Come on. You're my older sister. You could have said something."

"I don't want to talk to you if you're going to attack me."

"You could have been there for me." Sue simply did not understand how two sisters could have lived their entire lives without ever mentioning something so important. Surely, Maggie must have been curious.

"I suppose you think I didn't want to be. All I knew was that it was a girl and that Mum told me never to say anything, never to bring it up. She said she would handle it with you."

"Oh, so you did know. You never really believed the story about the circus." She was baffled. "I can't believe it," Sue continued. "And guess how Mum handled it."

"Well, I can imagine that she gave you bloody hell and told you not to sleep around and..."

"No, none of that," Sue said. "She eventually made some restrictions about dating and stuff. But do you know what she did?"

"No, I don't know. I'm waiting for you to tell me."

"Oh, get off your high horse."

At that point, Maggie slammed down the receiver with an abrupt bang. Sue felt as if she had been struck. "Bitch," she said, even though in the next breath she knew she wanted to talk to her sister. She dialled the number again.

"Hello," Maggie said.

"Don't hang up on me, okay. I don't like it."

"Well, all right. But don't start in on me. I'm on your side."

"So this is what she did, Maggie. She never said a word. She told me never to bring it up. Just like she told you. And after that, until this week, I never have. I didn't even tell Jerry. Can you imagine? I had a child and I never told my husband. I never told one single soul," she said slowly, emphasizing the last three words. Then she continued. "But Florence knew there was something. Florence got me to talk about it. Hans, too. He said there was something I needed to look at."

"Hans?"

Only then did Sue remember she had not told Maggie about Hans. "You and I have a lot of catching up to do," Sue said.

"You have a man in your life. I can't believe you haven't told me."

"If you lived here I likely would have."

"Do you know, I'm not so sure about that. We've been trained so well to keep things to ourselves."

"Well, he doesn't really qualify as a man in my life. We might be friends as time goes along. I don't know."

Sue could hear Maggie's sigh. Then the words, "I don't think that's the point."

"No, I wouldn't think so. My baby is the point. But I have been involved with Hans, too." Even if now there was no future in it. "Everything is complicated. Except this woman, my child, wants to see me. Are there things about you that you want to tell me?"

"Oh, there must be, but nothing as momentous as either of the ones you've just mentioned. And I'm about to leave for the dentist. I'll call you tonight. Will you be there?"

*

After a long conversation with Maggie later in the evening, Sue slept deeply. She was awakened by the ringing of the telephone. The time on the alarm clock sad it was six ten. At that hour, she thought it could only be Hans, but he had said he couldn't handle seeing her. Since then he had not called. She reached for the receiver.

"Do you believe in magic?" Hans asked.

"What? Swans and things?"

"I'm calling from in front of your house."

"Oh, come on." Why was he doing this when he was the one who had called a halt to seeing her.

"I'm sorry I woke you up, but could I come in for a cup of coffee?"

"I want to go back to sleep," she whispered.

"All right," he said. "I'll hang up and leave."

She let the receiver fall onto the bed and her head sank into the softness of the pillow again. She was so tired. Her eyes closed. What was he doing in the city on Friday morning? He did not see clients then. And how did he know she had the day off and would be home? She picked up the receiver again, knowing that whatever was going on that she did not yet understand, she still wanted to see him.

"I'll unlock the front door," she said.

"I can make coffee and have it ready when you come downstairs."

"I don't want coffee." She knew she sounded cranky, but she was still too groggy to figure out what she wanted. Pulling on a pair of sweatpants and a T-shirt, she began to think again about her daughter. Would she look as much like her as Thomas did Jerry? It was a lot to absorb so quickly, even though it had been there, underlying everything, for most of her lifetime.

Hans leapt up onto the porch as soon as she opened the door. Reaching for her, he gave her a big kiss on the cheek. Then, he threw his jacket on a hook and sat in the armchair in the living room that had belonged to her father. It was covered now in a plain corduroy material.

"Can I sing?" he asked.

She looked at him in disbelief, no longer crabby, but not full of energy and enthusiasm either. Sing? His timing felt peculiar. Why was he here at all? Why was he acting as if very recently he had not been able to handle seeing her.

"I couldn't reach you last night," he said. "I tried for two solid hours. Your line was busy every time."

"So," she said. "It's not as if I was expecting you to call. Why are you acting as if I would have been? As if we saw each other the day before yesterday?"

Here he was as if he belonged with her. It was too much to grasp. Everything kept on changing. She recalled that after a visit to the north, Maggie had told her that the mine was gone. She said they only did open pit mining any more, that all the buildings on the surface that had supported underground mining that were once so familiar had been razed.

"They can't do that," Sue had said. "They're tampering with our childhood."

The nerve, the gall. Maggie had agreed, but there had not been anything they could do about it. She supposed everyone had that proprietary sense about their childhood, a feeling that extended into their lives, making most change difficult.

"I had second thoughts," Hans said now, hesitating.

"Men," she said. This was about what *he* wanted. Not what she did. "Right?"

He dropped his head contritely. "Well, men are different from women," he said. "But the truth is that I care about you. I like walking and talking together and going out to lunch with you."

She noticed the newspaper he had put down on the stairs. "Is that the *Sun*?"

"Yes."

"Don't tell me you read that lousy newspaper."

"I already read the *Star* this morning. In the doughnut shop while I was waiting to drive over here."

"What about your horses and all those other animals?" She wondered, had she asked him to come at this hour, if he would have. "And what are you doing here on Friday?"

"Friday is the day I woke up in the middle of the night and knew I wanted to see you," he said.

"Is that so?"

He put his arm around her.

"You know what?" she said. "All of a sudden you're moving awfully fast." She wanted him to stop so she could get her thoughts sorted out.

"Do you want me to slow down?" Hans asked.

"I want you to be who you are," she said, even though she would prefer him to do what he had suggested "But I am who I am. And I don't want to feel only that I'm along for the ride. I need time, at least, to catch my breath."

"Well, all right then," he said. "That's doable."

"I told Maggie about you yesterday."

"You did?" His tone expressed surprise.

"I did."

"What did you tell her?" He looked nervous, as if her sister might talk to someone he knew, or someone who knew Heather.

"Oh, nothing much." It struck her that there would have been a better time for this conversation. Almost any time but this moment. "Is that why the line was busy?" Now he sounded relieved.

"Yes," she said. "There were a lot of things I hadn't told her."

"Are you all right?"

"Well, not really. My life is like yours. All hidden and divided into compartments. How can I know what I feel?"

"I know what I want."

"And what about Heather? Did your psychic knowing discover different realities in the last few days?"

"That has nothing to do with it."

"You don't think so? Is she still in England?"

"You're impossible. But yes, she's there. I've told you that."

"Oh well," she sighed, wondering if Heather's long absence meant separation. A whole retinue of characters, from parents to friends to Jerry, perched on her shoulder, watching and judging, and found her wanting. It was not at all how her relationship with Jerry had developed.

"My love," Hans said.

She did not say anything, but she let him hold her and they found their way to her room. Afterwards, when he went into the bathroom, she pulled the sheets off.

"I don't believe this," he said when he came back into the room. "Aren't we going to cuddle at all? Are you just going to dismiss me like that? I was just getting rid of the condom."

"I know," she said. "Help me turn the mattress, will you?"

"You're kidding."

In her reading, when he had said he saw something new in her personal life, there had not been anyone or anything she could think of. How could he not have realized he would be the man he was talking about? And why were they performing such a complicated dance?

"No," she said. "I'm not kidding. It's time for you to go. I have other things to do. But I will tell you that I can't think of anything that I want more, other than to meet my daughter, than to spend time with you."

For a moment, his face was suffused with a grin. "Hallelujah," he said. "But even so, you're not going to make me eggs and toast with jam, or coffee?" He chuckled. "Or, at least, let me make some."

"None of the above."

"You *are* kidding."

"Well, yes, I am, but as soon as you eat, you can take your *Sun* and run."

He put some bread in the toaster and buttered a slice as she poached an egg. When he was finished eating the toast, he stood up and grinned.

"The 'Sunshine Girl' is on page 3," he said.

"Very funny. Just take it and get out of here." She shoved him gently through the door and closed it behind him. She almost needed to pinch herself to make sure this incident had not been just another dream.

*

Crumbs from the toast Hans had eaten cascaded onto the floor tiles and dishes were spread out on the counter. Sue sat over a cup of coffee, looking out the window. What was she supposed to do now? She had hustled Hans out of the house with the intent of going to Kensington Market, her list on the table with two cloth bags to take to the small stalls where she often bought fresh produce. She could have waited until Saturday morning even though she liked shopping when the area was less crowded. Now it seemed ludicrous not to have let him stay, not to have basked in his presence.

The telephone rang and she tried to ignore it. The house next to the rocks and bush where she had spent her childhood flooded her mind. Sometimes she longed for the solitude of a cabin in the wilderness. That she had decided to rent out the one she had shared with Jerry now struck her as foolish. When she'd spread his ashes and planted a tree in his memory, she had been distraught. How silly she had been, not able even to spend the night there on her own. She had driven out to the highway and taken a room in a motel before driving back to the city the next day. A week later, she had put the cabin up for rent. Yet there were times she still longed for the quiet, thinking she was ready to handle it. Maybe there would come a time when she could go to the cabin with Hans. She finally picked up the receiver just before the answering machine would have taken the call.

"May I speak to Mrs. Reid, please?"

"Speaking," she said.

"The social worker has made contact with your daughter," the woman's voice said. "Yes," Sue said.

"She'd like to meet you. If you're willing, I'll give your phone number to her."

"Yes, please."

"Her name is Gwen Bennett."

Sue did not know what to say. She could not imagine naming her baby Gwen, but she would have to get used to it. She had given up her right to name the child. She had given up everything.

"She'll likely call you in the next few days. Is there a time that is better for you?"

"Evenings usually." An easy question to answer. But what would she say when the time came?

"I'll let her know."

"Thank you."

For the next few days, Sue hovered over the telephone, expecting that as soon as she left the house the call would come and she did not want to miss it. Forty years after the momentous event, she would receive a call from this woman who was out there somewhere, connected to her even though the umbilical cord had long ago been severed. Even if Gwen looked like her, Sue could not picture her. Whenever the telephone rang, her hand shook as she picked up the receiver. It was just as apt to be a stranger's voice as it was to be someone she knew. This time, it was a man offering a free estimate on some painting. She put the receiver down again, wondering what kind of woman her daughter was. Why had she waited so long to do this? It felt unnatural not even to have been curious, not to have told anyone until now. She hoped Gwen had been raised in a home that cherished her. She hoped her daughter would be forgiving.

When it was time to leave each day, Sue walked out of the house reluctantly. It would be hours until she was back again. She would check her answering machine, but she was afraid if she did not take the call herself that this woman might give up. As it turned out, in the days that followed, no call came from Gwen Bennett. Sometimes, Sue wondered if she had been dreaming about the whole thing. Until, one night, there was finally a woman's voice on the answering machine and Sue listened to it a dozen times, trying to memorize the unfamiliar tone. The lilt.

It was a short conversation when she reached the number. "I'd like to meet you," Gwen said.

They agreed on a café on the Danforth for the upcoming Friday.

"I don't remember the name of it," Gwen said.

Sue wrote down the directions and checked her calendar, silently rearranging her plans for after school that day. No matter what, she would be there. It would not be a day off for her, but the time Gwen suggested was after school let out. Sue was almost afraid to ask any questions. Or to say how odd it was that they presumably lived within a few subway stops of each other. It boggled her mind to think that was possible, that they had likely been that close and never encountered each other. It was likely more appropriate for Gwen to do the asking and commenting. She hoped this unknown daughter would bring pictures of herself at different ages. The whole forty years was blank and she wanted to know something about the life Gwen had led. It seemed unlikely she would ever tell Gwen that some of the children Sue went to school with as a teenager thought that for those five months she was hidden away, about to give birth, she had left town to join the circus.

That night, Sue scarcely slept. She rehearsed what she would say. She did not imagine that when the time came she would wait for over half an hour, frantic that she might be at the wrong café with no way of getting in touch with Gwen. And if Gwen had run into some snag in her plans, she would not have a way of reaching Sue either.

"Are you Sue Reid?" a polite voice asked as Sue pored over her calendar to make sure she had marked the right date.

Startled, she looked up to see a woman with slightly greying hair leaning toward her. "Yes," she said.

"I'm Gwen Bennett. May I sit down?"

"Yes, of course."

Gwen wore a gold band on her left hand, a smooth hand with a few freckles. Sue looked from it to eyes the same hazel colour as her own, flecked with small dots like honey. Otherwise, there did not seem to be a resemblance. The younger woman was quite stylish in a dark suit with a red patterned scarf at the neck, her glasses modern with lightly tinted lens.

"I think I got the times confused," she said. "I'm glad you waited. I've wanted to find you for such a long time. I can't imagine that I could have almost bungled it."

Sue was at a loss for words. The juxtaposition of the memory of lying in the hospital knowing she would never see her baby's face, never hold her, and the face of this woman who sat down across from her left Sue reeling. She felt nauseous and dizzy. Tears sprang to her eyes, but she held them back. This was the most important interview of her life and she was wholly unprepared. She wanted reassurance, a sense of herself as a worthwhile person. This woman had the power to give that or deny it.

Selfish, an internal judge announced. *Selfish beyond measure.*

Yes, Sue thought. This is about my child and what she might be feeling.

Well, the judge intoned. *You finally got it.*

"I needed to know something about you," the younger woman said. "I don't know where to begin though."

"You were born in this city, but not because I lived here," Sue said. "I had relatives who did and this is where my mother sent me. I was sixteen. The boy never knew. He moved away from town not long after I returned. He didn't even know I was pregnant."

"I want to know about *you.*"

"Health?"

"Yes. And did you have other children? Do I have any half-brothers or sisters?"

At that point, Sue knew she was going to disappoint the

younger woman. What could she tell her that would give her a sense of connection? Here she was with only a deceased husband, a stepson she had not known about, and a married lover. Sue saw her life through this woman's eyes and found it wanting.

"No," she said. "I didn't." She wanted to say that losing her baby was so huge that she could never face having another child. But she could not utter it out loud, the disappointment kept at bay for most of her life. Instead, she asked Gwen if she had any brothers and sisters.

"Yes. I grew up in a large family," Gwen said. "I'm the oldest and the only one who was adopted. My father was a pilot. He died three years ago. I miss him. My mother is still alive. She lives in Kincardine."

"Does she know you're meeting with me?"

"Yes. She knew I wanted to find you. She always said she understood. She told me what she could about your background, but it isn't the same as hearing it from you."

There was something detached, almost clinical, about Gwen's demeanour. Sue wondered if she, too, was trying to restrain her emotions. There was no script for most situations of moment in one's life. There certainly was not for this one.

"Gwen Bennett," Sue whispered.

"What would you have called me?"

"I don't know."

"Surely you must have thought of names when you were pregnant."

"Naming you never occurred to me. You were whisked away the moment you were born. I never saw you. But Gwen is a lovely name."

"Yes. It's one of my mother's names."

Sue tried not to show any reaction, but she tightened her lips slightly. "Do you have children?" she asked.

"Yes."

"Well, I suppose I thought of names the way a teenaged girl

would. The movie stars. Something a little unusual. There wasn't anything like ultrasound then that told you whether your child would be a boy or a girl."

"It must have been awful for you."

"When I felt you rolling around inside me that frightened me. I scarcely knew how you got there, although I did know. I remember hearing my mother call to see if I could go to Toronto to stay with some of her relatives. She didn't know I was listening."

Sue could hear her mother's voice clearly: "This is a big mess," she had said into the telephone. "I never thought Sue would get into this kind of trouble." But Sue did not tell Gwen that, or that she had thought of her situation in that way also.

"How long did you stay in Toronto?" Gwen asked.

"Five months. I went back north a week after you were born. I never had a chance to talk to anyone. There were absences of other girls when I was in high school. If anyone was gone for five months or so, you always knew why."

"I have three children," Gwen said. "A boy and two girls."

"Are you married? A single parent?"

"Married. The children are actually young teenagers. I've worked most of their lives. I've been fortunate to do a lot of it from home."

"Are you happy?'

"I am really. Although I looked for you because not knowing where I came from, there was this void, you know," Gwen said, brushing her hair back off her forehead. "I always wondered. I didn't look like either of my parents or any of my brothers or sisters. They're all fair and I have this dark, curly hair." She shook her head as if to emphasize what she was saying. "I'm smaller than they are. Our interests are different. Not that I thought about it every day. But I did think about it."

"I wish I'd looked for you sooner, but I didn't think it would be fair to you," Sue said, knowing she might be making excuses for herself. "And I guess I've lived in a shell of sorts, putting my life into compartments," she acknowledged. "I didn't have much choice about it for the longest time."

She could see Gwen was looking beyond her. Sue studied her eyes as if there would be a reflection there of what the younger woman saw. A hand touched her shoulder from behind and a male voice said, "Sue." Looking up, she saw Martin and realized it was he who had distracted Gwen.

"I've been meaning to call to see how you're doing," he said.

"Hello, Martin. I'm doing fine," she said, a little irritated at this unexpected intrusion. But she knew it was not intended that way. If she had noticed Martin and he had ignored her she would have felt worse. "This is Gwen. Gwen, my friend, Martin. Also Jerry's friend. Jerry was my husband."

"Hello, Gwen."

Sue hoped Martin had something pressing to do and would not linger. She would not tell him Gwen was her daughter. How could she do that? This woman had never experienced her as her mother.

"When can you come over?" Martin asked.

"I'll call Emily later," she said. "I'm sorry I haven't sooner." She was glad that Martin did not seem to remember that she had suggested entertaining them in her home. "I've been busier than I expected to be. There's a lot of catching up to do when the time comes. I'm surprised to see you out here on the Danforth."

"Business," he said. "I'm just picking up a cake now, to take home for dessert."

"Nice to see you."

"Glad to meet you, Gwen," he said.

Gwen nodded. She watched the interaction like someone who was looking at an unfamiliar topographical map. The quizzical look, then the concentration to absorb new information. She did not appear to be at an understanding yet of what she was viewing, but how could she be? As Martin moved away, Sue turned her attention to Gwen again.

"Jerry died of cancer almost two years ago," she said. "I married late. He never knew about you. No one did. Until now. Jerry also had a child I never knew about. His name is Thomas. He lost his own mother just before Jerry died and came looking for Jerry."

That's enough, Sue, she told herself, surprised at how her words seemed to have run away from her. She felt as if she had been babbling.

"Sorry," she said.

"It's all right," Gwen said. "I want to know about you. You haven't had an easy life, have you?"

"Well, I've never thought about it that way. But I haven't really looked at it very clearly until recently and when I did I realized I wanted to meet you." She knew that was why she had avoided reflection on the past because buried there had always been the reality of this daughter. Her mother had been wrong to make her keep such a secret. Maybe some day she would be able to forgive her for acting as she had. It was surely what people referred to as "the times." You could not judge that kind of action by the same standards you acquired as you went through life. That old saying about hindsight surely applied to the discovery of her daughter and how she might have looked for her earlier.

"I would rather you didn't tell your friends just yet," Gwen said. "And not this Thomas either."

Those words would keep coming back to haunt Sue. Was Thomas, whose existence she had doubted, going to be an impediment for Gwen in letting Sue acknowledge and get to know her daughter? But she owed her daughter something. Surely, she owed her, at the very least, the respect of agreeing to what Gwen was asking of her.

"All right," Sue said. "What is it you'd like from me?"

"I need time to think about all of this," Gwen said. "And I'd rather you didn't try to contact me for now."

Sue drew in her breath as if she had been punctured. The

words came out of no where, altering the rapport they seemed to have been building. "I do understand. And I don't entirely."

"Well, I'm sorry about that. I can't expect you to. But I've waited a long time and now I need a bit more time. When I want to see you again, I'll contact you."

"Did I do something?"

Gwen shook her head. "No, it's not about you."

But it felt to Sue as if it must be.

"All right," she said. "Take as long as you need."

*

Even though Gwen thought her childhood had been almost idyllic, there were differences she imagined would not have existed had she grown up in a biological family. When she started to wonder about that other family, she had received love and support from the parents who had adopted her, making whatever route she chose to follow as easy as they could. Sybil Bennett was as good a mother to her as anyone could have been, but Gwen had wondered sometimes about where she came from. It might even have been easier to wonder about that when she had loved almost fiercely the father who had raised her, who had loved her as much as all his other children. Sometimes, it seemed, even more. They had shared a bond through a similar wry sense of humour. She could not imagine people anywhere who could have been kinder or more loving than Jim and Sybil Bennett. Not perfect, but almost.

She was distracted by bright colours in a flower shop and stopped to look. A bouquet of white daisies with yellow centres caught her eye and she reached for them. Then, carrying the daisies, she walked along the Danforth toward home.

Closing the front door behind her, Gwen let her bags drop to the floor. She breathed a huge sigh as she sat down at her computer in the small office where she wrote articles for magazines and newspapers. Here, in this house, she knew who she was. A writer, yes, but far more than that. Here, she was Tony's wife and a mother of three. She had parents and brothers and sisters with whom she had spent all of her life before meeting Tony, with whom she had ties that were based on that shared history, but how could she appreciate who she was entirely without knowing her birth parents? This lack had plagued her for a long time. Her mom had assured her she thought it a natural curiosity. Even necessary. Yet Gwen had sometimes worried that it might destroy all her bearings.

A breeze wafted through a window and she went out to the kitchen to open it wider. The flowers would look stately in a tall vase she found in the cupboard, a wedding present that had been given to them eighteen years earlier. She set it down on the counter that separated the kitchen from the family room. Both rooms looked out over a vegetable garden and a small birdbath.

Gwen had explained to the children about her birth mother. They loved their Grandma and had been baffled by the thought that Gwen might have another mother. As soon as she had a cup of tea, she would phone Tony to tell him about the meeting. Still somewhat aggravated by it, but unsure why, she went through the steps of making tea in the kitchen as if on autopilot.

At her desk again, she put down her mug and took out a sheaf of paper and scribbled some notes. A poem, perhaps. She was not sure. She hid such jottings in a drawer, always locked with a small key, her secret other life. What if she had been born to a hooker? Or a nuclear physicist? These things should not matter, but her vivid imagination painted pictures even her dreams could not envision. So these unfinished scraps expressed some of her quandaries.

All these years of dreaming of finding her mother to find a woman without other children, only the son of a deceased husband she had not met till recently, Gwen thought. The stark reality of this woman's life was not anything like she had imagined it might be. Would she be less uneasy if Sue had a son or a daughter, or perhaps both, who shared genes with her abandoned child? Gwen had never thought of herself as that before and tried to obliterate the thought for fear it reflected on the mom she had called by that name all of her life. She was not even sure she wanted to see Sue again.

Mulling over these thoughts, she went down to the family room where both the rowing machine and stationary bicycle looked formidable. These were machines Tony used, neither being her preferred form of exercise. A pair of sweats hung on a hook on the wall. She reached for them, then pulled on a pair of running shoes, wishing all the while they had a treadmill.

Tony found her sitting on the bicycle when he came downstairs half an hour later. Her hair was dripping.

"What's up?" he asked.

She got up slowly, her eyes glazed. "Ah well," she said. "How much easier life must be to know one's roots clearly."

He nodded. "How did it go?"

"I meant to call you."

"But?"

"I just needed to think. Or not think more likely."

He put his arm around her. "Where are the kids?"

"They're staying late at school," she said. "A project for Ted. Catherine has a swim class. I think Sybil said she was going to a coffee shop with her friends. You're early, aren't you?"

"Yes," he said. "I thought you might want to talk."

She nodded.

"Want a drink?" he asked.

"That, too."

7.

THE SUBWAY STATION at Broadview was milling with people of all ages and colours. As the train drew into the station, Sue found a place near the door so she would not be crushed in the rush to get on the train. As they crossed the bridge over the green expanse of the Don River and the ribbons of highways below, she stared at the tall buildings near the lake further south. She almost missed her stop and when she emerged was unaware of the familiar shops, did not even greet a man at the corner whom she knew well because he sat there every day, a pale blanket draped around his shoulders. She always smiled or said hello, calling him by name, whether she gave him change or not. This time she only thought of it too late.

The route to the house was so familiar that she followed the tree-lined street without seeing it either. Gwen probably would not want to see her again, she thought, and wondered if her daughter would have been more receptive if she had acknowledged how much pain losing her had caused. But the truth was that Sue had been relieved not to have to look after a baby. Although she had wanted to see and hold her, she had wanted all the other possibilities strung out ahead of her to remain intact. "I'm sorry Gwen Bennett," Sue whispered as she put the key in the lock of her own front door. "I'm sorry." Meeting her daughter now felt almost as difficult as the birth had been. Protected by her family then, the only apparent repercussion until now were all the years of her silence. Yet she would have been a different woman if she had never had this child.

From the front hall, Sue could hear the answering machine taking a message. It sounded like Hans's voice. She rushed to the kitchen to pick up the receiver. "Hang on," she said. "I'm here."

"I've been worried about you," Hans said. "Are you all right?"

"Not really." At the very least, she was preoccupied with a reality that was now tangible and it felt like it could take a long time to absorb.

"You saw her."

"How do you know? I mean, yes."

"And it didn't go well." He said this as if he were telling rather than asking her.

"No."

"I'm sorry. I should have warned you it might start off badly."

Sue sat down on the chair at the counter and leaned on one elbow. Tears formed in her eyes but did not fall. Until Jerry's illness, so much had seemed simple. But if she said so Hans would likely say that was based on what they had chosen not to share with each other.

"Do you want me to come over?"

"I have to mark papers," she said.

"Do you want to take a walk and drop by for a hug before you start in on them?"

"Yes," Sue agreed. "That's a good idea."

*

Surprised with the intensity of Hans's hug when he beckoned her into his office, Sue could feel heat rising between them. Uncomfortable that someone might see through the sheer curtains in his window, she still did not move away. Soon, a client would enter the waiting room on the other side of the wall. But what difference did her relationship with Hans make to anyone? She thought somewhat uneasily of Heather, far away in England and likely to remain there, when Hans pulled away abruptly.

"Oh my God," he said.

"What?"

"Time for an appointment."

She stepped back, glancing at the clock. Smoothed her clothes. "What I really want is a chance to talk with you," she said. "Can you come by the house later?"

He did not say anything.

"What's the matter?"

"Heather's back."

"You're kidding," she said.

"No, it's true," he said. "She came back early."

"Why do you let me get involved and then drop Damocles sword on me?" She grabbed her bag from the floor near the door, her red jacket and yellow bicycle helmet on top. Seizing them, she stormed down the stairs and unlocked her bicycle from the rail of the porch.

"Sue," Hans called as he came out the door.

She pretended she did not hear him as she rode away down the side street toward Bloor. She never wanted to see him again.

"He's a jerk," she muttered. "A jerk and a jackass."

"Sue," Hans's voice followed her.

She did not pay any attention. A man who could not make up his mind was not what she wanted. Rather one who put his hand just under her left shoulder blade to lead her effortlessly through whatever the music was asking for. A waltz. The rumba. The tango. She wanted to sail around the floor in the arms of this beautiful dancer, their steps in unison and their movement graceful. This was just not happening. They tripped over each other's feet depending on whether he was available or not. For a while, his attention had flattered her. She had enjoyed the flowers. The humour. The professions of attraction he had uttered. She should have taken the way Heather kept turning up in his conversation as an omen.

Now here I am, she thought. Rejected by both my daughter and my lover.

A car honked, jolting her back into the moment. Astride her bicycle, riding in heavy traffic on Bloor Street, her bright helmet and jacket offering some protection, she knew such lack of attention was still dangerous. She signalled a right turn and went north on a side street. She knew the area well. Before moving in with Jerry, she had lived in a house that looked out onto a park across the street and from her back bedroom she had seen trees. Sometimes, from a nest in the branches, a racoon had jumped onto the roof and scurried across it. One year, there was a family of them in a hole near the eaves that had to be evicted, the opening plugged. At the time, she had thought there were more racoons in Toronto than people.

In spite of this familiarity with her city, in her dreams her geography was still the northern rocks and bush of her childhood. The wide sky and the head frames of mines rising upward to greet the cloudless sea of blue or grey overhead were her signposts. It was there she had stood on the highway waiting for a shift bus to take her out to one of the mines a few miles from town. There she had worked in summers testing samples from underground for mineral content. How remote that place was now, not only in distance but also in time. She felt like an impostor. She loved a man who was no longer alive and another who still had a wife. And she was a mother, who had never known her daughter till now. A daughter who might choose never to see her again.

Giving birth must count for something, she thought. Surely. Another fleeting thought came as she realized she would soon be at work marking all those papers and that simply aggravated her loneliness. That Hans had known her meeting with her daughter would go badly at the beginning, but not to worry, was only slightly reassuring.

Ahead of her was a light that she pedalled toward. She then turned right onto Bathurst to ride the few blocks to a small grocery store. After she picked up milk, home was her destination.

When she arrived, she parked her bicycle beside the step in the backyard.

"Hello, Sue," Hans said on her machine. "I didn't mean to leave you thinking Heather was here to stay. She *is* here, but she'll leave soon. She intends to move in with her parents and look after them. And she's found work in London. I guess I'll have to find a lawyer. She doesn't want the marriage. Nor do I anymore. Please call me and let me know you're all right."

Sue felt confused, hearing that Heather was only back in the picture temporarily. Had she felt safe in knowing Hans's wife would return or was this new development even more than she could have wished for? Whatever she felt, she was going to have to get used to the shifting environment of her life now.

Hans added, "And don't worry about your daughter."

Sue sank down into the nearest chair. After all he had told her that had subsequently happened, she wanted to believe him now

*

In the space between waking and sleeping, Sue had travelled the distance to a child's world, to potholes in gravel roads and leaves burning in autumn bonfires. She could still hear the blasting under the earth and see the jack pine and poplar becoming denser the farther back she walked. Beyond that were more bush, occasional clear shining lakes, a few silver birches, and more rock. It was there, far from the edge of town, on a layer of pine needles under the trees, that her daughter had been conceived. Laying on the jacket of the boy with almost no name now, no face. The boy with dark hair and eyes who had likely been handsome in the way young boys just beginning to be men can be.

"I love you," he had said.

She had felt herself get wet as he held her, wanting something as yet incomprehensible. She had wondered what the hot, hard thing was pressed so insistently against her body. When her mother had tried to tell her about such things, she'd acted as if she knew already. Embarrassed, her mother had not persisted. Always pretending that she knew more, how complicated could it be after all, she'd had no idea how baffled she would be by sex when it happened. For a while, she had not even made the connection when her period did not come.

It was the nausea that had aroused her mother's suspicions. "We're going to the doctor," she had said.

Sue had thought her father might offer her reassurance, but he never mentioned it. A woman's secret. He died without ever acknowledging that she had given birth. It was like his absence after she was born. Maggie once said she had not understood why their father packed his suitcases then. There were two words for what he was doing: "war" and "overseas." Frightening words Maggie said she'd tried to fathom as she lay alone in her bed looking at the photograph on her wall of him as a small boy in a white sailor suit. Praying each night that he would come back, Maggie had not known if she was praying for the vulnerable child or the man in uniform who waved from the rear of the train.

After he left, Maggie crept into their mother's room whenever she was frightened. Their mother would ask if she had had another nightmare and she would hug her while Maggie looked at the picture of Dad, wondering what war was like. All she knew was how alone she felt. Sue could imagine it, sleeping in the empty bed she had once shared with Jerry. The pain and numbing fear that came with losing someone. After their father left, Maggie said their mother started to have headaches that made her frown and disappear into her darkened room, sometimes holding onto her stomach and retching. Nanny came north then on the train from Toronto to comfort her daughter and to see her grandchildren. Sue imagined her sitting in the kitchen, rocking the baby, the baby who was her, Sue, while Mum's face whitened at her own mother's questions, her hands so shaky her coffee spilled into her saucer.

Sue's mother would have glanced at a photograph of Dad in uniform. "He felt it was his duty," she probably said softly, head lowered.

"I still don't understand," Nanny would have persisted. "Leaving you alone with small children when he had a choice."

Nanny had never been without an opinion, no matter how much it might hurt. Maggie had told Sue their mother pushed back her chair and ran from the room then. It had not been long before she had another headache.

The loud ring of the telephone on the night table startled Sue.

"Hello," a male voice said. "It's Thomas."

"Thomas?"

"Did I wake you up?" he asked.

"I don't think so." Looking down, she saw she was wearing jeans and a sweater. "What time is it?"

"Nine."

She tried to figure out what that implied. "Is it morning or night?"

"Night," he said. "Are you all right?"

"I think so."

"I wanted to let you know Florence is doing much better. She's going to come and stay with Kate and me for a few weeks."

"I'm glad."

"Will you come and visit?" he asked.

"I'll try."

"I know Florence would like to see you."

"Something has come up," she said. "It may have to wait a little longer. Tell her I'll come when I can. Tell her I've found what I was looking for, but that it's not easy. I know I'm talking in riddles, but she'll understand."

"All right." He sounded bemused.

"How is Kate?"

"We're expecting a baby. I really called to tell you that." His voice rippled with excitement.

"That's wonderful," Sue said. "I'm so happy for you." The

thought of a lined bassinet with a new baby in it suddenly made her smile. "What great news."

"Thanks."

"How's Kate feeling?"

"A bit sick sometimes, but excited."

"When's the due date?"

"Not for seven months. It's really early, but we wanted you to know."

"Thanks," she said again.

"I wonder sometimes about raising a child," he said. "This happened almost too fast."

"I think you'll both be fine, you know. You and Kate."

"You sound more awake now," he said. "As if you know what day it is anyway."

As she hung up, Sue knew this would not be an unwanted baby. She recalled how much pain there had been when she pushed her baby out into the world. She had yelled in agony. The nurses came. She was scarcely able to sleep and had looked around for someone to console her. Afterwards, she went back to her grandparents' house on a quiet, tree-lined street in Toronto where the window of her room looked out onto the swing set in the yard next door. For a long time, this window's vista had remained her picture of Toronto, that and the mirror over her in the delivery room in the hospital.

In the middle of many nights, the sound of footsteps overhead had made a hollow sound on the floors as her grandfather limped around, checking the thermostat and turning the heat up. Afraid to go back to the north, she had nonetheless, desperately wanted to sleep in the warmth of her own bed in the house near the mine. She had wanted to be there with her parents and Maggie, even with her little brother, Wally. Even if he had always been a pest.

Instead she lived for the duration of her pregnancy with her grandparents where it was the unusual silence that had most bothered her. They were kind enough and saw that Sue was comfortable. Attempting to reassure her, they had told her she would take the train back to the north soon. Although Nanny wasn't a woman who could usually refrain from comment, they'd lived mostly in this unnatural quiet.

The Northland had travelled through North Bay, Temagami, New Liskeard, and Swastika to Noranda. It was the same train that her grandmother had taken north to visit when her father was overseas. It was to Noranda that her parents came to meet Sue when she returned after the birth. As they drove over the washboard gravel highway toward home, her father had said she could learn to drive the car as soon as the weather was better. And later that year, Sue drove around the block endless times, using a yellow flap that shot up from either the right or left side of the car to signal each turn, pulling up carefully at the stop signs. She had passed the test for her driver's license and her father had congratulated her, told her how grown up she was, but they had never once talked about the baby.

The telephone rang again. "Can I come and stay the night?" Hans asked.

"What about the animals?" she asked. "What about Heather?"

"Do you have to make comments like that?"

"I guess I do."

"Well?"

"Well, what?"

"Can I come and..."

"When?"

"I'm not very far away," he said. "I'm on my cell."

She should have known. Maybe some day she would get used to his spontaneity. She used to want life to be predictable, but that profound need had long ago dissipated. Hans's ways, which left her feeling unsettled, also delighted her.

"I miss you," he said. "You know I'm crazy about you."

"I didn't," she said lightly. "But I'm glad you're telling me because I'm kind of crazy about you, too." She could not use his words easily, words that for someone who was cautious about love, seemed far too effusive. And although she was not even sure she believed him, no matter how often he repeated himself, she was beginning to think there might be something to whatever was growing between them.

"Do you miss me a little when I'm not there?" he asked.

"Yes, of course. Terribly." She thought they sounded like teenagers. And it was that long since she had had similar feelings of being tugged between wanting someone at the same time as she felt somewhat crowded. The feelings had been there around the boy who had fathered her daughter. Then not until she was nineteen or twenty, when life seemed to go on without any crises, were there boys again, who, when they approached, set her hormones raging. She was far more careful then than she would have been had she not been through what she had experienced after that one brief interlude in the bush.

And now there was nothing to tell her why Hans's marriage had crumbled, even if it had, and she wondered if she ought to wear protective armour.

"Do I have time to get to the front door before you do?" she asked.

"Probably," he said. "But you'd better hurry."

*

Images of her daughter's dark curly hair and hazel eyes danced through Sue's waking and sleeping dreams. She recalled the sight of Gwen walking away along the Danforth. Without a telephone number or address, crumbs were all she had to piece together an existence for this woman. Sometimes, she woke up in the middle of the night to lie staring into the darkness. Why would Gwen want to see her only to then disappear again?

When the telephone finally rang and she heard the almost familiar voice again, Sue was as surprised as when the social worker had called a few weeks earlier.

"Would you like to come to my home?" Gwen asked. "The children will be at their cousins' place."

"Yes, thank you," Sue said warily, surprised by an invitation that implied a closeness she did not yet feel.

"I'm sorry it's taken so long to get back to you," Gwen said. "I had to prepare my children. They've known vaguely about you, but I had to be more specific. Also, I had to go and visit with my mother."

"Yes." All the things a thoughtful person would do, yet Sue had not imagined them. She felt as if she ought to have done so and was quiet, afraid she might say something that would precipitate another withdrawal, relieved as she listened to the sound of the voice continuing with the invitation. A date three days away. So soon, she could only hold her breath. A Friday.

"Will you be able to come then?" Gwen asked. "Late afternoon."

Sue looked at the calendar on the wall beside the phone for anything she might have planned for after class that day, determined to change it if necessary. She listened to directions about getting off at the Chester subway stop and going north on the street she exited onto to an old red brick house "with a porch my husband built recently."

"Yes," Sue said. "North. A new porch. Amazing, so close to where I live. Both of us on the same subway line."

"It is, isn't it?" Gwen replied. "See you Friday."

A new porch. What she would recognize as she approached the top of the street. Then she would meet Gwen's children. They were her grandchildren. Would they ever think of her as another grandmother? It hardly seemed likely.

"I look forward to it," she said. And she did, but she was apprehensive.

When Friday came, Sue closed the classroom door behind her and headed toward the street. She mulled over what Hans had said. This occasion would go well, not to worry. How she could keep from worrying about something so unprecedented, something so momentous, was a mystery to her. She was startled when a voice interrupted her thoughts.

"Hi, Mrs. Reid."

A tall youth flung his leg over his bicycle as she nodded at him. "Todd," she murmured. "Hi."

He said something about the weekend and she smiled as she turned away. There was no time to spare, she thought as she turned to hurry along the pavement. She would drop off books at the house before she set out for the subway. When she arrived, there was a motorcycle on the grass next door. Her fleeting thought was that the man who lived in a room on the third floor must be there. It was unusual for him to be around at that time of day as he usually sculpted in a garage a few blocks away. Once, she had gone there to watch him do the form for a bronze of a woman with her head in her arms. It now sat in front of a building on Bloor Street. Before she and Jerry had gone to Mexico, the man had loaned them a record to help with their Spanish. Jerry had come to watch the bronze in progress also. Later, when Jerry was dying, the man had listened to music with him for an hour one afternoon.

Since then, Sue had rarely seen him, but when she did he was always cheerful. Not like some of the vagabonds who had lived in the house a few years earlier. When they had left, the street had once again assumed its quiet character even with the constant ebb and flow of people only a short block away on Bloor Street.

At the corner, she stopped at a small gift shop. Inside, there were special teas and coffees, incense, boxes of chocolates. She did not know what Gwen's tastes were, but decided that even if she did not drink herbal tea herself she would likely find a use for it.

Arriving at the porch that had been described to her, Sue saw a brass knocker on cedar that had aged and darkened. As she raised her hand to knock, the door opened.

"Hi," Gwen said. "Come on in." She stood back, leaving

room for Sue to enter. "Thank you for coming."

She took Sue's jacket and hung it on a metal coat stand. Standing in the foyer, Sue could see a fireplace with a marble mantel in the room beyond them. The tiles were painted in bright colours of blue, green, yellow, and red. On the floor was a basket filled with logs. Sue handed the parcel to Gwen, who proceeded to open it.

"How did you know?" she asked.

"What?"

"That I like herbal tea?"

"I hoped you would."

Gwen brought in a tray and they settled into chairs near the fireplace. "My mother would like to meet you," Gwen said. "How would you feel about that?"

Sue tried to smile. It felt almost too sudden to have to confront the woman who had raised her child. In her own mind, she had not yet made this step. "I hope we'll have a chance to talk a bit more beforehand."

"Yes, of course. And I'd like you to meet my children before that, too."

Sue thought she ought to feel delighted, but instead felt sad. All that wasted time when she might have known this woman. Now, Gwen already seemed so familiar that it was uncanny. Not just small likenesses to her and other members of Sue's family, it was mannerisms that she recognized in herself, and the colouring of Gwen's skin and hair. There were so many ways in which a stranger might tell they were related. This suddenly pleased her.

"I have some photos to show you," Gwen said. "Of my family."

Sue saw in her children something familiar also. There were features that either she or Maggie had had when they were younger as well as resemblances to Maggie's children.

"I have a sister," Sue said. "You'd be able to tell that her children are related to yours. They're older now, of course."

"I'd like to see pictures some time," Gwen said.

Sue decided it was time for her to broach the possibility of Gwen coming to the house on Walken Avenue.

"Yes," Gwen said thoughtfully. "I'd like that."

After agreeing on a time, they went on talking. Sue listened intently as Gwen spoke about her children. Her face lit up then and Sue could tell how proud she was of them and of her husband.

"It's not the best of times for architects," Gwen said. "But Tony has done quite well, even over the downturn. With me working, we've been more fortunate than many. The kids do their share. Laundry. Dishes. Although you know kids."

She said it as if she assumed Sue, who merely smiled, did know. "Come look around," Gwen said.

Everywhere, Sue saw photographs of Gwen's children. There were some of Gwen as a child and one of her parents. She was not surprised that Gwen did not look at all like either of them, nor like any of the other siblings. Yet she could see they were a close family in the way they smiled at the camera and even cavorted together, clearly glad to be together. She felt a twinge of longing, not for the baby she had not kept at sixteen who had fared better in this family than in any environment she could have provided, but for the child she had never raised. For the unborn children she might have had. She found herself suddenly regretting the solitary way in which she had chosen to live her life.

Sue saw herself in a mirror as they walked up the stairs to the landing. A slim, handsome woman. She could also see that she had been beautiful once, that she might even be considered so still. The woman in the photographs of Gwen's family had a full figure with ample breasts and a round face. Sometimes she wore glasses, at others she was holding them in her right hand. Her clothing was neat, but old-fashioned with round collars and pendants from another era. Sue thought of her as a woman much older than herself.

"Do you mind if I ask how old your mother is?"

"Almost seventy."

So she was a lot older. When Sue thought about it that seemed natural. She had been so young herself when this woman and her husband had adopted Gwen. "Is she in good health?"

"Oh yes. Thank heavens."

"I'm grateful to her for giving you a home."

"All my life, I never felt that I was different from any of my sisters and brothers. She always made me feel loved and wanted."

"It's a relief to know that. You wonder, you know."

"Well, yes, I'm sure you must."

Sue nodded. If she could rewrite the past she would. One thing was certain: she would never have gone through a pregnancy at sixteen because she would never have succumbed to the flattery of a young boy who wanted only the satisfaction of the moment. Ah, but I cannot rewrite the past, Sue thought. And she could never tell Gwen that she had been conceived in such a cavalier way.

Gwen showed Sue the upstairs bedrooms, told her which one belonged to each child and then headed for the stairs to go down again.

"I'm grateful to you for giving me my life," Gwen said when they reached the kitchen.

Sue nodded.

"May I call you Sue?"

"Of course. I'm sorry I didn't ask you to."

"Can you tell me any more about my father?"

Sue stiffened.

"I'd like to find him, too," Gwen continued while she opened the refrigerator and took out some juice.

"He doesn't know about you. I thought I told you that. Perhaps I forgot." This was not something Sue had anticipated and she did not know how to respond. So much lay under the veneer that she had presented for so long.

"Yes, you told me. But I'd still like to find him. Maybe he would want to know."

The room lurched in a large, hazy circle. Plates on the walls appeared to be upside down and the photographs Sue had looked at so eagerly before now floated in space. It was as if she were lying or sitting on the ceiling, looking down on Gwen. She seemed to be horizontal or to be spinning.

"I can understand you might be curious, but I don't know what benefit there would be in telling him. And I have no idea where he is."

"I don't want to hurt you, Sue," Gwen interrupted. "But this is my life. I've lived for all these years wondering. Now I've met you and that's what I've wanted for so long. And there's still so much more to learn. Yes, about my birth family on your side. But I had a father. Even if all he did was plant a seed."

"Yes," Sue said. "That *is* all he did."

"I *have* hurt you."

What was she supposed to say? Sue wondered. Could she even bring herself to utter his name now? She did not remember her parents telling her she could not tell him, but it had been understood. It was difficult to know what might have happened had he not left town, how she could have kept it from him. But likely she would have. She had never told anyone else in that town. She had never told anyone *anywhere*, until Florence had begun to probe and Hans to intimate she had something in her past to deal with.

"His name was Peter Marshall," she said. "Probably a fairly common name. I don't know how you would begin to search for him."

"You could help me."

"How?"

"You could start by asking anyone you still know who grew up with you where they think he might be now."

"I don't know if I can do that." Sue was sure she could not. And yet how could she refuse?

Peter Marshall had had piercing green-blue eyes that she would never forget, that had seemed to see into her soul. Men do that when they want sex, she thought, but she had not known that soon enough. And he had likely just been learning himself. He had probably been filled with a longing he had not entirely understood yet either.

"Well, you asked how."

"I guess I did."

Gwen was silent.

"He was handsome," Sue said finally. "And clever. I remember that we were both good at algebra."

"Maybe he's a teacher or a scientist."

"Well, I suppose. Or algebra could just be a red herring."

Gwen looked disappointed. Her eyebrows, slightly plucked, were drawn together now to form lines over her nose. Her nostrils flared a little as she breathed deeply. As the tension in the room rose, Sue sensed that she was now an impediment.

"I could ask Maggie," she said. "My sister."

"Could you?" Gwen asked.

"Not that she'll know anything, but you never know."

"Will you call me if you find out anything?"

"Yes. Of course." Once she began to ask questions, other routes could open up. As she gathered bits and pieces of information, she could come up with something. It would be like a problem in algebra. She had loved problems. Why should this be different? In a country with the meagre population of Canada, surely she could figure out what had happened to a boy who had grown up with her in a northern mining town. There was Angus. Over the years, he had run into countless people from Maggie's and her childhood even though he had come from a different place. If he had ever met Peter Marshall, he would not have made a connection with their family. She would ask Angus. She would also phone the woman who had been the mine manager's daughter whom she still occasionally ran into at political meetings or movies in downtown Toronto.

"We'll find him," she said. "Or we'll find out what happened to him."

"Thanks," Gwen said. Her face eased and her eyes were warm again.

"When would you like to come to my home?" Sue asked.

"In a couple of weeks?"

"Well, then, what about two weeks today?"

Afterward, heading west once more on the subway across the bridge over the Don River Valley, Sue felt as if she were floating. One day she had known nothing about her daughter. Now, she had met her. Now, she could begin to get to know her. A flutter of anxiety marred the picture as she visualized Peter as a greying, balding man walking into it.

*

Hens clucked and pranced around his feet as Hans went through the wire door to gather their eggs, the clucking drowning out any other noises. Heather would soon leave for the day and he was avoiding any encounter with her by staying out in the yard longer than usual. He had already fed the horses. When he emerged from the henhouse, Rusty jumped up and down, ready to play.

He thought he saw Heather in the distance, opening her car door. When the engine turned over and growled, the sound turning into a hum as it disappeared down the driveway, he made his way back to the house. Soon, she would hand in her resignation. While in England, she had found a part-time job close to where her parents lived. Hans thought they had drifted toward this major change without either of them even aware it was happening. Or maybe she had been. But even when he had become involved with Sue, he had not intended that whatever cracks existed in his marriage would become insurmountable.

Inside, he put the eggs in the refrigerator, keeping two out to fry with bacon. There was a note on the counter and he left it there. I'm being ridiculous, he thought. He was going to have to deal with everything sooner or later. He put the bacon in the pan before picking up the note.

There's only one solution, he read. *We have to sell the farm.* But she knew he could not live without the farm. She knew that. He read further.

Please talk to a lawyer and get this in motion. I'm sorry that it's ended like this.

The bacon sizzled and he lifted it with a spatula to turn and move it to the side so he could crack the eggs open. He wondered if she had discovered his affair with Sue and had become vindictive. Surely, a lawyer would think of something he could propose to Heather so selling was not necessary. While his mind went on racing, he scrambled to find his calendar, his billfold, what he needed to take into the city for the day. Sheets still lay scattered on the bed, and the pillow was on the floor of the spare bedroom where he had been sleeping since Heather had returned.

On the road south to the highway, his thoughts were on his land and of how much he would miss it if it had to be sold. Whatever happened, he would have to find a place where he could have Rusty with him. Ever since his sister died, he had felt as if life were not unfolding as it should. He was often irritated by clients who had a sense of entitlement, and yet here he was, thinking he was special enough to deserve to keep this property in the rolling hills. He supposed he'd had more than he deserved, but that did not lessen his frustration.

After the leisurely drive south past farms and the occasional general store, he reached the 401, where all the vehicles seemed to travel at breakneck speed. He gestured to Rusty to stay down, but the dog seemed to know when the traffic changed without being told. Hans still gave his orders for good measure. It was just common sense to do so, he thought, but so many people had no idea how to handle animals.

At the Spadina Expressway, he moved into the exit lane and drove down to Eglinton. Traffic was heavy as he came off the highway and he thought the Don Valley Parkway would have been faster. At least it took you to the centre of the city. As he passed by the bottom of Sue's street, he wondered if this might be a day for him to find time to call her. But when he arrived at the building where he rented an office, he was already immersed again in knowing he would have to speak with a lawyer. As he put his sandwich in the small refrigerator in the waiting room that he shared with others on the floor, he was suddenly aware of a man sitting there. They nodded at each other.

When he checked the calendar on his desk, he saw that this man had been for a reading once before. He could tell because that information was written in next to the name. Usually, that made a reading slightly easier. With only five minutes before the appointment, Hans thought there was just enough time to check with someone for a legal referral. As he moved quickly down the hall, there was one door open. Approaching Marlie, a social worker who always asked a lot of questions, would mean he might have to reveal more than he wanted. But she was the most likely to know.

"A family lawyer," he said when he found her at her desk and quickly told her what he was looking for. If he remained light in his approach, why would she assume anything other than he needed the information for a client? Maybe he needed it for the man whom she would have seen on her way past the waiting room.

Her eyebrows moved up slightly as she reached for a small book in her purse and gave him two names. He thanked her and went back to his office where he closed the door quietly, sat down, and dialled the first number.

The receptionist squeezed him in. The first half-hour would be free. He could decide if he wanted to continue. This appealed to him even though he knew there would be no turning back. Heather already had a lawyer and wanted to sell the farm. That would be the big issue. He wondered if she might still reconsider, but he wanted to see Rosalind Clement, the lawyer he had just called, whatever happened. Heather was determined when she set her mind on something. What would her parents think? They both liked him. If they knew he had taken a lover, they would be angry. But how could they know? He wondered if he should fly over to England to see them. He could still try to convince Heather not to walk out on their marriage, but he did not want to do this if his interest was only about the farm and it almost seemed to have come to that.

Looking at the clock on the wall, he saw he was now five minutes late for his client. Even as he moved to the door, his thoughts were elsewhere. If he had enough money to buy Heather's share of the farm, it would solve the dilemma. But he did not.

As the man walked into the office, he hesitated near the chair on the other side of the table from Hans.

"Yes," Hans said. "That's the hot seat." He put a tape in the recorder on the table and when the man was seated and facing him, he turned it on.

"I've just moved into this great house," the man said. "I admired it for a long time and even thought of telling the owner to contact me if it were ever up for sale. But he didn't. It was just good luck when the time came."

"You're going to move to the United States," Hans interrupted.

"Didn't you hear me?" the man asked in an irritated tone. "I just moved. I have no intention of moving again. I just uprooted my family for this house."

"You're still going to move," Hans said.

"What the hell am I doing here?" the man asked loudly. "This information isn't worth paying for." He stood up and walked quickly out of the room.

Oh well, Hans thought as the sound of footsteps receded down the stairs. He stood up and sighed. Men were often more demanding than women. They only came if they had something specific to ask and only if someone they knew had recommended him. Now, he would not know what had drawn this one to make another appointment. Nor would he be paid for his time.

He was about to pick up the phone again when he heard his next client arrive. After he read for her, he went for a walk and came back to eat his sandwich. There was a message from Heather's lawyer. She wanted to sell the farm. Well, he'd known that. No doubt about it now. If he could block her until he could figure out if there were a way to keep it, Hans thought he would have to do just that.

"I'll have my lawyer get to you soon," was all he said when he returned the call.

When his day of readings was over, he headed out onto the road again. It was after seven and he was hungry and tired. There were still trucks on every side of him as he sped past the highway north to Brampton. His was the next exit and as he edged over into the inside lane a long truck passed him. He often thought of wheels he had heard had come loose and flown into someone's windshield and of truck accidents that seemed to have increased in the past year. Glad to leave the traffic on the 401 behind as he headed north to the farm, he turned on the radio to classical music.

When he parked near the gate and walked to the house with Rusty jumping excitedly around him, Heather was at the door.

"Hello," he said.

"I'd rather you didn't stay here," she said. "It would be better if you had some place else to sleep."

"Pardon," he said, though he had heard her.

She had been just over thirty when he married her and her daughter almost thirteen. Now, Heather was in her late forties and still attractive, with long hair streaked with grey. And she wore intriguing new reading glasses that slipped down over the end of her nose. Even so, it seemed the mystery in their marriage had vanished long before Sue had come along, and he knew he had not done enough to save it. Not that he could have, sensing something changing that he had not been able to pinpoint. It was deeper than the physical changes that seemed more a mark of her maturity, of her experience, of her beauty.

"I'm going out to ride for a while," she said.

He pictured her astride the chestnut mare, London Fog. She was handsome when she rode. A competent rider himself, he was hesitant about night riding.

"It's dangerous," he had said many times.

"You know we said we wouldn't interfere with each other," she'd said just as often, especially about riding. He stood aside, now, to let her go. He was suddenly overwhelmed with sadness, aware of the great gulf between them and a lack of understanding about what had happened.

When she was halfway to the barn, she turned. "Vivian wants to come out for the weekend."

"Oh Lord," he muttered.

Vivian now lived with her boyfriend in a condo in Toronto. He supposed Heather would find that sterile after living in the country. He conjured up an image of a fire in the wood stove and of warm cider. Perhaps one of the neighbours would come over to visit.

"Well, of course, you know I adore Vivian," he said. "But don't you think it's rather lousy timing?"

"I figured you wouldn't be here by then. I did ask you to move out."

"I didn't say I would do anything," he said. "Maybe you could go and stay with Vivian."

"You're so predictable," she said. "Forget it. I'll ride now."

"Be careful," he said.

She was already moving toward the barn again and the breeze carried his words in the other direction. He looked up at the clear sky stretching away in the distance, a sky filled with stars and with none of the blinding lights of the city to mute them.

Life went on like this for a week or two, with Heather not saying when she would return to England. He spoke with his lawyer about what to negotiate. There were phone calls with Sue. He spent hours walking on his land, unable to imagine leaving it. Unable to imagine someone else sitting in the living room with the rolling hills extending beyond the windows.

When he went into his office, he felt he was merely going through the motions. And yet, once a client sat in front of him, he was able to focus on whatever messages he was getting.

"I'm not worried about you," he said to one woman who had become somewhat of a regular. "But do you have something going on with your stomach?"

The woman hesitated. "Yes," she said finally.

"Thank you," he said. "I know you do and you're going to have to see a doctor. Whatever it is, it's something small. Don't worry. It will be fine."

After she left, his telephone rang. He did not expect anyone for half an hour, so he answered it.

"Hello, Mr. Jonker," a male voice said. "A cheque is in the mail. I owe you an apology."

"Who is this?" Hans asked.

"You told me I was going to move to the States. Well, you were right. When I went into work, the boss asked me to do the start-up on an office in Boston. I couldn't believe it. And not only that, it was only a day after seeing you that I found out."

"Yes," Hans said, recognizing the man now. "I could have told you more if you'd stayed, but you know it now."

They talked awhile and Hans learned how the man had felt about the move, given that at some level he had already prepared himself for something.

"Do you ever get it wrong?" the man asked.

"Oh sure," Hans said. "In my own life. All the time. But not very often with clients." He must pay more attention then.

"Well, thanks again," the man said. "And I apologize for walking out without paying. At the time, I didn't like what you had to say. But I did go to hear it."

*

Overhead, a spider web stretched from one corner of the ceiling to the far wall. Sue thought that the ice patterns on her window as a teenager had resembled the filigree of the spider's weaving. That time before, when her life had revolved around having to keep a secret, was fuzzy. A memory of a new boy coming across the schoolyard toward her crossed the threshold of her awareness. She had heard about him, knew his name was Peter Marshall, but she had yet to meet him. He would have arrived on one of the buses from an out of town property. She could no longer remember at which mine his father had worked. It might have been Golden Manitou where she had had a job in the assay lab in later summers. Or, more likely, it would have been East Sullivan, a mine that was closer to town. Peter used to ride his bicycle in along the highway in good weather. She did not think anyone from as far away as Manitou would have done that. They might have taken a shift bus if they had come at a time when they could not have gotten a lift any other way.

"So," he had said, winking.

At first, Sue thought this new boy must be talking to Rosie, the blue-eyed blonde siren of her teenage years, who had been standing behind her, but when she turned around, she was surprised to find Rosie no longer there.

"My name is Peter," he had said. "What about you?"

"Sue."

"Hi, Sue."

She did not know where his family had come from to arrive in Ile d'Or. Too shy to ask, she decided to ask her sister later. He was younger than Maggie so she might not have noticed him. As it turned out, he had an older brother in Maggie's grade, so she knew that their father was a geologist out at East Sullivan and that they had moved from some mine in northern Ontario to work there. Maggie also knew before Sue did when they were going to move again. She had not bothered to tell Sue because there wasn't any reason for her to think of it. She had not known that Peter was the one who got her sister into trouble. Anyway, everyone in the family knew they were not supposed to talk about that.

It was so recent that she and Maggie had finally opened that door that it was still sometimes awkward when they broached it. Nonetheless, they talked every time they had an opportunity. When it was not too late in Toronto, Sue would call her sister and on weekends, the rates were cheap enough that they could talk for as long as they wanted.

"Maggie, I found her," Sue had said on their last phone call.

"Who?" Maggie asked sleepily.

"You know. I told you. She's an adult now with a family of her own. Her name is Gwen."

"Gwen?"

"Um."

"Imagine. What does she look like?"

"Like she's related to us. Like your kids."

"That feels strange."

"I don't know what I feel. As if I've spent my whole life waiting for this, I think."

Jerry, when alive, had thought a lot about his impact in the public sphere. Whereas, what she had been moving toward all of her adult life she now knew had been this, to know the child to whom she had given birth. Sue felt sorry Jerry never knew his, sorrier than she could ever have imagined. Was it any wonder her husband had, in his final hours, doubted he had done enough in his life when he knew out there was a son he had not even told her about. Another phone call to Maggie.

"What is she like?" her sister asked now.

"She's friendly. I can't believe I didn't look for her sooner. She's going to come here in a couple of weeks."

There was silence at the other end of the line. She could imagine Maggie trying to absorb what she was being told.

"Maggie," she said. "She wants to find her father, too."

"You haven't told me who the father was, have you?"

"No. I will though. He never knew. The family left town and moved somewhere else the next year. I don't know if it would have been different if they hadn't, but I doubt it."

"So who was it?"

Sue hesitated. The shame of it, her mother seemed to be muttering in her ear. "Peter Marshall," she said. "And I need your help to find him. It's something I have to do for her."

"Peter Marshall?" Her sister's tone suggested she was astonished.

"Would I lie to you?"

"I'm just surprised, that's all. I didn't know you even went out with him. He was always hanging around that sexy Rosie something or other."

"That's true, but all the boys were."

"I wonder where the Marshalls went. There was an older brother, too. I had a crush on him. They disappeared before I finished high school."

So Maggie did not know. She must have thought her sister would be able to tell her and would call him for her. "Where do you suppose he'd be now?" she murmured. "Do you have any idea?"

"No, but I could ask Angus."

"That was going to be my next question."

"He's away at the moment. He went up the coast to look at a property for Amarpec. He should be back early Tuesday. I'll ask him then. I'm wondering what else you might do to track Peter down. Angus knows so many people in the mining world, but he could be anywhere. He could be doing anything. He could be a truck driver. Maybe a dentist."

"Funny. I was thinking maybe a high-school math teacher."

"Why?"

"He was good at algebra."

Maggie laughed.

"He was a good skater, too," Sue said. "And he skied to school sometimes on the highway, all the way from East Sullivan." The mine where she had worked was on the same highway that ran through La Vérendrye Park and the Laurentians on toward Montreal. It had been a gravel road in those days and it had taken forever to drive as far as Mont-Laurier. Once there, the rest of the trip to Montreal had been smoother and faster. Her father had often asked Sue to take the wheel once she had her license because her mother never liked driving on highways — driving around town had been the extent of her comfort level. Sue thought that was likely why both her parents had been so keen for her to pass her driver's test. Unlike Maggie, she had been excited about driving.

When she and Maggie stopped talking, Sue went back to sleep. She wanted to cocoon herself in the safety of the big bed, covered by her thick duvet. She did not want to talk to Hans, to Thomas, or to Florence. It felt as if she were on the verge of a discovery she was not ready to share with anyone yet.

It took only a few days to track down Peter Marshall in the Maritimes where he was indeed teaching math, not at a high school but at a small university. As fate would have it, the Marshall family had moved from East Sullivan and Ile d'Or to the mining town where Angus had lived. Likely, the only reason Sue had not known this sooner was because there had never been any reason for it to come up in conversation. After a few years, the family moved on from there as well, but not before both Angus, Peter's older brother, and Peter completed high school. They had not kept in touch, but Angus had run into Peter on an airplane a few years earlier on a flight to Ottawa.

All that information made it easy to look up a telephone number. Sue did not feel ready to tell Gwen yet, but knew she would not be able to hang onto the information for much longer. Then, before she could and before Gwen asked, Thomas called. Could he spend the night on a trip he had to make to Toronto? Sue said yes. She also spoke to Florence who was by then staying with Kate and Thomas.

"How are you, my dear?" Florence asked.

"You're the one who was in a car accident. How are you doing?"

"You know, my dear, these children have been so kind to me. As have you. I'm probably doing even better than could have been expected for a woman of my age. I won't say for an old lady because I know you'll disagree with me. But all the same. Now, you tell me how you are and what's been keeping you so busy."

"I found her, Florence. I found my daughter."

"I thought that was likely," Florence said. "I thought that must be what it was."

"Her name is Gwen."

"Have you seen her?"

"Oh, yes. Twice. And she's coming here this Friday."

"And?"

"Well, she's lovely. She's married with children I haven't yet met, but she wants me to. And to meet her mother. She's had a better life than I could have given her."

"Only because of your age and the circumstances at the time. It's just too bad you had to hide it for so long."

"She wants to meet her father, too."

"I hadn't considered that, but it does seem logical. How do you feel about that?"

"Pretty uncomfortable, but I've managed to find out where he is. I haven't told her yet, but I will soon. He doesn't even know I was pregnant so how he will deal with her, I have no idea. I've never had any contact with him since I discovered the pregnancy and left town."

"My dear, you have a lot of courage. I'm glad for you. And it sounds as if it's already been worth it."

"Yes."

"You know how fond I am of you, child."

"I'm almost sixty. I'm no child."

"You could have been my child."

Sue wondered if someone were to write a story how these pieces would go together. Maybe what these revelations were meant to teach her was something about the nature of love itself. There was a complex puzzle that was gradually clearer, but it never became clear enough that she could quite grasp it.

"Come and visit me as soon as you can fit it in," Florence said.

"Yes, I will."

The research Thomas had to do in the city was simple compared to the questions he asked her when he arrived that evening. He wanted to know about Gwen. This emerged over an after dinner coffee.

"You're a gourmet cook," Thomas said. "You make the best things."

"How's your cooking these days?"

"I'm learning," he said. "Kate can't eat all the same things now that she's pregnant. So that's another challenge. Not until after the baby comes, she says."

"Are you excited?"

"Of course," he said. "Although it's a little mixed. I don't dare say so to either Kate or Florence. I have all these feelings about never meeting my father, about my mother not being here to be a grandmother. I have this sense that I can't give a child roots when I'm not sure I have any."

"I can understand that."

"That's why I was angry when Gwen came along. I thought I was the child you'd never had and you actually have a real daughter."

"Oh, my goodness. She has a mother, you know. I gave birth to her. That's all I did." She hesitated. "I want to know her, to try to give her something or to make up for all the years she looked for me. A mother who likely had, in her mind, abandoned her. It doesn't change that you're Jerry's son and that I'm so glad you found me."

There was a glint in his eyes, but then it was gone and she thought she had imagined it. All the same, she knew she had said something that touched him deeply.

"Did you love my father?"

"Oh, yes," she sighed. "And I think he was trying to tell

me about you at the end. I didn't realize what he was saying was intended to open doors. Everything occurred so fast and I only got to reflect on it when it was too late. In the moment, it was like sitting on a train and seeing small figures in a landscape as you go by. Knowing you will never see the whole picture."

*

Emily noted the signposts of another season: the darkness coming early, the leaves falling, the cooler breezes, all moving inexorably toward winter. She worried about Martin shovelling, especially since his blood pressure had been up at his last doctor's appointment.

"It's exercise," he would probably tell her. "Shovelling is good exercise."

"Maybe," she would respond. "If you're already in shape."

Emily shook her head as if they were in the midst of this conversation. Martin was a good husband; his lack of concern about his health the only tension between them. He had run with Jerry when his friend was alive, but then, just as easily had sat and drank beer and consumed French fries as if that had no impact. She had not started to worry until pains in his chest had slowed him down while on their evening walks. At least he had seen the doctor and started to take the necessary medication. He even carried the nitroglycerine with him in the evenings now in case exertion caused some discomfort. Lately, he had started to watch what he ate and worked out more at the gym. While not consistent, he had, at least, started a sporadic regimen, which pleased her.

As she closed the front door behind her, Emily saw a pile of envelopes on the floor. On top was a small yellow one without a stamp, and only their names, "Emily and Martin," written on it. Pulling up the flap, she extracted a card with a small watercolour painting of wildflowers. It was from Sue. Such a lovely miniature, she thought. The woman is talented. Inside, was a note and she was surprised to realize it was an invitation for dinner on Saturday.

By now, they had no longer expected Sue to follow through on the offhand invitation she had issued in Stratford, but there could be many reasons they had not heard from her till now. Emily had even suggested to Martin that they ask her to join them one evening soon.

When Martin arrived an hour later and dropped his briefcase in the hall, she went out to greet him with a hug.

"Look at this," she said, handing him the card.

"That's beautiful," he said.

"Yes," she said. "Look inside."

"Well," he said. "Are we free?"

Emily nodded.

"Why not call her then and say we'll be there?"

*

On Saturday, they walked through the shadows of evening, punctuated by the hum of traffic and people's voices on Bloor Street a block away, toward the familiar address on Walken Avenue. They passed red brick houses with open cedar steps and small neat front yards. When Sue answered the door, Emily handed her a blooming houseplant and Martin a bottle of French shiraz.

"Thanks," Sue said.

"I'll open the wine for you if you have a corkscrew," Martin said.

Martin was likely the only person who could walk into Sue's house and feel so at home, Emily thought. But it was two years since Jerry's death. Sue had her own life now. Even a man who must come and go whom they might never meet so long as he was married. She did not suppose that married men planned to leave their wives. At some point, Sue might be devastated. Instead of feeling even a murmur of satisfaction, Emily felt sad for her.

Martin headed to the kitchen behind Sue. Emily followed more slowly. She heard the murmur of their voices as Sue pulled out a drawer and handed the corkscrew, in the shape of an anchor, to Martin. She watched him open the bottle and was unsurprised when he began to talk about *Prime Time*.

"I wasn't going to sail without Jerry." He had been adamant, as if the presence of the boat would haunt him. He was relieved when finally Sue had agreed with him a few weeks after Jerry died.

"No, I know that," Sue said, her long skirt rustling as she moved. "We made the right decision."

After Sue checked the oven, they went into the living room. Emily picked up a photograph of Thomas. "Such a delight," she said.

"Yes," Sue agreed. "The only reason I might have kept *Prime Time*, but how were we to know that?"

Martin looked distracted, then sipped his wine. He surveyed the scene as if looking for what was familiar. Emily thought he probably did this whenever he'd come to the house since Jerry died, looking for Jerry in that exploration. Emily leaned against the back of her chair and slipped her shoes off.

"There's something I want to tell you both," Sue said.

Ah, thought Emily. The man.

"This is good news," Sue said. "Although not easy to talk about. But it's something I want to share with you."

Emily could see a puzzled frown on Martin's face as Sue told them about Gwen. What she felt was recognition of what might have been underneath Sue's cool exterior that she had never been able to fathom.

"I'm so glad you've been able to meet with her," Emily said. She caught Sue's surprised look. It would take time, but Sue was now someone she wanted to know. Would it be possible? When she heard Martin comment on the surprise of an election outcome, Emily knew she had lost the thread of the conversation.

"I have to check the oven again," Sue said, putting her glass on the table and rising from her chair. "And soon we can all come to the table." She had set the big one in the dining room with three place mats at the end nearest to the kitchen.

"Smells good," Martin said.

Emily followed Sue and picked up the plates for the table. "Anything else?" she asked.

"Soon."

"Thanks for sharing with us," Emily said. "I imagine you've been living on a roller coaster."

"Yes," Sue sighed. "But it's all worth it."

"I'm sure it is," Emily agreed. "When things settle I hope you and I will be able to get together."

Sue turned as if she had heard an unexpected and sudden sound. "Thank you, Emily," she said. "And sooner or later, I hope you and Martin will meet my daughter. Actually, Martin already has, but I did not say who she was when he saw us at a café on the Danforth."

Walking home after they had had a last cup of coffee, Emily put her arm through Martin's. "You never know," she said.

"What?"

"Secrets."

They did not talk for awhile.

"I think Sue and I could be friends," Emily said.

"I thought you already were," Martin said.

Emily almost laughed aloud, but managed not to.

"Not really," she said.

*

Sue twisted her hair nervously as she waited for Gwen to arrive for lunch. Over forty years after the birth, this young woman's existence meant something quite unexpected to her. She did not know what it was like to have raised a child, but she still felt a strong connection that was different from her bond with Thomas. But he did not need to know that this bond with her daughter was closer in a way she did not yet understand. Maybe it was not a good idea to make comparisons. This was her daughter and she hoped to find common ground that would matter to Gwen also. And Thomas did seem to know that she was fond of him. She had bought some gifts for his first child, due the following spring. Jerry's grandchild. Even though she was glad Thomas and Kate were not waiting to start their family, it still struck her that no one would have offspring if they focused on the on-going crises that occurred around the world. Even during her own childhood when the fear was of Russian planes sneaking in from the north. Her mother had counted planes for the Distant Early Warning Line then and ten or twenty years later there were people who had started to build bomb shelters in their yards.

Outside her window, the trees had shed almost all their leaves, with only the occasional one clinging to a bare branch. In early November, the branches looked grey. Sue could paint them that way, but preferred to paint a tree in sunlight when the trunk and branches were flecked with traces of orange, mauve, blue, and yellow. Soon, it would be the second anniversary of Jerry's death.

A knock at the door brought Sue quickly back into the moment and she moved quickly toward it.

"What a lovely house," Gwen said as she came over the threshold. "Have you lived here for a long time?"

"Jerry and I lived here for ten years. So you could say it's been a long time."

"It's strange to realize how close our homes are, just a few subway stops from each other," Gwen said. "We might have passed on the street often for all we know. If one of us had glanced at the other, we would have thought she was a stranger."

"So much to fill in, isn't there? Do you want to see some pictures?"

"Of course."

Sue had spread albums out on the dining-room table. There

were pictures of Maggie, Sue, and Wally as children. Of the town where they grew up. Of the mine shaft. Pictures of Maggie's three children at various ages. Gwen pored over these.

"Cousins?" she murmured.

"Yes. They're your cousins."

"I think I look a little like you did when you were a teenager."

"How does that feel?"

"Oh, I'm glad," she said. "I love my Mom, but it's odd to be part of a family and to look very different from the others. Sometimes, I saw strangers looking at us. I could almost tell they were perplexed. You know, why do the others all look similar and then there's this girl with dark hair who doesn't seem to belong?"

"I've found an address for your father. Angus knows him."

"Angus?"

"Maggie's husband. That would make him your uncle. He's not in touch with him now, but he saw him a few years back on an airplane. I looked up a telephone number and I've written it down for you."

"Did you call him?"

"I didn't want to do anything until I knew what you wanted."

"It might be a good idea if you spoke to him so my call won't come as a total surprise."

"You're probably right." Sue could imagine an entire panoply of reactions that included outright denial. Anger. Maybe curiosity. She was the one who needed to hear whatever they were.

"Do you mind?"

Sue fiddled with her fingers. She would do almost anything this woman asked. Gwen deserved that, but that did not mean it was easy.

"What would you like me to say to him?" she asked.

Now it was Gwen who was pensive. She must have already thought about it, but Sue could not tell anything from watching her face before she answered.

"No," she said finally. "You feel the way. All I want for now

269

is that he knows I exist. Let him know I'd like to call him. Ask him what a good time would be."

Sue absorbed this information at only the most superficial level. It was too frightening to go deeper. She was suddenly furious this man had lived a lifetime with no idea of what she had gone through. The birth of a baby and the attitude of the times had been the defining moments of her life. Because of them, she had never had another child. Because of them she had become an activist. She had worked for a woman's right to decide on whether to continue with a pregnancy, although she might well have chosen to proceed even if she had had another choice, even with all the odds stacked against her. Would she be able to talk to this man who was the father of her daughter without her anger seeping in? And yet, it was those defining moments that had brought this woman here, sitting almost comfortably with her now.

Sue, she told herself, there's nothing to be gained from anger now. Maybe there never was.

"Did you say your name was Walters before you married?" Gwen asked.

"I did. And my mother's maiden name was Desjardins."

"Then I must have some French heritage."

"Right back to the early settlers in Canada."

She could see Gwen was pleased, as if it explained something, perhaps the colour of her hair or her love of a language.

"What about my father? Do you know where his ancestors came from?"

Sue shook her head. "I know nothing. Peter was in my life for no more than a fleeting moment. A couple years at most as a schoolmate and then what led to your birth. Anyway, I don't imagine many teenagers have much interest in their ancestors."

"I thought that in a small, isolated town you might know these things."

"I didn't pay much attention then. Instead, there's all the angst. The changes in your body. The fears that come with knowing you're not a child and that even so you don't know how to look after yourself, that you're dependent on adults. And I was dependent on parents who loved me, but wouldn't talk about anything problematic. What do you make of that as a teenager? You think you're not all right and never will be. It appears that you didn't have that kind of childhood and I'm glad."

"No, you're right, I didn't."

Sue wondered about changing her name to Walters again. It was not anything she could have foreseen she would want in the aftermath of Jerry's death. Maybe she would phone Martin some time and make the arrangements to do whatever was required. She would have to find a way to explain it to him. Now that he and Emily knew about Hans, it might be easier. And everything had shifted slightly since she had told Emily about Gwen. Emily had already called Sue herself, not leaving it up to Martin. No longer did Sue feel judged, as if something like this, a secret long-lost child, was what Emily had suspected all along. She thought now Emily might even understand if Sue wanted to change her name, now that Sue no longer felt the name Walters implied secrecy. Instead it implied authenticity. She suspected Jerry would have understood why she wanted that now more than ever.

As Sue sat with Gwen in silence, instead of feeling it was uncomfortable and awkward, it felt natural. Then, they talked about Gwen at various stages of her life. The bedroom in the house in Kincardine. The younger children, her sisters and brothers. The family picnics.

"It's almost time for me to go," Gwen said when she had finished her tea. "I hate to leave, but I like to be there when the children arrive home from school. Even though they're quite able to manage, we check in with each other then. Sometimes I think they merely tolerate this little ritual, but I suspect they'd miss it if it didn't happen."

"That sounds very nice," Sue said, a tinge of sadness in her voice.

"Will you call me and tell me what happens when you contact my father?" Gwen asked.

"Oh yes, of course," Sue said. "I'll do that soon. As soon as I figure out what to say." She would have to think about a lifetime of what the birth had meant for her, not wanting to open up something she could not manage. She was not sure what it would feel like to open Pandora's box. Would she *go over the edge?* as she and Maggie had often referred to it. All she knew was that she did not want to. She had been in that uncomfortable state when she discovered she was pregnant. And again when they took her baby away without letting her so much as hold her. Beyond the baby's cry at birth and her immediate disappearance, Sue had, ever since, managed to erect rock-solid walls.

"I'll be interested," Gwen said.

Sue hoped to go on with her life as best she could. She hoped that she and this young woman would find paths to share and explore together. She would not go over the edge. Not with Hans, Thomas and Kate, Maggie and Angus, and Martin and Emily in her life. And of course, Florence, who had, in ways she could not fathom, given her the courage to move toward this reunion. She might begin to lose her grip, but if she shouted out, she was confident they would be there.

After she and Gwen hugged and Sue watched her daughter walk down the street toward Bloor, she sat quietly in the large armchair in the living room. After twenty or so minutes of breathing in and out deeply, she felt that some time in the next few days she would be able to handle a call to Peter Marshall. She would not belabour what to say. With information from Angus, she was fairly certain he would be the man who had the Nova Scotia telephone number. It ought to be easy to ask if he were the Peter Marshall who had lived in Ile d'Or in the early 1950s. She would say her name was Sue Walters and that they had known each other as teenagers. She would remind him that her sister was married to Angus Milroy.

"Yes, of course, Sue," Peter Marshall's voice replied two evenings later. "I remember you. Flaming red highlights in your dark hair. A free spirit. We used to compete in algebra."

Sue sat at the counter in the kitchen, her palms sweating. She could almost hear her heart beat and thought he must surely also hear it, or at the very least, the tremor in her voice.

"Yes," she said. "Yes, that's me. So you are the Peter Marshall I've been looking for."

"What a surprise," he said. "After all these years. I don't remember you being around when my family left Ile d'Or. We moved to a town in northern Ontario. We kept on moving."

"Um," she said. "So you never knew I was pregnant."

There was silence on the other end of the telephone.

"No one knew," she said. "No one talked about it. I was shipped to relatives in Toronto to have the baby."

"Why are you telling me?"

"Because you're her father."

"I don't understand," he said.

"You're her father."

Once again there was silence, but he had not hung up on her. Not yet anyway.

"She was adopted, Peter," she said evenly. "I never saw her. Until recently, that is. She asked me to let you know about her and to tell you that she wants to contact you."

"I, I, I," he stammered. "This is…"

"Yes, I know. It's a lot to deal with out of left field, but it's the truth."

"I know it could be," he acknowledged. "I have a family," he said. "A wife. I simply don't know how to handle it."

"Well, maybe you need some time to think about it, but Gwen is persistent."

"Is that her name?" he asked. "Gwen?"

"Yes, that's the name her family gave her."

"I don't know," he said. "I don't see what good it can do for her to call me or for me to meet her."

"I think you owe it to her." Sue was angry, but she tried to stay neutral. It would not help Gwen if she alienated him. If she still had unfinished business herself, it could wait until after Gwen did what she needed to do. She did not say "Coward," which was what she wanted to say.

"What's your number?" he asked. "I'll get back to you."

She gave him the number. "My name is Sue Reid now," she said.

"Do you have other children, Sue?"

"No," she said. "Other than a stepson who arrived on the scene late."

He did not pursue that avenue. If he were looking for sympathy, it must have dawned on him that he was not about to find it.

"I ... I'll get back to you soon," he said.

"All right."

When she hung up, Sue sat staring out the back window into the night sky. It was cold and the wind was blowing. She could hear branches on trees moaning. She did not know if she would ever hear from this man, but was prepared to give him a few days before letting Gwen know the outcome of the call.

*

Much to her surprise, Sue had scarcely noticed that Hans had not rung. Now, she began to wonder what might be going on, if perhaps he and Heather were in the midst of a reconciliation. The thought sent shivers up her spine and made her gulp for air. Sooner or later, she would know. It seemed beyond her and what could she do about it? It was his life and he had to deal with it. Although she would like to let him know she loved him. Maybe she would later, but for now, she dialled Gwen's number and waited for someone to pick up the telephone at the other end.

She did not want to disappoint her daughter with the story of Peter's hesitation, but there was nothing to be gained from calling him again. He had to come to terms in his own way with what had likely felt like a bomb to him. She could hear Hans saying that.

"But that's just common sense," she heard herself reply, disappointed that Hans would not have more to offer.

"Hello." It was Gwen's now familiar voice.

"It's Sue."

"I was just beginning to wonder when I'd hear from you. I was about to call."

"It's taken this long because Peter Marshall was thoroughly stunned when I told him about you. He lives in Nova Scotia with his wife and family. That's about all I know, except he teaches math at some college. He wanted to get back to me."

"So he hasn't called back?"

"Not yet."

"Would you give me his number?"

"Yes, of course."

Sue started with the area code for the Nova Scotia region.

"I promised myself that before the turn of the year I'd find out about both my birth parents," Gwen said. "Whether they were alive or not. And if they were, to try to see them. It's been such a long time to wonder. All these years something was missing even though they were also happy years. I've seen my Mom and she's excited for me. She looks forward to meeting you."

"I want to thank her."

"She wants to thank you."

Sue sighed. Layers and layers of tears lay beneath their words, but not the kind you shed easily. Later, in the wide double bed she no longer shared with anyone, she would probably start to shed them.

"I'm going to call him. It's too hard to wait and wonder."

Suppose Gwen met a blank wall or the fear she herself had encountered? "Yes," Sue said. "I imagine it's almost impossible."

"My kids want to meet you. What about after school on Friday?"

"Um," Sue said. "That would work." Eager though she was to meet them, the thought of these children frightened her. Within the next few months she would have acquired four grandchildren. By the time she saw Gwen next she would also have taken the steps to change her name to Walters again. In a city like Toronto, with the constant intermingling of people, the glittering shop windows juxtaposed with those lost souls begging on the streets or sleeping over grates, it was hard to remember that once, long ago, she'd had a life that bore no resemblance to the present. The town where her daughter had been conceived was a frontier town with open and silent spaces. She could lie in bed then and hear the sound of blasting in the middle of the night or the distant wail of a train. She could hear the mine whistles and the bell at the cookery. And she could go out the back door and walk for miles into the bush and never see another person. She remembered the rock across from the house and the blueberries that nestled in its crevices. She used to fill a red pail so they would have blueberry pie for dinner. Maggie had looked at her furtively after Sue had come back from Toronto. It was as if Maggie knew that even though she was the older sister, Sue had now experienced something that had made her different.

Sue, aware of her sister's covert, puzzled glances, had wanted desperately to talk to her, but she had been afraid to give Maggie anything she might use against her. Not that Maggie had done that since they were much younger, but as a child Sue had learned that her older sister had the capacity to hurt her.

"No discussion whatsoever," their mother had said.

Their father had said nothing.

So, they had not whispered in the dark or talked when their parents had not been around. There it was, something that could not be missed, but everyone pretended that absolutely nothing had happened. And for a while, Wally had seemed annoyed that Sue had come back at all. It seemed that those months of her absence had been a blast for him.

The telephone rang and Sue was relieved to hear Peter Marshall's voice.

"I meant to get back to you sooner," he said. "But everyone has had the flu."

So it was something mundane in the end, not an evasion nor something to engender anger either.

"You can tell Gwen to call me whenever she wants," he said.

"We talked earlier and she will soon. I gave her your number."

"What is she like?'

"She's a lovely person. You'll find out for yourself soon."

"I'm nervous," he said.

His voice sounded familiar, like the boy she remembered. They had done only what many teenagers before and since had when sensations they did not understand overwhelmed them. Although today's teenagers were different, no matter how much they knew, they could not know until it happened how the cravings of the body could surprise them.

"I'm thinking of coming to Toronto if she'd like that. Would I be able to meet with you as well?"

"Why not wait to see what comes of your conversation?"

"I owe you an apology."

It was so huge to hear those words and yet so insignificant in the light of the secret she had carried for most of her lifetime that Sue did not know what to say.

"I'd like to do it in person."

Sue had never expected to encounter him again or to have such an unexpected conversation. Coffee at a Second Cup or Starbucks? It hardly seemed like the venue for something so momentous. And how could she tell him what she was only beginning to realize, that having given birth to this woman now felt like one of the most important things she had done in her life? She regretted she had not been able to acknowledge her daughter nor to raise her. Yet here she was, a fully-grown and thoughtful woman.

"So, I'll be in touch," he said. "After I've spoken to Gwen."

"Okay."

"My wife and children know," he said. "It was a shock, of course, but they want you to know you have their support also."

Sue drew in a huge gasp of surprise she attempted to muffle. She had not expected to be touched and instead had been protecting every inch of herself from hurtful comment.

"Thank you," she said quietly.

"Thank *you*," he said.

8.

IN THE EVENINGS, bright red, green, blue, and yellow lights twinkled on trees and porches as the Christmas season approached. Occasionally, there were white lights only. The store at the corner had put up a fence between the sidewalk and a brick wall with Christmas trees poking out through the wire. One, Sue noticed, was tall enough that Jerry would have hauled it home and erected it in the living room in front of the window. He would have climbed up on a ladder to put the angel they had bought on its tip. They had seen the angel with its golden wings and a long gold robe in a store window.

"Do you have another?" Jerry had asked because it seemed too high up on the very tallest branch of the tree to retrieve easily.

"No," the storeowner had said. "But I can put something else there and get the angel for you."

Sue did not think she could bear to get out the large box of decorations they had collected over their years together. She wanted to do something different. Something quiet, even though it was not the first, or even the second, Christmas since Jerry had died. It was, nonetheless, the first she would spend alone on Walken Avenue. The house had changed, but these holidays always evoked memories. She had hoped that Hans might invite her to the farm, but with Heather still there that possibility had dissipated. She wondered if later Hans would walk over after work if she called him.

"Of course," he said.

Sue was mystified that she had not missed him these last weeks, probably because there had been such a flurry of activity for both of them. But suddenly his absence was so acute she had to see him. There was so much to tell him and she longed to feel his arms around her. She was grateful when he came through the light snowfall to her front porch. He carried yellow roses wrapped in light floral paper and when she opened the door, he practically lifted her off her feet with a big hug.

"Oh, woman," he murmured. "I've missed you."

"I've missed you."

He stood on the small piece of carpet inside the door and untied one dark boot, then the other, then put them on their sides on the boot tray.

"Where's your tree?" he asked.

"I ... I was thinking I wouldn't have one. Or maybe a small one. I wondered about going to your farm, but it hardly seems likely since Heather is there again." She was nervous bringing it up even as something that was not going to happen.

"Farm is up for sale."

"Oh," she said. "That must be difficult for you."

He nodded.

"What about the animals?"

"I'll keep the dogs."

"You'll keep the dogs."

"Yes, love. That's what I said."

"But the horses?"

"Heather will take them and board them somewhere. Actually, she already has."

"Will she keep them even when she's in England?"

"You know what? I didn't ask."

"Oh."

"You sound surprised."

"I am."

"I don't think you believed it was over, did you? Even though

I told you. But I can't blame you for that. I might have been dubious myself in similar circumstances."

Sue wanted to ask if he had made love to her again, but did not.

"I didn't," he said.

"What?"

"Whatever it was you were thinking."

"Oh come on, Hans," she said. "Surely you can't read my thoughts."

"Just an obvious thought," he said. "Don't worry, you're not transparent."

Would an ordinary guy have been tempted to sleep with his soon to be former wife when he was as fond of her as Hans was of Heather? But she was not about to prolong that conversation. He seemed glad to be here.

"Could I stay over?" he asked. "Otherwise, I'll have to start thinking of leaving before this snowfall makes the highways treacherous. I can try to phone a fellow who lives in the village to feed the dogs and take them out for a run. Even if Heather is there in theory, she might not be. "

Sue wanted to ask why he had never called anyone to attend to the dogs before, but then thought he'd probably never thought of it. And was surprised to find she was not even sure she wanted him to stay. Already, in the time alone since Jerry's death, she had taken on the habits of a single woman again. And was unsure she could cope with the big burst of exuberance of this man for longer than a few hours. He would leave the toilet seat up, turn the television on when she wanted quiet, and generally spin her life out of control. But she wanted him with her and could hear that intrusive judge telling her she would get used to it.

Well, I do love him, she replied to the voice in her head. *Well, get on with it then,* the judge said.

"Sure," she said aloud.

"I heard some hesitation."

"It's the answer that counts, isn't it?"

She watched him make himself comfortable on the couch in the living room. He lifted the cup of herbal tea he had carried in from the kitchen and sniffed it.

"Woman," he said. "I'm crazy about you."

"Well, thank goodness," Sue said. "Because you've grown on me." She laughed. "The thing is, I'm crazy about you, too." She was beginning to realize it would be possible to connect their two lives, rife as they were with long and complicated histories. It was time for change. It was time for risk again. It was not as if she lacked years of experience to fall back on. Wisdom, Maggie might call it. But you could still be foolhardy, even knowing better.

"Maybe you'll sing in the shower," she said. "I'd like that."

"I do want you to come out to the farm," he said. "I don't want to be there at Christmas though. I was hoping I could spend it with you in the city. And that maybe once Heather has moved out we could go out for a few days afterwards. I think she might go to her daughter's until she moves back to England. Or I hope she will. Then we could use the place. We could go skiing. How does that sound?"

"As long as you don't expect me to cook a turkey."

He laughed. "I'd like to cook a turkey," he said. "I love cooking."

It was then the power went off and darkness descended. Out on the street, all the twinkling lights stopped flickering. It was also then that her whole life gathered in a crescendo and she could see she was not who she thought she had been any longer. Hans put his arms around her and drew her to him and while some part of her was frightened, she could not bear to be that other woman. The one who was hesitant and diffident, terrified of intimacy. No, she was not that woman.

"How long since you've seen the northern lights?" he asked.

"Years." But rather than seeing them in her mind as he spoke, she saw formations of geese flying south in the autumn, the sky suddenly full with huge Vs and all around the sound of honking. She remembered being indoors, ensconced in some quiet corner, when she heard the signal of fall in that great flight. She had rushed outside and stood looking up. The northern lights were like that, too, the green and purple and white streaks — a sight that took over everything. There had to be sky unlit by tall city skyscrapers for it.

"We could drive north some time and spend a night far enough up to see them."

This was what she loved about this man. He could take a dream and put her in it. Jerry had been like that with music. Some piece she barely understood would acquire beauty with his observations and his rapt attention.

"Yes," she said. "That would be wonderful."

The lights came back on and the telephone rang. She pondered waiting for the answering machine to pick up the message, but realized it might not after the power failure. Everything seemed impossibly bright. Glare jumped off the ceilings, the television screen. She had difficulty adjusting her eyes to make the transition. The telephone brought yet more interruption.

"Sue Walters, please," a man's voice said.

"Yes."

"It's Peter Marshall again," he said. "I know I should have told you I was coming, but I decided suddenly. I'd like to meet with you. And would you let Gwen know I'm here?"

Gwen had made contact with Peter and they had talked enough to establish a link, but he did not feel he ought to call her without any warning.

Sue could see Hans studying her, his eyes thoughtful. She never knew what he might know, although he had likely picked up something in her tone. Surely not that the next morning she would walk along Bloor Street to the neighbourhood coffee hangout and meet Peter, the father of her daughter.

She hung up after saying she would do that.

Hans remained quiet.

"Well," she said. "The father."

"That's good," Hans said. "I'll take my things upstairs if that's all right with you. I'd like to use the bathroom."

"Go ahead."

He had his own toothbrush now, a green one she had bought for him. He had not moved in, but it was a statement and they both knew it.

*

The next morning, Sue waited for Peter to come in the door across from where she sat in the coffee shop. Would she recognize him? Sometimes, after forty or so years, the younger face seemed to peer through whatever marks and wrinkles had changed it. At other times, she could not imagine where the friend she once knew had disappeared. The man who came through next was too young. Then there was a woman. After that, a man who made her start as she realized he was, unmistakably, Peter. His hair was now grey and receded slightly at the temples, but she still knew him right away. He wore large spectacles with black frames on his nose and he was slightly heavier across the chest and in the midriff, though he did not have the huge belly she had imagined.

"Hello, Sue," he said, coming over to where she sat on a stool at the window. "I'll get a coffee and join you. I would have recognized you anywhere."

"I would have recognized you, too."

"Would you like anything else?" he asked.

"Thanks, I'm fine for now."

He put his coat on the back of the stool next to her and went over to the counter. When he returned, he had a mug of black coffee and a scone with butter.

"I called Gwen," she said. "She's expecting to hear from you today. She's looking forward to it."

"Thanks."

As they sipped their coffee, both of them stared through the window onto Bloor Street where a procession of people walked by. One woman with grey hair and a large purse stopped at the window of a clothing store across the street and then moved on to the delicatessen next to it. The languages on the sign were English and either Polish or Czech. Sue did not know which. This Toronto had changed from the one of twenty and thirty years ago when she might have considered going out for fish and chips a treat. Now, you could eat anything you wanted from any part of the world and hear languages you could only guess at. Thai food was one of her favourites, as was salmon cooked in the Native tradition with bannock on the side. One could develop eclectic tastes without ever travelling, although it often sparked the urge to travel. That, and seeing paintings loaned from some major collection in a far-off country, often made her contemplate the places she would like to visit. For a long time that had meant Europe, but of late, she had become interested in masks and there were so many cultures that created a variety of them. She thought it ironic that suddenly she had started a collection just at the point her own masks were being dismantled.

"I wish I'd known," Peter said. "I'm so sorry for what you had to go through."

"I don't think you could have done anything. In those days, it was easier if no one knew. After a while, when no one talked about it, I almost forgot. I can't now though. It comes swirling back as if it were yesterday."

"Where did you go? You were there one day and gone so quickly after. I wondered about you. Even so, I didn't make any connections. I guess I was pretty naïve."

"All of us were. But you were a gentleman even then in some ways boys often weren't. There weren't any snickers when I came back so I figured whatever story my parents told about some illness was believed and that you didn't say anything to anyone."

"A whole lifetime has passed without either of us knowing Gwen was out there."

"Well, I knew she must be somewhere, but I didn't want to think about it. I buried it so deeply it was as if it hadn't happened. I'm a widow, you know. I was married late and we didn't have any children. I didn't even tell Jerry, my husband, about the baby."

She could tell by the sudden narrowing of his eyes that what she had just said was inconceivable.

"I'm deeply sorry," he said. "You've had to live with this. For me, it's a new discovery."

*

Sue wondered what Gwen and Peter would say to each other. She had told Sue how much she missed her father since his death and Sue knew the parents she had lived with were her real family.

"Not often that you get to choose exactly the child you want," her father had told Gwen.

She would discover her birth father to be a decent man also.

This story was now no longer so unusual. Forty or even fifty years later, more and more accounts were surfacing of people who had had children no one had ever heard about in the circles of the birth parents. Sue had tried to take consolation from this, the child born to teenagers, the father unaware, the mother sworn to secrecy, but it had not helped. She picked up her keys. Before she could put them into her purse, the telephone rang.

"Could you come and join us?" Peter asked.

"I'm sorry," she said. "I'm just leaving to go back to work."

"Well, could we have lunch together tomorrow?"

You don't get it, she wanted to scream. You might be her father, but you can't walk in after all these years and take over, as if you're part of anything except the heated moment of conception.

"I need to think about it," she said.

"I'm sorry," he said. "I feel more rushed because I'll be heading back east tomorrow."

"There isn't any rush, you know. She's here and she's lived in the same place for a long time."

"She asked me to come to meet all of her family at some point."

Sue closed her eyes and sighed, putting her hand over the receiver. This was not welcome news, even though Gwen had told her that was what she wanted. Even though by the time Peter returned to the city on another visit, Sue would have met almost everyone. She had no reason to feel that she would be eclipsed by Peter.

"Whatever develops with Gwen will take time," Sue said finally, aware once more of being thrust into a situation so new that she had no way of knowing how to deal with it. Everything was full of surprises. Even this man who was the father of her child was almost a stranger, creating, with each contact, something unexpected for her to consider.

"Yes, of course," he said.

"I don't want to seem ungrateful for the way you're being so gracious," she said.

"I think I understand," he said.

"Okay then."

"You have an interesting life," Peter said.

"I suppose that's true, but how do you know?"

"I do, that's all."

She had not told him about Thomas and Kate and she wondered what else he knew to cause him to consider her life interesting. Maybe he could see the potential in the contact with Gwen for step-grandchildren soon. Sooner than he knew with the prospect of the imminent birth in Stratford. What would that child call her? Just plain "Sue"? It was hard to imagine being called "Nanny" or something similar after having her grandmother of that name in Toronto dominate her life when she was quite young. As the train had rushed south when she was five or six, she had imagined walking into Union Station with its high vaulted ceilings and finding Nanny waiting for her at the door where the passengers converged to leave the trains. Gramps had always been there with her, leaning on his cane. Nanny had shaken the hand of the porter when Sue stepped down onto the platform and Gramps had given him some money. It was a tip, he had told Sue later.

"Thank you for looking after our granddaughter," Gramps had said. He was used to the situation as Maggie had visited on her own the previous summer. It was yet to be Wally's turn.

"Have a good time," the porter had said to Sue.

She had smiled at him. He had been the first black person she had encountered other than in photographs. It seemed hard to believe now, as the city became increasingly diverse, that she had ever assumed it could be any other way. As a small child, her eyes full of new sights, Sue had been mesmerized. Sometimes, she missed that child who had found the world such an exciting and bewildering place. Now, it seemed as if life might be changing again. The child she had been, so filled with wonder, seemed to be merging with the woman she was becoming.

"Listen, I'll be in touch," Peter said. "In the meantime, thanks for everything."

As she put the receiver back in the cradle of the telephone, her caged emotions threatened to overwhelm her. All she could think to do was to walk briskly down to Bloor Street and let her feelings gradually dissipate. She thought again about those early trips that had ended in Union Station. As soon as Nanny and Gramps had all of Sue's luggage in tow they had gone to find the car. Old Bessie, Gramps had called it. He had sat in the front beside Nanny, his withered left leg, the outcome of childhood polio, preventing him from driving. Anything could happen when Nanny started up Bay Street between the high towers. She muttered if anyone drove their car too close to hers. Sometimes, she had even yelled out her window. When that happened, Sue had put her head down, hoping to make herself invisible.

As she walked now along the few blocks that ran west through the Annex, Sue heard people speaking many languages. There was the noise of voices, of traffic, of a distant siren. She revelled in watching people and noting how much more lively the city had become since she had first moved to it. If you live long enough, you get to see both your world and yourself changing as if through the lens of a kaleidoscope, she thought.

When she arrived back at the house, there were two new messages.

"Sue," Gwen's voice said. "Thank you for making it easy for me to meet Peter. You're very kind and very generous. Give me a call when you have time. My mother is coming to the city for Christmas and she wondered if she might meet you then. I hope so."

And the other message: "I'll be working a little late and then going out to the farm for the night," Hans said. "But could I bring my things in tomorrow and stay through Christmas?" Could he bring one of his dogs?

Sue was suddenly excited, as she visualized spending the season with Hans. It was what she had longed for before it was even possible, except possibly for the dog. She could just imagine Rusty pacing at the door to get out and then finding how the city confined him, the way it also did for Hans. She would make sure there was a celebration that would make it special for Hans, although she could not imagine Rusty would be easily fooled.

*

Thomas awakened to the sound of ice cracking on branches outside the window, glad to find when he looked at the clock that he had slept until eight o'clock. He stepped carefully out of the bed, trying not to awaken Kate. He hesitated when she groaned slightly, then crossed the room and opened the door carefully.

He did not smell the aroma of fresh coffee emanating from the kitchen as he usually did in the mornings since Florence had come to stay after the car accident. Surprised not to hear her voice as his footsteps approached the kitchen, he called out her name in a low voice. There was no response. Maybe she had not heard him. When he found the kitchen empty, he walked quickly to the hall that ran from the kitchen down past the master bedroom to the room where Florence slept. The quiet of the house felt odd. Florence had talked of going home soon, but they had all agreed she should stay until after the holidays so she could spend it with the two of them and Kate's family. She had insisted on making the stuffing the night before, and he had been there when she put it in a bowl in the refrigerator.

When he knocked on Florence's door, there was no answer. He pushed it open gently. There she was with the duvet pulled up to her chin, still asleep. As he approached the bed, he thought her opaque colouring strange.

"Florence," he whispered, reaching out carefully to touch her hand, stretched outside the duvet and across her chest. It was cold. An image of his mother in the hospital bed, mouth hanging open, eyes staring at the ceiling, flashed across his mind. A nurse had come in and closed her mouth and eyes, but they had fallen open again.

Thomas had spent an hour alone with his mother before two men from the funeral parlour arrived to wheel her out to the hearse. He had never talked to anyone about how painful it was, how alone he had felt, knowing she was gone somewhere but not anywhere he would ever be able to sit as they once had and chat with her again. He had sat with tears streaming down his face, telling her he loved her, telling her he would miss her, as if she could hear him. But he had had to say those things, to spend quiet time with her before he could take whatever the next step was. To figure out what it was. And finally, he had gone to call for the undertaker to come and figure out what to do from there. When he saw his mother again at the funeral parlour for the last time, her eyes were closed and the coffin was ready to be shut for the service and cremation.

"Oh my God, Florence," he said. "What do I do now?"

The door behind him slammed shut and he jumped. Florence must have forgotten to shut the window, he thought, as a breeze blew across the room. Kate came in with her dressing gown pulled tight around her.

"I think Florence is dead," he said, his voice expressionless.

"What?" Kate said. "I'll call my doctor." As if there were something that could still be done to revive the older woman. As if she could put off the awful truth of the still body lying right there in front of them.

Thomas stayed with Florence. He could not remember the names of any of her relatives, and then realized he did not know any of them. He would have to find out. He shook his head, as if to rouse himself.

"The doctor will be here in fifteen minutes," Kate said, coming to his side.

If it were a nightmare, he would soon wake up. "I ought to call Sue," he said.

"What do you want me to do?" Kate asked.

"I don't know," Thomas said.

"This is awful."

"Yeah." He started out of the room.

"Where are you going?" Kate asked. "I don't want to be alone in the room with..." She stopped.

"Come with me. I'll call Sue."

"She's too far away to do anything. Besides, it's Christmas."

"I'm going to call her."

Hans rolled over as the dog he had brought with him, a mix between a Border Collie and a Golden Lab, started licking his arm.

"Have to feed the mutt," he said.

Sue wanted to lie in bed with his body against hers. Sighing, she wondered why he had not brought Rusty, whom she knew by now.

"Merry Christmas, love." He rolled toward her.

"Merry Christmas."

"I'll bring you breakfast in bed," he said as the dog started to make small unhappy noises.

She found it ludicrous that she was jealous of the dog. "Don't go yet," she said, reaching down and stroking his abdomen. Not jealous, she thought. Slightly annoyed. Hans was here and even so she could not have him all to herself on Christmas morning.

"Dog can wait," he whispered.

"Phew," she said with a smile of victory.

"Did you know I'm still crazy about you?" he said.

"It crossed my mind."

After a while, she started to moan and the dog began yowling. Hans groaned as he held onto Sue and moved quickly. Then, he fell back onto the bed.

"Okay, Jenny," he said finally. "I hear you." He stroked Sue's cheek. "Now that was a greeting!"

He disappeared down the stairs. A little later, she heard the back door open and close, thought the dog must be out behind the house now in the tiny yard, and fell asleep to whistling and chopping sounds from the kitchen. When she next awakened, it was to the sight of Hans presenting her with a tray.

"When in the world did you do this?" she asked.

"When you were sleeping," he said. "Stuffing is made, too." He took out a small package wrapped in red paper and handed it to her.

Inside was a pair of small gold earrings. "I must be dreaming," she whispered.

"Good dream?"

"These are so beautiful. I am so grateful. Thank you, lovely man."

The telephone interrupted them and he reached for it. "Merry Christmas," he said, before handing the receiver to her.

"Sue," Thomas said. "Everything was really quiet and Florence wasn't up early like she usually is."

Sue held the receiver slightly away from her ear. "Have you called the doctor?" she asked.

"She doesn't have a doctor here. We called the one Kate goes to. She's coming over. But there isn't anything she can do. It's too late. Florence is gone."

"Oh, my." Something that almost constricted her breathing rose in her throat as she heard Thomas gulp. Hans moved to put his arm around her shoulder.

"Sue, are you still there?" Thomas asked.

"Yes, yes, I'm here," she said. "What would help most? We could come." She looked at Hans and he nodded. "We could be ready to leave in an hour."

"Oh, I couldn't ask that," Thomas said. "After all, it's Christmas."

Hans mouthed the words, "We can go."

"It's all right," she said. "Hans and I will be there in a couple of hours. Make it three."

Thomas let out a long sigh. "This is awful. And she wanted to be here for the baby."

"Yes, of course."

When Sue hung up, she began to cry softly. Florence had accepted everything about her, something her own mother had not been able to do, even though she had loved Sue. Once more she had lost love that could never be replaced.

"I'm here," Hans whispered. "We'll go together."

"Yes," she said. "Thank you." And then, "Is it still snowing?"

"No, and the forecast says there won't be any more for a couple of days."

"Sometimes I think it might be better to have more than one mother," she said.

"What do you mean?"

"Florence was like another mother. Someone who gave me permission to say and think about things my own mother never did. My mother lived as if the most important things never happened. You told me there was something I had to deal with, too."

"Well, you have. That's what you've been doing. And Florence knew what was important. I suspect she loved you and knew you loved her."

"I suppose," she said. "What about the dog? What about Jenny?"

"She's game to travel."

While Sue took a shower, Hans packed his shaving gear back into the small pack he had brought.

"We can use my car, love," he said as she came downstairs into the front foyer. "Jenny is used to it and I don't mind driving."

"Thank you." Too dazed to concentrate, Sue was grateful. If not for Florence and for Hans, she would not have found the daughter who had been taken away from her. Florence had, in her own gentle way, encouraged Sue to undertake such a search and to transform her life in so doing.

Sue packed an extra pair of slacks in her suitcase. Not knowing when they would return, she also rustled in the drawer for more underwear. The telephone rang again and she reached for the receiver. "Merry Christmas," Maggie said. She had just awakened in Vancouver.

"Merry Christmas," Sue said. "We're just leaving for Stratford."

"I didn't know you were going there for Christmas."

"Florence just died."

"I'm so sorry," Maggie said. "Are you all right?"

"I don't know."

There was a pause at the other end of the line. "I'm sorry," Maggie said again.

"I met Peter Marshall."

"My goodness. And?"

"He surprised me. Very apologetic. Very accepting."

"It leaves me breathless."

"Yes."

"Angus wants to wish you Merry Christmas, too."

Sue spoke to her brother-in-law. At the same time, she wondered if Florence had left any instructions about what she wanted for her funeral. If Thomas did not know, she had no idea. It had never dawned on her that it might one day be her responsibility, nor had it likely dawned on Florence. Although her request that Sue act as executor of her will and the information about the safety deposit box in Chatham might have alerted her. She did not imagine there would be time to go there before they had to make decisions.

It was later than they had intended when she and Hans set out for Stratford. Light snow was still falling.

"I'm glad you're driving," Sue said.

Beyond the worst of the traffic, Hans muttered that the next intersection was Mississauga Road. "The route to the farm," he said. "When I left, it looked as if there'd be enough snow for skiing soon."

There had not been any purchase offers yet, but the agent expected more clients once Christmas was over. Hans had not figured out where to live yet and she could not imagine him in an apartment in the city. He was someone who needed to be free to roam fields and swim in rivers and ponds. To take photographs of nature. To listen to bird calls and frogs croaking.

Strains of Handel's *Messiah* drifted through the car. Snowflakes formed shapes on the windshield and quickly disappeared with the sweeping arc of the blades. There was not much traffic. Every so often, the dog stretched up behind Sue and tried to lick her cheek.

"Oh, Jenny," she said. "Puhlease! I'm not into kissing dogs."

Hans laughed. "She likes you."

"Yeah, but all the same!" She smelled the distinct odour of dog.

They drove quietly for a while as Hans concentrated on the road and Sue watched the snow fall. She had so wanted to see Florence.

"I have a message for you," Hans said.

"What are you talking about?"

"A message from beyond."

"Suppose I don't want to hear it," she said.

"Actually, you do."

She brushed her hair back off her forehead with an impatient flick of her hand.

"It's Florence."

"That's crazy."

"When people die, they usually hang around for a while to make sure we know they're all right."

Sue sighed heavily. Jenny leapt up behind her again, put her paws on the seat, and started licking at her ear.

"Don't scare me like that, Jenny," Sue said. "Next thing you know I'll think this spirit is in the car."

"Well, she is. She can't lick your ear, but she's here just as surely as Jenny is."

Suppose he also got a message from her mother? But both her parents had been dead too long to have messages for her. Anyway, their lives had been lived on a less spiritual plane even though they had insisted on a religious upbringing for their children. The Bishop of Moosonee had baptized Maggie. The local minister had baptized Sue because by that time there had been one.

There were photos of her mother holding Sue in a long white baptismal gown taken outside a wood frame church. Two women, dressed in hats and suits with nylon stockings and high heels, had stood together with their babies in this barren place of rock and trees. You could not see the stockings in the photos, but Sue could imagine them with dark lines up the back, perfectly aligned for the occasion. Likely, they had been ordered from the Eaton's catalogue. Everything had come from Mister Eaton in those days or else from the general store on the main street called Mulholland's. When Sue and the other baby, Bonnie Wilson, were older, Bonnie had stolen from Mulholland's. She had been able to get out of that store with almost anything, but at some stage Sue had stopped being her sentry. She had not wanted to be a part of it. Not because she was being particularly honest, but because her mother had successfully instilled the fear of God in her. Or more to the point, the fear of being spanked and grounded and of losing her allowance. So although she was no angel, Sue had no desire to be caught stealing.

"Florence is saying she wants to remind you that she left her will in a bank in Chatham. Thomas has the key to the safety deposit box. And she wants to be cremated."

"Please, Hans. Stop."

Hans began to slow down and to move over to the paved shoulder.

"What are you doing?"

"You said stop."

"I meant not to tell me any more about Florence."

"Look, love, she isn't going to go away and be able to rest unless you listen."

"If you weren't here, she wouldn't have a way to talk to me."

"Well, we don't know that, do we? And anyway I am here."

Sue was quiet. He was at the point where almost everything in her life intersected now. She looked across at him, his eyes firmly on the road ahead. His hair had been cut shorter in the last weeks and his beard was gone. She could only see part of his right eye, but she could imagine both of them. He glanced at her quickly and then back to the road.

"You're wearing the earrings," he said softly.

"Yes."

"She says she's glad you're with me. She wants you to be happy. And she wants you to remember to meet Gwen's mother as soon as you get back to Toronto, and not to stay in Stratford so long that you won't be able to."

"Oh my goodness, I almost forgot. But how did you know? I didn't tell you." She did not say that most of what he had told her he could have come up with himself rather than attributing it to Florence. But she had not told him about meeting Gwen's mother. And she could not remember if she had mentioned Florence's will and where the key was.

"I'm just telling you what she's saying."

By then, they were at the turnoff for Kitchener and would soon be heading for Stratford. If the weather were not any worse along that stretch of highway, they would reach their destination within the next half-hour.

*

Thomas was at the window when he saw a car drive up and park along the curb. A man helped Sue out onto the sidewalk. Lights on a tree beside the front walk flickered through the soft snow cover. He went to open the front door before Sue could knock.

"Come in," he said.

A holly wreath with red berries he had hung quivered as they all swished by it.

A shiver ran through Thomas's body as Sue hugged him. He took their coats, then hung them in the front hall closet. Sue hugged Kate, too, as soon as she turned around. Hans came in behind them, shaking snow off his boots.

"I don't think you've met," Sue said, introducing Hans.

Thomas nodded in Hans's direction and the two men shook hands. "The doctor just left," he said, looking at Sue. "Do you want to see Florence?"

Sue followed him to the back of the house where he pushed open a door. Florence was still lying on her bed.

"She's passed on," Thomas said. "The doctor said so."

Sue stood still, her gaze resting on Florence.

"Someone from the funeral home is coming soon," Thomas

said. "Do you want to be alone?"

"Yes, thanks. For a little while."

Thomas backed out of the room and walked toward the sound of voices in the kitchen. When Hans and Kate heard him, they both turned.

"Kate's showing me around. You have a lot of nifty gadgets," Hans said. "Just tell me what you want me to do, you two."

Thomas did not know Hans, but he was prepared to let him do whatever he wanted. Cook the dinner. Make phone calls. Any older person who seemed able to take over would do at that moment. The gifts beneath the tree, like the new blouse and sheer nightgown he had bought for Kate, and the tiny outfit for the baby with a reindeer on it, would sit there unopened. Maybe some day they would unwrap presents. He did not know when. He turned to Hans.

"Okay," he said.

Kate looked at him with a worried frown.

"You all right?" she asked.

"I don't know." Would he ever be all right again? First his mother, then Jerry. Now this wise and loving older woman who had become so much a part of his life. He sat down and cupped his forehead in his hands.

"This is tough," Hans said. "You may even need to cry."

Thomas looked up at him, a surprised frown crossing his face. He was not used to anyone making this kind of comment, least of all a man. Before anyone could say more, the tears began to stream down his cheeks. Kate put her arms around him and Hans opened the refrigerator.

"I'll make grilled cheese sandwiches," he said, but no one heard him.

*

Florence's head was turned slightly toward the wall and her eyes were closed. Sue took her hand and was shocked by how cold it felt. Not like ice or something from the refrigerator. It struck her then that the name of the chill in the room was death. Even so, the older woman looked peaceful. Perhaps Florence had known. Like Hans, she had often seemed prescient.

"Oh Florence," she murmured. "I had so much to tell you."

She had the distinct impression that Florence heard her. It suddenly occurred to her that all the people she was surrounded by she had known only since Jerry's death or shortly before it. It was reassuring to remember that Maggie, Angus, and their children were also in her life. With Maggie, history stretched back to a time even before her birth. Wally, remote though he usually remained, was part of that history also. Now, so was Gwen.

"Oh, Florence, I so wanted you to meet her." Tears flowed freely. After a while, she became aware of a cool breeze and went over to the window. She thought Thomas or Kate must have opened it. She glanced back at Florence.

"Goodbye, dear one," she murmured, going over and pulling the sheet up so that only the older woman's head was left showing. A small woman in life, she seemed even smaller now in death.

"Peace," Sue whispered, touching Florence's forehead gently.

She found the others in the kitchen. Hans was putting cheese on slices of whole wheat bread and heating a frying pan.

'We were going to go to my parents for dinner," Kate said. "I just remembered. Florence made stuffing."

"We'll never make it," Thomas said. "Maybe we could just drop in on them later."

The sound of footsteps came from the front of the house and then the bell rang. Thomas looked at Sue.

"I think we'd all feel all right if you answered the door," Hans said.

There were two men waiting on the steps. A dark vehicle was parked at the curb behind Hans's car.

"We're here for..."

"Yes," Sue said.

They followed her to Florence's room. She gestured to them to go in. Sue could hear the murmur of their voices from where she stood just outside in the hall. A few minutes later, the men appeared again. As she watched them go through the front door and down to the hearse, Sue was thrust back to the day Jerry's body was taken away. Grateful to feel Hans beside her, she watched the door of the hearse being opened and the covered body placed gently inside it. She continued to watch as the dark vehicle moved slowly out onto the street and toward the corner.

Thomas closed the door and turned to her. "What do we do now?" he asked.

"Someone will have to go to the funeral home," Hans said.

"Maybe you'd come with me," Thomas said to Sue.

"If you want that," she said. "Of course."

Both Hans and Kate nodded.

"Kate and I can figure out what to do for the rest of the day. We'll tell you what we've decided when you come back."

Sue reached for her coat in the closet, knowing Florence would have wanted her there.

They drove in silence toward the river and over a bridge into the part of town where the stores, municipal offices, and archives were. The Avon River was frozen and there was snow on the ice. Sue remembered her visit to the house in Blenheim, and how she had waited for Florence to have a nap before they had a discussion about Jerry. And when she had been in the hospital in London, so close to death, she had been aware enough to tell Sue she ought to search for her daughter. Now, Sue was only beginning to grasp that there would be no opportunity to tell Florence about Gwen, about what this young woman meant to her. How unlocking her secret seemed to have made room for living life quite differently. She was sad she would never get to thank her.

The funeral home was quiet. There was a woman at the front who guided them to the room where Florence's body was resting. The man with whom they spoke about arrangements was dressed in a dark suit with a tie that matched. He seemed alarmed that they did not want a traditional funeral service, betrayed by his startled eyes and brows that came forward like a mastodon's, but he smoothed out his features with one hand and inhaled audibly. He kept on nodding his greying head as they described their wishes. Cremation. A memorial service for the family. No visitation.

"All right," he nodded. If that was what they wanted.

When they arrived back at the house, Kate greeted them at the door. She said her parents and her sister were going to bring their turkey over so they could have dinner together. In the meantime, a casserole had arrived from a neighbour across the street. This was the beginning of a stream of offerings from people who already knew there had been a death in the family.

"I'll put some in the freezer," Kate said.

"I wonder if they do this when babies are born," Sue mused.

"Probably," Kate murmured.

"The town where I grew up was like that."

At that point, Sue was not thinking of her own pregnancy, but of when she and Hans could return to Toronto. Once Thomas and Kate were with her family, she would have done what she had come to do. Her place was elsewhere now. Seeing Gwen in two days and meeting the mother who had raised her baby were what she was thinking about. She did like the general atmosphere of this town and knew people would now take over and do whatever Kate and Thomas needed. She had not thought southern Ontario, so long established, unlike the frontier mining town of her northern childhood, would have the same sense of community spirit. But even Toronto, after so many years of living there, often seemed like a small town to her. Rarely did she go out without encountering someone she knew, her neighbourhood stretching east and west on the Bloor subway line four or five stops in each direction. It was her city, her neighbourhood. She especially claimed the strip of Bloor Street a block from her house and was aware of small changes there on an ongoing basis. She noticed what man claimed sitting rights in what doorway. Occasionally, it was a woman. She noticed which one put out a hand in search of change and who was doing poorly. Sometimes, she stopped to talk. The smiles she received from the regulars when they chatted warmed her. When she was away for a day, they seemed worried about *her.*

"Have you been sick?" they would ask.

"I hope everything's all right," they would say.

Everything might not be all right, of course, but other than to mention some detail, like a hacking cough, she had spared them the minutiae of her life. It dawned on her that in the quick exodus she and Hans had made that morning that she had not taken Christmas treats to any of them.

*

On the drive back to Toronto the next day, Hans turned on music. "Easy listening," he said, thinking that after spending their last hour in Stratford at the funeral home for a brief time with Thomas and Kate, something that did not challenge the mood of quiet reflection was appropriate. And for the moment, Sue seemed glad to have as background something that was soothing. He figured Jerry would have hated it, would have wanted something with far more distinct rhythm. Maybe the songs of Pete Seeger. Jerry had been political, after all. He was glad to be distracted by Sue's occasional comments.

"It's hard to believe that we could have such a lovely dinner with death lingering over the feast," she said.

"Um," he agreed. "Kate's family made that happen."

"So did you."

"Thanks," he said. "I tried."

"I forgot about the men on Bloor Street," she said. "They would have been expecting me. Especially Al. He's always there."

"You fill a void in their lives," Hans said. "Not many could be that generous." He glanced at her briefly, noticing that this comment seemed for a moment to upset her.

He was not surprised that when they arrived back at the house in downtown Toronto, she went in only briefly and picked up some small packages and then went quickly out again and down the walk toward Bloor. He made no move to follow her; instead, he headed in the opposite direction with the dog, thinking there must be somewhere he could buy flowers. Bright colours. Not a poinsettia. Just something that would brighten the day and make it slightly festive. He wondered what Heather was doing at the farm. A wave of nostalgia swept over him. Soon, she would be gone and he felt sad that whatever they had shared was now finished, that love could gradually change and even evaporate. While he felt some warmth for her, he also felt angry at the thought that the oasis in the country they had created together would soon disappear. He wanted to pat the nose of a horse and see its nostrils flare. He wanted to hear goats and chickens around him. He had no idea what his life would become without being able to experience the animal noises and smells, to watch them in the fields, to feed and care for them. He wondered if he would be able to stand living in a city again.

Jenny ran ahead and a woman coming toward him stepped aside.

"Supposed to be on a leash," she muttered.

"Dog's harmless," he said with a big smile.

"There's a law."

No sense of humour, he thought. Going to have an ulcer. Oh, turn it off. This was not more than anyone might think under the same circumstances, but he felt he ought to tell her to watch out for an ice patch. Otherwise, she was about to slip and break something. An ankle? A wrist? Something.

"Be careful," he said. "There's some ice up ahead."

"Oh, get lost," she said.

"Well, Merry Christmas and Happy New Year to you, too,"

he muttered. As he continued on toward Bloor Street, he heard a loud shriek and turned to see the woman lying on the ground.

"I'll call an ambulance," he said, bending over her.

"Oh, no."

But he dialled 911 as a small crowd started to gather. A car stopped on the road. Soon after, a siren sounded and an ambulance careened around the corner. People came down from their front doors to the street. Hans slipped away when the paramedics took over and continued his walk, looking for flowers.

When he returned to the house, he found Sue plunked down on the couch. She seemed to be staring at nothing.

"Hi," he said. "I've brought you something."

She smiled, but he had the sense she did not see him. He took the paper wrapping off the bouquet and went to find a vase.

"There's something under the sink," she said.

So she did see the parcel, he thought. He reached down to find two vases near the bottle of dish soap. He took out the smaller one and ran water into it, then emptied a small packet of fertilizer that accompanied the flowers into the water. As he arranged some dark ferns to frame the white, pink, and red blooms, he started to hum.

"Something for you," he sang as he went back to the living room.

She was not there.

"Where are you?" he called.

She opened the bathroom door across the hall and came out into the room.

"Oh my," she said. "Those are beautiful." She watched him set them down on the mantel among Christmas cards strung out on a thin red ribbon. "Thank you."

Jenny started to squeal.

"C'mon, dog," he said. "You had your walk."

"Maybe she's hungry."

He did not want to say that the dog would prefer to be in the country.

The next day, Sue went to the nearby strip on Bloor Street where she knew she would find her homeless friends who had not been at their usual haunts the previous night. Perhaps they had slept in a hostel or rented a cheap room if they had the money. One of them often stayed in one of the few bank entrances or in all-night coffee shops or on grates in the sidewalk. She used to be able to have a conversation with him, but he seemed to have deteriorated. Known best to her was Al, the man with a regular place right at the bottom of her street. He had fallen on hard times and there seemed to be some element of addiction or mental illness that he struggled with. Whatever it was, he sat in the same spot day after day with his pale shawl around his shoulders and a tin cup held out to passersby.

"Hi, Al," she said.

"Hi," he said. "Merry Christmas."

A slight smile played across his lips and extended to his eyes — the pleasure of recognition.

"Merry Christmas," she said. "Sorry I didn't make it then."

"Were you ill?" he asked. "I haven't seen you for awhile."

"I was in Stratford for a couple of days. Family stuff."

She handed him ten dollars and a package wrapped in red-and-white paper, a ribbon, and a bow. He looked up and a tear ran down one cheek.

Oh dear, she thought. She wanted to be helpful, to make a difference in people's lives. Nonetheless, she felt there was always, in her generosity, an element of atonement. She was guilty and needed to do this to assuage her guilt. Was it a legacy of childhood events long before the conception of Gwen, long before her loss of innocence? Perhaps it was the outcome of the persistent admonition that she go to church or what she had heard there. Yet as part of a Protestant tradition, there had been no emphasis on confession. Many of her friends had confessed to the big priest with the quivering belly at the Catholic Church on the main street. Most of the rules of the predominantly Catholic town had emanated from his presence. She had been relieved she had not had to confess to that priest. Her mother's watchful eye had been plenty to contend with.

When Sue arrived back at the house, Hans opened the door. He seemed anxious to see her.

"Gwen called," he said.

Jenny poked her head through his legs and tried to squirm out between them onto the porch.

"You've been out, Jenny," Hans said. "Just be patient. We'll be going in a little while."

"Are you leaving?"

"I have to make sure everything is ready for the real estate agent to show the property. And I want to feed the animals."

"Is something the matter?"

"No," he said, but she could see that he was eager to be on his way. The city must be getting to him. Or maybe he *was* worried about the animals. He always missed them. He always missed the country. He had told her how he liked to be up high enough there to feel the breezes, see the wide sky, smell the farm air. "You know," he had once told her. "If you look toward Toronto in the summer, you can see a large yellow cloud over it even on a fair day."

"It's nothing really," he said. "It's just me. I get restless. I don't like to be away for long. Besides, you have Gwen to call and it will give you time for that."

Everything he said made sense, but Sue did not want him to go. She recalled previous times he had left hurriedly, upset about something. Afterwards, he was always apologetic. "And if you ever want to convince me to stay, just strip," he had joked. She could do that, but after they had laughed, he would still want to go. And it was clear he was leaving now to give her space as well as to get out into the country. To her surprise, she realized she needed it. A call with her daughter was not incidental. It was likely Gwen wanted to suggest when Sue would meet Gwen's mother and family. She thought of them as her daughter's *other* mother and *other* family, but in reality *she* was the *other* one.

Hans began to pack the bag he had brought with him. He had a hairbrush and shaving gear as well as a change of underwear, a fresh shirt, and a sweater.

"Do you always take that bag with you?"

"Well, not this one exactly. I always have stuff in the car, but I packed this time for Christmas with you. But there are all kinds of reasons in the country for being well-prepared, especially in winter."

He sounded a bit impatient, but she decided to ignore that. "Okay," she said. "Point taken." But she marvelled at the swift change in atmosphere. "You seem cranky."

"I'm sorry," he said. "I don't mean to be."

Sue was unprepared for Hans's call only two hours later.

"Heather's still here," he said. "I can't say much."

"*Sacre bleu*," she muttered, a blasphemy emerging from her childhood. She tried to swallow it. There must be some explanation. He did not deserve so much anger and she was not sure why she *was* angry or why she was directing all of it at him. She was silent. She thought Heather would have gone to the city with her daughter.

"Listen," he said. "It'll be sorted out soon."

"Um," she said, but she was dubious.

When he hung up, she banged her fist on a table. Surely he did not expect her to be happy at this news. She took the vase of flowers he had given to her and threw the flowers in the bathtub. When he called, she would tell him to go fly a kite.

When he did phone, he sounded contrite. "I bet you threw out the flowers," he said.

Sue took in a deep breath. "Not yet," she said, knowing she could still retrieve them. "So what's going on?" She was aware she had jumped to conclusions and that if she loved him she ought at the very least to hear him. She wanted to tell him she was going to see Gwen the next day and that they had spoken earlier.

"She wants to stay at the farm for New Year's to do some cross-country skiing."

"I thought she was at her daughter's." Sue could tell he was annoyed with the situation, surprised at it himself.

"I didn't expect this, but what can I do? I refused to leave when she asked me to, so she's been going back and forth between the farm and her daughter's condo. I never know what to expect. But she did come with Vivian to sign papers. The place is still half hers.

Sue was silent. You could love someone even when that person had hurt you; you could go on even after someone died, she thought. What could she say? Sometimes, saying nothing was the wisest choice. Probably Heather needed this time to say goodbye to the farm, but Sue was hardly going to say that.

"I'm not planning on staying in the same house with her for New Year's," he said. "I want to be with you."

"Do you still love her?"

He hesitated. "In a way, I suppose I do. It doesn't change how I feel about you though."

"So when will I see you?" she asked.

"Soon," he said.

When she hung up, Sue wondered if it had been as difficult for him, as tiring, to deal with her grief over Jerry as this was for her. She climbed the stairs to her room where she lay down and fell asleep.

*

Sue dreamed of dogs and horses. A knife with jewels in the handle. A glistening blade. When she awakened, it was to the sound of a thumping noise against her window. Her body was rigid again, her jaw clenched. Yet she felt relieved to know that what had been so vivid was not real after all.

She crossed the room to the window and looked down toward the front of the house. Hans stood on the street below making a snowball. He grinned up at her as he leaned back and threw it at the glass panes that separated them. Sun streamed down on the morning newspaper on a small table near her. It was open to a partially done crossword puzzle. What starts with "H" and has four letters? She had printed "hammer" down the side column already, so the first letter for the four across was "H." If it were meant to be a Dutch name, "Hans" would work. But that was not the clue; the clue was "A full house in poker."

The snowballs continued to thud against the glass. Sue felt as if she had come across a long bridge to the other side. No matter what the journey, Jerry would have died. And Thomas would have turned up. She would have had to face the void of losing Jerry and then the bridge across it without the fore-shadowing of any appointment with Hans. It was odd how sometimes everything changed after taking some unexpected step. Imagine if she had never come across that listing in *Toronto Life* before Jerry died. She would not have called to make an appointment with any psychic without that push and who knew what she would be doing now. She might not have set out to find her daughter. Not having Gwen in her life now seemed unthinkable.

She heard Hans's key in the lock and his footsteps as he came through the door and up the stairs.

"Surprise," he said.

Sue could feel his cool cheek against hers as he hugged her as well as the warmth of his body.

"Say something," he said.

The sun shone through the window in a long streak of light filled with particles that spread into the room.

"Well," she said, "'something' is a word, but it's not the one I'm thinking."

"What one are you thinking?"

"Hallelujah!" she said, his optimism starting to course through her.

He smiled and moved over to the crossword puzzle. "I'll find a word in this for you," he said. She watched him sit down, pick up the pencil, then lower his head over the newspaper.

"What starts with 'H' and has four letters?" he murmured. "A full house in poker." He paused, peering down at the puzzle with full concentration. "'Hand?'"

"I think you're right," she said, leaning over his shoulder so she could see the clue. "Try it."

"It works," he said, printing the letters "A," "N," and "D" in the allotted spaces. "Hallelujah."

Sue shared his pleasure at figuring this out at the same time as she wondered how she had missed something so obvious. She wanted to know how long Heather would stay in Canada, but decided not to ask. He would always love Heather in some way. All she could hope for was that the woman's ghost would not continue to intrude on them.

Before long, Hans was engrossed again. As she watched the intensity of his concentration, she thought if he could actually predict the future nothing they did made any difference. Still, whatever he said and whatever she believed, she was continually faced with making choices.

"What about if I sold this house?" she asked.

"Are you really considering that?"

"I don't know," she said. "But you did ask me to say something. Wouldn't that qualify as 'something'?" Glancing up, she saw Jerry smiling at her from a photograph on the wall. She knew more about him now, but he still remained in many ways a mystery. You could not know everything about anyone, she thought. Not even a husband. Nor would she even want to. There was so much she would probably never know about Hans either. It seemed likely they would argue at times. The sudden flare-ups when they did not understand each other would emerge. It seemed more natural than her marriage. And she understood now that the effort to preserve some semblance of perfection in any relationship was futile.

"Maybe we could buy a small piece of land in the country somewhere." She could feel her legs tremble again as she voiced thoughts so new to her they startled her.

He turned to look at her as if he could not believe what he had just heard either. "Do you mean that?" he asked.

"Yes," she said. "I do mean it." Even though she knew that once the words were uttered, she could not pretend she had not said anything, not even if she went on trembling at the thought that she could lose everything again. Jerry's death had come early. It could happen to anyone. This reality would always haunt her.

"I wouldn't want to be too far from Toronto," she said, "nor Stratford either. And I don't want to be a farmer or live on a farm." Her voice became stronger.

"Surely we could have chickens," he said.

Sue noticed how hopeful he looked, his blue eyes watching her intently. Under his banter and flamboyance, she felt his vulnerability.

"Lots of fresh eggs." Sue smiled.

"I suppose I'm going to do the cooking."

"I might help a little."

"We'll have dogs. And cats," he said hopefully.

"Rusty and Jenny, of course," she said. "But we'd have to draw the line somewhere, wouldn't we?"

"Somewhere," he said. "Another word." He started to hum again.

The sound soothed her and she was glad of his presence, of the dream they were already beginning to build together. A dream that would include her daughter and Thomas, of course. The list went on. The tune Hans was humming became clear to her. Was it where they would find their new home? *Somewhere, over the rainbow...*

"Maybe we ought to start looking," she said quietly, aware

there could be times when courage would fail her, relieved that this was not one of them.

*

It was after Christmas celebrations and before the beginning of another year that Sue met Gwen sitting in the restaurant where they first met on the Danforth. She was at a small table with her eyes glued to a book, holding her head up with one hand. Everyone was away, Gwen had told Sue on the telephone. A change of plans. Her mother was in Kincardine and the kids and their father were skiing. Sue's meetng with Gwen's mother was to happen now in early January.

"Hi," Sue said.

Gwen looked up, startled. "Oh, hi," she said, closing her book.

"Good read?"

"I like mysteries."

"My father liked them, too." Sue did not say that, at some point, most of them seemed contrived to her.

The waitress came by and Sue ordered some carrot cake with a coffee.

"I don't read them for the plot," Gwen said. "Sometimes I even skip ahead and see how it works out, then go back and keep on reading. I often wonder what people do in extremes. I don't think anyone ever knows for sure. Like torture. I like to think I have strong ethical principles, but how do I know what I would say or do were I tortured?"

"Hardly light reading. Or even light mystery. I think my father read them for diversion."

"I don't usually."

"I gathered." Sue tried to find the words to ask if it had something to do with the decision she had made when Gwen was born. Something about justice. She feared she would say the wrong thing if she did. "Does it bother you that the main characters are so often either in police work or forensics?" she asked instead. While she knew it was the point of many of these novels, that the character was a detective or forensic specialist, she liked the occasional story she found where this was not the case.

"It doesn't matter really what the characters do for a living if you're interested in something beyond the crime itself. Good and evil. What would make a good character give up scruples to commit a criminal act, for instance."

Sue nodded, although it was a bit confounding. For her, if fiction did not distract her from the horror of the news, for instance, it did not interest her. She had a small gift in her purse and she slid the box across the table. Gwen explored the tissue in the tiny packet until her fingers revealed a pair of small silver hoop earrings.

"They're exquisite," she said, but then frowned. "It's too bad, but I can't keep them."

"I don't understand."

"I – I – I." Gwen's face became a mask, expressionless. "You see," she said. "My mother could never give me something like this. I…"

"They're not terribly expensive."

Gwen wrapped the earrings in the tissue again and put them back in the box. "Thank you," she said. "It was very thoughtful of you." She put them into her purse.

Sue did not understand, except that the topic had now been dismissed. She suspected there would be a lot more uncomfortable moments between them. How could it be otherwise?

"I hope you'll find you can wear them," she said. "From what you've told me about your mother, I suspect she'll be glad you have some token from me to mark finally finding each other."

Gwen did not respond to this comment, except to nod slightly.

"You met Peter," Sue said. It sounded almost like a question, but it could as well have been a statement.

"Yes."

"How was that?"

"It was strange to know that he had no idea I existed until

you told him. I was glad in a way. He wasn't able to make any decisions when I was born he would later regret, I suppose."

"Do you think sometimes we know things even though we think we don't?" Sue thought of Thomas. She would rather Jerry had told her, but now she saw there were little intimations that had made it impossible not to know there was something, like his visits to Florence when he had never asked her to accompany him.

"So you think Peter knew about me?"

"No, but I think he'll put it together some time and realize that he should have tried to find out what happened to me when I disappeared from town. I think he didn't because he couldn't face that I might have been pregnant. He's likely relieved now, especially when his wife and kids have been so accepting."

Maybe some of Hans knowing came from that intuitive sense, although Sue was convinced he also knew future events that were too far ahead for intuition. Sometimes, he made the most remarkable and detailed predictions.

"He seems a gentle person," Gwen said. "I'm glad he's my father."

Sue watched the younger woman.

"I think the father I had would like him, too."

"And your mother?"

"Well, she already thinks she'll like you."

"I was talking about Peter," Sue said, but she recognized the note of hope and optimism in Gwen's comment.

"Oh yes, of course. Yes, she'll like him."

Gwen opened her purse, removed a tiny gift bag from it and reached across to hand it to Sue. "Something for you."

Sue fiddled with the bag, thinking of the earrings and then of Florence. She had not told Gwen much about her except that she had died and that she was the one, along with Hans, who had encouraged her to look for her daughter.

"Then she was special," Gwen had said. "Hans must be, too."

From inside the bag, Sue pulled out a tiny picture frame with a photograph of a child at around two years old. Dressed in overalls, she had dark curls forming a fringe around her head. Holding a small plastic shovel and smiling at the camera, the child seemed about to jump up and down. Sue wondered what the photographer had said.

"It's you," she said.

"Yes."

"Thank you." Sue could not think of anything else to say, but she understood how generous a gesture this was. Her very first photograph of her child. It was monumental.

"You're welcome." Gwen beamed.

There was still the underlying fear, Sue thought. Even faced with this reality, from all the years she had not known where her daughter was still lingered that fear of what she had done to ruin her own child's life.

"You have a lot of courage," Gwen said.

Sue shrugged.

"Well," Gwen said. "You risked I'd be angry and unforgiving."

Courage is what it takes and takes the more of / Because the deeper fear is so eternal, Sue thought, remembering this line from a poem. Then, she recited it out loud.

"That, too," Gwen said. "I was afraid, too. That you might be disinterested or difficult. And maybe only curious."

"I guess my deepest fear was that you'd been hurt or neglected. Or both."

"And mine was that I would never find you. I looked for years, you know, and had about given up. That was awful. As long as I could hope you'd turn up, I felt reassured. But when I thought you might have died or just not bothered to look for me, I couldn't stand it. Especially that you might be dead. I thought I would find you somehow if you were still alive. I always believed that. Or almost always."

Maybe this was her guilt, Sue thought, what she had to atone for with gifts to the homeless on the streets of the city. Her daughter had been looking for her for half a lifetime and she had done nothing until very recently to make that search successful.

"I'm sorry," Sue said.

"For what? You're here."

Sue felt bereft of words to express the thoughts that flooded through her. Florence's lifeless hand. Sitting across from a lost daughter. Meeting Jerry's son. Loving Hans. It felt as if she were finally ready for all of it.

"It didn't have to be quite so difficult for you. I could have made it easier."

"You weren't ready, I guess," Gwen said.

"I guess not," Sue replied. "Until now."

Gwen nodded.

Sue was tempted to say something like "Hallelujah." Instead, she just reached her hand across the table.

Acknowledgements

Thanks to Margaret Arthur for the germ of an idea that kept on growing. To Katherine Wallace and Barbara Wehrspann for reading different versions and their perceptive feedback. Paula de Ronde, too, with her probing comments about whatever I have asked her to read. Elizabeth Greene and Heather Wood for sharing the journey.

To my agent, Margaret Hart, and my editor, Luciana Ricciutelli. Both Margaret and Luciana have helped bring my three books thus far to publication. Both are talented and dedicated women to whom I am profoundly grateful.

Moosemeat Writing Group for ongoing critique and good humour. What an interesting, talented group this is, so fortunate I am to have found it.

As always, I am grateful for the support, encouragement and enthusiasm of my family. Andrea, Mark, Max, Phil, Therese, Stephanie, Michael. Geoff, Skye, Gillian, Stacey, and all the Winnipeg Cossers continue to be my ongoing support. As also are my friends. Ruby for her enthusiasm and special launch parties. Larry. Carol. Michèle. Gwen who would recognize her mystery reading namesake. Lee and Ron. Brydon et al. Ray and Shirley. Joan, Gene, Huong and Frank, Liisa and Gerry. Nelson, Anne and other northerners. Catherine. Colleen and

Dieter, Trish, Lisa, Gero and other dancers. Neighbours. The community in the LIFE program at Ryerson. My McGill friends who have stayed the course. The wonderful women I met working at the Helpline. The list goes on. And on.

I am grateful as well for my northern childhood. And for my mother who taught the neighbourhood children to dance. And for the people in my life who continue to dance!

The lines, *"Courage is what it takes and takes the more of / Because the deeper fear is so eternal,"* are from Robert Frost's poem, "A Masque of Mercy," in the *Complete Poems of Robert Frost* (New York: Holt, Rinehart and Winston, c1962).

Photo: CA7 Creative

Mary Lou Dickinson's fiction has been published in the *University of Windsor Review, Descant, Waves, Grain, Northern Journey, The Fiddlehead, Impulse, Writ* and broadcast on CBC Radio. Her writing was also included in the anthology, *We Who Can Fly: Poems, Essays and Memories in Honour of Adele Wiseman.* Inanna published a book of Dickinson's short stories, *One Day It Happens,* in 2007, and her first novel, *Ile d'Or,* in 2010, both to excellent reviews in *The Globe and Mail,* among others. She grew up in northern Quebec and currently lives in Toronto.